THE HOLLOW MAN

Oliver Harris was born in north London in 1978. *The Hollow Man* is his first novel.

Oliver Harris

The Hollow Man

JONATHAN CAPE
LONDON

Published by Jonathan Cape 2011

2 4 6 8 10 9 7 5 3 1

First published in Great Britain in 2011 by
Jonathan Cape
Random House
20 Vauxhall Bridge Road
London SW1V 2SA

www.rbooks.co.uk

Addresses for companies within The Random House Group Limited can be found at:
www.randomhouse.co.uk/offices.htm

The Random House Group Limited Reg. No. 954009

A CIP catalogue record for this book is available from the British Library

ISBN 9780224091220

The Random House Group Limited supports The Forest Stewardship Council (FSC), the leading international forest certification organisation. All our titles that are printed on Greenpeace approved FSC certified paper carry the FSC logo. Our paper procurement policy can be found at
www.rbooks.co.uk/environment

Mixed Sources
Product group from well-managed
forests and other controlled sources
www.fsc.org Cert no. TT-COC-2139
© 1996 Forest Stewardship Council
FSC

Typeset in Minion by Palimpsest Book Production Limited
Falkirk, Stirlingshire

Printed and bound in Great Britain by
CPI Mackays, Chatham, Kent ME5 8TD

For Emily

God give me strength to lead a double life.
Hugo Williams, 'Prayer'

1

HAMPSTEAD'S WEALTH LAY UNCONSCIOUS ALONG THE EDGE
of the Heath, Mercedes and SUVs frosted beneath plane trees, Victorian
terraces unlit. A Starbucks glowed, but otherwise the streets were dark.
The first solitary commuter cars whispered down East Heath Road to
South End Green. Detective Constable Nick Belsey listened to them, faint
in the distance. He could still hear individual cars, which meant it was
before 7 a.m. The earth was cold beneath his body. His mouth had soil
in it and there was a smell of blood and rotten bark.

Belsey lay on a small mound within Hampstead Heath. The mound
was crowded with pine trees, surrounded by gorse and partitioned from
the rest of the world by a low iron fence. So it wasn't such an absurd
place to seek shelter, Belsey thought, if that had been his intention. His
coat covered the ground where he had slept. A throbbing pain travelled
his upper torso, too general to locate one source. His neck was involved;
his right shoulder. The detective stood up slowly. His breath steamed.
He shook his coat, put it on and climbed over the fence into wet grass.

From the hilltop he could see London, stretched towards the hills of
Kent and Surrey. The sky was beginning to pale at the edges. The city
itself looked numb as a rough sleeper; Camden and then the West End,
the Square Mile. His watch was missing. He searched his pockets, found
a bloodstained serviette and a promotional leaflet for a spiritual retreat,
but no keys or phone or police badge.

Belsey stumbled down a wooded slope to the sports ground, crossed the playing field and continued along the path to the ponds. His shoes were flooded and cold liquid seeped between his toes. On the bridge beside the mixed bathing pond he stopped and looked for early swimmers. None yet. He knelt on the concrete of the bridge, bent to the water and splashed his face. Blood dripped from his shaking hands. He leaned over to see his reflection but could make out only an oily confusion of light and darkness. Two swans watched him. 'Good morning,' Belsey said. He waited for them to turn and glide a distance away then plunged his head beneath the surface.

2

A SQUAD CAR REMAINED IN THE EAST HEATH CAR PARK WITH the windscreen smashed, driver's door open. Blood led across the gravel towards the Heath itself: smear rather than spatter, maybe three hours old. Faint footprints ran in parallel to the blood. Belsey measured his foot against them. The metal barrier of the car park lay twisted on the ground. The only impact had been with the barrier, it seemed. There was no evidence of collision with another car, no paint flecks or side prangs. The windscreen had spilled outwards across the bonnet. He stepped along the edge of the broken glass to a wheel lock lying on the ground and picked it up. It must have come straight through the front when he stopped. He was lucky it hadn't brained him. He put the lock down, collected a handful of wet leaves and wiped the steering wheel, gearstick and door handles.

He left the car park, onto the hushed curve of road leading from Downshire Hill to South End Green. He walked slowly, keeping the Heath to his left and the multimillion-pound houses to his right. Everything was perfectly still. There is a golden hour to every day, Belsey thought, just as there is in a murder investigation: a window of opportunity before the city got its story straight. He tried the handles of a few vehicles until the door of a Vauxhall Astra creaked towards him. He checked the street, climbed in, flicked the glove compartment and found three pounds in small change. He took the money and stepped out of the car, shutting the door gently.

He bought a toothbrush, a bottle of water and some cotton wool from an all-night store near the hospital. It was run by two Somali brothers.

'Morning, Inspector. What happened?'

'I've just been swimming. It feels wonderful.'

'OK, Inspector.' They gave shy grins and rang up his purchases.

'Still haven't made Inspector, though.'

'That's right, boss.' The owners didn't look him in the eye. If the damage to his face worried them, they didn't seem inclined to enquire further. Belsey collected his change, took a deep breath and walked up Pond Street to the police station.

Most London police operated out of modernist concrete blocks. Not Hampstead. The red, Victorian bricks of the station glowed with civic pride on Rosslyn Hill. Above the station lay the heritage plumpness of the village and, down the hill, the dirty sprawl of Camden Town began. Belsey sat at a bus stop across the road watching the late turn trickling out of the station, nocturnal and subdued. At 8 a.m. the earlies filed in for morning parade. He gave them five minutes then crossed the road.

The corridors were empty. Belsey went to the lockers. He found the first-aid box and took paracetamol, a roll of bandage and antiseptic. He removed a broken umbrella from the bin and prised his locker open: one spare tie, a torn copy of *The Golden Bough*, but no spare shoes or shirt. Belsey returned to the corridor and froze. His boss, Detective Inspector Tim Gower, stepped into the canteen a few metres ahead of him. Belsey counted to five then padded past, up the stairs to the empty CID office and sat down.

He kept the lights off, blinds closed, grabbed the night's crime sheet and checked he wasn't on it. A fight in a kebab shop, two break-ins, a missing person. No Belsey. He searched the desk drawers for his badge and warrant card and they were there, oblivious: *E II R, Metropolitan Police*; a crown in a silver explosion. So this was what was left of him.

He ran a check on the totalled squad car and it came up as belonging to Kentish Town police station. Belsey called.

'This is Nick Belsey, Hampstead CID. One of your cars is in the East Heath car park . . . No, it's still there . . . I don't know . . . Thanks.'

Belsey locked himself in the toilet and stripped to the waist. He studied his face. A line of dried blood ran from his left nostril across his lips to his chin. He ran a finger along the blood and judged it superficial, apart from a torn lip, which he could live with. His right ear was badly grazed and his right cheekbone hurt to touch but wasn't broken. Dark, complex bruises had begun to bloom across his chest and right shoulder. He cleaned the wounds and spat the remaining fragments of broken tooth out of his mouth. He looked wired, both older and younger than his thirty-eight years. His flat detective eyes were regaining light. Belsey removed his trousers, dampened the bottoms and rinsed his suit jacket so the worst of the Heath was off. He hung his coat up to dry, put his trousers back on, then returned to the office. He looked under his colleagues' desks for a pair of dry shoes but couldn't see any.

The call room had sent up a list of messages for him – calls received over the past few hours. They had come from several individuals he had not spoken to for years, and some distant relatives and an old colleague. *You tried to get hold of me last night* . . . He didn't remember calling anyone. A vague dread pressed at the edges of his consciousness.

He opened the blind in front of the small window beside his desk. The night had evaporated, the air turned hard, with thin clouds like scum on water. It was an extraordinary day, Belsey sensed. A midwinter sun hung pale in the sky and there was a clarity to it all. A man in shirtsleeves opened up a chemist's; a street cleaner shuffled, sweeping, towards Belsize Park tube station. City workers hurried past. Out of habit Belsey wondered if he should cancel his cards, but the cards had cancelled themselves a few days ago. His old life was beyond rescue. It felt as if without the cards he had no debt, and without the debt he was free to run.

The important thing was to stay calm.

Belsey smoothed the sheet of jobs on his desk: one fight, two break-ins, a missing person. His plan formed. The control room had put an alert note by the missing person half an hour ago. It meant they thought someone should take a look, although adult disappearances weren't police business, and it was probably just the address that caught their eye: The Bishops Avenue. The Bishops Avenue was the most expensive street in the division, and therefore one of the most expensive in the world. No one pretended the rich going missing was the same as the poor.

He stuck a message on the sergeant's desk – *On MisPer* – and signed out keys for an unmarked CID car. Then he went downstairs, checked there was enough petrol in the tank and reversed onto Downshire Hill.

3

HE DROVE STEADILY. THE OCCASIONAL LAND ROVER PASSED, commuters dangling cigarettes out of tinted windows. But the worst of the school run was half an hour off, the traffic still fluid. Belsey climbed to Whitestone Pond, past early joggers, past the Spaniards Inn, and turned left, down into the secluded privilege of The Bishops Avenue.

Stand-alone mansions lined the road, each asserting its own brand of high-security tastelessness. The Bishops Avenue provided a home to sheikhs, princes and tycoons, running broad and gated for a kilometre down from the Heath to a dismal stretch of the A1 and across the main road to East Finchley. It was a world in itself, inscrutable and aloof from the rest of the city. A woman stood on the drive of number 37 with a black jacket over a cleaner's pink uniform. She was pale, blonde, smoking with rapid, shallow puffs. The house behind her loomed with gormless pomp. It boasted two storeys of new red bricks, white windowsills, white columns either side of a black door with a high-gloss sheen. Tiny trees in black pots guarded the front. A flagless white pole stood in the centre of the semicircular driveway; pink gravel led around to the back of the property.

The woman gave a glance at his injuries and then at his police badge and went with the latter.

'I haven't touched anything.' She spoke with a Polish accent and a line of smoke out of the side of her mouth.

'What's your name?' Belsey said.

'Kristina.'

'And you clean for the missing individual?'

'Yes.'

He walked past her to the steps. 'Anyone in?'

'No.'

Belsey looked up at the shuttered windows. He climbed the four smooth stone steps to the door but the maid held back.

'They lived alone?'

'Yes.'

'Are all the alarms off?'

'Yes.'

'When did you last see him?' Belsey said.

'I've never seen him.'

'You've never seen him?'

'No.'

'How do you know he's missing?'

'There's a note.'

Belsey pushed the door. It opened to reveal a hallway the size of a small church, with marble floors and a chandelier. At the back, two curling flights of red-carpeted stairs parted around a tall, waterless fountain. Belsey stepped in. His damaged form appeared in elaborately framed mirrors. He climbed the red stairs to the first floor and checked three bedrooms with white carpets and scatter cushions, and a bathroom with stone sinks, a jacuzzi and soap dishes like gold scallop shells. He found face wash made out of Japanese seaweed, and rolled-up towels tied with silver ribbon. He didn't find any suicide. Most home suicides were found in bathrooms, less often in bedrooms. The occupier wasn't in. Only one of the bedrooms appeared to have been used recently, its bed sheets tangled. Belsey opened the cupboards until he found a pair of snakeskin loafers. He took his wet shoes off and slipped the loafers on. They were loose but perfectly comfortable. There was a wallet on the bedside table filled with cards in the name of A. Devereux. No cash. He checked the bedside drawer but found only cufflinks and a Harrods carrier bag. He put his old shoes in the bag and took them downstairs.

The fridge in the main kitchen had an inbuilt TV and radio. It had a display that told you when the contents were about to go off. Right now it said 'chicken portions' although Belsey couldn't see any chicken inside. He found one bottle of champagne unopened, some granary bread, cheese, jars of olives and marmalade, semi-skimmed milk and half a microwave goulash. The milk smelt fresh. The freezer contained a bag of prawns and a bottle of vodka. He couldn't find any coffee. There was a stainless-steel toaster on the side, beside a rack of wine bottles. He put two slices of bread in the toaster and filled the kettle.

Belsey wandered the length of the ground-floor corridor while the kettle boiled, admiring the new books on shelves and modern art on the walls. The frames were florid and golden, the art bare and abstract. He walked through a dining room with glass candlesticks and floor-length drapes, to a study with oak panelling and a billiards table set up on a Persian rug. The suicide note was on the table's baize, black ink on headed stationery.

I'm sorry. For a long time I thought I could continue the way things were, but this is no longer the case. For the past year I have felt as if the sun has gone out. Please believe that I know what I am doing and it is for the best. I have tried to ensure that all paperwork is in order so that you have no cause for further aggravation.
  Alex Devereux

How polite, Belsey thought. There was no addressee. Maybe it was for the staff. Who signed a suicide note with their full name? The paper was heavy, watermarked. It carried the Bishops Avenue address and a motto: 'Hope Springs Eternal'. Belsey checked Devereux's handwriting against paperwork in the desk and it matched. He felt the temperature of the taps in the en suite bathroom and checked the window locks. A door on the top floor opened when Belsey pulled the bolt. It led onto the roof. Belsey stepped outside and exhaled in wonder. An infinity pool rippled in the morning breeze, encircled by deckchairs. No corpse floating. Below him, beyond trellis panels, Belsey could see the lawn and a tennis court, the edges of the property, playing fields and then the Heath itself, branches scratching the sky.

He wandered back down into a main living room and experimented with the control for a plasma screen above a marble fireplace. He buttered his toast and read the note again while he ate. Then he went out and threw his ruined shoes into the back of the unmarked car. Kristina was sitting on the wall.

'Any signs Mr Devereux was in trouble?' Belsey asked.

'No.'

'How long have you been working for him?'

'Two months.'

'Anything unusual about the house today?'

'No.'

'Vehicles missing?'

'I don't know.'

'What line of work was he in?'

'He was a businessman.'

'No kidding.'

Belsey walked around the side of the house to the garden. Frost coated the lawn. There were sculpted pathways, wrought-iron furniture, the usual cameras and razor wire. No one pretended the rich killing themselves was the same as the poor, but no one pretended it was for different reasons either.

The maid handed over her keys to the place with an air of solemn ceremony. Maybe this was what they did where she came from, Belsey thought. Maybe they saw it all the time.

'Would you like a drink?' Belsey asked.

'No,' she said.

4

Belsey drove by the East Heath car park. They'd collected the squad car. All had been cleared away, even the broken glass.

He tried to think what CCTV would have picked him up last night, which cameras would record a driver's face. He parked beside the depot on Highgate Road and sat in the car for a moment. Then he got out and walked towards the shabby business of Kentish Town Road.

What had he done?

He walked into the Citizens' Advice Bureau and took a leaflet entitled 'Managing Bankruptcy'. Then he walked to the Tote bookmakers. They had a plastic unit in the corner with hot drinks and snacks. He had just enough change left for a coffee. Belsey took a seat at the back. He swallowed four paracetamol. He read the leaflet – *Make a list of your everyday outgoings. Be honest* – then turned it face down.

The previous night had marked a division in his life. This is what Belsey sensed. It was a fire break. He felt his way backwards from the crashed car into the night that led to it. The car belonged to Kentish Town. He must have been looking for a final drink, to have ended up in the Kentish Town area. Now he remembered going into a store on Fortress Road to buy cigarettes and his wallet was gone. That was a block from Kentish Town police station.

He drank his coffee watching the day's first gamblers walk in. A flutter, he thought. What an expression. He got up and left them to it.

A probationer manned the front desk of Kentish Town police station:

rookie-fresh, nineteen, with bleached blond hair. Belsey showed his badge.

'Nick Belsey. Hampstead station. I heard you had a squad car go AWOL.'

'That's right.'

'What time?'

'Reported 3.17 a.m.'

'Inspector Gower's asked for the tapes.'

The new boy looked uncertain. 'Our car park tapes?'

'That's right. Do you know where they're kept? The hard disk?'

'Yes.'

Then DC Robin Oakley appeared in the background and Belsey's heart sunk. Belsey had been on training courses with Oakley; he drove a Nissan GT-R and collected martial arts weapons. He had a big mouth.

'Nick,' Oakley said, eyeing Belsey's cuts. 'What happened to your face?'

'Did anyone hand in a phone or wallet last night?'

'Why?'

'I lost mine,' Belsey said.

Oakley thought this was very funny. 'Anyone hand in Nick Belsey's wallet?' he shouted. 'Could be anywhere, Nick. Know what I mean?'

'No.'

Oakley grinned. The rookie looked confused. 'Should I go see about the car park?'

'That's fine,' Belsey said. 'Leave it.'

'What's happening in the car park?' Oakley said.

'Nothing. Have you got a cigarette?'

They stepped outside. Oakley fished a ten-pack of Superkings out of his breast pocket and passed one to Belsey.

'What are you like, you crazy bastard?' Oakley said.

'Did you see me last night?'

'Half of London saw you.'

'Where was I?'

'Have you spoken to your boss?'

'Gower? Not recently.'

Oakley's face twitched with the urge to laugh. 'Where did you end up?'

'Why?'

'Nick, you've got to speak to Gower.'

'OK. What did I do?'

'At one point you were in Lorenzo's.'

'Christ.' Belsey closed his eyes. Lorenzo de Medici's was a cocaine-fuelled dive behind Tottenham Court Road. By day it was a mediocre spaghetti house, but it had a 5 a.m. licence and an alcoholic owner who couldn't control his own stock. The walls were painted with bad copies of Renaissance masterpieces and the toilet sinks were usually stained with blood.

'What time was I in Lorenzo's?'

'Does it make a difference?'

'Did I have my phone?'

'You were phoning *everyone*. You were telling them to come to Lorenzo's. You said it was your birthday, mate.'

Belsey opened his eyes. Oakley smiled, shaking his head. He tossed his cigarette into the road, patted Belsey on the arm and headed inside.

Belsey finished his cigarette then walked back to the car. Memories were cracking through: he knew he had been at Lorenzo's now, in the very early hours – he remembered trying to sell his jacket to the owner. He had been trying to explain to someone in the bar how he had over-leveraged himself and they found this hilarious. 'Overleveraged,' they kept saying. They were having to shout over the music.

'Now I'm going on a retreat,' he said.

Belsey had a leaflet from a health food shop: *Anxious? Uncertain? We are an interfaith community offering healing retreats in Worcestershire.* There was a drawing of a cross-legged man glowing with enlightenment, beams radiating from his body. *Become like a child whose soul is empty. Peace of mind is already yours.*

'You're going to rehab?'

'It's not rehab. It's a healing retreat,' Belsey said.

'A retreat from what?'

He remembered at some point being in a car with a man who said he worked for the Foreign Office and this man had track marks on the backs of his hands. And now he saw the start of it all, standing in the front hall

13

of a B&B in King's Cross with his worldly possessions in two bin liners at his feet. The last of his cards had been declined.

He had known this moment was coming, but it had been astonishing to be in it. Machines had started spitting back his cards a fortnight ago. The first few times it happened he had gone through the motions of speaking to call centres, chatting to polite young men in Mumbai and Bangalore. He had sat in front of pub napkins with a pen in his hand as if some calculation was demanded of him. *Ego is the gambler's greatest enemy*. That was all he could think: one phrase from a book stuck on repeat. What had he done? He had been clever enough to keep the debt moving and not clever enough to sacrifice a lifestyle to pay it off. He had been too brave – that was the simple truth: stupid with a confidence beyond all reason. His gambling acquaintances would say he had gone on tilt – out of control, throwing himself towards his own end. Was that what he'd been doing: trying to find a way out through the bottom of his overdraft?

His final few days of credit had been the wildest; buying presents for strangers, setting up debits to charities, a last few reckless, euphoric punts on distant rainfall and elections in Central Asian republics. At the time he thought he had broken through to an insight, but he saw now it was a kind of hypothermia. It began when the pain of the cold had passed and you were washed with miscalculated serenity. He had looked away for a few days and when he looked back his finances had begun consuming themselves. Pay cheques no longer covered interest payments, let alone such extravagances as accommodation.

The B&B owner had been apologetic as he moved Belsey out. There was nothing he could do. It was a small business. Belsey's room had already been occupied by a thin, nervous-looking family – to whom Belsey left the bags of his belongings. He didn't have the heart to carry them anywhere. He was thrown out along with a young, bright-eyed Afghan – Siddiq Sahar – who was about to get married, cast upon the street.

'I've been refused asylum and you've been refused credit,' Siddiq grinned. He seemed OK about it. He said he'd sorted his own paper-work anyway. They stood smoking in front of the Continental Hotel's flaking facade, Belsey in his detective's suit and the Afghan in a flight

14

jacket with the Stars and Stripes on the back. Sunlight fell across the scaffolding of St Pancras Station onto dusty pavement and dirty shop windows. They had got to know each other quite well in the month of Belsey's residence. Siddiq had come to the UK via Moscow. He said he'd been a tour guide in Moscow and a political prisoner in Afghanistan. He liked to grease his hair and help female tourists.

'Are you working today?' he asked.

'I've got the day off.'

'I need a witness,' he said. 'A suit and a witness. I will give you fifty pounds.'

'What kind of witness?'

'For my wedding.'

The bride was a Slovak from Edgware, a red-haired girl with a dirty laugh, ten years older than the groom. They exchanged vows in Marylebone Town Hall, married by a woman with a clipboard. Belsey tried to refuse the money afterwards, and when Siddiq insisted on paying, Belsey had bought champagne with it. They were in a tourist pub by Madame Tussauds. He hadn't intended to drink. After four bottles between the three of them they moved to a bar beneath a Christian Science reading room. That was the wedding reception. They seemed very happy together. Belsey wondered if there was anyone he could bring himself to call, to borrow money from – enough for a night's sleep at least. The answer was no.

Memories rushed in now. By 9 p.m. he had found his way to a memorial do for a dead policeman, a dog handler who had known his father and who'd died recently in a road accident in France. Men from Dogs Section, some Drugs Squad, crowded the Ten Bells in Waterloo, near where they trained the dogs; old coppers, men with high blood pressure and market-trader voices. It was dark outside. He had broken through to a state in which every moment flowed effortlessly to the next and he could not go wrong. He was having an adventure; everything would be resolved. Belsey made loud greetings to men he barely recognised, men from his childhood, when his father was in the Yard. They had aged. For a brief, terrifying moment he saw the future intended for him. Someone bought brandies.

'Your old man, he was a great murder detective, but he never went home, you know what I mean?' *No, no, I don't.* Someone was trying to talk to him about his father. *What does that mean?* They'd brought a sniffer dog and someone had put a black armband on one of its legs.

'It's crying.'

Everyone laughed. No one was crying. Then Chief Superintendent Northwood arrived, the Borough Commander, in his parade uniform, with a framed photograph of the dead man. Northwood had his wife in tow: Sandra Northwood wore heels and high, platinum-blonde hair. She was a handsome woman in her fifties, who achieved another layer of brittle glamour with each of her husband's promotions. Northwood himself towered over her, rigid with self-importance. He had hated Belsey since an incident with a fire extinguisher at Hendon police training college. He made a speech.

'Dogs are the heart of the police.'

Someone said: 'A man who loved dogs more than he loved life.' Belsey raised a toast. He stood on a chair. Music played.

'This is what Jim would have wanted,' everyone agreed, getting legless.

Then Belsey was dancing with Sandra Northwood, her soft body warm in his arms. 'Oh,' she breathed into his ear and giggled.

She said: 'I remember your father. I remember when you seemed so young.' And she touched his face as if searching for some way back to that past. Her hands smelt of hairspray. 'Nicholas,' she giggled. Her eyes were unfocused. He wondered if she'd been sleeping with his father; wondered who hadn't.

'Were you sleeping with my old man?' he asked. 'Sandra? Can you hear me?'

He paid for the cab out of Sandra Northwood's purse. She was beside him. So this is where the Borough Commander lives, Belsey thought, looking at a low, detached new-build with shrub borders. Where was the Commander? The lights were off. Belsey helped Sandra in. The house was empty. Belsey went inside to see what it was like, the Chief's home. The furniture looked very new. Some of it had been kept under plastic. Sandra poured them wine from an open bottle on the sideboard.

'My husband says you're one of the best.'

'Thank you.'

'Handsome, like your father.'

She fell asleep on the sofa. Belsey went upstairs, looked in the bathroom cabinets, found Northwood's Masonic regalia in a chest in the bedroom and put it on: apron, gauntlets, collar. He was gloriously wasted. He took the regalia off. He stole twenty pounds from one of Northwood's jackets, urinated in the bath and backed out.

5

You've got to speak to Gower, Oakley had suggested, and apparently Inspector Gower felt the same way. Belsey received a summons as soon as he arrived back at the station. They sat in Gower's office, door shut. It seemed to Belsey as if they had been sitting a long time looking at each other.

'How was the memorial last night?' Gower began eventually.

'Fitting.'

'You know I worked with him once. He was a fine dog handler. A fine policeman.'

'Yes.'

Gower had a silver moustache and wore pale linen suits; a solid detective, a manager rather than a maestro. He read Belsey's injured face. *I've been going through a bit of a hard time*, Belsey should have said. That would have been appropriate. But it was not entirely true, and he had decided honesty was to be his strategy. He wanted to say: *I have been going through a good time*, which was closer to the truth and always a more dangerous situation.

'Do you know anything about a squad car that went missing from Kentish Town?'

'It was on the Heath.'

'Why?'

'I don't know,' Belsey said. 'But I believe I'm responsible. I'd like to request a transfer out of London.'

Gower stared at the desk now, as if he was the one in trouble, which he may have been, and Belsey felt sorry that such a dedicated officer should be drawn into his own misfortune.

'You are our best detective,' the Inspector said quietly.

'What I'd like,' Belsey said, 'is to transfer out of London. As far away as possible.'

Gower looked at him. Belsey felt calm, strong even. Books on criminal law lined the Inspector's shelves alongside bound magazines on birdwatching. Belsey read the spines. He studied the family photos, some of which were turned to face the guest as if to say: look, look what we are fighting for. Twenty years ago Tim Gower had been Lance Corporal Gower, patrolling the streets of Northern Ireland. Belsey had tried to get him to talk about it at a Christmas drinks, but Gower refused: 'Long time ago now.' Belsey respected Gower but felt he might not have the resources to deal with this particular situation.

Gower transferred his gaze from Belsey's face to the window and then back again.

'What's happening to you?'

'I think I may be having a religious experience.'

The Inspector nodded slowly. 'What troubles me is that I don't think you care,' he said.

'That I'm having a religious experience?'

'About keeping your job.'

'I would like to.'

'Maybe you don't care enough about yourself.'

'I'm proud to be a police officer,' Belsey said. But it sounded overzealous. He did not want to be sent to counselling again. He wondered what they would talk about this time. 'What I'd like,' he said, 'what I think I need, is a change of scenery.'

Gower shook his head, not like a refusal but as if Belsey had picked up the wrong script.

'Northwood's not very happy about something. He's requested a review – about what exactly I'm not sure, but it concerns yourself. I need to know what you've done.'

What *had* he done? Irreparably angered the man at the top, Chief Super

19

Northwood – the man using Camden borough as his personal stepping stone to high office: the man whose pervasive power, in Belsey's opinion, seemed to be based on a lot of threats and not much efficient thief-taking. This was in spite of his recent, much publicised promise to halve crime in the borough over the next three years. He was a politician.

'With all due respect, sir, fuck Northwood.'

Gower opened a desk drawer, slid one sheet in and took another out.

'No, Belsey. We don't fuck Northwood, or anyone else for that matter. You're not in Borough now.'

'I haven't been in Borough for six years.'

'You know what I mean.'

Borough was his first posting as a constable, first years in CID. He fought to keep the memories at bay: all of them, but especially the good ones.

'I'm going to suggest you take a break for a while,' the Inspector said, 'regardless of what happens.'

'I don't want to take a break.'

Gower uncapped his pen and started filling in the form. The police had forms for every eventuality. Belsey needed to fill in a form for Mr Devereux. That had been quite a home to go missing from. What had Devereux felt life was lacking? Maybe he'd just made enough money and was checking out, job done. Belsey let his eyes rest on the photographs of wetland birds on the Inspector's wall. He imagined Gower in military uniform on a road-block, County Armagh, watching the birds. Eventually Gower capped his pen.

'I've spent ten years dragging this police station out of the depths. I'm not having one man and his crisis drag it back down.'

'What do you mean by crisis?'

'This isn't a game.'

'I'm just curious what you mean by the word "crisis".'

'No one's doubting you're good, Nick. But you're not as good as you think you are. You're not worth a whole police station and more.'

'I've never thought that,' Belsey said. Gower studied the form. He asked Belsey to sign it. Belsey signed it without looking.

'What's that?' Gower nodded to the book in Belsey's hand.

'*The Golden Bough.*'

'What's it about?'

'The pagan origins of Christianity, folk culture, myths.'

'I thought it might be about birds.'

'There are birds in it. Bird cults.'

'Bird cults.' The Inspector sighed. 'The initial review will be tomorrow. They'll assign a representative. I'm going to ask you to write down what happened in advance of that.'

'Starting when?'

'When the trouble started.'

Belsey laughed. Yes, he thought. *Where my honesty ceases, there am I blind.* Gower was right, he should record the journey that had brought him here. An extravagant holiday to Cyprus, a bar tab for seven hundred pounds, an awful spread on last year's League One play-offs. Or the first bailiff's letter, with its archaic language of goods and chattels, as someone somewhere began to cut their losses. He would write about that: his nobility, taking out one final loan to pay off the woman who was leaving him and ensure no debt collectors came knocking at what had briefly been their home. Perhaps he could start the whole thing with his first night as a constable, looking up at the windows of the Aylesbury Estate, lit against a vast and starless sky. How much of this did Gower want to hear?

The Inspector moved his seat. 'That's all for now.'

'Can I ask you a question?' Belsey said.

'Go on.'

'You're a birdwatcher.'

'Yes,' Gower said warily.

'What do you do once you've seen them?'

'Nothing.'

'Nothing?'

'Belsey –'

'Do you write it down?'

'You're out of control, Belsey.'

'I think I'm in control,' Belsey said.

6

'HE WAS HAVING A DIG IN HIS BALLS. I KICKED THE KITCHEN door and he's got one foot up on the sink. He said, I saw you coming. I said, why'd you start fixing if you saw us coming? He said he didn't know when he'd next get the chance.'

Belsey stepped into the office. His colleagues went silent: Derek Rosen leaning heavily against the edge of Belsey's desk, Rob Trapping watching with a grin on his clean-shaven face.

'Then what?' Belsey said.

'He took the pin out and there was blood everywhere,' Rosen said. He flapped a tabloid and began to read.

'How did it go?' Trapping turned to Belsey. He was only twenty-three years old, six foot four and still in love with the idea of being a detective.

'Really well.'

'We could have done with you yesterday,' he said. 'Knifing outside the job centre.'

'I heard.'

'Turns out it was Niall Cassidy's boy, Johnny. We haven't found him yet. Apparently you know him from the good old days.'

'I thought he was in a Spanish prison.'

'Comes back from a two-year stretch in the Balearics and stabs the guy who grassed him. Straight from the airport. Stabs him in the thigh.'

'What was that about? Jet lag?'

Trapping laughed. His mobile rang.

'Jet lag,' he said. He left the room, laughing, answering his mobile: 'Detective Trapping here.' Belsey sat at his desk. Niall Cassidy: another name from his south London days. It felt as if something was slipping; whatever mechanism kept the present and past from leaking into each other had broken.

'The prodigal son,' Rosen said. 'I've had someone here looking for you. From a company called Millennium Credit Recovery. Mr Walls. Like the ice cream.'

'Like the ice cream.'

'That was his line.'

'It's a good one. I've never met any Mr Walls.'

'No. Apparently he's never met you.'

Rosen turned back to his paper. Belsey admired the blue sheen of his jowls, the fine network of red veins starting to cover the skin. Mr Walls, he thought; which of his creditors had sold on his expired dreams to Millennium Credit Recovery? What could he say when they eventually tracked him down? *Let no debt remain outstanding except the continuing debt to love one another; for love of one's fellow man is the whole of the law.* St Paul. Patron saint of London.

'Have you heard of an Alex Devereux?' Belsey said.

'Who?'

'He lives on The Bishops Avenue. Devereux.'

Rosen's face went thoughtful. He looked up from his paper.

'No,' he said. 'Why?'

'He's disappeared.'

'Not a crime last time I looked.' Rosen grinned. His teeth were yellow. He turned to the sports pages and his face went slack again.

Not a crime, no, Belsey thought. Every man and woman's right. He ran Devereux's name through the Police National Computer. It came back clean. He picked up the phone and called three morgues, twelve hospitals, River Police and central records but got no hits. Belsey filed Devereux as a Missing Person: *MisPer*, rhyming with whisper. Then he sat at his desk watching the street grow dark. The morning's tide flowed back: commuters relieved of their day's duty; children with au pairs, holding new paintings. Belsey stared at a report about an arson attack in Chalk Farm, a thirty-five-year-old man who had set fire to his old school. Then it was six o'clock and Trapping was in the doorway with a coat over his arm and a hopeful expression.

'Drink, Nick?'

'Not tonight, Rob. Loads on.'

Belsey waited until the office was empty. He typed 'shame' into his PC and looked at a picture of a dead Nazi officer lying in a stream, a guard from a camp who'd shot himself. Once he was sure he was alone, Belsey printed the picture and locked it in his desk drawer. He rested his head on his arms and closed his eyes and wanted to go home.

The Wetherspoons on the Finchley Road could be found on the top floor of a shopping and leisure centre, beyond the gym and interior design store and the eight-screen cinema. The whole place was washed with a comatose serenity. Belsey let an escalator lift him past water features and artificial plants to the pub. It was large, and bathed in a dim blue light as if to stop people finding their veins. Belsey walked to the furthest corner, sat down and listened to a CD get stuck and no one care. He liked the Wetherspoons. It felt like a departure lounge. He liked bars in chain hotels and airports and train stations; places with no smell and no attempt to mean anything. In these places an individual could gather their thoughts.

Belsey checked his companions: several pensioners, meditative at their individual tables, a couple with the hurried intimacy of adulterers, neat staff talking Polish and an office party kicking off. It was a redundancy, Belsey guessed, by the quantity of empties on the table. Floor-length windows looked out over six lanes of the Finchley Road, as if any view was worth seeing. Belsey put his hands in his pockets and watched the cars, wondering if this was a crisis. They say no one changes until they hit the bottom. He'd always imagined it like a crash, but perhaps it was like reaching the bottom of the ocean, with everything a little weightless and unreal.

The office workers were drinking hard, encouraging on the weekend oblivion. It was Wednesday. They had their ties low, blouses open, company card behind the bar. Belsey got up, circled the group and walked to the barmaid.

'Can I put three pints of Stella on the tab?' he asked.

'Of course.' The girl poured his drinks and rang it up and put the receipt behind a MasterCard on the back shelf. 'Anything else?'

Belsey picked up a menu. 'Do you recommend this City Platter?'

'It's very popular.'

'I'll get one of those. And a vodka tonic, double, maybe some pork scratchings.'

'OK.'

'Sorry if we're being a bit rowdy,' he said, as she fixed the vodka.

'Someone leaving?'

'Someone leaving, someone joining. Everyone's celebrating. It feels like everyone's moving somewhere. How long have you been working here?'

'Three weeks.'

'How are you finding it?'

'Fine.'

'It's one of my favourite places.'

Belsey drank the vodka tonic at the bar and took the pints and pork scratchings to his table. He felt, momentarily, a longing for his phone; felt the impossibility of being contacted, like a static charge. Incommunicado, he thought. He would have liked to contact his bank, more than any of his friends and family. It was a morbid longing; he did not know what he would say. At least the bank already knew his shame. He could apply for bankruptcy. Moral bankruptcy too. But he wasn't convinced he wanted to be saved. His predicament was a force at his back and he wanted to be propelled. *Not a crime last time I looked.* To vanish. To start again. He could sense an extraordinary option growing on the horizon.

Belsey drank the pints in quick succession. While he drank he tested his soul for a sense of failure, pressing gently inwards like a crash victim touching their ribs. But he couldn't feel it. He needed sleep. Images of bus shelters, railway stations, shopping centre doorways passed through his mind like a sequence learned in childhood: the body-sized surfaces of the city in which a man may lie and not be disturbed. The platter arrived: chicken wings, garlic bread, cocktail sausages, potato wedges, nachos, some sour cream and barbecue sauce. He ate steadily.

There was always Iraq, of course. An old acquaintance from training college had tried to persuade Belsey to go out there. Simon Nickels worked for a private security contractor in Baghdad. Belsey had got a call out of the blue.

'Drinks at the police club. On me. All the old boys.'

Who were the old boys? Belsey wondered. When he got there it was only Simon, standing at the bar. He had grown a moustache. Belsey possessed a vague memory of him passing out in a bath at a party.

'You should come over. Sunny there. Choice of three pools.'

'Three, you say.'

'And we give you weapons training. Beautiful gear they've got. Top of the range.'

'That's not very enticing.'

'There's a golf course, a cinema. Everything you could want.'

'There's a golf course and a cinema in Finchley.'

Nickels wiped the froth off his moustache. He had a tan line on his ring finger where a wedding band had been.

'It's City banker money. You say to yourself: play a bit of squash, stay in shape, don't hit the bottle too much, in a couple of years you've got the mortgage paid off and the kids' university fees sorted.'

'I don't have any children.'

'You will.'

'Who else are you seeing while you're over here?'

'Only you,' he said. 'Only you.'

That was three weeks ago.

The barmaid went to clear tables. Belsey stared at the fruit machine. Each pub's small monument to chance. To supposed chance and the machinations behind it. He studied the game and make. He took a pound out of the tips saucer, considered calling the security contractor, then put it in the fruit machine instead and lost.

At eight thirty he was in the North Star, a small, functional pub with flat screens over its Victorian trimmings. He watched the news over the shoulder of one of the local after-work alcoholics who was talking about anal sex and derivatives. The news showed a young dark-skinned man moving in slow motion over a chain-link fence. The businessman was buying drinks for everyone and then he stopped and Belsey moved on to Ye Olde Swiss Cottage.

'Was I in here last night?' he asked.

'You were in, for sure.'

'Did I leave a phone?'

'No.'

The Cottage was built like a Swiss chalet, abandoned in the centre of a bad-tempered traffic junction. Few risked the crossing to enjoy its dour Alpine charm. But the pub had a side room with a good pool table. Belsey played two frames, won both, and when a fight started he moved on. The Adelaide, the Enterprise. At some point he crashed a birthday party in the Camden Holiday Inn. He was happy there. And then he was outside again. Everything was fine. He moved down the ladder gracefully from the Neptune to the Cobden Arms to the Sports Bar which had karaoke so raw it felt like Greek tragedy.

'Singing, Nick?'

'Not tonight.'

'I want you to meet my friend. Anne, Nick's a detective.'

'A detective!'

'Not for much longer.'

'I've always wanted to meet a detective.'

'I'm not going to be one for much . . .'

But he was OK. Into the back streets of Hampstead, where the world seemed gemmed and out of an advert; the houses themselves fat jewels with rustic tables behind basement windows. And the Heath always beside him, a shadow; and then he was crossing the Heath in primeval mud again, through trees that seemed half familiar like the ghosts of a thousand old friends.

Belsey was halfway to The Bishops Avenue before he realised what he was doing.

*　*　*

The road was deserted, fantasy homes unlit behind their gates. It seemed as if part of the fantasy was that you didn't even have to be there, present in your own life. Guards slept in booths beside the larger houses. Water features sang softly to the night. Number 37 hung back from the road, shrouded in darkness, mourning. Belsey rang the bell. He felt forms shift, the ghost of Alex Devereux approach the intercom and retreat. The house itself appeared larger in the gloom, heavy with emptiness. Belsey unlocked the front gate and walked into the grounds. He climbed the steps and knocked. After a moment he unlocked the front door and stood on the threshold, waiting. He moved inside and sat on the edge of the hallway's fountain while his eyes adjusted to the dim interior. Then he got up and familiarised himself with the alarm system, made sure it was all off, and shut the door.

Belsey left the lights off. He felt his way through grey shades of luxury to the second floor and opened the door to the roof. A hazy moonlight caught the undulation of the pool's surface. It looked like treacle. Belsey let his clothes fall to the floor and dived in.

The water was freezing. Belsey surfaced with a gasp. But it felt good, his body naked in the cold water. It woke him up. He floated on his back, gazing at the light pollution. It felt as if the water itself was a kind of wealth and he was floating in it.

He swam a few lengths and dried off, went down to the kitchen, heated a tin of soup and took it with bread and cheese into the lounge. He ate, watching his silhouette in the television screen. Then he stood up, unlocked the French windows and walked out. A security light came on. The plants and garden furniture froze as if caught in nocturnal conspiracy. A fox stared back. *Hello, friend.* Belsey lowered himself to his heels and it ran into the undergrowth.

The garden extended to tall wooden fences with cameras at each corner. He wondered where the tapes were kept. There was what looked like a small bandstand and a rock garden with shallow pools of dark water flowing down to a pond. He couldn't see any fish. He returned inside, locking the door and then – this surprised him – wiping his prints off the handle with a corner of curtain. What was he doing here? He explored the house, testing the silence for an enduring impression

Devereux might have made upon it. He found a room with nothing but a card table and two decks of cards in neat piles, face down. A door in the basement led to a small cinema with three rows of cushioned chairs and a smell of damp. There was a small bathroom in the basement, with its own TV screen in the wall and a lot of colourful glass bottles by the sink.

Belsey returned to the bedroom. A cordless telephone sat on the bedside table, beside a book entitled *Ten Secrets of Effective Time Management*. Well, you found one secret to time management, Belsey thought. He smelt Devereux's sheets. He smelt the clothes in the cupboard and detected cigar smoke and a heavy aftershave he didn't recognise. There were no photos anywhere. Perhaps he had taken them with him. There were security cameras in the front hall and study but he couldn't find the control panel or hard drive. A floor-length mirror filled the centre of the right-hand bedroom wall. Belsey spent some time admiring the polished glass, the bedroom reflected in it, trying on Devereux's clothes: double-cuff shirts; wide, unfashionable ties.

He went back to the kitchen, emptied the bin onto the floor and sifted through the rubbish with his foot: junk mail and catalogues. No food packaging. No tissues. No DNA. He looked for a passport in the bedroom and study, found an old fax machine, a bottle of Bell's and a box of Cuban cigars, but no documents. There was a framed photograph of St Petersburg's Winter Palace on the study wall and a model of an ocean liner in a glass case beside the window.

For the past year I have felt as if the sun has gone out . . .

Belsey returned to the lounge, lay down on the carpet and let the darkness enclose him. He turned on the TV and poured himself a cognac from a decanter on top of a cabinet. So this is wealth, he thought. And, after another glass: this is the most exciting thing I have ever done. The phone rang. It felt like an electric shock. There were phones all around him ringing, a digital trill from the study and kitchen and, fainter, from rooms beyond. Belsey walked to the study and stared at the phone on the desk and the suicide note on the billiards table. He listened closely, as if the significance of the call might be discerned from its ring. It rang for over a minute then stopped.

7

BELSEY WOKE ON THE LIVING-ROOM FLOOR IN A DRAB LIGHT. Above him, the crystals of a chandelier hung like tears too expensive to fall. The clock on Devereux's home entertainment system said 6:15 a.m. He knew where he was. He rolled beneath the coffee table and covered his face with his arm but sleep had gone.

Devereux's shower sprayed water at different heights, with a touch-screen panel so you could program yourself a hydro massage. The shower cabinet was big enough for three or four. That would be a party, Belsey thought. It would be nice to bring someone back here, add some female company to the mix. He spent ten minutes washing, used a variety of exotic creams, then wrapped himself in a thick bathrobe bearing the gold monogram *A.D.*

He checked his face in the mirror. Even in the soft glow of the fluorescent mirror lights it wasn't a pretty sight. But he was passable. His right ear looked raw and there was faint bruising on the side of his face. There would be a scar on the right side of his jaw where the cut was deepest. A souvenir. The rest was superficial.

His own clothes stank so he went to Devereux's bedroom and laid some suits on the quilted eiderdown. Devereux favoured pale greys, blazers, ties with flags and yachts, shirts in yellow and pink with Savile Row tags. They struck Belsey as the clothes of an international figure, a man who did business not work. He chose an outfit: Armani suit with a touch of silver to its grey, a pink Ralph Lauren shirt and a tie with gold-and-navy stripes. It looked awful and he loved it. The suit hung just past his wrists, loose at the waistband, but it went well with the snakeskin shoes. Devereux's wallet remained beside the bed. Belsey put it in his pocket for the weight.

He checked the road from the front window and when he was sure no one was passing he stepped out, skipping down the front steps. He walked to the north end of The Bishops Avenue, where its grandeur dissipated into the suburbs. East Finchley. The tanning salons and charity shops were waking up. The cafes had started to open. He tried the first one he got to.

'Could I have a coffee?' he said. 'I don't have any money but I'd like a coffee.'

The woman laughed. 'You want a coffee?'

'A small one, thank you.'

'No,' she said, and laughed again.

He went into a Costa Coffee on the high road. 'Someone cleared my coffee,' he said, and pointed to an empty table.

'Sorry about that, sir.' They made him a fresh one. Belsey sat down and dealt out the contents of Devereux's wallet. There were a lot of cards for expensive hotels: Mandarin Oriental Geneva; Ritz Carlton Moscow; Florida Marriott. Devereux was a man who collected hotels as if these places were the significant acquaintances of his life. He was a member of a club called Les Ambassadeurs with an address in Mayfair. He used a Barclaycard, black Amex, silver Visa and Diners Club. There was a receipt for a meal at Villa Bianca in Hampstead four days ago; Devereux paid for two glasses of wine, salmon tortellini and a mozzarella salad. There was a loyalty card for a coffee shop on the high street. Finally Belsey pulled out a clump of business cards. On these he was '*Alexei Devereux, Director, AD Development*'. The company had a Paris office on Rue de Castiglione, an NYC operation on Fifth Avenue and a London address in EC4.

Belsey returned to Devereux's house, blocked caller ID on the kitchen telephone and dialled the London office.

'AD Development,' a woman answered.

'Can I speak to Mr Devereux?' Belsey said.

'I'm afraid he's not in the office. Can I take a message?'

'No,' Belsey said. 'Thank you.'

He hung up and called the Paris number.

'*Bonjour*,' a woman said. He hung up.

Every bank has a police liaison team. Belsey called the dedicated CID hotline for Barclays, gave his code, and was put through to the head of external investigation.

'External,' a man said.

'Is that Josh Sanders? It's Detective Constable Belsey, at Hampstead.'

'Nick, how's business?'

'Slow. I'm waiting on a warrant for an account of yours. I was wondering if you could speed things up. Can I read you the number?'

'Go for it.'

Belsey read off Devereux's account number. Sanders typed it in.

'Mr A. Devereux?'

'Yes.'

'Not one of our most active customers.'

'When was the account last used?'

'Four days ago: withdrawal of sixty pounds, Hampstead High Street.'

'How much does he have?'

'He's two hundred overdrawn.'

'He's overdrawn?'

'Went over a week back.'

Belsey thought about this. 'Any debits set up?' he said.

'None. He's only had the account a couple of months.'

'Payments?'

'There's a purchase on it last week: Man's Best Friends.'

'Man's Best Friends?'

'Sounds like a pet shop. Customer present transaction, Golders Green. Would that make sense?'

'Not much is making sense right now,' Belsey said. 'Do you have his pin number there?'

'You know I can't give you that, Nick.'

'I know, Josh. Just a joke. Thanks for your help.'

Belsey put the phone down. An idea, humorous at first, had persisted until the humour faded and the core of possibility remained. He wanted a plane ticket. He wondered if Devereux could help him raise the cash for that. He sat down with one of the cards and a sheet of Devereux's paper and practised Devereux's signature. It wasn't easy. Alexei Devereux had an ornate hand. It seemed to belong to another age – the signature a brand might use when selling you overpriced grooming products. After ten minutes Belsey had it good enough to pass. He found car keys on a Porsche fob in the cutlery drawer and after some searching made his way through a small door at the back of the kitchen into the garage.

A Porsche Cayenne SUV sat alone beneath strip lights, fat and mean as a tank, with blacked windows and glinting hubcaps. It was the only car in a garage big enough for five. Belsey climbed in. You could get comfortable in a Porsche Cayenne. The dashboard carried a DVD player with touch-screen monitor and GPS. There was almost ninety thousand on the clock which seemed a lot. Belsey switched on the satnav and scrolled through recent journeys stored. Most started or ended at Heathrow. A lot involved central London hotels. Belsey read it as a rental vehicle but couldn't think why Devereux would be driving a rental. He checked the glove compartment and found a manual, a dust cloth and some Prada shades.

A button on the wall lifted the garage door. The front gates opened a second later. Belsey eased up the ramp into the city.

It took Belsey a moment to get used to sitting above the early-morning traffic in the SUV. He expected resentment from those navigating the narrow roads of Hampstead but people pulled aside for him, respect-fully. It was like being police. Belsey drove to Camden, parked behind the Buck Street market and walked to a 24-hour convenience store with a jumble of souvenirs and cheap hardware at the back. The staff were sleepy and careless. He knew the store let you sign for card payments – they were always calling Hampstead trying to report fraudulent trans-actions. For the same reason, he also knew their CCTV was permanently broken. After a minute's browsing Belsey selected a bottle opener, a Zippo lighter and a penknife that said 'London'. Start small. He found the silver Visa and slid it out of Devereux's wallet, moving his fingers over the raised letters of the name.

'Do you have a gift-wrapping service?' he asked the girl on the till.

'No.'

'OK.'

She looked at the credit card, turned it in her hands, swiped it and stared at the machine.

'It says I should contact the card issuer.'

'Really?'

'Yes.'

'Why would that be?' Belsey watched her eyes slide to the phone and back. He knew why it would be: something had been flagged on the system. Maybe it was a new card, or Devereux had changed addresses, or been travelling abroad. He should just choose another credit card. He watched the shop floor and couldn't see any security. A door in one corner led to fire stairs; a back exit would lead to Camden High Street and there was an alley from there to the crowded market.

She shrugged. 'Sometimes it says that.'

'OK.'

'Do you have any ID?'

Belsey showed Devereux's business cards and his club membership.

'I'll have to make a call,' the girl said. She had a memo stuck to the till with the relevant phone numbers, called Visa and read out the security code and Devereux's name. Belsey counted his breaths. 'Yes,' she said. 'He's here now. Yes. OK,' and to Belsey, 'It's OK.'

'Can you ask them how much credit is left?' Belsey said.

'How much credit is there?' she said. 'Fifty? Thank you.' She hung up. 'Fifty thousand,' she said.

'Fifty?'

'That's right.'

Belsey chose a greetings card that said 'Goodbye' and bought that as well.

He drove through the Square Mile, parked on Tower Hill and checked Devereux's business card: *AD Development, St Clement's Court, EC4.* He wanted to know a little more about the man before he borrowed his money. He wanted to know if he was dead or alive.

A colder wind blew through the City these days, but Belsey still felt a thrill when he entered the place: the sense of grind, the sheets of glass and bone-coloured stone; austere, baroque, loaded. He loved the churches stranded among all the finance like ships run aground. He used to do some church sitting in the City, a few years ago. There was an organisation that sat in churches to keep them open. He'd got the idea off a heroin addict he'd decided not to arrest, and it had appealed to him for a while – he had just started at Hampstead and was trying to clear his head. Until then, he had barely spent two minutes in a place of worship, had never received a moment's religious instruction. He thought he'd start with the real estate. It had been a phase, the same distinct period in his life when he started stealing books from the pubs they were meant to decorate; dusty hardbacks on history and philosophy. He'd even read the Bible, and it was better than he expected. So much was about dissatisfaction, leaving places, being lost. He saw these books now as props with which he'd tried to construct something: a life that was more than a job, perhaps. It hadn't worked. But the churches, at least, had been peaceful. Each carried its own flavour – some bright and serene, others unspeakably lonely, like being in a cell.

Belsey walked around the back of Monument, through the tail end of the morning rush hour in its winter uniform of dark coats and scarves. Basement windows looked down onto rows of unmanned terminals. Every building advertised offices to let. But the crowd had not thinned. It took him a while to find St Clement's Court, moving from the main roads onto progressively smaller and more crooked side streets. He found the plain front of St Clement's Church, then realised that a slender gap between the churchyard and an anonymous office block beside it was in fact the entrance to an alleyway. On one side of the entrance a plaque said 'Here lived in 1784 Desiley Obradovich, Eminent Serbian Man of Letters'. On the opposite wall was an equally weather-worn notice, engraved in metal, with a disembodied hand pointing into the permanent dusk of the alley: Entrance to 37–41 St Clement's Court.

The passageway was one of those chaotic formations that made the City feel like it had been eroded through limestone. Belsey went down it. By some quirk of the medieval warrens, numbers 37–41 turned out to be a single black door in a narrow, brown-brick facade at the end of the cul-de-sac. Belsey wondered if it had once been attached to the church; a parsonage, maybe. AD Development had the property to itself. It presented one leaded window to the world, the lower half quaintly curtained off like a French restaurant. There was a single brass bell with a brass plaque polished that morning, carrying the firm's name.

Belsey climbed onto the churchyard wall and peered over the curtain. The glass was fogged but he could make out a young woman at a desk in an office. There was no one else. She looked cold, in a cardigan and heels, writing something. Belsey climbed down before she noticed him. He realised he was wearing Devereux's clothes. He removed the tie and jacket, reasoning that these were the most conspicuous items, and left them folded at the side of the building. Then he rang the bell.

The door buzzed. He entered a hallway with gold fittings, a large framed mirror and flowers on a table. The side door into the office was already open.

'Come in,' the young woman said, through the doorway.

The office was well worn, oozing old-money charm and suggesting a comfortable few centuries of clever business. It had furniture for four or five, but only the girl was present. She was a brunette, in heavy make-up that failed to disguise how young she was. An old electric heater blew at her ankles. One woman's coat hung on a hatstand beside three dented bottle-green filing cabinets. There was a large mahogany table at the back with an upholstered armchair that might have been antique. Dusty green curtains filled the wall behind it. Someone had arranged a decorative stack of pine cones in the fireplace. The carpet was worn.

The girl watched him expectantly. She looked like an intern.

'Is Mr Devereux about?' he said.

'No.' Her face faltered. 'I'm his assistant. Can I help?' It was a strange face, he thought; not plain but not quite pretty, with liquid eyes and incredibly pale skin.

'Do you know where he is?'

'No.' She twisted a Kleenex in her hand.

'OK. When was he last in?'

'Is there a problem?' she asked.

'No. I don't think so. Is this his office?'

'Yes.'

'Does AD Development have offices upstairs?'

'No. This is the office. Who should I say called?'

'Don't worry about it.'

He was on his way out when she said: 'Excuse me.' He turned. She'd let a little more anxiety reach her face.

'Yes?'

'Do you know Mr Devereux?' she asked.

'Why?'

'Well, I'm a little concerned. I should have seen him. I haven't seen him for a while, in fact.'

Belsey considered his options.

'When did you last see him?' he said.

'A couple of days ago.'

Belsey walked back in, closing the office door and pulling up a chair from the side.

'I'm an old business partner,' he said. 'Perhaps he mentioned me. Jack Steel.' He shook her hand.

'Oh. Yes, maybe.'

'You must be . . .'

'Sophie.'

'Sophie, I'm also concerned, to be honest. I got a call last week and he said . . . well, he sounded upset. He wanted to say goodbye. I didn't really understand what he meant at the time.'

'Goodbye?'

'Farewell. Was he meant to be in today?'

'He always is. At least once a day. I don't know . . .' She trailed off.

'What about the other offices – Paris, New York? Have they heard from him?'

'No.'

Belsey got up, walked to the desk at the back and sat down again. He slid the bin out from beneath Devereux's desk and removed the foil wrap of a cigar, an empty carrier bag and a receipt from a local coffee shop.

'When did you last see him?' he asked.

37

'Friday.'

Belsey opened the desk drawers. The girl made a noise.

'I don't know if you should –'

'I know what I'm doing.'

The drawers were filled with cardboard wallet files in an assortment of colours. He emptied the files onto the desk and searched for bank details. She watched him, slightly horrified.

'How did he seem?' Belsey asked.

'On Friday? Distracted, I guess.'

Distraction: that was the danger. Do not become distracted. The paperwork didn't give much away.

'What do you think was distracting him?'

'He said something about being down to his last million.' Belsey tried not to smile. 'I think he was joking. I mean, I don't know if he was joking. I didn't think too much about it at the time.'

He stood up, turned to the green curtains, pulled them aside. They were covering bare bricks. He let them fall.

'Is the business going all right?' he said.

'As far as I can tell.'

'Hard times.'

'What's going on? Is he OK?'

'Are you able to access the company accounts?' Belsey asked.

'No.'

'How much do you know about operational workings?'

'Nothing. I mean, I pay in cheques. Mr D handles all the big transactions personally. Mr Devereux, that is.'

'Mr D?'

'Mr Devereux.'

'Were you sleeping with him?'

'Was I what?'

'Sleeping with him. Having sex.'

'No.'

Belsey opened the lower desk drawer.

'Those are his private papers,' she said.

'We need to find out what's going on.'

Belsey took out a file and emptied it. It contained a desktop diary. Belsey flicked through it: a suicide's diary could look distinct. There was a lot of scrawl over the previous month – names and times, sometimes three or four days blocked out – 'NY', 'Madrid'. Then it thinned out. Then it became blank. No plans for summer, no plans for spring. Only one incongruous entry, tomorrow night: 'Dinner'.

'He was having dinner tomorrow.'

'Oh, he was always meeting people.'

'After that it looks like he was winding down.'

'What do you mean?'

She looked like she might start to cry. Belsey took the empty carrier bag from the bin and filled it with an assortment of papers while she blew her nose.

'What should I do?' the girl asked.

'Hold tight,' Belsey said. 'If I know Alexei he'll be lying low, waiting to surprise us all.'

8

BELSEY RETURNED TO HAMPSTEAD POLICE STATION. HE SLID the 'Goodbye' card into his drawer, then placed his new Zippo and the penknife on his desk and admired them. He pocketed the lighter. He glanced through the stolen AD Development paperwork and decided to study it in detail later, when he had time to concentrate. For the moment, at least, he still had a job. *Work while it is day. The night is coming when no man shall work.* There were messages for him: from the hotel where he'd been staying, a loans company, an ex, a second cousin he hadn't seen since a wedding in 2004. People wanted to know why he wasn't answering his phone.

He called the ex from the office line.

'I am. I just don't have it.'

'But I spoke to a man on your number.'

'What did he say?'

'He said he wasn't you. Are things all right, Nick? Someone said you'd gone missing.'

'Missing? I'm here at work.'

'You sound different.'

'I am different.'

'Are you OK?'

A note in his in-tray instructed Belsey to attend the headquarters of the Independent Police Complaints Commission at 3 p.m. They hadn't wasted any time. Someone wanted him out. He looked at it and wondered if he'd gone missing. Maybe he was on the run. There were people on the run who were perfectly still. He folded the IPCC note into his pocket, stood up and stretched.

It was a relatively quiet day. Most of the other Hampstead detectives were at a training session in Enfield. The station was short-staffed and Belsey had to process a sixteen-year-old with a kilo of cannabis resin. Afterwards, he took the hash and bought some cigarette papers, begged a couple of Silk Cut and returned to the station.

He sat in the rape suite, smoking. It was comfortable there. That was the idea, he supposed: a sofa, some dried flowers, a side room behind a curtain. No one would look for him in the rape suite. He considered his plan as it stood and what he needed to do: investigate flights, locate his passport, raise a little travel money. Now he had decided on his course of action Belsey felt at peace. He hadn't smoked hash since his early twenties. He thought of his expectations then, the thrill of police work, the crew he ran with. They would compete to see who could travel the furthest in a night, while supposedly on duty. One time he stuck the sirens on and made it to Brighton. He remembered standing against a rail beside the sea, feeling spray on his face and staring into the blackness. It felt like being on the edge of everything he knew. He had made it in forty-two minutes, down the M23. If it was this easy, he thought, how far could he go in a night? In a week? At that moment every cell in his body wanted to run. Looking out over the sea, he thought: moving is the most important thing in the world. And he had forgotten that, as you do with the most important things.

He spent five minutes gathering papers for a court visit next week that would not take place. He would be gone. The case concerned a husband who'd tried to kill his family after he'd lost his job. The bank had cut his overdraft facility, the neighbours smelt gas. Belsey was glad he would not be there to see it all unfold. The justice system would find itself temporarily without a cog, but it would survive. At twelve thirty he returned to The Bishops Avenue.

New shoe prints led towards the house, parallel with his own. Heath mud, size nines where he was size eleven: no treads, some pale dust on the outside of the left sole where they had tried to skirt the pink gravel.

41

The visitor must have walked around the building, trying to see if anyone was in, then approached the bell. Belsey crouched to the bell. It was metal and would pick up good prints. He stepped back and looked at the windows. No lights on. None of the curtains had been moved. He emptied the mailbox attached to the front security gates. Then he climbed the steps and let himself in.

'Hello?' he called. There was no answer. Belsey flicked through Devereux's post as he walked through the house, tearing open envelopes and discarding the junk. He thought there might be a pin number or, less immediately useful, a bank statement. But he was also now intrigued by the enigma of Alexei Devereux. What had brought this situation about? Where was he? As a good detective, Belsey did not like mysteries, and as a bad one he found too many. In his first week of CID, Inspector John Harlow – the only DI he ever truly respected – had seen it in him: *It will be your downfall, Nick Belsey. Not knowing when to call it a day and stop asking bloody questions.*

He found three pizza-delivery menus, a letter from a call-forwarding company encouraging him to upgrade his service, and a lot of catalogues: for office supplies, outdoor sports equipment, children's educational toys, health supplements and designer luggage. Devereux had also received several brochures about tooth whitening. Belsey read them then checked his own teeth in the bathroom mirror. They were streaked with coffee; the gums appeared to be falling away.

A foul smell had begun to permeate the house. Belsey lit a scented candle from the bathroom. He sat at Devereux's desk, took a fountain pen and some headed sheets ('AD Development: *Hope Springs Eternal*'), and popped the cap of the pen. He wrote: *Hello, I am here*, and watched the ink soak into the thick paper. Then he took a fresh sheet and wrote his name and date of birth at the top. He wanted to write a confession. He wrote: *I have been a police officer for twenty-one years*, and then his mind went blank.

He couldn't ignore the stench any longer. It smelt like rotting meat. Time to clear the fridge out, Belsey told himself, and tried not to think what else it might mean. The smell was getting worse by the minute. Belsey walked to the kitchen but there was nothing rotting in the fridge, or any of the kitchen cupboards, or the bin. A single fly crawled across the tiled floor.

Belsey crouched down to see it: a bluebottle, shimmering, turquoise. Belsey lay on his stomach, inching closer until he could see the jewel-like eyes and the twitching of the individual legs.

Calliphora vomitoria. Nature's pallbearers. It crawled to Belsey's fingers and inspected them for signs of life. He had an awful feeling.

There were two flies circling the light fitting in the living room. A third flew in from the hallway. The Calliphoridae could smell death ten miles away, but Belsey sensed he wouldn't have to go that far. He followed another up the stairs.

The smell was strongest in the bedroom. He covered his mouth and nose, checked behind the curtains, under the bed, the wardrobes, but couldn't find any body.

He walked down the corridor. The next door led into a laundry room the size of an average bedroom, with cupboards, rails, wicker baskets, two washing machines and a dryer. Belsey opened the cupboards and took the lids off the wicker baskets. He opened the washing machines and dryer. They were all empty. The room was large, but not large enough to hide a corpse, and he couldn't understand what came between the two rooms to fill the rest of the first-floor corridor. Belsey walked back and knocked on the wall. It sounded hollow.

He walked back to the bedroom. He looked at the right-hand wall and the floor-length mirror. He pressed on the surface of the mirror and it shifted. He pressed on the edge and it swung open.

The mirror hid a small room. Belsey peered inside. A middle-aged man stared back from a swivel chair, suited, his throat sliced open and crawling with maggots. The space was rigged as a safe room: windowless, with electromagnetic locks, a phone and two CCTV monitors on a small desk. It had its own chemical toilet in the corner and a stack of mineral water and tinned food. Blood had reached the ceiling and the walls: shallow brown drops, held at the point where gravity had lost interest.

Belsey walked back downstairs.

He'd never been sick at a body and wasn't going to start now. He went out to the garden and crouched down breathing the fresh air. It wasn't enough to clear the smell from his nostrils though. He took a scarf from Devereux's wardrobe and made some strong coffee, drank half and watched it cool, then he poured the rest onto the scarf and tied it around his face. He found a pair of rubber gloves beneath the kitchen sink and went back.

The copper smell of blood provided a low note alongside the appalling sweet reek of decomposition. Carotid arteries fountain up to twenty feet on a good day. Blood had dripped back down into the corpse's face, streaking his scalp, dappling the front of his shirt. The man's eyes were covered with an opaque yellow film. He was heavy-set, balding, with fading golden hair cropped close; clean-shaven with a dusting of post-mortem stubble. Gases bloated the corpse but you could still make out a characterful face, like an emperor in decadent times; a strong nose and a full mouth. He'd had the muscle to dig deep and had done so with feeling. Belsey couldn't help being impressed. A paring knife lay on the floor beneath his right hand.

On the desk in front of the body was a slim, bloodstained brochure: 'The Reflections Funeral Plan' – motto, 'Everything Settled'. It carried a photograph of two swans floating on water. Inside, various prices for cremations and funerals were listed, averaging on two and a half thousand with interest. You paid in instalments. 'It's a good feeling when you know everything is in order, with no loose ends, and that your family will be spared undue distress.' No loose ends? Belsey thought. Family? Devereux's family seemed a long way away. Devereux had clipped a cheque for £3,200 from his UK current account, dated four days ago, made out to Reflections Ltd.

Belsey used the brochure to scrape some of the maggots away from the wound. Devereux had several cuts – short, parallel nicks high beneath his left ear: the trial cuts of the suicide, as they eased themselves into it. On his fourth attempt he dug deep, so deep he didn't even make it across his throat; the incision petered out beneath the larynx. The job was done, though. There were no other injuries – no defence injuries on the arms or hands. Belsey didn't particularly want to dwell on the larvae crowding the man's nostrils but he persuaded himself to take a look. They were getting on well, still unhatched, over a centimetre long. In a sealed environment, at winter temperatures, that placed the death between three to five days ago.

Belsey checked the room's electronics. A sticker on the CCTV hard drive said 'British Security Technologies'. The system was off. Belsey switched it on, looked for recording history but the drives were blank. He switched it off again and wondered about this. Certainly, as police, you learned that security technology got bought a lot more often than it got used. But then it wasn't always filming several million pounds.

He searched the suit. The pockets were empty.

He left the safe room, cleaned his prints off Devereux's wallet and placed it back beside the bed, found the last two days' envelopes in the bin and put them in his pocket. Then he left the house and locked up.

Belsey walked to Hampstead police station, to his office, and made a cup of tea. He gathered up the paperwork from AD Development. Then he went to a phone box outside the station and called the number for the station's control room.

'Hi. I'm the manager of a cleaning company in Hampstead. Could you pass a message to Detective Constable Nick Belsey? Tell him there's still no sign of Mr Devereux, the man missing from The Bishops Avenue. He asked us to let him know.'

He walked back into the station and picked up the message, drove over to The Bishops Avenue, let himself into the house and radioed for an ambulance.

'I've got a body here,' he said. 'No, there's no need to rush.'

9

THE AMBULANCE CREW ARRIVED WITHOUT LIGHTS OR SIRENS: two men and a woman moving with the businesslike pace of paramedics calling on a corpse.

'Wow,' they said as they came into the house.

They climbed the stairs, trying to guess how much it cost. 'Fifteen million,' 'Twice that.' Then they stepped into the safe room and saw the infested body.

'Yep, he's dead.'

'Did you try any CPR?' the woman asked, and they all laughed.

None of the brass came down, just a pathologist, his assistant and a photographer. The paramedics wandered through the house taking pictures on their mobiles. Soon the pathologist's assistant had joined them, gawping. No one rushed the job.

When photographs had been taken and the pathologist had pronounced him dead, the crew wrapped the body in plastic and carried it on a stretcher to the ambulance.

'He'll be in St Pancras Mortuary if you want him.'

'Thank you,' Belsey said.

'Who'll be doing an ID?'

'I'll check for a next of kin. I don't know. He lived alone.'

'OK.'

'I should have found the body the first time,' Belsey said. 'I should have looked more carefully.' He shook his head. The ambulance

46

pulled out. A security guard from the house across the road watched it go.

Belsey went back inside and shut the door. He opened all the windows. Why in the safe room, he thought. But suicides sometimes liked to tuck themselves away, to let the emergency services find them rather than a loved one. Or, in the absence of a loved one, their cleaner. And there was something fine about retreating into safety to slit your throat. He thought about the set-up: the funeral payment plan, the pragmatism of the cheque. It had been a tactful death, all things considered.

What were the implications for himself? Belsey wondered. Who would come to claim the house? A couple of hours ago, the remnants of Devereux's life had seemed a lucky find. The sight of his body had made them appear more starkly abandoned. He sensed greater freedom, and greater responsibility.

He called Land Registry and ran a property search. 37 The Bishops Avenue was owned by a lettings company called Home from Home who described themselves as VIP relocation specialists: 'for business leaders and their families; service includes school search'. They were based on Hampstead High Street. Belsey called the office and got a man with a very smooth, camp voice.

'You rent out the property at 37 The Bishops Avenue?'

'Yes.'

'To Mr Devereux?'

'We can't disclose details. Is this press?'

'It's police. When did he start renting it?'

'This is police?'

'Hampstead CID.'

'Perhaps if you'd like to come into the office.'

Belsey called the Driver and Vehicle Licensing Association. Sure enough, the Porsche came up as a hire car. City Inter-Rent – offices in Heathrow, Marylebone and Croydon.

Everything became a little less substantial.

The DVLA said Devereux got his UK licence three months ago. They came up with a date of birth: 2 February 1957. It made him fifty-two years old when he took his life.

Companies House had no AD Development incorporated in the UK, which meant they weren't trading as a limited company: no shareholders, no accounts to return. It was odd but not unheard of.

The phone began to ring and wouldn't stop. Belsey paced Devereux's bedroom and let it ring. He picked up the invoice from RingCentral ('Your Phone System, Everywhere'). It made him curious. RingCentral offered a service for companies that needed to divert calls. Belsey imagined it was the kind of thing you'd use when transferring location or understaffed. He thought of Sophie alone in the AD Development office.

The ringing stopped. Belsey lifted the cordless phone on the bedside table. He hadn't used it yet. He pressed the button to redial the last call made from it. A woman answered.

'Hello?'

'Hi,' Belsey said.

'Is that you?' she said. In the background Belsey heard traffic, someone laughing. He hung up. A moment later he lifted it again and called St Pancras Mortuary.

'You've got a body coming in from N2. Alexei Devereux. I've got an individual who can ID it. Send someone to this address.' He read off the office address for AD Development. 'It's Mr Devereux's office in the City. There's a girl there who worked for him. She's called Sophie. I don't have her full name.'

'OK.'

'She doesn't know about it yet. Be gentle.'

'Of course.'

Belsey used to be the one they sent to break the news. That was in his uniform days. He had got the nickname Angel of Death because he volunteered. Someone had to do it, and his colleagues were grateful. And there had been a very grim satisfaction to performing a task that could not go well and for which you were blameless. It had been a while since he'd made one of those visits.

He went to the study and sat down with the paperwork from the AD Development office. There were a lot of enquiries and proposals, a lot of acronyms: SSI International, NK Trading, Saud Holdings and LV Media, all discussing stakes in an AD operation. There were a lot of people looking to invest in Alexei Devereux, it seemed. He, in turn, was always up for a deal. A stack of letters concerned his enquiries about land in Sharm el Sheikh and Abu Dhabi. He appeared to have interests in banks, sport, media, hotels and gambling. Belsey imagined he must have contributed in some way to Devereux's fortune. It allowed him to feel a small sense of justice in whatever stratagem he was pursuing.

A significant amount of the paperwork gave the name Alexei Demochev. It tended to be older business: faxes and correspondence from Russia; Moscow lawyers and accountants, sometimes writing in Cyrillic, sometimes English or French. Belsey checked the number on the aged fax machine in the study and it was the machine to which they'd been sent.

At the bottom of the pile was a page of newspaper in Arabic, torn out roughly along one side. Belsey was ready to disregard it as scrap when he saw that one of the articles had been circled in blue biro. Four inches of closely printed calligraphic script were accompanied by a grainy black-and-white picture showing an Arabic man in a light-coloured suit shaking hands with a blond man in frameless glasses. The blond one was younger. Both were smiling. The date was given in Roman numerals at the top of the page: Monday 9 February. Three days ago.

The circle of biro lent the clipping an urgent significance – that and its proximity in time to Devereux's suicide. Did Devereux read Arabic? The impenetrability of the writing was frustrating. Belsey reclaimed Devereux's wallet from the bedroom, folded the article twice and placed it inside. Then he returned the wallet to his pocket and felt better.

One course of action involved arranging ID in Devereux's name but with his own photo. A driver's licence or passport. That would be easy enough. He could use the Bishops Avenue address to open an entirely new bank account, complete with credit card and overdraft, then reacquaint himself with the kind people at No Worries Loans dotcom, except this time with a credit score that would open up an unsecured twenty-five grand.

But it would take time. And Belsey sensed there was something more ambitious he could pull off, involving the money already there. He had been given the sparkling playground of Devereux's life, and he hadn't seen half of it yet. He didn't buy the poor Russian businessman act.

He needed to find out a little more about his target. He needed to stay awake.

Galaxy Drug Store occupied the centre of a run-down parade of shops in East Finchley, sheltered between a William Hill and a Chinese take-away. Its sign was missing the final 'e' but the window display made up for it, flashing 'All-night Pharmacy' in neon. The window was crowded with film posters and international phonecards, and told the passing custom that they had DVDs for hire. Belsey walked in.

The maximum amount of ephedrine hydrochloride legally available without prescription in one sale was 180mg. The only product commonly sold within these restrictions was ChestEze tablets which bundled 30mg of caffeine, 18.31mg ephedrine and 100mg anhydrous theophylline, the last being a member of the happy family of xanthines, a pharmacological cousin to caffeine. They came in packs of nine.

Belsey walked up to the counter where a teenage assistant stood picking at his skin.

'I've been told I need a product called ChestEze,' Belsey said. The boy looked at him doubtfully, then went to shelves behind the counter and fetched a pack. He placed it down between them. Belsey made a show of reading the small print: *for relief of bronchial cough, wheezing, breathlessness and other symptoms of asthmatic bronchitis.*

'Could I get two packs?' Belsey said.

'I can't sell you two, I'm afraid.'

'One's for my father. I got the bronchitis off him.'

The boy raised an eyebrow but went to fetch another. He seemed easy game. Belsey asked him to wait and found some air freshener, vitamins and a pack of Sudafed as well.

'I don't have a pin for it,' Belsey said, taking out the Amex.

The boy briefly closed his eyes with a weariness beyond his years, then he pressed a button and passed Belsey a chewed biro.

Belsey took his bag of supplements and walked to the public library on the high road. He asked for a guest code for the PCs, logged in and searched for Alexei Devereux. The top few hits looked credible: one was an article in Russian from the *Khiminskaya Prada* and one an article from the *Wall Street Journal*. You had to pay to view the *Wall Street Journal* article in full, but it began: 'Of all the new crop of oligarchs to set their sights beyond Russia, Alexei Devereux is perhaps the most intriguing'. The *Eurasian Trade News* website dropped his name in a list of five men 'changing the face of the Russian entertainment sector'. It didn't say how. It said he was 'notoriously reclusive'. Later it said, 'the enigmatic Alexei Devereux is personally responsible for pumping two billion dollars into the ailing sports network TGT'. The *Novaya Sayat* newspaper linked a spike in Posky International shares to talks of a Devereux buyout. Posky operated in the leisure and retail sector. The piece was an inch-high column to the side of a general stock graph from 2007. Only the *Moscow Business Gazette*, dated to last October, gave something of the life: 'Ultra-reclusive, ultra-successful investor', Devereux was one of 'the Christmas List', ten men who pioneered the second round of sell-offs over Christmas 1998. It said Devereux had gone into political exile after his ties to opposition politicians made life increasingly untenable in Russia.

Belsey read the last article twice. The implication was that he had gone into exile shortly before the piece was written, which was ten weeks ago. It said he had bases in Paris, London and New York and would probably be welcome in any of them. But no one knew where he'd gone. No one knew where his businesses were going.

Belsey returned to the house. The smell of putrefaction had begun to fade. The insect life had moved on to its next show. He sprayed the air freshener then found the bottle of champagne in the fridge and opened it. A recommended adult dose of ChestEze was one tablet in four hours. He took three with a glass of Veuve Clicquot. He shut the safe room and tried to forget it was there. He was slightly horrified by his actions, and yet this horror was a place to be for the moment.

Belsey looked at the American Express credit card. It became valid only five days ago. He called the customer services number on the back.

'I have a new credit card here,' Belsey said. 'But I never received a pin for it.'

'Would you like us to dispatch a new card?'

'I just need a pin number.'

'We'd have to dispatch a new card as well.'

'That's fine. And you send the pin separately?'

'That's correct.'

'How long would that take?'

'Two or three days.'

'Can you do it special delivery? I don't want to lose another one.'

'I'm afraid not, sir. But it should be with you in the next few days.'

'That's fine.'

'I just need to ask a few security questions. Could you give me your date of birth?'

'Second of February, 1957.'

'And your postcode?' He lifted an unopened catalogue of gardening equipment and read it off the address label.

'Your mother's maiden name?'

'Demochev,' he tried.

'That's not the name I have here, sir.'

So he'd hit a wall. Belsey wondered how he would get Devereux's mother's maiden name. He pictured a dense archive of Soviet-era paperwork. It had always seemed touching to him, the use of maiden names as security; this private knowledge of our mothers' pasts. It didn't touch him now.

'I'm an orphan,' he said.

There was a pause. 'OK, sir. Is there a particular name you gave us? A password?'

'I've forgotten.'

'We would need to receive that before we can dispatch a new card.'

'OK.'

Belsey hung up. He gave it fifteen minutes then called the Card Fraud Unit's offices in Temple.

'Any reports just made on this individual's card?'

'Not as far as I can see. Want to make one?'

'No.'

Out of curiosity Belsey called City Police and the Serious Fraud Office. He ran Devereux and his company past them but they knew nothing, were uninterested and, by their own account, busy enough already.

It takes the average person twelve months to discover that their identity has been stolen. That was for the living. If this was what he was doing, stealing Devereux's identity, then it gave him some time. He felt ready to pick up where Devereux had left off. If he was going to be born again it would be nice to be someone rich.

Belsey set about his first systematic search of the premises. There were a lot of things he would have been interested to find: a will, a chequebook, the driver's licence or any other photo ID, pin numbers, passwords, address books that might contain them, a laptop. He started with the study. The study had an elaborate dresser consisting of two alcoves joined at the top by an arch, with shelves in the alcoves, drawers beneath them, and then small cupboard doors. Everything was empty but for blank paper, yellowing newspapers in French and Italian; old catalogues.

The chest of drawers in the bedroom and the living room were also empty. Belsey searched behind the artworks for a concealed safe but found nothing. He looked under the dining-room table and found folded tablecloths and a box of crystal wine glasses.

He found a dusty sauna in what he had originally thought was a walk-in wardrobe. On the ground floor, beside the kitchen, he discovered a utility room that Devereux probably didn't know about, with a washing machine, ironing board, tools for cleaners and gardeners, bottles of cleaning products, floor polish, mops and overalls.

Not a single item of use to him.

The phone began to ring again. It seemed to announce the peculiarity of his situation. Each ring was the splash of oars pushing him further away from shore. Belsey sat in the study and looked at the model ship and the Winter Palace, the will to plunder momentarily deserting him. Devereux's possessions felt like words left hanging mid-sentence. They seemed to want to say something. About loneliness, perhaps. Exile was a feeling; he understood that. Belsey looked around and sensed

53

someone trying to make a strange place look like home. Maybe it explained the non-committal rental style.

What had Devereux thought of, sitting here? Money worries? A deal gone wrong? A country he'd never see again? Belsey imagined snow-covered fields, farm machinery, a dirt track. There were peasant women selling honey cakes to travellers; factories with muscular men and flags. He walked to the window then sat on the floor and looked at the space beneath the desk and the antique chair. Something glinted on the floor. Belsey crawled under the desk to the object. It was a watch, supposedly a Rolex: silver and heavy. The face bore the Rolex logo, but the second hand didn't glide, which was a giveaway. Devereux didn't strike him as a man for fakes, but then it seemed Devereux might not have been all he once had been. It was still a watch, ticking and with ambitions. It had five dials on the silver face and a lot of buttons to play with. Even fakes could go for several hundred pounds. Belsey liked it. One of the dials showed the phases of the moon.

He put it on and went to the wine rack in the kitchen. He opened three bottles and tried them all: a burgundy, Clos des Lambrays Grand Cru; a 1996 Riesling from Alsace; finally an Italian red from Piedmont, 1989. He decided the only moral thing you could do with wealth was destroy yourself with it. He looked at the fake Rolex on his wrist and drank the burgundy then took the Riesling up to the pool. The light was turning grey. Belsey kicked his shoes off and sat on a sunlounger. He wondered what you did once you had achieved luxury, what you discovered on the far side of it. He decided he should learn more about time management. His career had been a substitute for time, he saw now, but the career had come apart in his hands. He didn't know what would replace it. He wanted to talk to Alexei Devereux.

He made one last search of the premises. He hadn't investigated the garage any further because it had seemed empty. But a second check showed he had overlooked a wheelie bin in the front corner, by the electric door. He lifted the top and saw a blue recycling bag, half full; tore it open and saw paper.

Belsey took the bag to the living room and emptied it on the floor. The various documents preserved the form of whatever single file had contained them. The papers involved correspondence relating to some-thing called Project Boudicca. At the top of the pile was a fax from lawyers representing the Hong Kong Gaming Consortium regarding 'what we hope you will find is an arrangement convenient to both parties'.

The proposed arrangement involved the split for a deal: 80 per cent payment to AD Development and 20 to a numbered account with the Raiffeisen Zentralbank Austria. The fax gave account details. 'Please consider this correspondence sensitive.'

Belsey sat on the floor surrounded by the bin bag's load. He felt himself swimming above a new depth of wealth, the water colder and darker. Behind every great man is an anonymous account. This one was a Sparbuch. Sparbuchs were so anonymous that the Austrian banks were no longer allowed to supply them, but old accounts changed hands on the black market. The bank didn't ask you for a name or address. They gave you a small savings book, the *Sparbuch* itself, and you chose a pass-word. That was it. It was useful to have an Austrian accent, or a helpful Austrian attorney, to ensure no flags were raised. Then you were free to drop as much money in and take as much money out, and all you needed was the password. No incriminating statements, no correspondence, no free pen. Mostly people liked to visit the bank in person but funds could be transferred by wire or telephone. They called it wealth protection and police called it a dead end.

Belsey couldn't find the savings book itself. But, incredibly, he had the account number, the *Kontrollnummer*. It was crazy to think he'd get further. But it was true that more than half of people write their pass-words down somewhere. Seventy-five per cent reuse the same one again and again.

Belsey dug through the pile of discarded documents and saw the account mentioned in correspondence with a law firm called Trent Horsley Myers and a firm of accountants on Sloane Square. Finally there was a letter to the solicitors from Raiffeisen Zentralbank Austria, confirming that they now offered twenty-four-hour telephone banking and there were no formal restrictions on the amount an individual could deposit in one day, although sums over 500,000 euros would take forty-eight hours to clear.

Belsey had found the buried treasure, he felt certain. He called the number on the bank's correspondence.

'*Guten Abend,*' a woman answered.

'*Guten Abend,*' Belsey said. 'I'm calling from London. I have an account with you and I need to make an urgent payment out of it.'

'Of course, sir. Can I have your password?'

'I don't have the password here. I have the account number.'

'I'd need your password, sir.'

'This is urgent. I have a contractor waiting.'

'I can't do that, sir.'

'What would I need to transfer money out?'

'Account number and password.'

'And I could do that by phone?'

'Of course.'

'What if I've forgotten my password?'

'You'd need to bring proof of identity into one of our branches and speak to a security adviser.'

'Thank you.'

Belsey hung up. The money was there, he could smell it. *We brought nothing into this world and it is certain we can carry nothing out.* What had the PA said? Down to his last million. He could believe that Devereux was moved by poverty to take his life, but poverty was relative. One man's bankruptcy was another man's nest egg. It was just a question of advancing carefully.

Belsey considered his next move. Then he saw the time. He was late for the end of his career.

10

THE IPCC HEADQUARTERS WERE IN HIGH HOLBORN: A GLASS-walled office block with a Starbucks on the ground floor. Belsey parked the Porsche Cayenne round the corner and walked in. The headquarters wore a neutral mask; blue carpets, floor-length windows, code-access doors in pale pine. He'd been there once before, after a death in custody, and hadn't enjoyed it much then either.

'Belsey. Here for a review.'

A front-desk man looked at him, checked something and sent Belsey, accompanied by a guard, to the second floor. There was an open-plan space with a lot of civilian workers at flat-panel monitors. The guard departed and a man came up to him.

'Nicholas Belsey?'

'Hi.'

'Frank Sacco. I'm your lawyer, Riggs and Jenkins.'

He shook Belsey's hand. Sacco was a short man in an olive-green suit and slip-on shoes, face glistening as if he'd slicked the hair and continued slicking his face. Riggs and Jenkins supplied all the lawyers for internal investigations. It meant Belsey's case had already reached the union.

'Pleased to meet you,' Belsey said.

'Anything we need to discuss?'

'Do you know much about identity theft?'

'It's not my speciality.'

'Let's go in.'

Sacco led the way to a corner office. Inside were two men and a woman – one man and the woman sitting behind a desk with a file, the second man standing, looking out of the window. Belsey walked in and shut the door. The seated man was Barry Gaunt, from the IPCC. Belsey recognised the commissioner from television, where he talked about what went wrong at riots, police who had acted violently. He was too broad for his M&S suit, with a pink face and a thick neck. The standing man was tall, with rat-like features. The woman had a bob and a dark orange trouser suit and craft jewellery. So they've brought in a counsellor, Belsey thought. From the office you got a view of Kingsway, the old tram tunnel, Red Lion Square. People were filing in to Conway Hall.

'Please, sit down.'

Belsey and Sacco took the empty seats. The counsellor spoke first, which was never a good sign.

'I'm Janet, from the Mental Health Assessment Team.'

'I'm pleased to meet you, Janet,' Belsey said.

Gaunt spoke: 'Barry Gaunt from the IPCC. This is Nigel Herring, from Camden Borough headquarters.' He waved towards the tall man. Herring avoided Belsey's gaze. Belsey knew the name: Northwood's attack dog, risen to Inspector purely by virtue of kissing Northwood's arse. A shifty character, with his finger in too many pies. He wore a Masonic ring and an unhealthy pallor.

'What do you understand about this situation?' Gaunt asked.

'This situation?'

'About why you're here.'

'Because I stole and crashed a squad car.'

'OK,' the counsellor said gently.

'Chief Superintendent Northwood wants you to explain yourself.'

'I don't know if I can explain myself as such. Things happened, and I am ashamed of what happened, and understand that procedures will . . . proceed.'

'It's not just this, though, is it?' Gaunt said.

'You mean with regards to that night?'

'With regards to everything.'

'With regards to everything, no. It's not just this.' Belsey said.

Gaunt looked half bored, as if he resented being drawn from serious riots to the small and insignificant riot of Belsey's life.

'Where were you going?' he asked.

'I think I was actually trying to get to the Heath. In that sense I succeeded. I woke up the following morning on the Heath. Am I suspended?'

'Should you be?'

'Don't answer,' Sacco said.

'Would it be a paid suspension?' Belsey said.

'Are you in financial difficulty?' the counsellor asked.

'Yes,' Belsey said. He put his hands into Devereux's jacket. Then he took them out again and checked the time. He thought: who drops a watch? If you drop a watch, you hear it. You pick it up. And you don't drop it anyway, because it's on you.

'Do you enjoy police work?' the counsellor asked.

'No more than I'm meant to.'

'Would you like to talk about what it means to you?'

'Can I ask you a question about dreams?' Belsey said.

'Let me ask you a question,' Herring interjected. 'Did you enter the Borough Commander's home on the night of 11 February?'

'Yes.'

'With his wife?' He sounded exasperated.

'Is that an offence? You'll have half the Met –'

'Watch yourself.'

'Watch yourself,' Sacco said.

'Is this on the square, Nigel? Know what I mean?'

'You're running out of lives, Belsey.'

'Yes.'

'Yes what?' Gaunt said.

'Yes, I entered it.'

'Why?'

'I was curious.'

Herring turned back to the window with his hands in his pockets.

Belsey thought about money laundering. Even if he could get access to Devereux's personal stash he wouldn't be able to transfer it into his current account without setting off alarm bells. Sudden changes in wealth did that. Transfers from dead businessmen to bankrupt detectives did that. And he needed a financial set-up that could travel. He'd spent several months seconded to Anti-Money Laundering and knew the game. There were three stages to each wash: placement, layering and integration. Placing money meant establishing some door through which you could get dirty cash into the world of finance. It meant finding a vein. Layering was the web you weave, the movement around shells, offshores, numbered accounts, making it untraceable before the third stage: integration. Because no one wants a big cheque from the Bank of Downtown La Paz. But get it into the City of London and it's legitimate. EC1 was every money launderer's dream. Just half a mile away . . .

'Northwood says you've got previous,' Herring said.

'Does he?'

'Trouble at Borough. Question marks.'

'Chief Superintendent Northwood has some form of his own, doesn't he?'

Herring began to speak but the counsellor intervened.

'Let's concentrate on the specific incident,' she suggested, with gentle exasperation. 'Try to explain what occurred.'

'Not a great deal occurred. I apologise for taking the car. I've been going through a rough time.'

'Had you been drinking?'

'Of course I'd been drinking.'

'Would you say you have a problem with alcohol?'

'No.'

'Any other substances?'

'Ritalin. If I wanted to work here,' Belsey said, 'would I have to be close to retirement? Older, I mean?'

Herring tightened his lips. 'We're going to need a urine sample.'

'Where would you like it?' Belsey said.

Gaunt opened his desk drawer and produced a small pot, which he rested on Belsey's edge of the desk as if to avoid contaminating himself. Is that all he had in there? Belsey wondered. Receptacles for urine?

'OK, sure,' Belsey said. He took the pot, went towards the toilets, then he kept going to the lifts and out of the front doors.

11

Belsey looked up 'Company Formation' in a Yellow Pages in Holborn Library and found what he was looking for.

Ocean Wealth Protection and Private Banking Assistance. Same-day Company Formation Agent. Start a new business in 3 to 5 minutes: £32.00 – Tax Havens and Privacy Solutions.

Privacy solutions sounded right. He knew an international business corporation – an IBC – could be set up in somewhere like Antigua with the click of a button, complete with an office address and even board directors provided by the Antiguan authorities. Your name didn't come up on any paperwork but you could steer money through. Ocean had a walk-in office in Belsize Park just a few minutes from Hampstead Police station. Belsey knew the street: a parade of estate agents, cosmetic surgeons and boutique clothes stores. He imagined Ocean looked at home there. He was correct.

He parked the Porsche Cayenne outside their office, making sure Ocean had a good view of it. He got out, straightening his suit, and rang the intercom.

'Straight up the stairs.' There was a positive note to the voice. Belsey climbed narrow steps to a door marked Ocean Ltd. The office was run by two men, one young and one old, with computers and little else. The older one had the faded sparkle of a player, hair cropped close, gym-build. He looked like a bank robber trying to dress as a banker. The younger one wore a white shirt with braces and a pink tie with a fat knot. On the wall was a map of the world with coloured flags pinned to a lot of small islands. A free-standing fan moved cigarette smoke towards a double-glazed window where it rolled back towards the desks. Belsey was gestured to a seat at a bare desk in the centre of the room.

'Coffee?'

'Black, thanks.'

Belsey glanced at the walls. Around the map were a lot of plaques and certificates that told you little other than the outfit knew how to look cute. The older man poured the coffee.

'How can we help?'

'I'd like to buy a company,' Belsey said. He took a sip of good, strong coffee. 'I need to cover my back.'

'What kind of thing were you thinking of?'

'Two IBCs somewhere offshore, maybe Antigua, with nominee directors and a trading record. I want a postbox address that can't be traced to me and an anonymous deposit account in the name of one of the shelf companies, somewhere untouchable. But I need it respectable enough to transfer medium sums into a European current account without drawing attention.'

They leaned back, nodding. The younger agent balanced a pen between his index fingers.

'Sounds like you know what you're doing.'

'I need an idea of prices.'

'It depends on the jurisdiction. For an off-the-shelf company, the British Virgin Islands is attractive: Crown property, starts at eight hundred and forty. Jersey is twice that, but then it's a major financial centre. Otherwise there's Dominica, the Seychelles, Anguilla. All the companies we sell will have records going back at least three years. Dominica's the cheapest that we'd feel comfortable recommending.'

'What's on Dominica?'

He flipped a small laptop open.

'We could sell you, for example, the Dutch Export Import Trading

AG, set up March 2005. Or the American Auto Management Corporation, a couple of months older. Each comes with a law firm as nominee director, so that any dealings remain confidential. You get power of attorney so you can manage the company. There's no reporting requirements.'

'And the bank account?'

'If it was me I'd go for Cyprus, but that will be fifteen hundred. Otherwise, maybe St Vincent, which is US dollar accounts only but you can receive or transfer money in all major currencies. Minimum deposit would be around two grand; you pay the deposit to the bank, not to us. It's totally anonymous but they do ask for references. It's a tough climate out there. You don't look like a terrorist to me, but . . .'

'Any that don't ask for a reference or minimum deposit?'

'The Island of Niue.' He pronounced it Nee-oo-yee.

'Niue?'

'A chunk of coral in the middle of the Pacific Ocean. Three hours' flight from New Zealand. Self-governing member of the British Commonwealth, mostly home to seagulls and the registered addresses of Japanese telephone-sex companies. And the Bank of the South Pacific, as it's known. Essentially, you give us an address of your choice and we type up a bill and fax that to them. It will do. They'll charge a one-off fee of two hundred dollars for admin.'

'Perfect.'

'Great. What else? We can do you a Certificate of Good Standing for ninety-five pounds, a virtual office in a city of your choosing which can hold mail and forward calls. That's around seventy per month. For twenty-five pounds we can even give you a rubber stamp of the company.'

'What does that do?'

'It's a stamp made out of rubber, with the company name on it.'

'I'll get one of those.'

'OK.'

'How does this call-forwarding service work?'

'However you want. When someone dials your company it goes through to them. They answer the phone and say this is X company, so-and-so is in a meeting, and then they call you to pass on the message.

64

Or not. They can wait for you to call, or pass messages once a week. They can sing the caller happy birthday, if you want. It's your call, you see?' He grinned.

'I see. I've got a lot of money in an Austrian account that I want to transfer. What works best for that?'

'Niue will be fine. We can use one of the IBCs to set up an account on the island. That will come with a local office address, which is a statutory requirement, but we'll throw in a virtual address package which means you can operate from anywhere in the world and not worry about unwanted bureaucracy.'

'That would be great.'

'Of course it would.'

Belsey sipped his coffee. He felt, for the first time, what every career criminal must feel at least once and never forget: the possibility of getting away with it; the knowledge of policing's limits, the limits of international cooperation, and the space of freedom beyond them. He gazed out of the window and thought of tropical seas. *Wash me whiter than snow*, the prayer went. *Wash my sins away.*

'What's the total?' Belsey asked.

'For an address, two shelf companies and a bank account you're looking at six grand, tops. Probably more like five thousand eight hundred.'

'I don't have the money on me right now.'

'Sure. Come back when you do. It's all ready to go.' The young man looked up from his screen and smiled.

Belsey tore a parking ticket off the Porsche's windscreen, binned it and drove to a travel agent's on Hampstead High Street. All the assistants were busy. He took a seat in the waiting area and thought of the last time he'd been out of the country: a weekend break to Palermo, a spur-of-the-moment thing with a blonde estate agent who had been a witness in a club shooting. They'd gone straight from the Old Bailey. That was last May, his only holiday in five years. But he remembered the feverish promise of those days, of places in which London seemed a long, dark dream; *that* was the kind of place he was going.

He took a brochure and scribbled a list of non-extradition countries on the back. He knew the police forces that were hard to liaise with. There'd been several cases where they tried to liaise with Libya. It was impossible; no one spoke English, no one answered the phones. To Libya and then . . . on, further. *They give you weapons training. Play a bit of squash, stay in shape . . .*

'Can I help?' A young woman called him over.

'How much is a flight to Libya?' Belsey asked.

The woman ran a search on her computer.

'Right now, starting at two hundred and twenty, one way, Tripoli.' She tilted it so he could see.

'Including tax?'

'No.'

'What's the cheapest flight you do?'

This check took a moment longer.

'Dublin,' she said.

'I need somewhere further away than Dublin.'

'How about Bremen? That's in Germany.'

'How much is that?'

'Four pounds without tax. Probably twenty-eight with.'

'Flying from Stansted?'

'That's right.'

'What does the train to Stansted cost these days?'

'Return?'

'Single.'

'Hang on.' She wheeled her chair over to a colleague then wheeled it back.

'Nineteen.'

'Thank you.'

He walked out of the travel agent's and into a cafe, took a newspaper from the bin and wrote in the blank spaces of an advert: flight, taxes, train. He listed the prices for each one. And he felt a quiet satisfaction at seeing the bottom line – forty-seven pounds to start his life again. Then he wrote five thousand eight hundred pounds alongside it, the rough figure quoted by the company formations agent. That would keep

66

alive the possibility of a more dramatic regeneration. But it meant significant start-up capital.

He turned the page over and wrote a list of Devereux's possessions in the margin and, beside it, a column of what he thought he could get for them.

12

His passport wasn't in the CID office. Obviously he'd used it when he went to Sicily. He couldn't remember the last time he'd seen it.

Belsey had been searching for a few minutes when a phone call came in. 'Belsey?'

'Yes.'

'Mike Slater. We've got word there's been a body found on The Bishops Avenue. A suicide. Any idea about that?'

Belsey caught his breath.

'None at all, Mike. Tell me about it.'

'I'm serious, Nick. I've been holding off running a feature on your recent exploits. Now I need a story.'

'A body's not a story.'

'It is on The Bishops Avenue.'

'Let me get back to you, Mike. Keep me out of the paper. I appreciate that.'

Belsey put the phone down, cursing loose-lipped paramedics and over-eager journalists. Mike Slater was editor on the *Hampstead & Highgate Express*, a man whose crumpled charm and air of world-weariness disguised a passion for journalism that had kept the *Ham & High* a respected local weekly for two decades. Slater was on friendly terms with Belsey but he could smell a story in NW3 when one was ripening. Trapping entered the office.

'Nick.'

'Rob. That stabbing suspect, Johnny Cassidy, have you found him?'

'Not yet.'

'You said he was Niall Cassidy's boy.

'That's right.'

'Is the old man still a fence?'

'Well, he's not head of neighbourhood watch, put it that way.'

'Still in Borough?'

'Nowhere else would have him. Used to be your neck of the woods, didn't it, Nick?'

'I passed through.'

'Best not to stop, eh?'

He picked up a file and walked out. Belsey pondered. Lack of funds was holding him back. The violent homecoming of Niall Cassidy's son could be a stroke of luck. He needed to shift a lot of stolen goods very quickly and he wasn't going to use one of the high street's new pawnbrokers.

He grabbed his coat and the keys for Devereux's Porsche and decided on a trip down memory lane.

13

Belsey crossed the river on Blackfriars. The sun was setting. Halfway to the Old Kent Road it felt like he began to fall. The elastic of time had snapped and he was falling backwards through his once-promising career, down through Borough towards Elephant and Castle.

He left the riverside glitz behind him. Beyond the redevelopment, in the timeless Victorian shadows, the landmarks had not changed: the estates in which he'd learned his trade, the pubs where he'd tried to forget it again. But the pubs were boarded up now. Places that had been derelict to start with and whose survival had seemed testament to something perverse and unyielding in life were gone. The Eagle, which had been a copper's pub, bore anti-trespass threats on every window. His favourite memories of himself, bathed in an amber light of whisky and lager, had been boarded up. Barely out of his twenties when he'd last worked these streets, fresh to CID and high on it.

By some grimy miracle the Wishing Well had survived. It stood alone beside a railway arch, on a backstreet of mechanics and lock-ups. The legend 'Take Courage' remained faint on its side, painted onto bricks still blackened by nineteenth-century smoke. Handwritten sheets promising 'Live Music Saturday' obscured its front windows.

Belsey parked the SUV and walked in.

Niall Cassidy and his gang sat around a tin of cigarette filters, a transistor radio and a *Racing Post*. They were metal thieves – that was the current game, at least: they stole manhole covers and electrical cable to be melted down and sold abroad. Previously they'd connected to low-key amphetamine importation, and still did as far as Belsey knew. Most operated a complex portfolio of crime. Light from street lamps trickled in through dirty strips of glass above the taped sheets. A sign said 'Welcome Home Johnny', but Johnny wasn't home. What had Trapping said? Two years in the Balearics, comes back and stabs the man who grassed him. Now lying low, it seemed. The Well had been robbed of its celebration.

'Afternoon, lads,' Belsey said.

'Bellboy, my son.'

'Nicky, long time.'

'Not long enough.'

'How's the land of the rich?'

'Better than in here,' Belsey said.

The snug bar was dingy. There was a pool table in a separate room behind it, in the deep end of the gloom. Cassidy nodded a greeting but kept his mouth shut. He looked like a man who'd been trying to get drunk and failing, a man whose jewellery was weighing him down.

'What have I missed?' Belsey said.

'Nothing. It's been shit.'

They grinned toothless grins, stroking faded tattoos. The landlord, Rod Thompson, was a wreck of a man with emphysema. He was pale as a corpse now, but retained the residual instinct of a wise publican. He set Belsey's drinks up with a wink.

A pint of Stella and a shot of Jameson. Belsey drank the whiskey at the bar, watching the group. He'd interrupted a discussion: doubtless about Johnny and his unfortunate chain of events. Conspire literally meant to breathe together. He considered this as he watched the Well. Back in smoking days this had been tangible in grey wisps of Old Holborn. Now they sat in the clear air like fish out of water: Dell Patterson, one of the half-dozen postmen from the Nine Elms depot sent down a few years ago for skimming credit cards; Trevor Hart, who dealt in untaxed tobacco and diesel; Brendan McCarthy, who had just got out of Wandsworth having served two years for GBH on his brother-in-law.

These were individuals shrunk so far back into themselves that you saw a no-man's-land behind the eyes, an undecorated space, then a shut room with furniture piled against the door. Porridge heads. And Wandsworth was hard time by all accounts. In the old days Belsey would have made a point of checking in with Brendan, having a probationary chat. You got the prison gossip, of course, but these were also the ones to watch, the newly free, spasming.

'Belsen, boy. Pull up a seat.'

'Is that a new suit, Nicky?' Trevor asked.

'I just bought it.'

'One of us must be doing something wrong.'

'Both of us, I imagine,' Belsey said, drawing up a stool.

'What happened?'

'I got promoted.'

'To what?'

'El Presidente. I'm the boss now.'

'You look more like a pimp every time I see you.'

Belsey sat for a moment and enjoyed being back in the Wishing Well. He did not like to think about what wishes were made here. People threw small change into the urinal with an irony he found hard to gauge. He admired the cigarette-burnt surfaces and yellowed posters of County Kerry tourist attractions. Once upon a time the Well had been an IRA pub, an outpost of that underground network that sheltered beneath the Westway. It was still a good pub for hiding. The old boys were in at 11 a.m. – you'd see them lining up outside, punctual as clockwork, waiting for their cells to be unlocked. With discipline like that you could hold down a good job, Belsey would tell them. Hypocrite.

'We heard the crap.'

'What have you heard?' Belsey asked.

'Trouble up North.'

'We heard you had some enquiry. Sounds like nonsense.'

'It's not nonsense.'

'It's a different force now, the Met.'

'Different world. An honest copper like you . . .'

How word spread, Belsey thought. Cassidy had remained silent. Now he stood up with his pint and his phone, his keys and his fags. He looked towards the door.

'Fancy a game, Niall?' Belsey said.

Cassidy turned and stared hard at the detective.

'If you say so.'

They turned the lights on in the back and racked up. Cassidy lit a cigarette from a fresh box of Marlboro Golds and balanced it on the edge. No council inspectors were going to make it to the back room of the Well. Its own landlord never made it. Sticky glasses crowded the woodwork. Belsey broke and potted six. Cassidy took his shots badly. Belsey was on a roll; he was surprised by his form, all things considered.

'Where is he?' Belsey said.

'Who?'

'Who do you think?'

'I don't know.'

'He's your son. Why's he skipped his welcome-home party?'

'I don't know.'

'What's this talk about a stabbing outside the job centre?'

'No idea, Nick.'

'Other people have an idea.'

'They haven't fingered him for that.'

'Like fuck they haven't.'

Belsey cleaned up. Cassidy's mind wasn't on it. He lit a second cigarette off the first and Belsey watched his face in the light of the cherry. Belsey had met the son once or twice. Johnny had been a good footballer, trials at Arsenal, and when that didn't work out a cage fighter, part of a crew that trained at Legend's Gym behind North Lambeth tube station. That was before he went to Ibiza and discovered love. A few months later he was smuggling it from Holland. Belsey fed fifty pence into the table and racked up again.

'What are they saying?' Cassidy asked.

'Three witnesses.'

'With a name?'

'With his full postcode, Niall. It was 3 p.m. outside the job centre. Not quite the perfect crime.'

'He was just joking about.'

'Fucking funny. I remember last time someone slotted me. I couldn't stop laughing. I thought I was going to wet myself, Niall. Know what I mean?'

'What do you want?'

'I heard it was a fancy knife. Not the sort of thing he would have had on the plane. Where'd he get that?'

'I haven't got anything to say, Nick. I haven't seen him.'

'Where did you get the cigarettes?'

'What?'

'The health warning. *Fumar puede matar*. That's Spanish, isn't it? Filthy habit in any language.' Cassidy's face fell. 'Want to put some money on the next game?' Belsey said.

Niall Cassidy chalked his cue. Other times he would have been calling Belsey pig scum by now and describing the delights that awaited him when he ended up in Pentonville. But the wind had gone out of his sails. It happens, even with the dedicated.

'It's the paperwork I'm worried about,' Belsey said. 'It's all paperwork these days. Mountains of the stuff. It's why you never see us on the streets any more.'

'I know. I reckon you need a holiday, Nicky. Look, how's this?'

He took a roll of dirty notes out of his back pocket and put three hundred in twenties on the table. 'Reckon you could do with getting away for a while. Treat yourself.'

Belsey counted it, kept twenty and returned the rest. 'I *am* going away. But I'm going to need a fuck of a lot more than this.'

'What are you after?'

'Six grand.'

'Don't treat me like a cunt, Nick.'

'You haven't heard what I've got to say. Because I'm asking if I can do *you* a favour.' They weren't playing any more: standing with their cues upright on the ground. The light above the table caught the lower half of their faces but not the eyes. There was no sound from the pub. 'Put a tune on the jukebox,' Belsey said. 'Something lively.'

Cassidy did. That alone told Belsey he was in control. Interview-room practice, get them cooperating on small things, dancing with them, leading them. He figured Cassidy had reached a point. And besides, the things you can do to someone are nothing compared to what you can do to their family.

The music came on. 'Careless Whisper'.

'I said something lively.'

'What's this about?'

'There's a brand-new Porsche Cayenne parked outside. I'm going to give you that with a TV and a DVD player.'

'What are you doing?'

'Because you're my millionth customer, you see, Niall. And now I'm out of here. I do you a flat-screen TV, video, blender, microwave. Everything a modern home requires. Porsche thrown in, and an amazing trick where Hampstead CID lose all Johnny's paperwork. I'll make sure no one touches him. I need six grand in cash by the end of tomorrow.'

'Six grand? Jesus Christ, Nicholas, what are you up to?'

'I'm going on my toes, Niall. I'm starting again.'

Cassidy stared at him. 'I'm straight now. The whole family's straight.'

'I know,' Belsey said. 'I know. Me too.'

14

A REGULATION 163 NOTICE SAT IN HIS IN-TRAY: NOTIFICA-
tion of the IPCC investigation. It didn't mention any suspension. Beneath
it was an envelope from the Mental Health Assessment Team. He removed
the items and dropped them in the bin. Trapping walked into the office
with his arms full of old Offender Profiles.

'Nick. IPCC trying to get hold of you. And a lawyer, from Riggs.' He
dropped the files on his desk.

'OK.'

'What's that about?'

'I'm being headhunted. They want me to lead a new anti-corruption
squad. What's the paperwork?'

'Have you not heard? We just got John Cassidy in.'

'In here?'

'He's downstairs. Our friend Tony's giving a statement.'

Belsey walked down to the cells, swearing. He checked the board: John
Cassidy, number 5. He walked to the cell door and slid the shutter. Johnny
was sitting cross-legged on the floor with his back against the wall. The
pose took Belsey by surprise. He had his eyes shut. He looked in good
shape. How long had he been out of cells? A day in Spain waiting for
the flight, two in London on the run. Belsey could hear Johnny's brief
arguing with the custody sergeant at the end of the corridor. He went
over. The legal aid was an obese, raw-skinned man called William Balls,

or Billy Balls-Up, depending on whether he was present. Balls wore a shiny navy suit and always stank of stale smoke.

'Detective Constable Belsey,' Balls said, spotting a more pliable representative of the force.

'Boss.'

'You know Tony, don't you? Mad Tony? You wouldn't call someone like that a reliable witness.'

'Mad Tony's not his real name. Where is he?'

'Waiting outside the interview room,' the custody sergeant said.

Belsey found Tony Cutter sitting bent over his knees in the corridor. He was shaking. He used to steal steaks from Tesco and sell them to women on the estates. Every few days they'd bring him in with his coat stuffed and the station filled with the smell of thawing meat. Now he made his money begging and selling on prescription drugs. Psychosis and alcoholism contended for the upper hand. The corridor reeked.

'Nick.' His face lit up. Tobacco smoke had stained one side of his face and the teeth that remained.

'Tony. How's life?'

'I saw it, Nick. I was just having a beer. I didn't want to get involved. It looked like God's work.' Belsey checked his ink-black pupils.

'Is that right?'

'God's own handiwork. It's evil, Nick.'

'Certainly sounds it.'

Belsey walked back to the cell corridor. The Custody Sergeant was nowhere to be seen. Balls sat on a plastic seat, wiping his forehead with a blue hand towel.

'Let's get some air,' Belsey said. They stepped out to the car park. 'Tony's not going to be a problem,' he said.

'It's not him I'm worried about. They found twenty grams of ketamine and a converted replica in the freezer of Johnny's girlfriend. She's rolling over, washing her hands of him.'

Belsey groaned. 'How did Johnny know he was grassed?'

'It's not rocket science.'

'He knew where to find him.'

'The job centre was an OK bet.'

'Why don't you claim that police leaked the informant's name to him. Make some noise about it. Mix things up.'

'Did they?'

'I don't know. I doubt it. Is he getting bail?'

'Trying.'

'Does his old man know?'

'Not yet.'

He returned to the office and sat down, shattered. The best laid plans of mice and men . . . It was not, on reflection, the best laid plan. He washed a ChestEze down with some cold coffee. It would be very important to divide his mind, to watch out for what he was doing. Sleep on the plane – that would be his mantra. He went to the front desk.

'I've locked myself out of the office,' he said. 'Can I get the master key?' They gave him the master key. He went upstairs, let himself into Gower's office and sorted through the day's post until he found the IPCC envelope. He took the envelope and locked up and returned the key.

He'd be fired when he chose to be fired.

He called the Well but Niall wasn't in. There was nothing else he could do for now. He drove back to The Bishops Avenue. There were no more footprints outside the mansion, not as far as he could see in the glare from the security lights. Belsey hung back, watching the house, walked past it twice, then entered.

Home sweet home.

He walked into the safe room and stared at the solidified convex drips, the streaked map of blood on the wall. He sat in the swivel chair and picked up the Reflections Funeral Plan and admired the swans. Swans sing their own funeral song – wasn't that what the legend claimed? Never sing a note until they are dying, then they begin. Belsey unclipped the cheque and held it, then slipped it back into the brochure and left them on the desk.

He went to the living room and began unplugging the electrical goods. He worked methodically: hi-fi, cabinet speakers, DVD player. He left the

TV in the living room for the moment and took a smaller model from upstairs. Then he took the microwave from the kitchen and the trouser press from the bedroom. He found a screwdriver and stepladder in the utility room and started unscrewing the smaller chandeliers. The curtains were open and Belsey went to draw them. At the window he saw he was too late. The security guard for the house opposite stared back at him through the darkness.

On The Bishops Avenue, neighbourhood watch came with a uniform. Belsey crossed the road. The house facing Devereux's own was built from pink marble, modelled on the Acropolis. It had its own name – 'Summer Palace'. Belsey showed his warrant card to the security guard.

'How long have you been working here?' Belsey said.

'Five years. Why?'

The guard had an Israeli accent and sharp, grey eyes.

'The man who lived opposite, we're investigating his death. At the moment it looks like a straight suicide but I'd like you to keep an eye out for anyone acting suspiciously.'

'OK.'

'Did you ever see him around?'

'No.'

'You'd notice.'

'Right.'

'Vehicles coming in and out?'

'Cleaners, gardeners. That's all.'

They both watched a moped idling at the roadside, checking a map, trundling on.

'Is your boss in?' Belsey said.

The guard waved him towards the front door and lifted a radio to his mouth. Expensive set-up for a doorbell, Belsey thought. The owner answered in a camel-hair coat and silk scarf, holding his car keys. He was thick-set, broad-shouldered, with a lot of children running around in the background.

'I've got some questions about the man who lived opposite,' Belsey said, badge out.

'What happened?'

'He died.'

The neighbour glanced briefly at the sky and muttered Hebrew. He bounced his car keys but didn't say anything, looking at Belsey, waiting to hear what the proposition was.

'Did you know him?' Belsey asked.

'No. I only spoke to him once. He seemed a very cultured man. He said I should come over for drinks, but I'm rarely in the country.'

'Do you know his name?'

'Mr Devereux.'

'What do you know about him?'

'He had a hard time of it.'

'Why's that?'

'All his family, I believe, perished in Russia many years ago.'

'Perished?'

'Prisons. I don't know. I heard this from Russian friends of mine. Everything he had he made himself. Every penny.'

'How did he make it?'

'He was an entrepreneur. I'm not sure of the details. But he believed in capitalism.' The neighbour gave a slight smile. 'Before it became fashionable over there.'

'When did you last see him?'

'I haven't seen him since that first time. I'll ask my wife, she sees everything on this street.' He went to ask his wife and came back shrugging.

'Never seen him. Have you asked the guard?'

'Yes.'

'Let me know if I can do anything else to help.'

Belsey walked to the shops and bought superglue, Sellotape and talcum powder. It left him eleven pounds of Cassidy's twenty. He asked for a carrier bag. That was everything he needed for a DIY fingerprint kit. Back at the house he took one of the jars from the fridge. *Glass is every detective's dream*, as an instructor at a CID forensics training day had put it. Belsey had never forgotten the phrase. He took the anglepoise from the study and covered the bulb with glue, then switched it on and wrapped the bag around the lamp with the marmalade jar inside. The glue vapours would stick wherever there was grease, and then you could dust the surface with a little talc and it was as good as anything a lab would send you.

Nothing. Belsey checked another jar, then a toothbrush, then the cover of a catalogue. He peeled Sellotape samples of lamp switches and TV screens. There were no prints. Devereux didn't like using his fingers. Belsey took a torch from the garage and patrolled the house, searching surfaces, anywhere he knew he hadn't made contact himself: the handles of drawers, the rim of the jacuzzi, window frames, the underside of toilet seats. There wasn't a print in the place.

He sat in the lounge and thought. Maybe death was not enough for Devereux. Maybe he had to wipe all traces of himself from existence. *I have tried to ensure that all paperwork is in order so that you have no cause for further aggravation.* The Marquis de Sade left instructions in his will: he was to be buried in a copse, in the woods of his property, the ditch covered over and strewn with acorns – *in order that the spot become green again and my grave may disappear from the face of the earth as I trust the memory of me shall fade out of the minds of all men . . .*

Bullshit. The place was scrubbed clean. Someone had done a job on it.

The cleaner would be a place to start. Belsey called three cleaning companies in Hampstead. Eventually he found the company that employed Kristina – Sprint Domestic Cleaners – and reached her on her mobile.

'Mr Devereux's home, on The Bishops Avenue – did you clean it before you called the police?'

'I didn't.'

'When did you last clean it?'

'I mean, I didn't call the police.'

'You didn't?'

'No.'

'Who did?'

'I don't know.'

'What were you doing there?'

'I was trying to decide what to do. Then you arrived.'

This threw him. Belsey called the control room.

'Do you have details of the person who called in a missing person report on the morning of Thursday the 12th?'

It took them three minutes to get the record up.

'Yes, the details are here.'

'Was it a cleaner?'

'No.'

'Who was it?'

'Detective Inspector Philip Ridpath.'

'It was called in by police?'

'Yes.'

'Who's Ridpath?'

'Someone in the Yard.'

Belsey felt himself pitched deeper into uncertainty. He wrote the name on the back of an envelope.

'What department?'

'The Financial Investigation Development Unit.'

'Financial Investigation?'

'That's correct.'

Belsey thanked the control room and put the phone down. Things suddenly felt a lot more dangerous. He had walked into a scene that already had Yard attention. His first instinct was to walk away again, fast. But a deeper, more insistent voice told him he had a lead to follow. Finally he reasoned that he would be safer knowing what he had stumbled upon. It was seven thirty. He tried the number for the Financial Unit, just in case anyone was still around. A man answered with a nasal drawl.

'Sergeant Midgley speaking.'

'I'm looking for an Inspector Philip Ridpath. Is he still in the office by any chance?'

'I believe so.'

'Can you put me through?'

'Not right now.'

'Why?'

'He's not answering his phone.'

'He's not answering his phone?'

'He's busy.'

'We're all busy,' Belsey said. 'What the hell is this?'

15

BELSEY DROVE THROUGH VICTORIA, THROUGH THE GLUM
suburbs of government. Whitehall's outlying muscle clustered inelegantly
alongside the cheap hotels and chain restaurants. Belsey had never liked
the area. Buildings either crouched to the ground or were the size of
cruise ships. Humans shuffled in the cracks between public-sector slabs
as if it was the buildings they were serving. Belsey turned onto Broadway
towards New Scotland Yard.

The Kremlin, they called it. But Rome would have been a closer analogy.
Like Rome, it was regarded with suspicion by its satellite districts, as a
place where nothing actually happened, and to which everything was
bound. To most police it was a still point in the centre of the machine,
endless paper jammed in its endless wheels. The twenty featureless floors
of mirrored windows enhanced the impression. From the outside it
always looked empty. It never was.

Belsey parked around the corner, far enough away not to have the car
bomb-disposed. He straightened his hair and tie in the rear-view mirror,
then approached the Yard, stepping over the slabs of anti-terrorist
concrete, past armed guards in bulletproofs.

All white-collar departments got high security. Belsey knew it wasn't
going to be easy. They operated a system called sterile corridors, which
meant even officers from other Yard departments needed permits to
get through. He went through the visitors' entrance, signed his name
and department at the front desk and said he had an appointment

84

with Ridpath concerning a tax exile. He was given a pass 'to be worn around the neck at all times' and taken up to the fourth floor, where he showed the pass to get through the outer security of Economic and Specialist Crime. Then he had to talk his way into the warren, past Film Piracy, Stolen Vehicle, Computing, until the corridors were narrower, the pot plants thick with dust, and he was in the Financial Investigation Development Unit. The Yard has odd-shaped hollows worn by operational requirements, by a need for obscurity. It has nooks and byways into which careers fall, or lead themselves, away from daylight.

At the front desk for Financial Crime he used Ridpath's name again.

'He said it was urgent.'

'Hang on.' The guard checked a list. A few, late-evening loiterers. Plain-clothed men and women passed the desk, glancing at Belsey. 'Is he expecting you?'

'Certainly is.'

Eventually the guard escorted Belsey through the department, past closed doors. They arrived at an office with a sign saying 'Financial Investigation' and the guard knocked.

'Come in.'

The office had its own steel security door with hinge bolts. Inside, one man with greased black hair sat in the large, neat room, polished boots up on his desk. Belsey guessed that this was Midgley.

'Visitor for Inspector Ridpath,' the guard said.

'He's busy . . .' Midgley began.

'I think he deserves a break,' Belsey said. There was a wooden door at the other end of the office. Midgley shook his head and smiled. Belsey walked past him. He knocked on Ridpath's door and a small voice said: 'Who's there?'

'Alexei Devereux,' Belsey said. There was a long silence. Eventually the door opened.

Ridpath stood in the doorway. He was Belsey's height, but a little wider, in a white shirt and paisley tie a few decades old. His eyes were small and dark but not without fire, and he sported a neat mous-tache, like the admission of a harmless personal foible. It drew attention to his plump, clean-shaven cheeks and his baldness. There was an overall carelessness to the man, like someone who'd been put together from badly written instructions. Behind him was a window-less office filled with papers: stacks on the floor and on top of cabinets and desks. It felt as if the space that remained had been carved out with effort.

'What is it?' he said.

'You called about a Mr Devereux.'

'Who are you?'

'Detective Constable Nick Belsey.'

'Detective Constable?' he smiled. He looked at his assistant, who smiled back.

'Excuse me,' Belsey said, stepping into the office and shutting the door with Midgley on the other side. Now it was the two of them, face to face.

'What do you want?' Ridpath said.

'I want to know about Alexei Devereux.'

Ridpath walked back to his desk and collapsed into an old cushioned chair. He waved with wary hospitality towards a spare seat and Belsey sat down and studied the Inspector. It was terrible, he thought, in the twenty-first century, that you could tell a man lived alone by the state of his shirt collar. Ridpath moved some papers.

'A routine inquiry. I can't recall the exact nature of it.' He found a file and flicked through it, then seemed to give up.

'What does AD Development do?' Belsey said.

'I don't know. If it's something to do with Devereux, then I'm not aware.' He spoke with the faintest of Yorkshire accents, like a man who'd spent a career trying to lose it, but it had clung on, honest and stubborn, and made Ridpath seem honest and stubborn too.

'Did you speak to him?'

'No.'

'What happened? Why did you call him in as missing?'

'I can barely remember. I must have been told to contact him. He wasn't at his home, so I contacted you. Or your station, at least.'

'When did you try to contact him?'

'Won't you have all this information at Hampstead?'

'Who said anything about Hampstead?' Belsey said.

'What do you mean?'

'You said Hampstead.'

'Isn't that where you're from?'

'I am. But I didn't say it.'

'*He* was in Hampstead.' Ridpath's voice was quieter, eyes steely. 'Devereux.' There was something he wasn't saying. Belsey suspected they were building a case and didn't want it poached, a case concerning things far beyond one body in a Hampstead mansion. 'He's been showing a lot of cash around the place,' Ridpath said. 'I just wanted to ask him a few questions.'

'How are you with a Ouija board?'

This stopped him. He closed the file. Then he carefully moved it to a different area of his desk. The graveyard. It must happen all the time, Belsey thought. Death stealing his cases.

'Well, I can't say I'm surprised,' Ridpath said.

'Why's that?'

'People who walk around with half a million pounds in cash need to have acquired it from somewhere, and those places aren't always good for their health.'

'What makes you think he had that?'

'Ten days ago I got a Suspicious Activity Report from Christie's on Old Brompton Road, an auction house.'

'I know what Christie's is.'

'According to the SAR he paid for a painting with five hundred grand in paper money. Maybe that's just how he likes to operate, but it means they're obliged to inform me and I'm obliged to look into it.'

'Did you know who he was?'

'No. I was just doing my job.'

Belsey nodded. Perhaps the ideal detective would be barely conscious, he thought, operating their small lever in the network of machines that was justice.

'Does his death strike you as suspicious?'

'I imagine it's all fairly straightforward.'

87

'Do you?'

'Listen, I investigate financial crimes. Dying is not a financial crime.' He leaned back with the satisfaction of a man who has chosen his portion of mystery. Belsey liked him. He liked people who didn't want to be liked. Ridpath was charmless.

'What are AD Development up to?' Belsey asked.

'Is that his company, then? I've no idea.' Ridpath checked his watch.

'When did you first try contacting him?'

'Monday. I tried a couple of times on Monday and Tuesday. Then I gave your station a call.'

'What's in the file?'

'Nothing. Just the initial report.'

'Show me.'

Ridpath stared at him. 'No.'

'Why?'

'You're not authorised.'

Ridpath took a bag of something from his desk drawer and stood up. It was an old loaf of white bread, starting to crumble. Apparently their meeting was over. Ridpath walked to the door and opened it. Midgley was standing a few feet away trying not to look interested. Belsey followed Ridpath through the office to the corridor and along the corridor to a window which opened a few inches, and looked down through darkness to the Thames.

Ridpath lay crumbs in a line on the windowsill and watched the pigeons swoop. Belsey wondered if he brought the bread from home. He wondered if he ever went home.

'I don't know how you got in here,' Ridpath said coolly, 'but I'd advise you to have one of the security see you safely out. It can be a bit of a maze.'

'I can see that,' Belsey said.

Ridpath went over to a vending machine and waited for what the machine described as a cappuccino. The drink arrived and he ate a spoonful of thin froth with a plastic stirrer. The financial investigator licked his lips.

'Do you not have anything else you should be doing?' he asked, when Belsey still hadn't moved. But he seemed more curious than resentful.

'If you hear anything more about Devereux, will you let me know?' Belsey said.

'I doubt it.'

'Me too.'

16

BELSEY DROVE TO KING'S CROSS AND PARKED A FEW BLOCKS away from the mortuary. He walked along the busy, lamp-lit streets with his head down, thinking: what was Ridpath's game? What was in the file? Thinking also: well, some people like using cash, even with six figures involved, even in Christie's. Especially in Christie's. It was only recently that auction houses had started trying to clean up their act.

But the big thought, the one he couldn't shake, was that Devereux wasn't his little secret any more. Devereux was in the system, and the system never forgets. It doesn't know what's important, but that means it can't be told what's unimportant. It wasn't good news. It meant someone might take an interest at any time – in the money, in the body, in the nice set-up on The Bishops Avenue.

He passed the British Library, turned onto Midland Road, and by the time he raised his head he was at the back of the Eurostar terminal. He gazed at the gravel strip beyond the chain-link fence – between the fence and the tracks. If he could get to that, to the train as it pulled out . . . People must do it, jump off again as it slowed towards Brussels, disappear into the Belgian night . . .

He arrived at St Pancras Coroners Court and Mortuary. A foundation stone set into the small, Gothic building announced the pride of John William Dixon and Samuel Richard Lamble at having erected it on behalf of the Sanitary Committee in 1867. Broken concrete steps led up to the door. Beyond it, St Pancras Gardens sheltered beneath a canopy of bare branches. The solemn red bricks of old workhouses towered over the scene. The ghosts of slum children rustled in the trees and reflected in the long, sad windows. Belsey took a lungful of night air before going in. The whole place seemed touched by death – not its grief or terror but a cold, quiet oddness. Death with a finger to its lips. So it was a fine place to put a coroner's court.

He knocked on the dirty glass door of the court and wondered who was on night duty. After a moment Dr Angela Hawks appeared, white-coated, shaking her head.

'We're closed, Nick.'

'I'm here for the after-party.'

She sighed and let him in, locking the door again. He was going to give her a kiss on the cheek but she'd turned and was off into the murky world of wood panelling and formaldehyde.

He followed her to the morgue, a small room with a single steel table, linoleum tiles on the floor, cracked off-white tiles on the right-hand wall and thirty small, numbered doors on the left. A skeleton, ragged, missing its lower jaw, lay on the table.

'Look at this fellow,' Hawks said. 'What do you make of it?'

Belsey walked the length of the gurney and back: scraps of cloth the same grey colour as a clump of hair clung to bones stained green. Some clay remained on the bones. 'Male,' Belsey said. 'There's lesions on the bones. Syphilis perhaps. A nick at the top of the spine, blade nick. Maybe died from a blade at their throat.'

'When?'

'Where did you find him?' Belsey said.

'E1.'

'Skull and teeth stained green from copper waste, so he was buried before the Royal Mint was built. Deposits on the skull. Buried in what?'

'Lead.'

'That's why he's still got some hair.'

'He's Roman. About 200 AD's our guess.'

'What brings him to the land of the living?'

'The shopping centre under construction. Already excavated a whole medieval graveyard and now they've found it's built on top of a Roman one.'

Belsey peered into the Roman's empty eye sockets.

'The first thousand years are the most crucial in a murder investigation,' Belsey said. 'We might have missed our chance. Has he got a name?'

'Hadrian. We're going to rebury him, but we're waiting for someone who knows the correct Roman rituals.'

They were respectful with the dead, according to council stipulations; unnoticed and unthanked for it. Belsey liked them for that. The world was most careful with you when you cared least.

'Has the coroner been for that suicide I sent you?'

'Not today. He was at a fire on the M11.'

'Anything worth mentioning?'

She covered the Roman skeleton with a blue sheet, checked a chart in the lab and unlocked door number 29, dragging the long shelf out on greased wheels. Belsey took a pair of disposable gloves from a Kleenex-style box on the side and helped unwrap Alexei Devereux.

She'd shaved some of the hair away to check the skull. There was the usual Y-shaped incision down his front. The throat had been sewn up and the eyes sealed shut. It felt strange seeing the body again, having occupied the life. Belsey felt a pang of guilt. But more powerful was a sense of kinship. Devereux, old friend, Belsey thought. Me and you.

'Anything in his stomach?'

'Some red meat, greasy. He hadn't eaten for several hours. A few mils of alcohol in the blood but nothing dramatic.'

'Did the secretary ID him?'

'Yes.'

'How did she seem?'

'Young. Upset. A little nauseous. Cried over my floor and said she couldn't believe it.'

'Did she call him Mr D?'

'Why?'

'That's what she called him. Mr D.'

'Cute. Do you mind if I have a cigarette?'

Hawks hung up her white coat and they went to the roof. It was windy.

There were three mildewed armchairs and a free-standing ashtray among the chimneys and aerials. She lit two cigarettes and passed one to Belsey. In the bleak wilds behind King's Cross he could make out hydraulic arms swinging out over a landscape of loose gravel. Closer to the mortuary was the Regent's Canal, rippling black and orange, cluttered with houseboats.

'Christ, it's beautiful,' Belsey said.

'You think?'

'Ever hot-wired a houseboat?'

'Not for a while.'

'It can be done. I arrested someone for it once.'

Hawks smoked with her arms folded, one elbow cradled in a hand, leaning against a Gothic clay chimney pot. Her sandy hair fell just short of her shoulders. Belsey remembered a party for a retiring pathologist, when they were outside looking at the moon and she took his arm. It was instinctive and innocent. Maybe that was why he never did anything until they were leaving, when he made the clumsy pass. Strange, calling them passes, he thought. A passing-by, a gone.

There was a houseboat called *The Duchess*, with the name painted on the prow. Through its windows he could see a living room in miniature, an armchair, an old stove. There were pots of flowers on the deck.

'We could climb on and sail away,' he said.

'Shall we?'

'Just follow the canal to Limehouse, join the Thames; through Essex, out to the sea.'

Hawks took a long pull on her cigarette and studied Belsey's face. 'I heard you were having some kind of review.'

'Who told you that?'

'I forget. Is it true?'

'I'm conducting a review. I'm in a period of transition.'

'Where are you transiting to?'

'I don't know yet. I had an out-of-money experience.'

Hawks laughed. For a second she looked younger and less wary. Then she crushed her cigarette under her heel.

'You look shattered.'

'I'm having trouble sleeping.'

'Come on,' she said.

They went back in and stood either side of the waxy corpse.

'Are you done?' she asked.

'Give me a moment.'

Hawks went and sat on a stool by the side counter. 'What are you thinking?'

'What's the mistake people make when trying to slit their own throat?'

'Is this a joke?'

'Maybe.'

'I don't know. What is it?'

'They tilt their heads back.'

'I'm not laughing.'

'Tilt your head back.'

She did. He came over and touched her throat, running a finger along the muscle.

'That's the platysma; it's a fine muscle. It's not easy to hack through.'

'Maybe he didn't.'

'I found him with the head back,' Belsey said.

'And?'

'Could you see it being murder?'

'I'm not a police detective. There's nothing to make me think foul play – there are trial cuts, a tapering wound, no other injuries. That's all I can tell you.'

'What do you know about Boudicca?'

The pathologist stared at him. 'Is she involved?'

'I think she may be.'

'Queen of the Iceni. Burnt London down. You still find Roman coins that melted together in the heat.' She looked at the clock. 'It's quarter to nine, Nick. Why am I doing your history homework for you?'

'I'm trying to broaden my education.'

'Try the coroner tomorrow. Maybe he can broaden your education.'

Belsey binned his gloves. They washed their hands together at the sink. Belsey said: 'Did you know the first coroners were meant to go to shipwrecks to see how much treasure there was for the king? That's what they were for.'

'I didn't know that. What do you want me to do with Mr Devereux?'

'Just get rid of him.'

She dried her hands. Then she looked up at Belsey, wearily.

'No. Hold on to him for the moment,' Belsey said.

17

HE PICKED THE CAR UP AND HEADED NORTH, TRYING TO outrun a growing sense of doom. No passport, no cash, a body begging for an investigation, a Porsche Cayenne filthy with his prints. A seven-year-old would see that the whole thing stank.

It started to rain, a malevolent rain that took its time with cold, heavy drops that streaked the windscreen. The world did not seem a good place for habitation. *Judgement falls, and through the water that saves the occupants of the floating ark, the rest of life is destroyed.* Belsey drove through Hampstead Village. For a moment he felt there was a car tailing him, then it disappeared. He thought: tomorrow I'll come clean. Maybe he could still take the suspension, do some sick time, move quietly to the Home Counties with a police flat and uniform duties and a voluntary arrangement to pay off his debts. For the rest of his life. He'd resign himself to debt, time measured in debt. To being police.

Belsey turned off Heath Street onto Church Row to the Church of St John. He needed a moment's peace. And it was beautiful, in the darkness, with the rain easing. The church boasted a Hampstead graveyard out of a Gothic imagination, crooked and overgrown, with maze-like back ways and small districts of thick holly opening onto the occasional weather-softened bench.

He sat on a bench beside a fenced chest tomb and knew he would not come clean. He intended to flee London; his first instinct had been right. And it would have to be soon. He felt it not as a plan but as fate.

Whatever happened, he was out of London within the next forty-eight hours. He didn't need more nonsense with numbered accounts and a suicide that didn't feel right; not with obsessive–compulsive Yard cops interfering and God knows what other international agencies keeping watch. He would just flog a car and TV to Cassidy and buy the cheapest ticket he could find.

And suddenly everything looked different. He was in the realm of last sights and last goodbyes.

A last night as a billionaire.

Hampstead didn't offer many pickup joints. Belsey wondered where to drive for a final roll of the dice, just one conclusive exploitation of his Hampstead mansion and its king-size beds. All the obvious destinations felt like a step backwards, the usual tired bars and clubs. And, he realised despondently, only eleven pounds of his assets were in disposable cash. He leaned back and thought maybe he'd spend the night in the cemetery. Then he became aware of a light seeping between the graves, coming from the windows of the church crypt.

He walked over. Through the window he saw into what served, by day, as a nursery. The child-sized chairs were stacked in a corner and twenty adult ones had been arranged in a circle in the centre of the floor, sixteen filled with men and women, pensive beneath the nursery's strip lights. The women outnumbered the men.

Belsey stepped back. Then he smoothed his hair and reknotted his tie. He found the stone steps to the crypt and descended.

A small, arched door led into the nursery. Children's paintings decorated the walls. Jars of water along the window ledge held dirty brushes. Belsey went over to a table with a stainless-steel urn and a plate of biscuits. He made a cup of strong instant coffee. If it was going to taste like tar he might as well get a kick out of it. He found an empty chair, sat down and didn't look around.

The meeting started.

'Welcome,' the leader said. 'My name's Aidan.'

Aidan said hello to the old faces and welcome to the new. He wore heavy-framed glasses and held a folder of self-help literature. An estate agent with bad shakes was introduced by his wife. She was there to help him through it. 'Whatever it takes,' she kept saying. She had brought fruit cake for the group, and offered it to Belsey. Belsey took some cake. Beside the estate agent sat a gaunt boy of eighteen or nineteen in the blue-and-orange uniform of a supermarket chain, then an older man with a tattoo of a tiger up one of his arms and a bomber jacket under his chair. Five or six people arrived as the meeting got going: Hampstead drunks – retired judges, an old actor, women of the Conservative Party. Belsey tried not to look too closely.

A woman arrived late, and took the seat opposite Belsey's own. She was about his age. She smoothed a hand over auburn hair and crossed her legs. Her skirt was tiny and it was a long way down the legs to a pair of sleek black heels. But he looked at her because she had green eyes that might have been crying recently, and when she glanced up at him he felt a shiver. She looked professional, beautiful and awkward, like someone who'd found themselves alcoholic in the way you find something spilled on your shirt.

'Hi,' she said in a low voice. 'Sorry I'm late.'

The room turned to her and then away, the men turning a little faster than the women. But the new arrival scanned the place, eyes bright and quick. Her gaze held Belsey's a second too long. He checked his memory for recent victims, witnesses, suspects; fellow police and barristers. He'd never seen her before.

When it came to her turn the woman said her name was Charlotte and she'd been dry twenty-two hours, then admitted it was actually five. Her voice was confident until it cracked. She'd fallen off the wagon, she said, but was determined to make it work this time. She knew she couldn't do it alone. She was a fashion buyer for a popular high-street department store. She was thirty-two years old. Everyone clapped. Belsey watched her eyes and checked for clues: light make-up, plain silver-chain necklace. No wedding ring, he was pleased to see, although there was nothing a wedding ring ever stopped and sometimes it made the whole thing simpler.

When it came to his turn Belsey said his name was Jack and he hadn't drunk for ten years. He said he'd come that night because a friend had killed himself. He looked up a couple of times during the first half of the meeting and the woman was still watching him. She looked away each time.

'What does a moral inventory imply?' the group leader asked. 'Firstly, that we are thorough, that there is no corner of our soul that remains cluttered with excuses . . .'

Belsey walked up to Charlotte at the break, as she was standing beside the hot-water urn.

'Welcome,' he said.

'Thank you,' she said, then, 'Ten years. I can't imagine not doing anything for ten years.'

'Well, it's really not worth imagining.' Belsey smiled and she smiled. She measured some instant coffee into a plastic cup. 'You've made the hardest step,' he said. 'Coming here tonight.'

'Is that right?'

'No.'

'I'm Charlotte.' She shook his hand. 'I guess you heard me say that already.'

'Jack.'

She made a coffee and held it, standing with her hip against the edge of the table. Belsey wondered if five hours sober was an exaggeration as well. She blew gently through the steam and shot glances around the room.

'Are you local?' she asked.

'Local enough,' Belsey said.

'Lucky you.'

'I love this area.'

'It's encouraging hearing about people who've kept control for so long,' she said.

'Sure,' Belsey said, and took a sip of coffee. 'To be honest, I thought this was Sex Addicts Anonymous.'

'Really?'

'I'm kidding.'

She laughed.

'It must feel good, being sober so long.'

'It feels rubbish. The coffee doesn't taste any better either,' he said, and poured the rest down the sink.

Charlotte sat next to him for the second half of the meeting. There were readings from the AA book and another discussion. But Belsey had lost concentration now. To finish off, the estate agent stood up and told the group about his experiences in care homes and how he had forgiven his abusers as God had forgiven him.

'We think we are strong,' the man said, 'and then, when we discover we are weak, we think we have failed . . .'

Charlotte started to cry. Belsey put an arm around her shoulders. There was a lot of talk from the group about taking things slowly and attending as many meetings as possible. Then they all stood up and held hands to say a prayer. Belsey felt the small bones of her hand in his own.

Afterwards a couple of the members came over to Charlotte and hugged her. There was a trading session of inspirational cards and leaflets. The estate agent's wife insisted Charlotte keep the leftover cake. She said God was looking out for her. The next time Belsey looked round Charlotte had gone.

He helped empty the urn and stack chairs and arrange the children's ones. Belsey wondered if the daytime nursery was aware of the room's night-time function. He imagined the adult chairs stacked in the corner during the day, like a lesson they weren't ready for. He left through the church itself. It had a painting he remembered from the only other time he had been inside, when the donations box was stolen. It showed Christ among shepherds. There was writing above and below him: 'He makes me lie down in green pastures, he leads me beside quiet waters.' 'Quiet waters' made him think of the reservoirs above Walthamstow marshes, which he had helped dredge once looking for a missing toddler.

He left the church. There was a figure standing alone under a street lamp, waiting.

'Hey,' she said.

'Charlotte.'

'What a bunch.'

'Now you know why it's anonymous.'

She grinned. She shrugged inside her coat and looked around. Church Row was empty. It had stopped raining.

'Are you driving?' he asked.

'I probably shouldn't.' She glanced at the keys in her hand. 'Are you going to tell me not to?'

'No.'

'Did you say you lived around here?' Her eyes were wide and bright. She looked at the street lights. Each had a halo and sprinkled its light across the wet stones.

'Yes. A short drive away.' Belsey patted the Porsche. 'This is my car. Would you like to come back for a while?'

18

THEY DROVE UP HEATH STREET, PAST THE PRIVATE ART galleries and Mediterranean restaurants to Whitestone Pond. It was a clear night now. The pond had frozen. The SUV hadn't elicited much of a reaction from Charlotte. But then, Belsey thought, she was a classy young woman. How rich did he seem? They passed a burger van that served the night's community of men looking for other men among the trees and turned onto Spaniards Road.

'You live along here?' Charlotte said.

It was a dark road. If she knew the area, she'd know there were only mansions ahead, and if she didn't, it looked like wilderness.

'Just a minute along here. But we can stop and I'll pay for you to get a cab if you want.'

'No, it's fine. This is my direction anyway. It's all so beautiful. I'd forgotten what Hampstead is like at night.'

'This is Dick Turpin's old haunt,' Belsey said, reaching for small talk. 'The highway robber. They used to have what they called gibbet elms along the side of the road to display the bodies of executed criminals.'

'Nice touch.'

He sensed she was uneasy. But then it hadn't been him waiting to pounce outside the meeting. He made a conscious effort to keep things light-hearted.

'All these old street lamps are listed,' he said. 'I love them. You know there used to be ten thousand lamplighters in London, in the days of gas. Every night they'd come out.'

Where had all the lamplighters gone? Belsey imagined them seeing the first electric light and knowing it was over, raising money to set sail; following the horizon of darkness.

'Oh. They're beautiful lamps.'

'So if you're not local what were you doing at the meeting?' he said.

'I had some work locally.'

'Fashion buying.'

'Exactly,' she said, but without conviction.

They passed the Spaniards Inn and he wondered which one of them was being played. A block later he turned left onto The Bishops Avenue.

'Oh my God.' She laughed. 'Who are you?'

He parked a few houses up from 37 and they walked. He kept one eye on the security booths across the street, another on the parked cars, the bushes and the shadows that led up to Devereux's. They reached the gates.

'Here we are.'

'What is this?'

'Home.'

He led her across the drive, up to the front door and she was silent. Wealth had come between them. He opened the door.

'Are you living here alone?' she said, when he turned the hall light on and the stairs and fountain appeared. It all struck him now as stiff, like a stage set.

'At the moment.'

'You don't get lonely?'

'I get very lonely. Would you wait here?'

Belsey went to the bedroom and locked the safe room. It smelt fine now. He closed the window. What was he doing? It was reckless to the point of suicidal. Maybe it was a way of forcing an endgame. A lot of criminals commit crime to give them an excuse for running. He understood that. And it would make it easier giving up the wealth if he'd exhausted its potential. One way to defeat a vice is to exhaust it. He needed to exhaust the ghost of Devereux.

He went to the living room and hid the empty bottles and slid the cognac behind the sofa. He picked up any envelopes or paperwork with Devereux's name on. Devereux's home would still carry traces of its previous occupier but he couldn't sterilise the place. He had cover stories thought out. Rich uncles, absent bosses. More than that, he had the heady invulnerability of a man trying to get laid twenty-four hours before leaving the country.

'Come in,' he called.

Charlotte stepped tentatively into the room and gasped, looking at the shelves and the carpet and the books.

'All these books. And art.'

'Where shall we sit?' Belsey said.

She sat down on the sofa. She didn't seem too upset any more. She slipped her coat off and Belsey admired her neck.

'Do you have a dog?' she said.

'No. I don't think so. Why?'

'There's dog hair on the sofa. I'm allergic.'

'Can I see it?'

She pointed at the hair. He took it to the free-standing lamp and studied it. She was right.

'There's no dog,' he said. 'I don't know where this came from.'

'Can I get a drink? I mean water, coffee,' she added hurriedly.

He went to the kitchen and made coffee, thinking about dog hair. *Man's Best Friends. Customer present transaction, Golders Green. Would that make sense?* He thought about the suspiciously perceptive fashion buyer who'd invited herself into his home. His borrowed home. When he took the coffees through, Charlotte was browsing the shelves.

'How did you get so rich?' she asked with a child's frankness.

'Do you want to know the truth?'

'Please.'

Belsey sat down and sipped his coffee. He watched her heels denting the thick carpet.

'I used to have nothing. Less than nothing. I drank – that's all I did. And one day I told myself I was going to stop drinking. And at the same time I told myself – for every drink I didn't have, I'd do some business.

I'd make an extra penny. An extra pound. Every time I wanted to destroy myself I'd become rich instead.'

'Really? That's so impressive.'

'Yes.' He took another sip. He had always wanted to be a self-made man. 'And I found, if you do something because you want to, because you know there is a purpose, it changes you. If you do it with all your heart.'

She sat back on the sofa beside him and took her mug.

'Thanks.'

'I was in the army. It taught me a lot about what's valuable. Now most of what I do is with disadvantaged children.'

'You were in the army?'

'Forward operations. Like a scout. I'd radio positions for the planes.'

'Are you religious?'

'Why?'

'They say you have to put your faith in a higher power. It's the first step.'

'That's what they say.'

'So, do you?'

'It's not hard to find a higher power,' Belsey said. 'It would be hard to find a lower one.' He laid his arm across the back of the sofa so that it was almost touching her. She was still thinking about his words, glancing around the room again.

'Not meaning to be presumptuous,' she said, 'but I'm thinking you're quite a powerful man.'

'I'm rich, and I know people, and people will do things I tell them.' Belsey felt light-headed talking like this. His fingers were brushing her shoulder. 'But that's not power. For many years I had all that and yet I couldn't stop myself taking a drink, even though it was destroying me. So, money is not power. Money makes no difference.' He tried to remember what the leaflets said. 'There's no problem that a drink won't make worse.'

'Except sobriety.'

'Take one day at a time.'

'I don't think you're being entirely honest with me,' she said suddenly, turning to face him. His left hand froze half an inch from her skin.

'Why's that?'

'You haven't been dry ten years.'

'What makes you say that?'

'Because I know people who have.'

Belsey nodded. He sipped his coffee and looked at her.

'Well, Charlotte,' he said, 'what if I put it to you that you're not a fashion buyer?'

Now it was her turn to frown. 'Go on, put it to me.'

'How much writing does it involve?'

'Why?'

'You've got a writer's bump on your right hand.'

'Maybe I keep a diary.'

'Maybe.'

'So what am I then?' she said.

'You're a journalist.'

'How do you make that?'

'The bump, and you called it a popular high-street department store. That's newspaper anonymity, no one talks like that. And you just called me on my lies and yet you're still here. You're not police, or you would have taken the edge off the private-school accent a long time ago. So I'm thinking you do investigations of another kind. You were nosing around the Hampstead drunks.'

'So why were you there?'

'I was looking to get laid.'

She took a slow breath, as if regaining balance. 'OK, which paper?'

'If I get it right you take your clothes off.'

She considered this.

'Underwear?'

'Of course.'

'If you get it wrong?'

'I take my clothes off,' Belsey said.

'Shoot.'

'The *Mail*.'

She watched him carefully. 'Why?'

'Just an educated guess.'

'I want you to tell me why.'

'Am I right?'

'Tell first.'

'The clothes, the style. Some poor bastard's got a drink problem and you're set to shaft him.'

She smiled. 'So close.'

'What is it?'

'*Mail on Sunday.*'

He looked at her. Then he started unbuttoning his shirt.

'Wait,' she giggled.

'For what?'

'Just wait.' She laughed.

'Well, in that case,' he said, and brought the cognac out.

Charlotte fetched glasses from the kitchen and joined Belsey on the sofa, kicking off her shoes. She curled her stockinged feet beneath her. They drank a lot of cognac. With each top-up they leaned a little closer.

'It's a particular bastard with a drink problem,' she said after the third glass. 'And it's not just a drink problem.'

'What is it?'

'I shouldn't be saying this. He's probably your neighbour or something. Milton Granby heads the finances for the Corporation of London – the lot that run the City, the Square Mile.'

'Not my neighbour as far as I'm aware.'

'Well, that's who I was looking for.'

'Why?'

'Have you ever seen him there?'

'I wouldn't know him to look at.'

'Not many would.'

'So what is it, if it's not just a drink problem?'

'It's why he's drinking.'

'Go on.'

'Oh, the usual. Rumours about a massive hole in the City's finances.

It's a world within a world, as I'm sure you know. Ancient, eccentric. Some say more powerful than the government itself.'

'I know a bit.' Belsey was familiar with the policing arrangement. City of London Police operated independently from the Met and the relationship was mixed. The first time Belsey went to a City station a white-haired inspector rapped his knuckles on the Metropolitan shield in Belsey's wallet: *Even the Queen has to ask permission to enter the City walls* . . .

'Half the time it thinks it's in the twelfth century and the rest of the time it operates like a cut-throat venture capitalist,' Charlotte continued. 'Recently, on the investment side, it's been associated with several shaky funds. It's a bit of an embarrassment, a hole in the Corporation's own account books. Milton Granby's one of the most powerful men in the Square Mile and no one's heard of him. And he's corrupt, that's what I'm saying. I'm not just interested in screwing him for a drinks problem. He's supposed to be planning something drastic. I shouldn't have told you all this.'

'I guess I've failed as an avenue of research.'

'Yeah, I gave up on that a while ago.'

They faced each other for a few seconds more. Then he leaned in and kissed her.

Another door opens, he thought. The most mysterious. She pulled him close, then, after a moment, leaned back to see his face. A woman chasing sleaze, Belsey thought, and all she'd found was this. He wondered at his own corruption. It seemed a big word. He thought of the bent cops he had known: disappointed men, not without talent, harder than the criminals they chased. Usually there was a hole in one book or another, an addiction to drink or fast cars or women. The rumours would start, then one day the individual would disappear, transferred to desk work or off on sick pay. And then there was DI Neil Tanner, found hanged in a lock-up in Dalston before they'd had the chance to sack him.

Belsey poured more cognac. After another three glasses they walked up the stairs to the bedroom and sat on the bed. She gazed at her reflection in the mirrored door of the safe room.

'Come behind me,' she said. 'Look at us. Anyone would think we knew each other.' Charlotte laughed. He was behind her, holding her, his arms beneath her breasts. She was drunk. 'Do you like it here? In front of the mirror? Seeing the prey you've dragged in?' She lay on the bed, with her head hanging over the edge so she could see the mirror upside down. He ran a hand up her thigh. 'You're a bad man.'

'Am I?'

'Yes.'

He lifted her top and kissed her stomach. 'Why?'

She reached down to the floor and then curled up, brandishing a hair clip.

'I don't think this is yours.'

He took the hair clip from her and lay back on the bed, wondering what exactly he had got himself into. She tutted disapprovingly. Then she crawled across his front, her fingers finding his shirt buttons, and he stopped thinking.

They watched themselves in the mirror like they were watching two strangers. Afterwards she shut her eyes and he held her, listening to her breath slow down. She fitted well in his arms. It was a long time since he had slept with someone who didn't know he was a policeman; it made him wistful, and at the same time renewed his eagerness to move on. There was more reinvention ahead, he felt. Belsey untangled himself and went to the bathroom. He examined the hair clip. He stuck his head under the cold tap, and by the time he came back she'd rolled herself up in the duvet, out for the count. He opened her handbag, found a purse with a bankcard in the name of Charlotte J. Kelson and returned it to the bag.

Belsey went downstairs and poured himself a large whisky. He felt better than he remembered feeling for a while. The whisky gave him a warm glow. For a while Belsey admired the study, with its fireplace and mahogany desk and worn Persian rug, and he felt a spreading gratitude for the rich. They were guardians of the world's beauty, passing these fine houses and attractive streets down generation to generation. He had a sense that wealth could have made him a better person.

He browsed Devereux's shelves: biographies of statesmen, guides to London, books on antiques, English country houses and Russian history.

He took down a book about the cavalry in Russia.

The long hours on horseback were the happiest and most relaxed moments in this restless and strange existence. Never was the uncertainty of the day and of fate accepted with less care than in the early mornings when the squadrons assembled, when the cool morning breeze ruffled the manes of the horses and made the pennants flutter.

Belsey would have liked to have been in the cavalry. He could have gone into the Met horse section. Riots, football matches – these were the places you found horses now. He thought of his riot training, as a cadet, in the ghost town in Staffordshire kept solely for the purpose. He saw the empty streets before him, the shells of homes and shops and pubs echoing with the rattle of truncheons on shield plastic. Older officers, friends of his father, would still sometimes speak of the miners' strike, and Brixton, Broadwater; these were shared rings through their careers, battle scars.

He took down the *Everyman Illustrated History of London* and imagined Devereux buying it after arriving here, excited by his new home. One page had been turned down at the corner, then turned up again, but the book retained the memory and opened.

Boudicca.

Perhaps the most total destruction London suffered was at the hands of the fierce warrior queen, Boudicca.

Devereux had underlined her name. The book continued:

Boudicca was a queen of the Brittonic Iceni tribe who led an uprising of the tribes against the occupying forces of the Roman Empire.

Belsey skimmed the account. After a flogging and the rape of her daughters by the Roman Emperor, Boudicca rose up. AD 60 or 61.

The Iceni destroyed Camulodunum (Colchester) routing a Roman legion sent to relieve the settlement.

On hearing news of the revolt, the Roman governor Suetonius hurried to Londinium, the twenty-year-old commercial settlement that was the rebels' next target. Concluding he did not have the numbers to defend it, Suetonius evacuated and abandoned it. London was burnt to the ground.

He read on until he got to Boudicca's defeat at the Battle of Watling Street.

The warrior queen poisoned herself to avoid capture. Legend has it that she is buried on Hampstead Heath.

Belsey closed the book. He flicked the pages but no others had ever been folded down. No other names were underlined.

He pulled on a pair of suit trousers and one of Devereux's raincoats and stepped out into the garden. He followed the sculpted pathway, past the bandstand. Moonlight glittered the wet grass, which was slowly losing its manicured sheen. Belsey imagined Devereux in this garden, walking at night. He remembered the corpse on the gurney with its stitched throat. He felt the man's clothes around his living body. Then he began to check for ways into the property from the outside, making a survey of the walls and calculating what lay on the other side: other gardens, the grounds of Highgate School, the back of an old people's home. It wouldn't be impossible to get into the garden, force a French window, slit a man's throat in his sleep.

Belsey walked past the tennis court, past the pond. The rain had cleared some dead leaves away from a patch of freshly turned soil in the far corner, beside the fence. Two thin conifer saplings had been planted six feet apart, each attached to a support stake with a buckle tie. He crouched down, stuck his hands into the soil and pulled out bulbs which had been planted an inch deep around the trees. They hadn't started to sprout. The soil was a combination of topsoil and paler, clay-like subsoil and it stuck to Belsey's hands.

He went and rinsed them in the pond while he considered this. He didn't feel particularly inclined to investigate further. He wandered to a garden shed that contained two spades, a coiled hose and seven bags of peat but nothing else, around to a veranda he had not seen before, on the northern side of the house, with a swing seat and an abandoned ice bucket, then back to the tennis court.

There was a bang at the front of the house.

Belsey turned. Three more bangs – the side of a fist on wood. Someone was there.

Belsey left the lights off as he stepped silently back inside. He found a towel and wiped the rest of the clay off his fingers. Another three thumps: someone persistent; someone who believed the house was occupied. Belsey must have left the gate to the street open. He tried to think what the place would look like from outside. The study light was on but not the front rooms. Would the study be visible from the road? He moved back to the corridor, where Charlotte stood with a sheet wrapped around her.

'Who is it?' she said.

'I don't know.' He realised he was speaking very quietly. She stared at his raincoat.

'You can answer it if you want.'

'I'd rather not. I don't know who they are or why they're here.'

'You don't want to find out?'

'The house can attract attention.'

She looked at him curiously and wandered back to bed. Belsey checked the security screen in the front hallway. It showed a smart young man in frameless glasses and an expensive overcoat holding a newspaper over his head, and the emergency lights of an Audi convertible ticking at the kerb. The man glanced nervously up and down the street. Rain slashed the lenses of his glasses. He didn't look like he'd chosen the house by chance.

Belsey found Devereux's wallet, took out the clipping from the Arabic newspaper and unfolded it. He looked at the fair-haired man on the left of the photograph, shaking hands. He checked the screen again. He thought it might be the same man; it was hard to tell. Belsey waited in the living room. Eventually he heard the Audi start. The next time he checked the screen the man had gone.

He took the scrap of newspaper to Devereux's study and placed it under the desk lamp. The two men grinned back at him. The image had been cropped close, but you could see sky beyond them and the tops of buildings, office blocks, a church spire. So they weren't in the Middle East. It looked like London. At the very edge of the picture you could make out stonework, as if they had been posed in the doorway of a church, looking out to the city.

He leaned back in Devereux's chair. Again, the dead man's possessions seemed to gather to tell him something, but it was more urgent now: the artworks and junk mail and bare branches tapping the windows – trying to pass on a message he could not hear but needed to.

Belsey returned to the bedroom and saw the white sliver of a half-open eye.

'Who was it?' Charlotte asked.

'No one,' he said. She pulled the duvet over herself. He eased the door shut, went downstairs and lay on the floor, feeling his own lies and those of the dead creeping closer.

19

BELSEY WOKE UP EARLY. THROUGH A GAP IN THE LIVING-ROOM curtains he could still see night. It was not yet six: one-night-stand early, with the familiar jolt of recollection. He went to the bedroom and watched Charlotte sleeping with one bare leg hooked outside the duvet, then he stepped back downstairs and put coffee on and tried not to remember his dreams. Images surfaced: Gower, Northwood, a forest. They were out of uniform, in casual clothes. They carried spades and walked with purpose. Belsey wondered if Northwood ever dreamt of him. How did he appear in Northwood's dreams? How would he appear once he had fled? It was strange, he thought: that part of our existence which is in other people's dreams.

Belsey knew his way around the kitchen now. He had settled in. He'd had sex in the house; not just had sex in it but used it for the procurement of sex. If that was not confirmation of tenancy, what was? Today he needed to raise six grand off the sale of Devereux's possessions and set himself up with the financial infrastructure to empty the dead man's accounts. He had a sense that something was catching up with number 37 The Bishops Avenue. Ideally he'd skip the UK by nightfall, but Belsey suspected he would have to lie low until tomorrow morning. He was on his second cup of coffee when he heard a door open upstairs. He went to the hallway to see Charlotte descending the curved red stairs in one of Devereux's robes. She had a sleepy smile.

'I love these stairs,' she said. 'What a way to start the day.'

'Sometimes I slide down the banister,' Belsey said. 'It's still very early.'

'What time is it?'

'It's just gone six. You should go back to sleep.'

'I'm awake now. I figure I'll go home and change before work.'

'Would you like coffee first?'

She walked towards him. He didn't know what she was going to do. She kissed his cheek. Then she sat on a stool at the breakfast bar and they drank coffee, with the darkness loitering outside and the kitchen reflecting off the black windows.

'How are you feeling?' Belsey said.

'Good. Better than I have in a while. I enjoyed myself last night.'

'Me too.'

'It was unexpected.'

'That's my favourite kind of night. Would you like some breakfast? I don't know what I've got.' The fridge display was flashing a list of items: milk, eggs, fruit. He opened it. He couldn't see a breakfast in there.

'Who's Alexei Devereux?' she asked.

Belsey turned round. She was holding a clothing catalogue still in its plastic wrap, reading the address label.

'The previous occupier,' Belsey said. 'Where did you find that?'

'It was on the chair.'

'He's the previous occupier. I still get catalogues.'

'Is he the reason my robe says A.D.?'

'He left in a hurry.'

She raised an eyebrow, then tossed the catalogue aside. 'What is it you're not telling me?'

Belsey sat down across the counter from her.

'There's a lot of things I'm not telling you, Charlotte, but then I've only known you for ten hours. For a lot of that time you were sleeping.'

She finished her coffee and checked her watch. He looked at her face while he could, until she laughed and asked him what he was doing.

'There's nothing to eat,' he said. 'Do you want to be driven back to your car?'

'My car?'

115

'The one you left . . .' And then he saw her start to smile. 'There was no car.'

She grinned, victoriously.

Belsey drove her home. The streets were still desolate, a dawn chorus grating against the naked concrete of Archway. She directed him to a residential street off the Holloway Road. It was the kind of respectable, dark-bricked street he would have liked to live on himself had he managed to uphold his career, his decorum.

'It's not The Bishops Avenue,' she said with an embarrassed laugh.

'No,' he said.

'Stop by number 12.'

He parked and she didn't get out straight away.

'Maybe I'll see you again,' she said.

'Fingers crossed.'

'Think you'll be able to find me?' There was a glint in her eye.

'Easy.'

And then she was out of the car and he watched her and she didn't look back.

He returned to The Bishops Avenue. The day began to brighten. It had just gone 7 a.m. and north London was coming to life: personal trainers training, builders in the front of vans pouring tea from flasks. Belsey saw, momentarily, how he would remember it from his own exile, when memory had done its filleting and hung up its bloodstained apron. He'd be left with the sight of Hampstead in the morning: parking attendants and children in boaters. And he'd find something to miss about it, some part of himself which was left there. Maybe he'd think of the morning with Charlotte, the whole elaborate deceit of it all and he'd think: *Then I was myself, more than ever. What am I now?*

He spent a few minutes straightening Devereux's home, cleaning the coffee cups. Then, on an impulse, he called the *Mail on Sunday*, got a receptionist and asked if a Charlotte Kelson worked there. She did.

'Would you like me to put you through to her voicemail?'

'No.'

He hung up, stared out of the window and momentarily looked forward to a future that wasn't going to happen.

Belsey took the cheque made out to Reflections Ltd and studied it again. There was a door through which Devereux was meant to exit this world and Belsey was blocking it. He was trying to get out of London using the same exit. He went to the kitchen to make more coffee, but he'd finished the jar. This seemed significant. He noticed a girl in the uniform of a local private school walking slowly past, beyond the gates. She gazed at the mansion, looking through the kitchen window.

He slipped Devereux's suit jacket on and stepped outside. He didn't mean to follow the girl, but it happened that they were going in the same direction, along Hampstead Lane to the pond. A long way to walk to school, he thought. She turned down East Heath Road. He followed. At South End Green she disappeared and he stopped beside the doorway of Starbucks, appreciating the morning a final time: the busy triangle of the Green, bounded by the Heath to the north and the concrete of the Royal Free Hospital to the south. Supermarket delivery vans and pregnant mothers passed between the two, dappled by fresh sunlight.

And already he had a sense of something terrible about to occur.

The girl reappeared a few minutes later on the opposite side of the street. She glanced at Belsey, walked on towards Hampstead Heath train station, then turned and crossed the road towards him. Now he saw her face. He recognised her. Where had he seen her before? Eighteen years old in heels and make-up, with a quilted Chanel handbag and a white-tipped cigarette. Hardly a schoolgirl, but for the blue-and-gold jumper of South Hampstead High School. She looked at Belsey's suit, Devereux's suit, as she stepped up onto the pavement. She was staring at it. A chill spread from the small of his back to his chest and stomach.

'Morning,' Belsey said. He gave a smile and a nod. He had a growing feeling of recognition, but his brain wouldn't make the final connection. Something didn't make sense. She met his eyes a final time. Then she flicked her cigarette butt into the road, where it streamed like a distress flare, and walked past him into the coffee shop.

He stepped closer to hear her voice.

'Latte with vanilla,' she said. 'Takeaway.'

'Grande.'

'Yes.'

The first shot shattered the glass. Belsey dived instinctively to the floor. The impact of bullet on glass had been clearer than the shot itself, but he knew the sound of rifle fire. Another three shots came in quick succession, a second's silence. Then the screaming began. Belsey crawled to the cover of the parked cars and tried to formulate a course of action. He heard a fifth shot, then a sixth. It was a high-powered rifle, firing from a distance. The crack of each shot echoed off a block of flats across the junction. Belsey checked the street: people running, people at the bus stop gripping each other, covering their heads; no one aiming a gun. There was a sound like a sudden shower of rain as the rest of the Starbucks window collapsed. Two more shots rattled into the store, unimpeded now. Belsey was calculating the angle they were coming from when it went silent. After a moment he moved, crouching, into the cafe, through the space where the window had been.

A display unit lay on the floor with bags of coffee beans across the tiles, blood spatter on an upturned table. The alarm rang shrill and point-less over soft jazz and the sound of a tap running. A woman in Starbucks uniform hid behind the counter.

'Police,' Belsey said, scanning the store just in case, checking furniture behind which someone could hide. 'Get away from the windows. Go into the back.'

The barista looked up, blank with shock. Belsey studied the coffee shop again: one old woman cowering in the corner, a young East Asian man in Starbucks uniform clutching a bleeding arm. A male customer in blue overalls knelt behind an armchair, and the schoolgirl lay on her side in the storeroom doorway. She must have been moving towards shelter, Belsey thought. There was no gun around. No more shots either, just the alarm, the jazz and a strange silence underneath it all.

Belsey walked through the cafe towards the girl. Blood dripped down a free-standing sign that said 'Create your moment of goodness'. Bullets had passed through the sign into the sofas, opening them out. Yellow stuffing hung in the air.

The girl twitched. There was a dark, wet gap where her left shoulder should have been. Blood spread across the front of her school shirt.

'Don't try to speak,' Belsey said, kneeling. He undid the shirt. He saw, among the general blood, darker entry wounds in the abdomen and chest and knew there was nothing he could do now. She was a few inches from Belsey's face, gazing through the ribbons of blood into his eyes. He pressed both hands against the chest wound. Even as he tried against all odds to staunch the flow he was thinking: *Those were hollow-tipped bullets – to do that kind of damage. And who runs around Hampstead with a rifle and hollow tips?*

'Don't speak.'

Because she was trying to speak. The girl reached for something, found a stack of paper cups on the floor and gripped this. Then she opened her mouth again and a bubble of viscous blood formed at her lips and burst. She closed her eyes. Was there some sacrament to perform? Belsey thought, as the blood dribbled down her chin; a police detective's ritual: *You have the right to remain silent . . .*

When she was dead he took the cups out of her hand and left the body for forensics.

He called Central Operations from the coffee shop's phone.

'I've got a code three, Starbucks South End Green, shots fired. Detective Constable Nick Belsey present, requesting urgent assistance. One fatality, at least one other wonded.'

'Is the scene secure?' the control room asked.

'I reckon so.'

Sirens filled the air now, approaching from Hampstead, Kentish Town, Camden and Highgate, homing in. But for the moment the scene was his. Commuters stared into the shattered shopfront. He turned to the closest pair, young men, and told them to keep everyone else across on the other side of the Green. Beside them was a man in council overalls, a man in a suit and a woman in jogging gear.

'Stop the traffic,' Belsey said. 'Go up Pond Street. You –' he turned to the jogger – 'go up to Keats Grove, and you on Fleet Road, stop all traffic. Now.'

Paramedics in green began to mass outside the hospital, waiting for the all-clear: the upper tier of the car park had a fringe of nurses and patients in dressing gowns, staring down. The first two response vehicles arrived a moment later, police drivers strewing their cars across the road and pavement, nudging the folded tables of adjacent cafes and the vegetable crates of the health food shop. Belsey saw his boss, Inspector Tim Gower, jump out of a Ford S-Max a few minutes after them, in civilian clothes, striding towards the carnage. Gower saw Belsey.

'Are you hurt?'

Belsey realised he was covered in blood.

'I'm fine.'

'What happened?'

'Someone started firing into the Starbucks. It sounded like a rifle.'

'Did you see them?'

'No.'

'Any idea which way they went?'

'I've no idea.'

Gower put an order out: no more vehicles until they had armed officers present. Belsey gave a brief rundown of what he knew: eight shots five minutes ago, no sign of any gunman.

'Don't go anywhere,' Gower said. He turned to the other officers and ordered tape boundaries and then yelled at the civilians to clear the area.

Armed Response turned up three minutes later, followed closely by Homicide and Serious Crime Command. After ten minutes of well-drilled swagger from the boys with guns, the paramedics and scene-of-crime officers were allowed to move in. Five minutes after that, a white tent covered the front of the Starbucks like a belated airbag. Forensic officers tagged the area with numbered flags. They searched the sky and talked about rain. The girl was carried out on a stretcher, beneath a blanket, and there was an awkward hush that lasted all of thirty seconds before work resumed.

Belsey gave his account to one of the Homicide team, DS Joseph Banks.

'I didn't see anyone drive up. I didn't see anyone run away.'

'How many shots did you hear?'

'Eight. Like a hunting rifle. It was at some distance.'

'Other people are saying ten or more.'

'No. There was echo. I wouldn't say more than eight.'

'From where?'

'I don't know. But it was the girl they wanted.'

'The schoolgirl?'

'Three shots, one to her shoulder, two to the torso.'

'If that's right.'

'I saw it.'

'What were you going to be doing today?'

'Going into work,' Belsey said. He watched Chief Superintendent Northwood climb out of the back of an armoured, metallic-grey BMW, uniformed, capped, glowering. His driver remained in the front. All other officers paused to acknowledge his presence, as if the whole event was stage-managed for Northwood's arrival. Those who knew him gave casual salutes; the rest retreated into the background. Northwood surveyed the panorama until his gaze fell on Belsey. This was, it seemed, the one detail out of joint. He marched over.

'What a surprise,' the Commander said, with quiet fury.

'Sir.'

'What the hell are you doing here?'

'I was getting a coffee.'

He stared at Belsey. Then he walked away, towards the crime scene.

'You know him?' Banks said.

'We're close.'

'Get yourself sorted. Go in. We'll pass any instructions through your station.'

20

It was a five-minute walk from the crime scene to Hampstead police station. Belsey chose to go up Pond Street, past the hospital, to avoid the bottleneck of emergency vehicles on South End Road. At the station he showered, borrowed a clean shirt and went to the parade room. The usual morning prayers – the 8.30 a.m., pre-shift meeting – had been converted to a murder briefing. Gower gave a breakdown of what they knew, then read a list of officers to go to the incident room and a list of those to remain on Rosslyn Hill assisting from there. Belsey wasn't assigned to either.

'Look,' he said to Belsey, when the other men and women had gone, 'I'm still waiting to hear from the IPCC, but I think it's best if we keep you on restricted duties. Away from Northwood. Someone's got to hold the fort . . .'

Belsey returned to the CID office and sat at his desk. He hadn't been expecting this. He leaned back in his chair with his eyes shut listening to the sirens on Rosslyn Hill and felt like he used to, aged eleven or twelve, hearing his father and his father's friends drunk downstairs. Shut out of the party. He had spent his life as a police officer trying to find out what people got up to downstairs, knocking on the doors of men and women's individual nights and peering in. He didn't like to be shut out of a murder investigation. Not when his shoes still had the victim's blood on them. Devereux's shoes.

His hope had been to flee the country this evening. He knew, without having to think, that his plans were on hold for now. It would look awful. And he couldn't bring himself to turn his back on a girl who had died in front of him. Not for the moment. Guilt was not just a matter of what you had done, but what you had chosen to run from – even if it was not your crime to start with. He could not run while her dying face was still fresh in his mind.

And he had recognised her.

The canteen was empty. Belsey turned the TV on. Sky News showed shots of the white tent; men and women beside the police tape being interviewed and their breath steaming. The ticker reported 'shock and confusion' over 'shootings in affluent London suburb'. There were no photos of the girl yet.

He thought of patterns: women get killed by the men who love them. Places of work get fired up by former employees. Walk into a coffee shop with five people inside and one of them will owe someone money, another will have slept with someone's wife. None of these clicked. Belsey moved through the events as his mind had preserved them, using the visuali-sation techniques he used with witnesses. He started with the morning he had been enjoying, the sunlight, the shape of branches against the sky. He moved in on the details: frost in the centre of each paving slab; a horn blaring somewhere on Fleet Road. Then he let the girl appear. And he looked harder than he did then. He saw the individual strands of her dark brown hair, the black quilt of the handbag, a chipped nail on the cigarette hand. The right hand. The girl looked back at him, her gaze passing back through him, and the more he thought, the more she stared, still staring, from wherever she was now.

He had seen her before today. He had seen her recently. When had he been into a school, or spoken to teenagers?

Tony Cutter arrived at the station, shaking and delusional, confessing to the crime. Belsey offered to speak to him.

'I had my suspicions, Tony.'

'I'm sorry, Nick. There's blood on my hands.'

'Things happen. Let's move on. Where are you sleeping these days?'

'Alice Ward.' The psychiatric ward of the Royal Free. It saw a lot of Tony.

'Looks like you've been on the street quite recently,' Belsey said.

'I was. Now they've given me a bed in Alice.'

'Cheaper than a hostel.'

'Cheaper than a hostel!' He laughed. 'I'm not going in a hostel.'

Belsey walked him back to the Royal Free. They attracted glances on Rosslyn Hill. With Pond Street taped off, the traffic had solidified, as if it was all part of a spreading rigor mortis.

'Can I ask you something?' Belsey said, as they approached the hospital.

'I'm in trouble, aren't I, Nick?'

'Did you ever work?'

'Work?'

'Did you ever have a job?'

'I was a handyman. And then I washed the buses, when I was married.'

'You were married?'

'Seventeen years, Nick.'

The police tape stopped short of the Accident and Emergency Department, allowing a narrow channel for ambulances. There was a thin crowd beside the hospital itself: nurses, visitors, patients on drips. All watched the forensics team. There was nothing to see and it was hypnotic.

'I'll be all right from here,' Tony said.

'OK. I'm hoping to go on holiday soon,' Belsey said. 'So you might not see me around. If you don't, then take care of yourself. Don't cause trouble.'

'Off on holiday!' Tony grinned.

'Bye, Tony.'

Belsey walked back to the police station and called Dispatch.

'Where's the incident room?'

'St John's. Downshire Hill.' They'd taken over the nearest church, which was common procedure for the initial days of a Major Incident Inquiry. The investigation was at speed, and there was no way Hampstead police station could accommodate it. The station gave him a number to call. He called.

'Any ID on the girl yet?'

'Jessica Holden, eighteen years. Hospital have just pronounced it DOA.'

The name wasn't one he knew. This only made his feeling of recognition more puzzling.

'Anything on her?'

'Nothing.'

'When's the press conference?'

'There's one in the community centre at ten. They're already starting to report on it and Northwood wants to get the facts straight.'

'Northwood?'

'He wants to get a statement out fast.'

Belsey sat back and remembered the panic, people taking cover, the girl's last gaze upon him. He ran Jessica Holden through the Police National Computer: nothing. Youth Records: nothing. He called Customs.

'It's Chief Superintendent Northwood's office here,' he said. 'Yes, I expect you've heard . . . Yes, we've got a name for the victim now and I want to run a check.'

According to Customs, Jessica Holden had a new passport ordered five days ago, fast track.

'Forty-eight-hour fast track?'

'That's right. Unused so far, sir,' the Customs officer said.

'How much did that cost her?'

'Two hundred.'

'When was she last out of the country?'

'Three years ago.'

'Suddenly she's in a rush to go on holiday.'

'Looks that way, sir.'

Belsey walked past the hospital, down towards the crime scene. News vans with satellite dishes crowded the patisseries. He felt a story breaking, like a wave crashing down on all their heads. If it bleeds it leads. But where?

Belsey's stomach cramped. He hadn't had a proper meal since the Wetherspoons.

At 10 a.m. the first reporters filed into Hampstead Community Centre. They'd halted the installation of a second-hand book sale and replaced it with cables, the first TV cameras and a chaos of orange plastic chairs. Northwood arrived five minutes late, sweating. He went to the front. Belsey stayed by the door, out of sight. It was crowded, yet quiet enough to hear the electronics whirring. For a moment he thought Charlotte might be there. He couldn't see her. Northwood cleared his throat.

'I'm going to keep this short. There will be a more extensive briefing at midday. At 7.45 this morning there was a firearms incident at the Starbucks on South End Green. One member of staff and one member of the public were hit. The member of the public was a young woman. She was pronounced dead at the Royal Free Hospital at eight thirty this morning and I can confirm that this is now a murder investigation.'

Belsey sensed the quiet thrill pass through the room; a death, a story, a dead-girl story.

'I can't give you any names until we've notified the families. The exact chain of events is unclear at the moment, but it appears that at least five shots were fired into the store from outside. Investigations are now concentrated on a group of individuals seen leaving the area on foot shortly after the incident, and we would call upon anyone who might have seen anything suspicious to come forward.' Belsey frowned. He wondered if he'd misheard but Northwood went on: 'We would implore acquaintances of those responsible for this terrible act to come forward. Don't be afraid to do the right thing. Someone out there knows why a young girl lost her life this morning. They can contact us in the strictest anonymity.'

He gave a Crimestoppers number, and a number for the incident room, and invited questions from the press.

'How many weapons were fired?'

'We're waiting for confirmation.'

'Do you know the type of weapon used?'

'Not yet. Our ballistics experts are looking at that now.'

'Is the staff member male or female?'

'Male. I don't have an age yet.'

'Do you have an age for the girl?'

'I won't be disclosing any more details about the victim until I've spoken to her family.'

'Can you confirm a possible connection with the shooting in Chalk Farm last week?'

'I can't confirm that, no. That is one of many avenues we are exploring. Obviously we are now going to concentrate all the resources at our disposal on solving this crime. You the press will play a vital role and I must ask you to be patient.' Northwood glanced at his watch and began unclipping his microphone. 'I hope to be able to tell you more this evening.' He ignored the rest of the shouted questions.

Belsey walked out quickly to avoid the throng. Someone grabbed his arm.

'Nick.' Belsey looked into the pale eyes of Miranda Miller from *Five News*. He knew her from a Soho bar they both used to frequent, an establishment so desperate they thought a police officer lent the place some class. He was a bright-eyed constable then and she was a cub reporter for the *Camden New Journal*. 'What the hell's going on?' Miller said.

'I don't know, but that was bullshit.'

'I owe you a drink.'

'How about owing me breakfast?'

They got a table at the back of the Coffee Cup cafe. Belsey ordered eggs and toast and a double espresso on her company card. Miller ordered orange juice. She launched straight into interview mode.

'Can you confirm it's gang-related?'

'No. But it's going to impact on property prices.'

'Come on, Nick. I heard the girl who got shot was eighteen.'

'That's why I like you, Miranda. You tell me news.'

'And I've got a leak from the Chief Super himself that they're searching for three teenagers.'

'He leaked that?'

'Straight to me. A robbery gone wrong.'

'It's not a robbery.' Belsey sipped coffee and when the food arrived he set about it hungrily.

'It's a robbery according to Northwood,' Miller said.

'Northwood doesn't know how to work this sort of investigation. He's in line for Assistant Commissioner and thinks this is going to be open and shut and get his face on TV.'

'And it's not?'

'It'll get him on TV. There's nothing straightforward about it, as far as I can tell. The whole thing's crazy. Have you heard anything else about the girl?'

'The victim? Nothing yet. Why are you so sure it wasn't a robbery?'

'There was no attempt to take anything.'

'What information do you have on that?'

'I don't have information, Miranda. I've got a hunch. It says you're being fed desperation and guesswork. It says there were two buses parked at the stand in front of the coffee shop and no one in front of them with a gun. But I don't have evidence and I haven't been asked to find any. Do you want another juice?'

'I've got a live two-way in ten.' Miller flicked open a compact. She checked her face and teeth. 'Do me a favour: pass the usual message to the parents. Put them in touch with me if there's going to be any interviews or appeals.'

'What are you starting at these days?' Belsey said.

'Two grand.'

'For their grief?'

'For an interview. Everyone gets the grief. And a photograph of her would be wonderful.'

'And what do I see?'

Miller snapped the mirror closed. She fished a fifty-pound note from her suit jacket and placed it on the table with a business card, drank the juice down and wiped her mouth.

'Did you know, Starbucks have requested we don't refer to it as the Starbucks shooting?' She grinned humourlessly. 'No "Starbucks Killer" or "Starbucks Victim".'

'They're quick. Didn't you once say you'd speak to your producer about getting me a show?'

'I know a guy who does police-chase videos. I can talk to him.'

'It'll be like that,' Belsey said, taking the money. 'High speed: but thought, not cars. But all the violence, all the crashes.'

'Promise you'll call me if you get a suspect. Even a wrong one.'

'OK.'

'A police source cast doubt on the gang-related leads. How does that sound?'

'Sounds like you've got yourself a story.'

'Give me a call soon, Nick. You're making me curious.'

Emergency Incident Room: St John's Church, Downshire Hill.

The street was one of Hampstead's most charismatic, with overgrown gardens behind high brick walls. Its sash windows now reflected back a stream of homicide detectives heading to the whitewashed church at its centre.

The temporary incident room had overwhelmed St John's. Belsey saw officers from Serious and Organised filing in, which meant someone somewhere had twigged it might be a hit. There were also reps from the specialist gang units, press officers, heads of forensic departments. He stepped in, showing his badge. The usually airy, classical-style church was a trading floor of investigation. One large whiteboard at the front carried lists of the officers visiting every Starbucks in the area, questioning every local jogger, dog-walker, milkman and rough sleeper who might have caught a glimpse of anything suspect.

'Nick, what are you doing here?' Detective Sergeant Karl Munroe, an expert on evasion, walked past clutching two phones and a notepad: Munroe knew where people went when they wanted to vanish, how they got money, what modes of transport they used. He was short, with tinted glasses and a stubble-shadowed face.

'Karl. Long time. Where's he gone?'

'It won't be far.'

'Do they have an address for the girl?'

'Lived with her parents on Lymington Road. Number 18. That's all at the moment.'

Belsey knew the road. He'd never visited that address.

'What are people saying?'

'It's a mess, Nick, I'll be honest with you. The best we've got is this report of a red motorbike heading north along Willow Road.'

'Witnesses?'

'All shaky. One saw two men enter the Starbucks. Another thought there were three. One said the gunman was black or Asian, and came out of a back room shouting in Arabic, maybe praying.'

'Nice to have a choice.'

Munroe smiled wanly. Belsey walked towards the back of the church hall, where they had the pictures up. They'd set up a pigpen with banks of phones manned by civilian workers. The phones were ringing. Dead girls did that. Beyond the phones were boards with photographs of the Starbucks. To one side were photographs of the girl on the floor where she'd fallen. *Jessica Holden*, Belsey thought. He looked closer. Then he knew where he'd seen her before, and the world lurched.

He caught the Northern Line to Bank, surfaced at Monument and walked past St Clement's Church to the office of AD Development.

The lights were off. The door was locked. The brass plaque had been unscrewed, leaving four small holes and some unpainted wood. A broken estate agent's 'To let' board sat propped against the front door. It hadn't been there before, but didn't look new either, suggesting someone had removed it and temporarily hidden it away. Belsey climbed up on the churchyard wall and peered over the curtain into the office. He tried to understand what he was seeing. The office was empty; not just of people but of furniture. He got down, fetched a piece of stone from the adjacent churchyard and smashed the office window. An alarm went off. He reached in, opened the window and climbed through, landing heavily among flaked plaster and broken glass.

All the cabinets and drawers had disappeared, along with the hatstand, desks and chairs. Even the carpet had gone, revealing old flagstones.

Belsey let himself out of the front door in time to see a couple of City constables turn into the lane, speaking on their radios. He pulled his badge out.

'I didn't see them. I just heard the alarm and took a look – the window's smashed. Can't see that there's much to take anyway.' The constables went over and shone a torch through the broken pane. 'Has this been empty long?' Belsey asked.

'Months. Like most of the empty offices around here.'

'The landlords should get some better security,' Belsey said.

He found Devereux's business card and called the London number from a phone box at the end of the alleyway. A young woman said: 'AD Development.'

'Can I speak to Mr Devereux?' Belsey said.

'I'm afraid he's not in the office. Can I take a message?' The voice was bright, scripted, Scouse.

'Is this a call-forwarding service?'

'This is AD Development. I can pass a message on to Mr Devereux.'

'Is Sophie there?'

'No, sir.'

'Jessica?'

'If I can take a message we will make sure someone gets back to you as soon as possible.'

'I'll speak to anyone in the office.'

'I'm afraid they're in a meeting.'

'This is RingCentral, isn't it?' Belsey said.

'This is the line for AD Development. Can I help any further?'

Belsey hung up and called the number on the estate agent's board.

'Yes, we're sole agents for that property.'

'How long has it been unoccupied?'

'Six months. The previous tenants needed somewhere with more space, but it's a one-off property. Very distinguished history. Would you like to take a look?'

21

LYMINGTON ROAD LED AWAY FROM HAMPSTEAD VILLAGE, down from the grittier side of the Finchley Road to West End Lane. The street separated a low-rise, red-brick estate to the south from Hampstead Cricket Club to the north. Finally, as it curved towards West Hampstead, a few of the original pre-war houses remained backing onto the tracks of the North London Line.

Belsey had no difficulty finding the victim's home. Number 18 was made conspicuous by a ragged front garden and the fluorescent constable on its doorstep.

'DC Belsey. Hampstead station.' Belsey pulled his badge out. 'Are the parents in?'

'They're in.'

'I was there earlier. I've been asked to speak to them.'

The doorman looked sceptical. 'OK,' he said. 'But we can't have everyone tramping through.'

Belsey stepped into a harsh, surreal scene. The mother was on the sofa, moaning something incoherent. The father sat in an armchair staring into space. They didn't look up when Belsey entered. A family liaison officer stood on the patio, smoking.

The house was crowded with dusty ornaments and books with broken spines. Belsey smelt it as soon as he set foot inside: a kind of poverty which eats away from within, an erosion fought against with the accumulation of valueless objects, artworks, papers, as if to stop the whole facade imploding. The wallpaper was starting to peel. Resentment had crept into the fabric of the furnishings. Belsey had lost count of the number of times he'd attended a supposed burglary and smelt the place, then moved a magazine and seen the unopened envelopes, always the unopened envelopes. And he'd wait to see the kind of insurance claim they put in and have to decide whether to report the burglary or the fraud or neither.

Belsey turned from the lounge. He trod silently up the stairs.

Police and thieves: both could find their way around a home with their eyes closed. Domestic lives fall into only so many patterns, as if there were some unseen magnetic field commanding the detritus of a family.

He walked into the dead girl's bedroom and it was all wrong.

Pop stars on the wall. Teen magazines. He checked the dates: two years old, three years old. A kid's notepad, school files. He ran a finger over the bedside table and watched a line form in the dust. Belsey looked through the cupboard and the drawers and found a lot of old super-market-brand clothes and not much else.

He went back downstairs to the living room thinking about the glamorous young woman he'd seen that morning. The mother had worn herself into exhaustion. The father hadn't moved. There were photo-graphs of Jessica on display: riding a horse, at a theme park, with grand-parents. She was an only child, it seemed. Belsey picked up a framed school photograph. Now he was sure: Jessica had been Sophie, Alexei Devereux's assistant. He put it back.

'Mr and Mrs Holden,' Belsey said. The husband looked up, blankly. 'My name's Nick Belsey. I'm a detective from Hampstead station.'

It took them a moment to process this. Feeling awkward, Belsey poured them all whisky from a bottle on the sideboard. He put their drinks on the table. The mother was shaking. Had he originally had it in mind to say something? The peace of her last moments; she spoke of you; she felt no pain. He downed the whisky, a cheap, sweet Scotch. Then he made his address.

'I want you to know Jessica passed away quickly. I was there and I think she suffered very little. I can't imagine what you're going through.

My job is to help bring whoever did this to justice and there's not a moment to waste. So forgive me if this seems intrusive.'

No one spoke. Neither of them had taken their whisky. He sat down.

'Would you mind if I asked you a few questions?'

After a moment there came the slightest shake of the head from the woman.

Belsey said: 'The job Jessica was doing, how long had she been working there?'

'She didn't have a job.' The mother's voice was hoarse.

'Did she work at all?' he said. 'Part-time? Anything like that?'

'No.' The mother shook her head. 'She was at school,' she said. 'Just school.'

Belsey took a moment to consider this. People have secret jobs, to go with secret needs for money. They have secret names to go with secret jobs. Teenagers find school insufficiently lucrative and skive into employment. Or maybe the mother was right: Jessica wasn't working. Then what was she doing?

'Was there a boyfriend?'

The mother started crying again. The father found his voice.

'Not that we knew of.'

'When was she last seeing someone?'

'She was too young for boys,' the father said. 'There was nothing serious.'

'But she went out sometimes, maybe to parties.'

'Of course.'

Belsey refilled his glass. He'd almost forgotten his promise to Miranda Miller.

'Have you spoken to any reporters?' he asked.

'We don't want anything to do with reporters,' the father said.

'Good. Because it's important you get it right. If you need to speak to anyone, this is the woman the police recommend.' He passed Miller's card. 'A public statement can help the investigation; it jogs memories, witnesses come forward. This will get you through to Miranda Miller from Channel Five. She wants to help.'

The mother examined the card as if it was meant to explain more than it did. Belsey stood up. He couldn't bring himself to procure photographs. He'd tainted the purity of their grief and could leave now. There was still dust on his fingers.

'She can help financially,' he said, nodding at the card. They heard him, but didn't look up. Belsey continued to the door. But he wasn't done.

'What was Jessica like?' he said, turning. They looked straight at him now.

'What do you mean?' the mother said.

'Was she outgoing?'

'She was a thoughtful girl. Always thinking.'

'Friends?'

'Yes, a few.'

But the mother was looking up at the corner of the ceiling; you saw it in interview rooms a lot. It meant she was struggling to remember.

'She hasn't been here much recently, has she?' Belsey said.

A silence. The husband looked to his wife.

'She came and went,' the wife said.

'Difficult girl? Lots of rows?' They couldn't bring themselves to nod. 'When was she last here?'

'A few weeks ago.' The mother's voice cracked. It was all about to get teary again.

'Have you told the other officers?'

'She knew there was always a bed for her,' the mother said. She covered her face with her hands. Grief is always guilt, Belsey thought.

'She was a young woman. There was nothing we could do to keep track of where she went,' the father said.

'But did you tell anyone she'd run off?'

'She hadn't run off.'

Belsey turned again and this time began to leave.

'Will you?' the mother said.

'Will I what?'

'Tell them.'

'If I get the chance.'

'Do you think it means something?' she continued, as if she hadn't heard him. 'Was the shooting something to do with Jessica?'

'I don't think so,' Belsey said. And it was a lie.

22

THE SOLID VICTORIAN BRICKWORK OF SOUTH HAMPSTEAD
High School nestled behind the Finchley Road at the end of a residential street now thronging with TV crews. They stood just outside the school gates, grabbing sound bites from any girl who would stop. There were plenty of them, crying, fixing make-up, going out on their lunch breaks to smoke. It meant everyone was distracted and Belsey could walk in unchallenged.

The echoing corridors were crowded with girls who stared as he passed. Did he look in a fit state to wander a school? He hoped he looked less strung-out than he felt. He remembered this sense of drive from the back-to-back shifts on other murder cases, body moving beyond fatigue, day and night taking on one shade of stress.

Belsey made his way through the school, asking directions until he found the headmistress's office. The door was open. The study looked unthreatening, bright with GCSE artwork and a lot of well-tended plants. In the background, a radio on the window ledge droned news of the shooting. The headmistress nodded to Belsey and continued to speak on the phone; she was younger than he expected, but with an authority that was hard to miss, in a well-cut suit and with blow-dried hair.

'No . . . Yes . . . No, we're not treating this as a threat to the school . . . Yes, we'll be letting parents know as soon as we can. Thank you.'

She hung up, gave an exasperated sigh. The phone started ringing and she unplugged it. Belsey showed his badge and she nodded wearily and beckoned him in.

'We're under siege here,' she said.

'I'll keep this brief.'

A woman's voice from the radio said: '. . . *a straight-A pupil with everything before her . . .*'

The headmistress paused a second beside the radio.

'Where do they get these ideas?' She shook her head then turned it off.

'From you?' Belsey said.

'Not me. Not from my staff. I feel terrible about what happened, and I'm sure she was perfectly pleasant if you got to know her, but she wasn't a straight-A pupil. Not recently.'

Belsey helped himself to a seat. He wondered what to make of this.

'Do you have a moment? I have a few questions.'

'I'm sure.'

'She was on an assisted place,' he said.

'That's right.'

'Her parents ran into financial difficulties about eighteen months ago, couldn't meet the fees.'

'Yes. How do you know?'

'Because I'm a Hampstead detective. What else do you remember about her?'

'She was contrary, stubborn. One of those girls you assume are well behaved because you don't notice them, then you realise they're shoplifting every lunch break. Not academically outstanding, not awful. But impossible to engage. The only piece of work I remember seeing was an essay on the First World War. I don't know why I remember that. It was good. We were thinking about Oxbridge at one point. But she didn't want to be here.'

'Where did she want to be?'

'Where does anyone want to be?'

'I don't know.'

The headmistress considered this. For a moment they sat there in silence.

'Neither did Jessica,' she said finally.

Belsey had a feeling he could get on well with the headmistress – in another situation, another life.

'Do you know if Jessica was working? Paid work, I mean, not school.'

'No. But she wasn't doing much unpaid work in school. She was probably going to be expelled.'

'For bad grades?'

'For non-attendance. We don't waste time on these things.'

'How bad was her attendance?'

'Of late, we'd be lucky to see her twice a week. Her parents didn't know where she was. The last week was the worst. She'd decided school was over. That's why I feel the press are barking up the wrong tree.'

'I think you're right.' Belsey nodded. 'What do you think she was doing when she wasn't attending?'

'I have no idea. But a girl like that . . .' She shrugged.

'What does that mean?'

'I've been running a school of teenage girls for half a decade now.'

'A girl like what?'

The head spent a while choosing her words. She chose: 'A girl who thinks being adult means getting in trouble with older men. She should have buckled down. Only she thought she was too good for all this.'

'School's wasted on the young. Don't they say something like that?'

'Not quite.' The headmistress plugged the phone back in. It rang. 'Will you tell your colleagues any of this, or are you afraid it might lose you media appeal?'

'I'll pass all this on,' Belsey said. 'I believe Jessica was caught up in something. I'd appreciate it, if you hear anything, if anyone knows what she's been up to, if they could let me know.' He took a pen and paper from the desk and wrote the number for his direct line.

The head considered this, before nodding.

'Of course. I'll have a think. Now, if you'll excuse me, eight-hundred and-fifty-one girls remain alive.'

23

BELSEY WALKED DOWN HAMPSTEAD HIGH STREET TO A SHOP
that sold handbags. He'd passed it a thousand times. Now it was time
to go in.

The shop was brightly lit and very bare. It was just Belsey, three staff,
a security guard and the handbags. He looked along the rows of bags,
each on its own plinth like a museum artefact. He saw the Chanel bag
that the dead girl had been carrying.

'I like this one.'

'Yes, sir.'

'How much is it?'

'Sixteen hundred and ninety-five.'

'Can you knock off the ninety-five?'

'No, sir.'

'I'm joking. Do you sell many of these?'

'Not too many.'

The store security approached nicely with one hand folded over the
other. Belsey thought of the struggling home on Lymington, the pre-
teen bedroom. Where did she stash stuff, he wondered. The equipment
for a second life, where did it live?

What had he stumbled into?

The assistant started straightening a row of wallets. Belsey looked out
of the front window and saw a Transit marked 'Pimlico Plumbers' with

a man in aviator shades sitting in the front looking back at him. Suddenly the man put the van in reverse and cut away into traffic.

'Thank you for your time,' Belsey said, walking to the door.

'Thank *you*, sir,' someone said to his back.

24

MURDER SQUAD HAD COMMANDEERED THE OLD WHITE BEAR for the purposes of refreshment and informal congregation, a pub the size of a postage stamp at the corner of two residential streets. There was a rule that said find the third-closest pub. No one liked to be seen drinking near to the incident room. The Old White Bear was halfway to Hampstead tube station and it was well hidden.

This was where Belsey knew he'd find them, CID men and women standing around a single picnic table at the front, coats on, smoking fast. This was where a lot of the most useful discussions would be held. The pub was providing bacon rolls on production of a warrant card. The officers looked drained: many had come straight from other inquiries and were busy pouring sugar into cups of tea. Few remained for more than ten minutes.

'We could do with you on this one, Nick.' DC Tom Shipton shook his head. He was part of a small crowd centred on a patio heater. Belsey had worked his first ever murder with Shipton, a pensioner killed with a samurai sword in Elephant & Castle shopping centre. Next to him was a stooped, middle-aged officer with shaving cuts whom Belsey didn't recognise, and June Glasgow. Glasgow was one of the most respected murder DIs in north London. She had long black hair, a black suit, plum-red nail varnish; no jewellery, not even a wedding ring, although Belsey happened to know she was civilly partnered with a young woman in the Home Office. But she kept herself interview-room bare. It became a habit: cards to the chest.

'How are they playing it?' Belsey said.

'Robbery,' Shipton said. He looked cold. He had his hands thrust into his overcoat pockets.

'It wasn't a robbery,' Belsey said.

'He said, "This is a robbery."'

'Who?'

'The gunman. This kid.'

'I thought it was meant to be a gang of them.'

'It's not clear at the moment. But there was a gang in the area earlier, near Gospel Oak.'

'Jesus Christ.' Belsey sensed an investigation running away under the momentum of its own mistakes. He'd seen it before. Glasgow watched him, with the curiosity of a good DI. She lit a Silk Cut.

'What about CCTV?' Belsey said.

'Nothing obvious,' Shipton said.

'Some teenage gangster comes in and fires up a Starbucks and no cameras get a whiff?' Belsey shook his head.

'People saw. He said, "Open the till."'

'Who says?'

'There's been other soft targets,' Shipton said. 'KFC.' But his heart wasn't in it.

'It doesn't get much softer than a fucking Starbucks,' Belsey said. 'What did he want? Muffins? How much do they keep in the tills?'

'No more than a hundred, but he doesn't know that.'

'How did he get away?'

'On foot.'

'After going armed? Munroe mentioned this red motorbike. What about that?'

'I haven't heard of any red bike.'

Belsey winced. Investigative disconnect. This was how hours got wasted and criminals went laughing.

'It wasn't a kid, and it wasn't a robbery,' he said.

'Then what was it?'

'And why do you care?' Glasgow said pointedly.

'Why do I care?'

'Why aren't you assigned?'

'I'm on other things.'

No one seemed to find this hard to believe. No one seemed too sorry either. There was a general stubbing of cigarettes, a shaking of heads and checking of watches.

'Where was she coming from, before the Starbucks?' Belsey said.

'She was seen earlier near Kenwood.'

'Whereabouts?'

'Bishops Avenue,' Glasgow said. Belsey took a deep breath. It felt like being tapped on the shoulder. Glasgow studied his eyes.

'With anyone?' he said.

'No.'

'What was she doing on The Bishops Avenue?'

'Walking. We don't know. We're doing door to doors later.'

'How much later?'

'Soon as we have the manpower.'

'Are you releasing that information about her whereabouts?'

'Ask Northwood.'

Belsey shook a cigarette out of Glasgow's pack and lit it with his Zippo.

'It's not on her way to school,' he said quietly, more to himself than to anyone else.

25

Every week or so a man went up to the Heath and exposed himself. CID had been putting a case together for a while. No one used to bother with flashers until it was noticed that they went on to pursue sex crimes of increasing severity. Perversion has diminishing returns. Now the flasher had done it again, getting bolder. Everyone knew this kind of thing headed only one way. So when Belsey got back to the station this was the job he had been assigned. The office was deserted – one message on his desk: *Heath flasher – 11.30 a.m.*

Three hours old. Belsey tore the message in half. It felt like a calculated insult. But then, he thought, maybe it was a blessing in disguise. Heavy grey clouds had begun rolling westwards. The Heath would be empty by the time the rain came. He could lose himself there. It would give him time to think.

He sat out the shower beneath an oak, deep in the woodland behind Spaniards Road. He realised how badly he had needed this moment of reflection. Images returned: the dead girl's eyes, her mouth shaping to a word. To a name? He saw Jessica in the office of AD Development, saw the empty shell of St Clement's Court, and then Charlotte Kelson with a hair clip in her hand. A woman in Mr D's life. A woman now as dead as him.

When the rain stopped he walked to the gardeners' hut. One of the Heath's keepers, Peter Scott, bent over a bag of dead leaves, unloading them onto a bonfire. He had a thin face with pockmarks in the cheeks.

His hands were stained with blue-ink scars that Belsey had seen on other men who'd done long sentences in category-A prisons. They had never spoken about it. The smoke gathered thick as wool among the damp branches.

'What are the Heath Constabulary for?' Belsey said.

'They said I should contact you. It's the same one, this flasher.'

'How do you know?'

'They all talk about his fingernails. Long, dirty nails.'

'You should be a detective.'

'She wouldn't leave her name.'

Belsey sighed. He crouched by the fire and warmed his hands. 'How are you doing?'

'Never been better.'

Belsey fed some dead branches into the flames and watched Scott work. They were often like this. The gardener was that rare thing: a good man to be silent with. When the last of the bags had been emptied Scott disappeared into the hut. He emerged a few minutes later with two mugs of tea and gave one to Belsey. They sat on logs outside the hut.

'What about that shooting?' Scott said.

'You heard about it?'

'It's on the radio. Are you not on that?'

'Not me. What are they saying?'

'Schoolgirl, innocent bystander, glowing future ahead of her.'

'I was told to hold the fort.'

'Is this the fort?'

'One of them.'

They drank their teas. Then Scott stood up and checked the sky.

'I want to show you something,' he said.

They walked deeper into the Heath. The edges of the world appeared sharp, as if the air had been polished by the rain. They walked past Athlone House, the red-bricked mansion that had housed the RAF intelligence school in World War II. Belsey imagined the men here, the classrooms with blackboards and aerial photographs of towns marked for destruction. Then they climbed past the derelict mansion, to a copse of chestnut trees on the edge of the Heath.

'Look.'

A few of the trees were branded with fluorescent-yellow crosses; the sort of marks used by workers digging up roads.

'What is it?'

'I don't know. They appeared a couple of weeks ago. Probably for a race. People come for a run, mark the route. They don't ask.'

'Show me some more.'

He led Belsey over a kilometre or so, showing him the trees marked with a yellow X.

'No plans to chop them? No disease?'

'There's nothing like that going on.'

'It's not a run,' Belsey said.

'Well, I don't know what it is. Continues down towards Highgate Ponds, and back across the East Heath.'

Belsey picked at some bark. It flaked, silver grey. This was what made the plane tree perfect for London, Scott had told him once, it shed its skin and the pollution with it; a lesson there. They came across another cluster of yellow crosses a moment later.

'Have you reported it?' Belsey asked.

'That's what I'm doing,' the gardener said.

26

Belsey walked down Heath Street to the village.

It was past 4 p.m. now, the time of a winter afternoon when Hampstead had a light of its own, silver and mauve; the colour of bags under the eyes of someone you loved and made tired. It came up from the ponds and hung about Downshire Hill and Flask Walk making the beautiful homes more cruelly beautiful.

An *Evening Standard* van pulled up outside the tube station with the headline on its side: 'Hampstead Rampage Horror'. A fresh pile of newspapers was dumped next to a distributor and a man purchased one without breaking his stride. Belsey admired the moment: the city as machine, bound in its rhythm of morbid fascination. He swiped a copy and read it as he walked.

'A Hampstead schoolgirl died this morning after a gun attack on a Starbucks in North West London . . .' They kept to the official line on her all-round abilities and general popularity. The school was in shock. They were arranging counselling. There was no picture of Jessica yet.

He continued down Hampstead High Street to the incident room.

The room had settled into its rhythm; off the boil now, but simmering. Already the investigation was moving out from its epicentre to the world. Belsey looked for June Glasgow but couldn't see her.

'Know where I'd find DI Glasgow?'

'Outside, at the back. Just finished interviewing witnesses.'

He poured two coffees from a pot beside the inquiry manager's desk and took them out. Glasgow leaned against the church wall, alone with her thoughts.

'Nick,' she said. He gave her a coffee. 'Just what I need.'

'Any joy with the interviews?'

'Waste of time so far.' She sipped her coffee. 'Nutters.' She passed him her pack of cigarettes and held out a light. After another moment she said: 'I've been drafted into a pile of shit.'

'Looks that way.'

'Northwood sees it as his.'

'It is.'

'But he's not a senior investigating officer. He shouldn't be steering. Did you see the conference? Now we've got fifteen papers leading with street gang.'

'What are your angles?'

'We don't have them. That's the point. That should tell us something.'

'Like what?'

'Like you're right, it wasn't a robbery. But I've no idea what it was. I've never worked anything like it.'

'But you've got ideas.'

'Something with no logic, so we shouldn't be looking for it. Maybe crackheads.'

'Crackheads are high visibility. You'd have witnesses from Charing Cross to Highgate.'

'Psychotic.'

'Same.'

'So what are your ideas, Nick?' she said, tired of the game.

'An assassination,' Belsey said.

'On who?'

'Who was in there?'

'A seventy-five-year-old woman visiting her sister in hospital. A cleaner from Uganda on his way to work. A Chinese student, twenty-one years old, who's been working at Starbucks two months. The store manager – a Polish woman tipped for big things in Starbucks management – and

149

a schoolgirl who's in the wrong place at the wrong time. We've checked them all. No history, no suspicious connections.'

'Only one of them was fired at.'

'The schoolgirl?' She shook a match and dropped it. Belsey knew what she was thinking: speculation like this wouldn't mean much to the chain of command around her. A senior-looking plain-clothed officer slipped out of the back of the church, down the stone steps to the road. He winked at Glasgow as he passed.

'The Magdala,' he said, lifting his drinking hand. Glasgow gave a non-committal thumbs up. Belsey watched him go.

'Who was that?'

'Ken Barber. From Gun Crime,' Glasgow said. But she was still puzzling over Belsey's theory. 'You're saying it was a hit on Jessica Holden.'

'Is there no way she could connect to anything?'

'Like what?'

'Like trouble, individuals with history.'

'Not so far as I'm aware.' Glasgow turned to Belsey. 'I heard you had some trouble of your own,' she said, as if maybe this was all about Belsey's state of mind.

'I'm all right.'

'I asked for you on the team.'

'And here I am.'

She looked at him dubiously. 'There's only one thing we found on the girl.'

'What is it?'

'A letter in her handbag sealed in an envelope. Her writing.'

'Saying?'

'Sorry.'

'For what?'

'It says something like "I can't do it. Sorry." A let-down letter.'

'Can't do what?'

'I don't know. It wasn't addressed to anyone.'

'Are you chasing it?'

'We're speaking to everyone who knew her. We haven't found any signs of a romance so far. If we find a love drama we'll follow that, but this doesn't look like the work of a jilted teenager to me.'

'I guess not.'

'I've got to get back. Thanks for the coffee, Nick.' She didn't thank him for his thoughts. Belsey watched her make her way back into the church, then walked to the Magdala pub and introduced himself to DI Barber. He was sitting at the back of the pub with a couple of the Murder boys. They looked glazed and tetchy. First drink since the call-out. But the Inspector seemed all right. Barber had heavy-lidded eyes and several gold rings. He fetched Belsey a chair. Belsey broke Miranda Miller's fifty-pound note and got four pints in.

'What were Jessica Holden's movements over the last few days?' Belsey said. 'Where was she yesterday?'

'Yesterday? She went to the gym. That was the last sighting before The Bishops Avenue. That's all we know.' The Inspector raised his glass. 'Cheers.'

'Which gym?' Belsey said.

'The posh one off Belsize Avenue.'

'Have you checked it?'

'We spoke to them. They said she went two or three times a week. Kept to herself according to most of the other users.'

'It's a nice gym,' Belsey said.

'It's got some nice clientele.' The men laughed.

'Which officers went in?'

'To the gym? I don't know. Why? You think this is health-related? You think she pushed someone off the treadmill?' The Murder boys laughed. Belsey laughed.

27

IT WASN'T A GYM, IT WAS A HEALTH CLUB – BELSIZE HEALTH
Club – and it made the distinction clear with a lot of high-mainte-
nance greenery and screens showing every satellite channel you could
hope to see. The building was on an expensive cul-de-sac. Vents spilled
the smell of chlorine across cobblestones. Membership bought you the
total absence of anyone without three grand a year to spend on Pilates.
Those with the money were arriving thick and fast from a day of
making it.

'I'm thinking of becoming a member,' Belsey told the woman on
reception.

'Hang on.' She called out, 'Mark.'

A man emerged in gym-branded shorts and a T-shirt that let his biceps
sell the benefits of membership. He shook Belsey's hand.

'Do you want to look around?'

'Definitely.'

'Follow me.' He patted Belsey's shoulder and led him into the gym.
'What's your name?'

'Nick.'

'Nick, looks like you could do with some relaxation.'

'Which machine's good for that?'

Mark laughed. 'What are you hoping to work on?'

'I want a six-pack.'

He showed Belsey the new equipment, the swimming pool, a room of exercise bikes. Belsey admired a growing army of men and women pedalling endlessly towards their own reflections. The man was talking about payment plans.

'And if there's an au pair or anything, we can get her put on your account half-price.'

'Perfect. Can I take a shower while I'm here? Maybe use the sauna?'

'I can sort out a guest pass.'

'That would be great. And I need a towel,' Belsey said.

Belsey took the towel to the changing room, undressed and folded his clothes. Some members got their own permanent locker. These were larger than the others; they had gold numbers and a little tag that said 'Premium'. Affiliates like himself had to put a pound in and he didn't have a pound. He entered the sauna and breathed in the smell of pine, watching the lockers until someone opened one and he could see how large they were.

He showered. The changing room was getting crowded. He helped himself to the free sprays and body lotion, dressed and went to reception.

'What do you get with premium membership?'

'It's what we recommend if you're serious about getting into shape. With premium you receive personal training, free classes, sunbeds, two towels and a locker of your own.'

'Did Jessica Holden have premium membership?'

It took them a moment to connect the name, then they looked uneasy.

'What is this?'

Belsey produced his police ID.

'I think some police came in earlier. About Jessica Holden?'

'Yes.'

'Did they ask to see her locker?'

'No.'

'I'd like to see Jessica Holden's locker.' He put his badge away. They stared at him. Belsey walked into the ladies' changing room.

'It's OK,' Belsey announced to the half-dressed women. 'This is a murder investigation.' He turned to the staff. 'Open Jessica's locker, please.'

They found a key, went to a locker and opened it. Inside were three suit bags and three Selfridges bags containing sets of office clothes, two basques, underwear from La Senza and Agent Provocateur, handcuffs, lube in sachets, six-inch heels, blindfolds in pink and blue, a new UK passport and a set of business cards that said her name was Emerald and she knew your 'heart's desire', at least within the M25 area.

It appeared the locker was spacious enough to fit a second life. And quite a life she seemed to have bought herself. Belsey looked at the business cards again, then told the staff that he needed to make a call.

They let him use the phone in reception. He called the incident room.

'Has any agency contacted you to say Jessica Holden was working for them as an escort?'

'No. Is it true?'

'I'll get back to you on that.'

The gym staff clustered close by, pretending not to listen. Belsey dialled the number given on Emerald's business card.

'Good evening, sir. You're through to Sweetheart Companionship. Can I help?'

'Whereabouts are you based?' Belsey asked.

'Are you looking for some companionship?'

'That's right.'

'Can I take your name?'

'I need to speak to the manager first. I have some unusual requests. Can you put me through?'

'What does it concern?'

'My request?'

'Yes.'

'Dead girls.'

She hung up on him.

Belsey thanked the gym for their assistance and walked out. He went to an Internet cafe on the Finchley Road and found the Sweetheart Companionship website. You could view girls by price or age or nationality; they advertised themselves with professional-quality shots, only partial nudity and vital statistics for those who wanted to imagine the rest. Half had their faces clouded. The home page kept the details of their work vague but advised that advance booking was necessary to avoid disappointment. All in all there were fifty-three girls of varying nationalities and price bands, all of whom may or may not have known his heart's desire. There was no Jessica. No Emerald. Belsey checked the agency's address and decided to visit in person.

28

Sweetheart lived on the top floor of a cramped Soho block on Poland Street, with narrow stairs leading past graphic designers and a TV production company. The door opened into a waiting area with a glass roof, a desk at the side and shots of 1950s film stars on the wall. It was turning 7 p.m., but then, Belsey guessed, it was a nocturnal kind of industry. A groomed middle-aged woman sat behind the desk, unfazed by his arrival.

'I'm here to speak to the manager,' Belsey said. She smiled him towards a seat, and after a minute the office door opened and Belsey was invited in.

The office contained a woman in a black trouser suit with a clip-board, and a man in an open-collared denim shirt with a tan and a greying goatee. The woman smiled at Belsey and left, shutting the door. The goatee gave a smile that was half a wink. Men here. Between you and me.

'Freddie Garth.' He shook Belsey's hand. 'Drink?'

'I'll have whatever you're having.'

He buzzed through for some beers and water. The office had a view over the jumbled Soho rooftops towards Greek Street. There were framed prints of racing cars, a photographer's white backdrop and a height chart. The desk was black, the chairs leather.

'So I'm in London for a while,' Belsey began.

'Of course.'

'And I wanted some company.'

156

'It can be a lonely city.'

'The thing is, I wanted someone young enough to be my daughter,' Belsey said.

The man nodded. 'Why not?'

'How young does it go?'

'You'll find all our girls are very fresh.'

'What do they do?'

'You pay for their company. Anything beyond that is between you and the girl. We don't involve ourselves. But I think you'll find most are very willing. In two years we've never had any complaints.'

'Let's say I wanted a girl called Emerald.'

Garth's jaw tightened. 'Let's say.'

'Any girls working under that name?'

'Not here.'

'Not any more, right?'

'Never.'

'So when did she start?' Belsey said.

'I don't know what you're talking about.'

Belsey pulled his badge. 'Try and think really hard what I might be talking about.'

Garth shut his eyes then opened them again. He was irritated. It was irritating, finding yourself involved in crime when all you were doing was being a pimp.

'Early last year,' he said, making himself comfortable in a way that said this was now a waste of his time.

'Well, she turned eighteen in September.'

'Do you have a warrant?'

'Do you?'

'We're all in order.'

'Not for selling seventeen-year-olds you're not.'

'I'm not talking to you until you show me a warrant. It's nothing to do with us.'

'The funny thing is, it's nothing to do with me either. So why would I have a warrant?' Belsey laughed. 'It's nothing to do with me and it's nothing to do with you.' He wondered where the beers were.

'Then perhaps you could leave.'

'And yet you took her off the books quickly enough.'

The woman came in with a tray of drinks and saw the expressions on their faces. She shot a puzzled look at Garth and he waved her out of the room.

'We took her off five weeks ago.'

'I could have done with that beer.'

'Let's make this quick. It's awful, what happened. But it's nothing to do with us and you don't need to be wasting your time here.'

'Why did you take her off?'

'She was fired.'

'Why?'

'She said she fell in love.' Garth's eyes gleamed.

'Is that bad?'

'We knew what it meant.'

'What does it mean?'

'It means someone thinks they're getting it for free.'

Belsey considered this.

'Maybe she *was* in love,' he said.

'It means she's turning tricks on her own. Sure, maybe she was loving it too. We see more of that than you'd think. It doesn't make it any better for business.'

'How did you know she was in love?'

'She became unreliable. I heard talk. She wouldn't turn up for jobs.' He shrugged. Belsey thought: poor Jessica. Didn't turn up for school and didn't turn up for work. A girl after his own heart.

'Did she do any secretarial stuff?'

Garth frowned. 'What do you mean?'

'Dress up in a blouse. Type letters.'

'She'd dress up as Mickey Mouse if it got your wallet open. This isn't a convent.'

Belsey nodded. He stood up and got some water from the cooler.

'She was seeing a man called Alexei Devereux. Tell me about him.' He stood beside the cooler so Garth had to twist to see him.

'We don't keep client records.'

158

'Bullshit,' Belsey said. 'Do you keep payment records?'

'Not lying about.' Now Garth spread his plump hands, suddenly placatory. 'I'm a simple man. I make a simple living.'

'It doesn't get much simpler.'

'All we sell is a chance to unwind. Most people just want someone on their arm, someone to have a nice meal with, go to a bar.'

'You're breaking my heart.'

'Anything else is between them and the girls.'

Freddie Garth looked very drained now. Drained of willpower and drained of useful information. Belsey could have told Freddie Garth more than Garth could tell him. The next detectives who turned up at Sweetheart's offices would find his revelations more startling. Then they would be just a step away from Devereux, and two steps away from Belsey himself.

Girl gets mixed up with crooked businessman. Girl dies. He could spend a lot of time trying to join those dots or he could solve the more pressing mystery of how to remove himself from their mess before the Murder Squad arrived.

Belsey left the Sweetheart office and headed back out.

29

HAMPSTEAD WAS HAVING ONE OF ITS NERVOUS SPELLS. THE population had retreated and the dark peace of the Heath rolled out through the narrow streets like a fog. There was a sense of quarantine. Sometimes, walking through the village at night, its wealth seemed to Belsey like a kind of disease. He felt the isolation it imposed, the undercurrent of fear, the surgery. A breeze scraped dead leaves across the spotless pavements. The only humans he saw were teenagers in parked sports cars, releasing the cloying scent of skunk weed into the night.

Belsey made his way to The Bishops Avenue. He wondered about Jessica's fresh passport, then the letter in the handbag: *I can't do it. Sorry.* She was meeting someone, he thought. Meeting Devereux, he tried to imagine. Had they been planning to flee together? Only Jessica got cold feet – and Devereux had already decided on a more absolute escape.

Then there was the shooting.

Maybe he was wrong about it all connecting. But he didn't think so. And the collapse of business empires could make people angry. *Go now*, he thought. He was too entangled with a man who connected to a fresh murder victim. The police could well be looking for him already. *Get out.* But getting out meant getting money. Cassidy was expecting his delivery – all he needed were the goods to deliver.

An empty beat car sat at the very top of The Bishops Avenue, close to the Heath. He could see a pair of detective constables moving house to house on their inquiries. They had passed Devereux's. Belsey crossed the road, away from them, and approached number 37 from the far side. When he was sure they were well away from the house he crossed back, and walked swiftly up the path to the front door.

He unlocked the door and went to the safe room, sat in the chair for a few minutes and shivered. He walked to the living room, turned on the TV and heard the headline: *Confusion over coffee shop shooting*. Sky were devoting a lot of airtime to it. Initial reports of a robbery had been questioned. Someone had paid Jessica's parents a visit and cleared out the photo albums: they had pictures of the girl at the front of a small stage in a satin dress, in a school line-up, one with friends in a Pizza Hut. But they'd failed to find the money shot, the heart-tug smile. Belsey crouched close to the screen. They seemed to favour the one of Jessica with friends. It wasn't a good picture. She looked like she'd been caught off guard.

He turned it off and finished loading Devereux's possessions into the Porsche, squeezing shirts and suits into the remaining space and choosing which household appliances would be most profitable. There was more than he could take in one load so he made a separate pile of spoils in a corner of the garage for later use. Finally he stood in the study. The Persian rug looked like it was worth something. He could tie it to the roof. After five minutes of pushing and pulling he had moved the billiards table clear and was able to roll it up. He stared at the carpet beneath.

A dark stain stretched towards his feet. Belsey crouched down and rubbed the carpet fibres between his fingers. Then he went and got a bottle of bleach from the utility room.

He put the bleach on the stained carpet and watched it bubble. An old Murder Squad trick: the peroxide was reacting with an enzyme called catalase and breaking down into water and oxygen. Which meant it was blood. He stood there, staring at it with part weariness and part wonder. He felt the pull of investigation and the pull of escape, and swore with frustration. Eventually he took some cotton wool and went to the safe room. He stood on the chair and swabbed the dried blood on the ceiling with the cotton wool. Then he took scissors and two freezer bags from the kitchen and cut himself a sample of bloodstained carpet. He sealed each sample separately and labelled the bags 'Blood: Safe Room' and 'Blood: Study'. He would sell Devereux's possessions first. But then he needed to pay a visit to Forensic Command. For the sake of his conscience and his curiosity.

After Hampstead's well-heeled menace he was glad for the more open threat of south London. Belsey drove through the estates, wondering how he'd explain the arrest of John Cassidy to his anxious father.

The Wishing Well was already Friday-night messy, brittle with an air of cocaine snorted off burnt cisterns. Men in bright shirts slapped each other's backs and a few tough-looking women laughed beside the bar. Belsey found the regulars in one corner, eyeing the fair-weather criminals.

'Where's Niall?' Belsey said.

'He's not here. Try the office. He said he'd be waiting for you. He's not happy.'

It had taken Belsey three years of favours and lock-ins to see the 'office', a derelict brick shed behind the Old Kent Road that had once been a Dairy Crest milk depot. It crumbled slowly behind high fences in a corner of wasteland. The brownfield site had been abandoned for years and was now meant to be turning into shops and key-worker housing, except the private backers had backed out leaving only barbed wire and a trashed Portakabin. It all lived behind huge dented gates that carried warnings about non-existent dogs; pitch black, away from the road, away from street lights.

Belsey banged on the gates. Chains slid through metal and they opened. Cassidy was on his own, a single red point of cigarette in the darkness. Belsey drove in, across compacted mud, into the depot.

Niall's 'office' housed an old JCB, a flatbed truck draped in tarpaulin and a lot of scrap metal. A meagre light dripped through its roof of translucent, cobweb-encrusted plastic, revealing a stained concrete floor and charging points along one wall for the milk floats. It had been the gathering point after many crimes, a perfect slaughter. The years of metal theft had left a chaotic jumble of scrap. Objects scattered about included magnets, manhole covers, roofing, parts of bus shelters. There was even fencing and decorative ironwork from cemeteries. The sour smell of old milk remained very faint.

Belsey left the headlights on. He jumped down from the SUV.

'There was a breakdown of communication,' he said.

'I'll say there was a breakdown of communication. What the fuck's he doing banged up?'

'Johnny's going to be fine. Trust me.'

But Cassidy's eye had been caught by the car and the load, and his trust followed that. The SUV would make his money back with enough spare to buy a few minutes with a decent lawyer.

'Have you got papers for it?' he said.

'What do you think?'

'You said there were papers.'

'That would be a silly thing for me to say.'

'You always mess me about, Nick.'

'That's my job,' Belsey said. But he could see Cassidy was satisfied with the haul. It was all mint. 'Take the plates off the Porsche before you do anything with it. Where's the money?' he said.

'Let's see what we're looking at first,' Cassidy said, and started moving Devereux's possessions from the car. Belsey helped him, trying not to feel too guilty about leaving the remnants of Devereux's elegant life in the corners of a milk depot. He admired the scrap, the ornamentation, the cemetery ironwork. Sometimes you could make out words: *Sweet is the sleep of those who have laboured . . . Love is stronger than death . . . Home at last.*

They sold the metal to China. Or at least they did before the bottom dropped out of the market. One time Niall and the gang stole an entire bridge, near Swindon. They'd never been done for it. Belsey always wondered how you stole a bridge. He liked to imagine it passing through the night; seeing it from a distance, travelling east on the M4.

'I heard about the Starbucks,' Cassidy said.

'What do you reckon?'

'Disgusting. A young girl like that.' He shook his head. He was sincere. Belsey had always admired the passionate moral protests of criminals.

Lest they be thought beyond humanity, perhaps. No, morality divided itself into ever thinner leaves.

'It was a rifle. Where would they have got that?' Belsey said.

'Not one of ours.'

'Whose was it?'

'It'll be contract,' Cassidy said.

'Why?'

'That's a job. A professional. And it wasn't anything anyone's heard about.'

Belsey picked a dusty milk bottle up off the floor. It was full of cobwebs. He put it back.

'Ever heard of a man called Alexei Devereux?' he asked.

'No.' Cassidy took a carrier bag from his jacket. 'Any more questions?'

'How do you steal a bridge?' Belsey said.

'You don't need the whole bridge, just the metal.'

'Do you melt it down in London?'

'Not personally. I want him out of there, Nick. I want Johnny out.'

'I'll see what I can do.'

Cassidy handed him the bag. It was filled with used fifties and twenties. Belsey counted six thousand in total and stuffed it in his jacket. He didn't need to count it twice. It had the weight of freedom. He was almost ready to go.

30

FORENSIC SERVICES COMMAND occupied a brutal concrete block at 149 Lambeth Road. It was a conveniently short sprint across the river from the Yard. It was a slightly longer sprint from the Old Kent Road, through the subterranean labyrinth of Elephant & Castle, and felt less convenient still when carrying six grand in a dead man's suit. Not the best part of town for cash transportation. Belsey kept alert, moving fast through the underpasses.

The Command, as it was known, didn't announce itself to the public as such, unless you counted the tinted windows and black security bulbs that lined its outer walls. Otherwise it looked like a multi-storey car park decorated with slat blinds. A giant '149' on the deep shaft ventilator stood in place of any formal identification – that and the occasional police vehicle dipping silently down the ramps.

'I've got something for urgent analysis.'

The security guard stared at Belsey. A sign said 'Welcome to Central Forensics' and underneath, 'Our Values'.

'I need to speak to the night labs,' Belsey said. 'It's concerning the Jessica Holden murder inquiry.'

This got a call put through. The guard spoke to someone in the Command Unit and Forensics Officer Isha Sharvani appeared a few moments later. Belsey was relieved to see a familiar face.

'Nick,' she said.

'Isha. I was sent round on an urgent. I know it's not very kosher. Would you run a check on these?'

She looked at the freezer bags with scepticism bordering on disgust. 'What job?'

'The Starbucks shooting. Just see if the two of them match. Give me a call at Hampstead. You've got my number.'

'Nick Belsey.' She shut her eyes in exasperation. But he knew she'd help.

The first time Belsey met Isha Sharvani it was 8 July 2005. The previous morning he had been on a drugs raid, standing in a crack house on Adelaide Road with a woman handcuffed to a sink. They knew there was something big on because response vehicles had been racing through Camden into town for ten minutes, sirens on full: unusual enough for morning rush hour, and all flavours of emergency service. And they kept coming, so you knew it was cars from the neighbouring boroughs as well. Belsey's team had killed their communications for the raid, and when they switched them on again there were call-outs to Russell Square and King's Cross, and then an all-units to Tavistock Square. Then the world slipped into Code Red.

They knew the drill. For two years there had been practice runs. The crack addicts got a momentary reprieve. Crime seemed suddenly reassuring, part of an everyday routine bleached by a brighter light.

All units to central London.

And so the next morning he had found himself with Sharvani collecting samples of clothing from select members of Camden's Pakistani community, ferrying them into Counter-Terrorism for analysis. The bosses had wanted someone Asian, preferably Muslim, to accompany him, and the fact that Sharvani was Hindu didn't seem to bother them. It was a strange few weeks. Belsey made good contacts at the Regent's Park mosque – intelligent men who knew Plato and Nietzsche as well as the Quran and were happy to discuss any of them – discovered a lot of hydroponic weed being grown by a group of Bangladeshi teenagers, and befriended Sharvani. He'd spent a lot of time at Forensic Command. He hadn't been back until now.

He wanted to put his curiosity to bed. Or, better still, to sell it on. Let someone else fathom the bloodstains of The Bishops Avenue. He wished he could fast-track the forensics procedure, wished he had a team to put in the legwork necessary to establish who'd been passing through Devereux's home.

The familiar clutter of abandoned market stalls at the back of Waterloo Station appeared, glimmering under the street lights. He needed to get back to Hampstead and stash the money burning a hole in his jacket pocket. But he was starving and there would be nowhere open at the other end. Belsey ducked into a greasy spoon on Lower Marsh. Taxi drivers, post-work street sweepers and parking attendants lolled in the fug of the cafe blowing on gloved hands, rubbing scratchcards and occasionally glancing up at an old TV set.

The news was rounding off with shots of a footballer coming out of hospital. Then it flashed back to the night's main story. Jessica's parents seemed to appeal directly to the assembled workers in the cafe. All they wanted to know, they said, was why. Who took their beautiful daughter from them? Belsey had witnessed it a hundred times: grief's appetite to know. Loved ones need to see the corpse, they need to see where it happened, look into the eyes of their child's killer. As if the past would be buried in these experiences.

It cut to a blonde girl, Jessica's age. They'd got her into a studio, making an appeal from behind a bank of microphones. 'Friend of Victim Appeals'. She cried well. She said: *Someone must have information*. She left flowers by the Starbucks and you saw she had expensive clothes. The camera got a shot of the message on the flowers: *Jess, RIP – justice will be done*.

Belsey bought a coffee and some chips and took his change to a payphone in the corner. He called Channel Five. Miranda Miller was out but her people were there and they knew who he was.

'Who's the blonde girl?' Belsey said.

'A friend.'

'When did she show up?'

'Earlier this afternoon.'

'Took her a while.'

'She was in shock.'

'I bet.'

He called the incident room. They said: 'She's called Lucy. We've had her in twice. Doesn't have anything helpful to say.'

'Are you sure?'

'I guess the question is whether *she's* sure.'

The CID office was empty when he got back to Hampstead. He transferred five hundred pounds to Devereux's wallet, then removed the bottom drawer of his desk and stuffed the rest of the money into the space beneath. He replaced the drawer and walked out, towards Pond Street.

They had the floodlights on in South End Green, casting strange shapes across the silent junction. Some of the pubs and restaurants furthest from the crime scene had opened, but they looked desultory, and many had stayed closed in a gesture of respect or resignation. The long shadow of the Gothic drinking fountain pointed towards the White Horse like a moondial. The artificial light caught all reflective surfaces: hubcaps, broken glass, frozen puddles. A van marked Express Glazing Contractors sat patiently, waiting to patch over the horror.

Belsey ducked under the tape and showed his badge.

'Who's in charge?'

'I am,' a wiry, grey-haired Detective Sergeant said. 'Who are you?'

'Nick Belsey. From Northwood's office. He's got a meeting with the Chief Constable in a couple of hours and wants to know the worst.'

'Dave Carter.' The Sergeant shook Belsey's hand, studying him cautiously. Belsey had always liked ballistics teams: quiet, precise men. Men of angles and velocity. 'What's the situation indoors?' Carter said.

'Chaos.' Belsey stepped into the tent. Carter followed him. The light was hazy through the canvas. It felt hallowed inside. A flag was stuck where a bullet had entered the floor. They didn't outline bodies any more, in case of crime scene contamination, but everything had been left where it fell and you sensed the space where a life had ended.

'How does it look?' Belsey asked.

'Eight fired. The first two shattered the window. One's in the back wall above the serviettes, one behind the coffee machine. We think the fourth must have clipped the Chinese lad and the third hit the girl. So did another two. One's embedded in the floor.'

'All from the same gun?'

'Yes. Something with a long barrel, not chromed.'

'Like a marksman's rifle.'

'Sure. Maybe a modified service rifle. Gas-operated, bolt action for accuracy. The bullets are 7.62 x 54mm. That's the kind of cartridge you find in military sniper rifles. Only these ones are hollow-tipped. The details suggest a gun that's probably ex-Red Army: the Dragunov, or the VSK.'

Belsey crouched down to the bullet hole in the floor.

'How many rounds do they take?'

'The Dragunov takes a ten-round box magazine. The VSK has twenty. The VSK comes with a silencer, though.'

'So it wasn't the VSK.'

'I doubt it.'

'See many Dragunov sniper rifles around these parts?'

'Not in my experience.'

They came ready for a mission, Belsey thought. He knelt and put a finger in the bullet hole, felt the angle then followed it in his imagination, out beyond the tent. They came armed to carry out a hit, were positioned at a distance with telescopic sights onto the Starbucks, getaway ready. And they weren't going to stop firing until the girl was dead.

'She would have been on the floor when it was fired,' Belsey said. 'Crawling towards the storeroom.'

'Maybe.'

'Look at the trajectory.'

'It could be ricochet.'

'Would a ricochet retain that kind of power?'

'Bullets are strange things,' Carter said.

Belsey stood up. He walked out of the crime scene and gazed at the hospital. He thought of Tony, safe in his medicated dreams. Where was Alice Ward? He looked up at the stack of windows. People jumped from the roof sometimes. Three or four each year. You could see bald patches among the ground-level greenery where they'd had to clear bushes away to find the bodies. He looked at the roof. Then he walked towards the hospital entrance.

The neon-lit reception had the unwanted air of a bus depot. Belsey continued towards the back stairs. He timed himself. He climbed ten flights to Gastroenterology, walked the length of the ward and pushed through a fire door. Narrow concrete steps led up to the roof.

Belsey hunched against the cold as he moved across the gravel surface. It took two and a half minutes to get from the front of the hospital to the roof. There was only one place on the roof where you could get sights on the Starbucks. It was around the back of an air-con unit, on a foot-wide strip of roofing tape at the very far edge. It was an acute angle onto the coffee shop's entrance but not impossible. The white tent appeared innocent at this distance, circus-like. The Heath stretched beyond it, placing the crime scene on the shore of a dark, ruffled sea.

Belsey checked the roof for cartridge cases, footprints, cigarette butts. What he saw was nothing. It looked like it had been raked clean.

He returned to 37 The Bishops Avenue. He didn't enjoy sharing it with a bloodstain. The phone was ringing as he walked in. Sometimes it would stop for a second, then it began again. He sat on the sofa and listened to the incessant force of individuals attempting to make contact with the dead Russian. He put the TV on. He thought: they didn't empty the gun; they had a mission and they'd completed it and then wrapped up. He tried to imagine the ruthlessness, the sense of invulnerability. And they knew Jessica Holden was going to be in that Starbucks that morning.

Belsey walked to the study and looked at the stain. The phone rang again. He picked up the receiver.

'Mr Devereux?'

Belsey remained silent, heart pounding.

'Mr Devereux?' A man with a Southern US drawl. Belsey cursed and hung up. He pressed the switch hook on the phone's cradle, let the phone ring twice, then released it.

'This is Jeff Cadden from Market Watch Financial Digest in Chicago –'
Belsey pressed the hook. It rang immediately. He answered.

'Hey,' a man said. 'Hey. What the hell –'

'Who's that?' Belsey said.

'Who's that?' the caller said.

Belsey hung up. It took ten seconds to ring again.

'Hello? Is that Alexei Devereux?'

'Yes.'

'Mr Devereux, I know it's late. My name's Mark Levine, I'm a lawyer for SSI International. There appears to have been some confusion –'

Belsey hung up, heard it ring, answered.

'Mr Devereux?'

'Yes.'

'This is Les Ambassadeurs restaurant. Regarding your booking.'

Belsey touched his finger to the hook. He'd had enough of playing PA to a dead man. But he stopped.

'Hello?' he said.

'Hello? Mr Devereux?' The man from Les Ambassadeurs was still there. He spoke with an indistinct Continental twinge. Belsey thought of the final entry in Devereux's diary – Friday 13 February: 'Dinner'.

'What did you say it was regarding?'

'Your booking. Tonight.'

'What about it?' Belsey said.

'Will you still be requiring it?'

'When have I booked for?'

'11 p.m.'

'What did I book?'

'A table for two in the restaurant area.'

'Yes,' he said. 'Yes, I still want it.'

'Of course, sir. We'll see you at eleven.'

Belsey opened Devereux's wallet and flicked through the hotels to the black card that said *Les Ambassadeurs* with a Mayfair address: 5 Hamilton Place. It said: *Private Members' Club and Casino*. A table for two sounded cosy. Just the idea of an 11 p.m. casino dinner was intriguing; Belsey could imagine what deals were made in that timeless world. He had just over forty-five minutes to get there. He wondered if Devereux's dining companion knew their date was off. They would be a useful person to speak to. It was a long shot, Belsey thought, but then he didn't have any other plans.

He found a Valentino suit at the back of Devereux's wardrobe: charcoal, single-breasted. There was no time to navigate the hydro massage. He chose a white shirt, put the suit on, splashed some Lacoste aftershave and popped a ChestEze.

Belsey hailed a cab on the corner of The Bishops Avenue. At Regent Street he directed it away from the lights and crowds into the backstreets of Mayfair. Everything shone slick and black under the street lamps. They continued down one-way streets of antiques shops and lawyers' offices into the cold shadow cast by Park Lane's hotels.

Les Ambassadeurs hid in the gloomy crevice between the Four Seasons and the Intercontinental. It shared the back street with a taxi stand and the hotel service entrances. Chefs and chambermaids crouched, smoking, in the niches. But the casino itself was a fragment of Georgian elegance. It occupied a town house, with freshly cleaned stonework and glistening iron railings. Belsey got out of the cab and paid. Three steps led up to wooden doors guarded by a man in tails and a waistcoat. A small, grey sign said *Les Ambassadeurs Club*. Belsey straightened his tie.

'Evening.'

'Evening, sir,' the doorman said.

He thrust the door open. Belsey skipped up the steps and walked into a long hallway with glistening wood and gold chandeliers. He took Devereux's member's card out of the wallet. Signs for the casino directed him up ornate stairs to a heavy door. Belsey pushed his way inside.

It was large but not so large as to lose the intimacy: twenty tables set up for poker, baccarat, blackjack, under a low ceiling of elaborately sculpted glass light fittings. The light was soft but bright enough for any sense of the hour to evaporate. There were no windows. Most of the tables hosted Middle Eastern men. There was a roulette wheel in a curtained bay with a cosmopolitan crowd, European and Japanese. Wooden blades turned lazily on the ceiling fans. A long bar lined the left-hand wall. At the back was a restaurant.

A young woman checked Belsey's card. She had a table beside the door with a leather-bound book.

'Good evening, Mr Devereux,' she said.

'Good evening.'

She checked the book. There didn't seem to be any pretence at recognition on the young woman's part, or any indication of concern. He was coming here, Belsey thought. But obviously not a regular. He wondered how many times Devereux had frequented the place.

'Table for two?'

'Yes.'

'It's ready whenever you are. Would you like to wait for your guest?' The woman saw him hesitate. 'Or enjoy the gaming rooms? We can hold the table for as long as you'd like.'

Belsey checked the time. Five minutes to eleven. He wanted to be ready if and when Devereux's date arrived.

'I'll take the table now.'

'Of course.'

He crossed the floor of the casino. When had he last been in a casino? Probably the Golden Nugget on Shaftesbury Avenue, which was as classy as it sounded and crowded with off-duty waiters from Chinatown. This was not the Golden Nugget. Between the restaurant and the bar sat a case of lobsters lit from beneath, casting marine forms across the ceiling. Belsey walked past the roulette and the lobsters to the restaurant. It was close to empty. He wondered why they had felt the need to confirm Devereux's booking. The heavy linen tablecloths were weighed down with a lot of silver and glassware. Each table had its own lamp. At the far end someone had painted an Italian garden on the wall. He was greeted by a maître d'.

'Mr Devereux.'

'Hi.'

Belsey was shown to a table away from the rest, where someone pulled out an ornate chair and someone else lit a candle. It was beyond eavesdropping distance, with a wooden partition that screened him from most of the room while keeping a sight on the doorway. Devereux chose it. He knew that.

'Thank you,' Belsey said. 'When do you stop serving food?'

'We're open all night, sir,' the waiter said.

173

'Of course.'

'Perhaps I can get you a drink.'

Belsey ordered a large Laphroaig and said he'd wait before ordering food. The whisky came. He drank it and looked around, wondering what was about to arrive and how he should greet it. The barman was shovelling ice into a shaker. Three American businessmen in the far corner of the restaurant were deep in debate. A whore in pearls sat at the bar sipping a mojito and looking hopefully in Belsey's direction.

He drank his whisky. He watched the clock. At 11 p.m. Charlotte Kelson walked in.

Belsey put his whisky down. There was no mistaking her. Kelson wore an expensive navy suit, gold necklace, her hair and make-up done. She studied the casino, eyes quick and beautiful as he remembered. Then she said something to the girl on the door and walked towards the restaurant. The Americans looked up, the whore glanced territorially, the barman flashed a smile.

Charlotte saw Belsey and froze.

They stared at each other. After a few seconds he lifted a hand and she continued hesitantly towards him. She got to the table but didn't sit down.

'What's going on?' she said.

'You tell me.'

She checked behind her, then the sides of the room, then Belsey. The barman had clocked this interaction. They both turned towards him and he went back to mixing his cocktail.

'Take a seat.' Belsey kicked out a chair. She looked around once more and sat down, holding her bag in front of her. 'Why are you here?' he said.

'I was told to be here.'

'By who?'

'I got a call an hour ago. It said to come here. To tell the people on the door I was meeting someone in the restaurant.'

'Who called you?'

'He wouldn't give a name.'

'He called the office?'

'Yes.'

'And asked for you by name?'

'That's right.'

'What did he say you'd find?'

'Information about the Starbucks shooting.'

The fans turned. Belsey became aware of piano music, very faint, coming from speakers in the plants.

'Who are you expecting to meet?' he said.

'Someone called Nick Belsey.'

It took his breath. Belsey drank the rest of his whisky while his mind spun. Someone knew he was going to be at the club, which meant they knew he'd been investigating Devereux, and that he'd picked up the call. Jessica saw him investigating, but she wasn't in a position to cause him much trouble. Why someone thought he'd want to provide information on her death he did not know. Maybe they didn't think that. Either way they were set on causing trouble. He watched the room out of the corner of his eye.

'Get a drink,' he said. 'Let's not look conspicuous.'

They flagged the waiter. She asked for a Pinot Grigio and he ordered another whisky. When the waiter had gone Belsey said: 'What did this man sound like?'

'Normal.'

'English?'

'Yes. As far as I could tell. What's going on?'

'Did you get his number?'

'I can't give you that.'

'Why?'

'I have a duty to my sources.'

'But you don't know who he is.'

'I don't know who you are,' she said.

The drinks arrived. Belsey felt eyes on him. The barman was practising shaker spins. The Arabs were being dealt cards. No one was watching apart from Charlotte, but he felt watched from all around.

'Who are you?' Charlotte said. 'Why did they tell me to come here?'

'I'm an undercover detective.'

'You're an undercover detective?'

'I work for what they call a Ghost Squad. I shouldn't be telling you this but I'm worried that you'll make more noise by not knowing. So know it and forget about it.' Ghost Squad was a good choice, he thought – there was more than one out there, entirely off the books for security reasons. Her contacts inside the force would only verify their existence and leave her vague on the details.

'You want me just to walk away and forget this?' Charlotte said.

'Yes.'

'I want to know what's going on.'

Belsey nodded. He could see that she wasn't going to be shaken off. This was her job and he got a feeling she was good at it.

'It wouldn't necessarily be safe for you,' he said.

'Is that a threat?'

'It's a warning. I'm not the one who's going to cause you trouble. Have you told anyone about last night?'

'No.'

'I don't believe you. But it's important that you don't tell anyone else.'

'I'm not making any promises. What's this Ghost Squad?'

'Not anything you'd have heard of.'

'Is it connected to Alexei Devereux?'

This stopped him. 'What do you mean?'

'I looked into things. 37 The Bishops Avenue is still rented by a Mr Alexei Devereux. I don't think you're him so I'm curious as to what you're doing in his house.'

'Why shouldn't I be him?'

'He's a Russian businessman, fifty-two years old. It so happens we got sent a letter about him a few weeks ago, along with a handful of other newspapers: a petition by certain members of the local community who weren't happy about his reputation.'

'Like what?'

'His racecourses. Am I right?'

Belsey thought this over.

'Mr Devereux's dead now,' he said. 'He took his life on Sunday. I can't tell you any more than that. How much do you know about these racecourses?'

'Nothing yet.'

'Did you run the story?'

'No. Only the *Ham & High* ran with it.'

He made a mental note. The *Hampstead & Highgate Express*. Maybe it was time to give Mike Slater that call back. Charlotte was looking around the casino now. The light caught her eyes and jewellery. She didn't seem scared. She seemed cautious, but in her element. She looked stunning.

'Have you heard of this Nick Belsey?' Charlotte asked. She stared at him with what he thought was accusation. He was not in a good position, Belsey understood that. But he wanted her.

'Nick Belsey? It doesn't ring a bell.'

'So why are you here?' she asked.

He started to wonder.

'I'm here because Alexei Devereux was going to be here. He'd made a booking.'

Now it was her turn to look puzzled.

'Who did you expect to meet?'

'I don't know.'

Charlotte considered this.

'What's it got to do with the Starbucks shooting?'

Belsey thought through what he knew and what he was willing to share. He decided it was worth tossing her some crumbs.

'Jessica Holden was a call girl. She knew Alexei Devereux. I think they might have known each other quite well.'

Charlotte searched his face for signs of humour and when she failed to find any produced a notebook.

'Don't write anything down,' Belsey said. 'Not here.' She put the notebook away. Belsey tried to see a few moves ahead, and couldn't even see what game he was playing. 'I'm going to ask you to hold off,' he said. 'For a day or so. Then I'll be able to tell you some more. But this isn't very safe, for either of us.'

She looked hard into his eyes.

'I'm going to want a story at the end of this.'

'Give me your mobile number.'

She took her notebook back out, tore a page and wrote her number. She slid it across the table to him.

'What network are you on?' Belsey asked.

'Vodafone. Why?'

'Some are more secure than others. We've got to be careful now, Charlotte. Give me one night. I'll be in touch tomorrow morning. But don't make things complicated for me. I'll have something for you, I just need to think how we'll get away with it.'

31

She downed her wine and left. There weren't many places to take it and he wasn't going to tempt her to dinner. Belsey watched Charlotte leave and then he went to the girl with the reservations book.

'Anyone else ask for me while I was dining?'

'No, sir.'

'Has there been anyone enquiring about me at all over the last few days?'

'Not to my knowledge. And it wouldn't be our business to discuss members.'

'Good. Do you have a fax machine?'

They had a phone and a fax machine in the members' study. Belsey called the control room at Hampstead station and asked them to fax through a Section 22 notice. Strictly speaking you needed the rank of Inspector to clear a request for phone records, but that just meant putting the right name on the paperwork. The form came through. Belsey filled it out for Charlotte's mobile, signed off as Gower and faxed it to Vodafone's data tracking department. The Regulation of Investigatory Powers Act would do the rest. It was terrible, he thought – Britain was turning into a police state. The results would come through to Hampstead station tomorrow. If he was still in the country, which seemed likely, and still alive, which felt less certain, it may just give him some purchase on his unknown antagonist. He returned to the casino, put another drink on the account, then a cigar.

'Been lucky, sir?'

'Not at all. Anywhere I can smoke this?'

Belsey was directed to what he thought was a side room but led outdoors to the 'Smoking Gaming Area'. This offered al fresco gaming beneath the stars: slots, electronic roulette, infrared heaters and a real tree. At the back was a waterfall lit by red and blue lights, cascading down film-set rocks. More coloured lights had been secreted in the plant beds. Belsey sat by the tree and smoked.

Who are you expecting to meet?

Someone called Nick Belsey.

It was personal. That changed everything. Had someone been watching them last night? After the meeting? *Information about the Starbucks shooting.* Again, he saw himself ministering to the girl as she died. He saw the office where he'd first met her. He couldn't hold the whole puzzle in his mind at one time.

When he looked up, the woman with the reservations book was standing in the doorway, accompanied by a tall, broad man in a buttoned grey suit. She pointed at Belsey and said something. Belsey made a split-second survey of exits and decided he'd need to get back inside rather than risk the security spikes of the garden wall. The man approached Belsey, smoothing the front of his suit.

'Mr Devereux?'

'Yes.'

'Your car's here, sir.' He said it with a small bow. Belsey thought about this.

'I was just starting to relax.'

'Shall I tell him to wait, sir?'

'Let me speak to him.'

Belsey stubbed the cigar and followed the manager out through the gaming rooms and down to the street. A man in uniform and peaked cap leaned over an S-Class Mercedes, wiping a rag over its gleaming black bonnet. Belsey approached.

'Are you here for Mr Devereux?' Belsey said.

'Yes, sir.'

The driver spoke with a Nigerian accent. He had sleepy eyes and fat cheeks. He put the rag away and produced a pair of bright white gloves.

'He ordered a car?'

'Yes.'

'When was it ordered?' Belsey said.

'Last week.'

'Are you going back to Hampstead?'

'No, sir. Not unless you'd prefer.'

'Where are you going?'

'I have an address.'

'Show me.'

The man reached into his jacket and produced a printout. He had a postcode for his satnav, there was no address. It was a WD5 postcode. Where was that? Somewhere on the Greater London outskirts.

'You've driven for Mr Devereux before?'

'No, sir.'

'Wait one minute.'

Belsey went back into the club. He splashed his face from gold taps, fixed his tie, ran a hand through his hair. That had been Devereux's plan, he thought. A late supper, then on. On to where? Somewhere, perhaps, that would explain a young woman's death. Belsey steeled himself for whatever trouble he was diving into. He returned to the street.

'Let's go,' he said.

Belsey climbed into the back of the car. Bottles and glasses sparkled in a rack at the side. A silver plaque in the back of the front seats said *Prestige*. A stack of company cards between the front seats showed a limousine. The driver got in and inspected Belsey in the rear-view mirror.

'Mr Devereux?'

'Last time I checked. Let's go.' Belsey poured a large vodka and slid low in his seat. The engine purred and they were away.

32

THEY CLEARED CENTRAL LONDON IN FIFTEEN MINUTES, heading north along the Finchley Road. Belsey had a sense of being carried along by the machinery of someone else's life; detached, curious. It wasn't an entirely unfamiliar sensation. The world through tinted glass looked edgy and poor. Then they were out of the suburbs, past Edgware, and still driving fast.

Where were you going, Alexei Devereux?

Belsey slid the partition screen to the side so he could see the driver. A cross hung off the rear-view mirror. Tall hedgerow blocked the view outside, occasionally dipping to reveal golf courses and business parks, storage warehouses, a Travelodge. Belsey noted signs for Porters Wood and St Albans. They were somewhere in Hertfordshire. Then they turned off the A41 onto a narrow, tree-shaded road dappled with moonlight. A notice at the turning said *Private. No Admission Without Invitation.* It didn't say what you might be invited to.

'Have we got an invitation?' Belsey said.

'You tell me, sir.'

'Of course we do.'

A minute later they slowed down: a section of fence had been dragged across the road and four guards in private-security outfits gathered around, two leading Alsatians on short leads. One of them said, 'Roll all the windows down, please,' and all the windows rolled down. Belsey breathed the night air, cold and coniferous. Another guard let one of the dogs sniff under the car. He leaned in to see the driver's papers and asked for a pass.

There was an awkward moment as they established the driver didn't have a pass and the driver twisted towards Belsey.

'Tell them it's Mr Devereux,' Belsey said. He didn't look at the guards, but sat with what he imagined was a look of expensive disdain.

'It's Mr Devereux,' the driver said.

The guard said something into a radio and after another thirty seconds came back with a respectful nod. The fence was dragged aside. He waved the Mercedes through and the windows slid back up. Two hundred metres further along the lane they passed another pair of men in navy blue jackets and black baseball caps. Belsey was trying to figure out what that meant when they arrived.

The house spread broad and grand across its front: slate grey, classical, with columns and a Union Jack limp on the top. Gold light shone through windows and open doors. The Merc approached slowly up a long drive flanked with dark topiary.

'This is it,' the driver said.

A footman waved them to a drop-off area around the side, where a lot of other Mercedes and E-Type Jaguars were parked in neat rows, some armoured, some with diplomatic plates. Belsey climbed out.

'You're going to stick around?' he said.

'Of course.'

Belsey climbed the steps at the front of the house, into a corridor with big paintings on either side. Two women with big hair and blouses sat before him at a desk with paperwork on a white tablecloth. They looked like they hadn't been expecting any more guests to arrive.

'Do you have an invitation?' one asked.

'I haven't brought it. I'm Mr Devereux. Alexei Devereux.'

The women were suddenly more attentive. They stared at him. 'Mr Devereux?'

'That's correct.' Belsey smiled and rattled his watch. He could hear a lot of voices ahead, a string quartet, the bubbling of expensive laughter and the gentle chiming of champagne glasses. Quarter past one. The party didn't show any signs of winding down. The younger of the women touched her hair and her friend smiled at him hungrily.

'Mr Devereux, we're so pleased to see you,' she said.

'I'm pleased to be here.'

They ticked him off a list. The strings stopped playing because someone was making a speech.

'Please,' the woman said. 'I think you'll find everything you need in the ballroom.'

'Thank you.'

Belsey walked through a pair of tall, polished doors. The ballroom was ostentatious even by the standards of ballrooms, with a sea battle on the ceiling and gilt-framed nobility in full length around the walls. A hundred people stood on the chequered floor, which made the room half full. One florid man in a tuxedo and tight silver waistcoat had taken to the stage and was making a slurred speech. A banner across the ceiling said 'The City Children's Fund', with gold and black helium-filled balloons nudging the stucco and chandeliers. The crowd bunched in groups of four or six beneath them, listening to the speech, with conspicuous security standing alone, earpieces in, hands behind their backs. Uniformed catering staff circulated with champagne. Belsey took a glass.

It was a hard crowd to read: wealthy, international, too glamorous for straight politics and too stiff to suggest many knew each other; a lot of Arabs, a lot of East Asian, a few white-haired men a little worse for wear with bow ties and a few expensively dressed women.

The speech droned on.

'We might turn instead to our ancestors for wisdom and I am grateful, my Lord Mayor, for your recent reminder at last month's Finance Committee dinner, of the advice of Cicero over two thousand years ago. "The budget should be balanced, the Treasury should be refilled and public debt should be reduced."'

Belsey looked for the Lord Mayor and didn't see him. He downed his champagne, took another glass and continued through a door at the other end. He wandered the house, into side rooms with cabinets of silverware and portraits of women in silk. Belsey idly contemplated stealing something. He couldn't see sensors. A ripple of applause spilled through the polished corridors. He returned to the ballroom, hoping to stand near some conversations and discover what it was Devereux had meant to attend. Then the inevitable happened.

'Have you come far?'

'Not too far,' Belsey said.

The man cornering him wore a military uniform with medals. He had very fine grey hair combed back to reveal a glistening scalp. He searched Belsey's person in vain for some identifying marks.

'How are you involved with the Children's Fund?' he asked.

'I work for AD Development. We're just over from St Petersburg.'

'Oh, St Petersburg is meant to be beautiful.'

'It is.'

'Been in the UK before?'

'I grew up here.'

'Whereabouts?'

'London.'

'Well!' This seemed to delight the man.

'What a great venue,' Belsey said. 'For the Fund.'

'It housed political prisoners, you know.'

'Really?'

'During the war. Here and Camberley House.'

'Lucky prisoners.'

Another man approached, stooped, with a champagne glint in his eye. The officer grabbed his arm.

'Richard, this man works for AD Development,' he said. He looked at Belsey. 'I didn't catch your name.'

'Jack,' Belsey said.

'Jack,' the military officer told his friend.

'Jack,' the friend said. 'Max has told us all about your company.' He shook Belsey's hand. 'Your generous donation.'

'This is Sir Richard Green,' the officer explained.

'Call me Dick,' Green said.

'I've heard a lot about you too, Dick,' Belsey said. He wondered who Max was.

'I want you to know you have our support.' Sir Richard gripped Belsey's elbow. He looked like a smooth bastard.

'Thank you.'

'What do you think of London?' he asked.

'He grew up here,' the officer explained.

'To be honest, I've had enough of it,' Belsey said.

'They say if you are tired of London you are tired of life.' Sir Richard smiled blandly.

'I'm tired of life in London.'

'Never live in a place you love,' the officer announced. 'You'll only be disappointed. Live somewhere you don't care for. My daughter lives in Hungary. They don't require you to like the country, and if you did they'd be slightly disappointed.' He laughed. A girl with a tray appeared. 'Have another drink,' he said to Belsey.

'Thank you.' Belsey swapped his empty glass for a full one. He heard a loud, nasal laugh and saw, across the room, the silver waistcoat – the speechmaker – surrounded by men in black tie, all laughing.

'Who's that?' Belsey said.

'The Chamberlain, Milton Granby.' The officer lowered his voice. 'He's been under some strain recently.'

Belsey turned again and stared. Well, well, he thought, what a turn-up: a man with a hole in his accounts. Granby's white hair offset a bright red face. It was an unfortunate combination but it didn't stop him commanding his surroundings. He had his chest thrust out and he carried himself on the balls of his feet, as if to achieve an extra few inches of height. It had the paradoxical effect of making him seem smaller than he was, someone who didn't occupy the volume of space that their status deserved. Belsey wondered what to make of his presence.

'What kind of strain?' Belsey asked.

'Oh, the pressures of public office. I heard you collect art, is that right?'

'Not so much any more,' Belsey said. 'Excuse me, I'm going to get some air.'

He lifted a full bottle of red and three glasses from a table by the door and stepped out onto a flagstoned walkway with views of a long, dark lawn. Belsey followed it around the building to the back of the kitchen, where the catering team were laughing and smoking.

'Here, this is from the boss.' He gave them the bottle and glasses. 'He thinks you're doing great.'

'Thanks.'

'Do you have a cigarette?'

One of them gave him a cigarette. He leaned against the grey stone of the house. 'I'm here with a friend. I don't even know what it's about.'

They looked at Belsey as if he should really be able to tell them that.

'Well, there's not many children here,' a red-haired girl said finally.

'And we're a long way out from the City,' another added, a thin boy with blond stubble and cynical eyes.

'What do you mean?'

No one answered.

'What's Milton Granby got to do with it?' Belsey asked.

'He seems to like the wine,' one said.

'I think he's the City,' the blond boy suggested.

'And we're the children,' another said. They laughed, but not like people having a good time.

Belsey walked back to the garden. He imagined for a moment he was Devereux: Devereux, sought by all, understood by none, having a moment to himself. He imagined this was how Devereux played it, turning up late, unannounced, as if he was no one. What would he contemplate as he wandered the grounds? History? The stars? Milton Granby, maybe. *Milton Granby's one of the most powerful men in the Square Mile and no one's heard of him. And he's corrupt, that's what I'm saying. I'm not just interested in screwing him for a drinks problem . . .* Who sent Charlotte to Les Ambassadeurs?

He followed a path to a pond with fountains, a long tray of black water with a sheltered pagoda at one end and stone vases with stone flowers in them along the side. From here you could see the lights of the M1. When he was briefly sleeping with a drama teacher in Luton, Belsey would cadge lifts from motorway police up and down the road. You got a lot of what they called walkers, illegal immigrants who had been dumped in motorway service areas. The police would find them

187

on the hard shoulder, wandering, utterly confused. The music started again. Belsey finished his cigarette, looking back at the house, and felt a brief, bitter-sweet guilt at squeezing Devereux's life for its last drops of privilege when the man himself had so clearly been done with it. The house was beautiful but it was not his party. One guest paced furiously on the front drive, dark hair, navy blazer with gold buttons, deep tan, a phone stuck to his ear. Belsey had seen him in the crowd around Granby. Right now he was having difficulty getting reception, checking his phone, checking his watch. Eventually he put the phone away, went over to the two women on the door and spoke to them, then turned to stare at Belsey.

Belsey stepped out of the lights and returned, through shadows, into the cover of the house. It was a little messy now. The organisers were trying to steer unsteady couples towards their rooms. The rest of the partygoers had gathered in the ballroom, where the trays now bore empties and the tables were being cleared. Some old boys were smoking on the front steps. Belsey bumped into Sir Richard Green.

'Jack.' He grabbed Belsey's elbow.

'Dick.'

'I just met someone who knows you from St Petersburg. You must come and say hello.'

Belsey felt a jab of foreboding and decided it was time for an exit. Sir Richard was leading him into the main room where a short, bald man and a large woman in a white dress were waiting.

'OK,' Belsey said. 'Let me get a drink. Do you want a drink?'

He turned out of Sir Richard's grip, walked through the hall to the kitchen and through the kitchen to a small window that looked out to the garden. He climbed through and continued around the side of the house to the waiting cars.

'Let's go,' Belsey said to his driver.

Someone ran across the gravel towards him. It was the guest with the blazer and the bad reception. Up close he was a giant of a man.

'Who are you?' the man demanded. His voice was deep, with a little rasp. Central or Eastern European.

'Why?' Belsey said.

'Are you Alexei Devereux?'

'Is there a problem?' Belsey asked. The man looked uncertain. Belsey felt uncertain. He decided to play it safe. 'I represent Mr Devereux. On behalf of AD Development.'

'We meet at last.' It was said with dark triumph. 'Max Kovar.' He spoke in a clipped way, as if he resented speaking at all and expected hired people to roll the words out for him. But his eyes had a fire to them. They looked too long and too hard. Kovar wore black leather gloves and now he plucked the right one off.

'Max, at last,' Belsey said. Kovar pumped his hand, as if working some machinery on which their relationship would embark. 'I'm on my way out of here, though. I'm sorry.' He found Devereux's wallet and removed a business card. 'Do you have these details? You can call me tomorrow.'

Kovar frowned at the AD Development card. 'You're his assistant?'

'That's right. I'm helping him settle into the UK.'

'Oh. Yes.' Kovar pocketed the card and shouted at the catering staff. 'Bring us a bottle of champagne and glasses.'

Drinks in the car park, Belsey thought. It seemed like Kovar wanted Belsey to himself. A girl brought them a bottle and glasses, served with the air of someone who was meant to clock off two hours ago. Kovar watched her walk away. Then he turned to Belsey and poured the drinks.

'Your boss is a hard man to get hold of,' Kovar said, holding two glasses in one gloved hand.

'He always says, if you can't get hold of him he probably doesn't want to speak to you.' Belsey laughed. He took his glass and watched Kovar's smile freeze. 'I'm kidding. Mr D has heard good things about you.'

'He has?'

'Yes. I've got to run in a second, though.'

'You cut me out,' Kovar said abruptly.

Belsey tried to read him. He couldn't place the accent: mid-European, with a touch of transatlantic. Generally offshore. If anonymous accounts could speak they would probably sound like Max Kovar. An expensive scent of pine and leather emanated from his person. No strong alcohol on his breath. He carried himself with the blunt arrogance of someone who was both rich and large.

'Perhaps we could speak for a moment,' Kovar said. 'Take a walk.'

'We're speaking,' Belsey said. 'Let's walk.'

They made their way to the sunken garden, slowly circling the pond. The temperature was plummeting now. The pond had gained a thin film of ice. It was a clear night, with a lot of stars. Their breath clouded around their faces.

'Don't trust Buckingham,' Kovar said.

Belsey nodded. 'You don't think so?'

'If I were you I'd shake free of him. I do my business tidily. Buckingham is a fool. I was disappointed to hear you were in discussions with him.'

'We discuss things with people, it doesn't always mean anything.'

'I know this territory.'

'Of course.'

'Buckingham's a fly-by-night, a criminal.'

'OK.'

They walked to the pagoda and turned. Kovar put his glass down and took a knife from his pocket. Then he produced a cigar. Kovar chopped the cigar and lit it with a silver lighter. They were a couple of hundred metres away from everyone. The smoke hung blue and steady in the cold air.

'I'm only over here for a few days,' Kovar said. 'Then I'm off again.'

'That's a pity.'

'Yes. Yes, it is.' He nodded. 'Did Mr Devereux get my letter?'

'I'm sure he did. He's not very good at correspondence. I'm sure you understand.'

'I was disappointed he couldn't find time to meet me.'

'He's so busy.'

'You know it is a sector close to my heart.'

'Of course.'

'And there is so much room for growth.'

'Yes.'

'We both know that. You would find it easier working with me.' He handed over a business card and looked away as he did it, as if embarrassed. The statement hung in the air. It was a threat, Belsey could tell that much. 'When I'm in London I stay at the Lanesborough.'

'It's meant to be a good hotel.'

'Let me tell you something,' Kovar said. 'I see myself as an artist first, a businessman second. I'm like Mr Devereux in that respect.' Kovar's sly face looked pleased with the words coming out of it.

'I can see that about you,' Belsey said.

'I think the beauty of our line of work is that we introduce new things into the world.'

'Yes.'

'People call us gamblers. Yes. There are men who make the right guesses. But very often they are the ones who have determined the outcome.'

'They're the men I don't play cards with,' Belsey said.

Kovar slapped him on the back.

'I have confidence in your boss. I don't have confidence in many men. Seize the crisis. That's what you say, isn't it?'

'Every morning.' Belsey could hear his old St Petersburg acquaintances approaching and wanted to be on the move. Kovar raised his champagne, gripping it, white-knuckled.

'To Project Boudicca,' he said. He said it like someone who has discovered something meant to be secret. He winked, waiting, as if it was time for Belsey to grant him admission. Belsey tried to see his face more clearly in the shadows. He could make out teeth, which might have been a smile or a snarl. He made out that dark glimmer behind the eyes.

'Boudicca,' Belsey said, and they touched glasses.

33

HE WAS OUT OF THE GROUNDS IN MINUTES, BACK IN THE
comforting speed of a Mercedes.

'Drop me at Hampstead police station,' Belsey said when they were
approaching Golders Green. The driver looked at him again, but didn't
say anything. 'You know where it is?' Belsey said.

'Yes, sir.'

'Let's get some speed on.'

The night had emptied. Mist wound its way around Hampstead's
brickwork. A panda car crawled through the empty streets, fog lights on.
That would be PCs Andrews and Robinson, Belsey thought, probably
silent together, thinking of their families. He had moved past tiredness,
on his own night duty. He had always thrived on it: the brief moment
when the sleepless gained possession of all; when the nocturnal made
their plans.

The Merc pulled up on Rosslyn Hill. Belsey checked the police-station
windows. The first-floor lights were off.

'It's all on the account?'

'It's all on the account.'

'Thank you.' Belsey got out. He wondered if you were expected to tip
chauffeurs. 'Here.' Belsey offered him Devereux's fake Rolex. 'You've been
excellent.'

'No, sir. Please.' The driver declined the gift. Belsey waited as he drove
off, then put the watch back on and headed into the station.

3.45 a.m. A civilian worker sat in the canteen, in the light of a muted TV. Occasionally a man in one of the cells would break into a few lines of song. Belsey climbed the stairs to the CID office. He left the lights off and turned on his computer.

Max Kovar had no domestic criminal record but he came up flagged on an international list, linked with a racetrack operator who shot his accountant in Berlin on New Year's Eve 2003. There was an investigation into some of Kovar's Madrid property deals the following year, involving a local official found at the bottom of a swimming pool, but no charges. Kovar was found in possession of seven doctored horse passports on the border of the United Arab Emirates, 23 June 2007, but he was shifting stallions sold to him by the Al Nhayan royal family and didn't even have to pay a fine.

Kovar had seemed very keen. He had seemed very rich. Belsey wondered if he had been given an easier means of exploiting Devereux's identity. He felt a tingle of anticipation. Kovar believed Belsey was a direct line to the oligarch. Belsey had been trying to steal Devereux's past, but what about his achievements still to come?

The City Children's Fund came up online as a registered charity. It had been set up to help deprived children of inner-city London. It also came up linked to stories of foreign donors buying favours through the back door. A group called Campaign for Open Government pointed out that it was set up at a time when several investigations were under way, looking at anonymous foreign donations to Granby and his associates. Milton Granby sat on the Fund's board of trustees.

Belsey gathered everything on Granby that was in the public domain. The Chamberlain lived on a very secluded residential road in the Vale of Health. The Vale was a privileged Hampstead enclave that got its name from being the only part of London to escape the plague. The Vale of Wealth, officers called it. St John's would have been his local AA meeting; Charlotte was on the right track. Hampstead police had him on the VIP list for fast response in case of emergency.

Most of the information regarding Granby appeared on the City of London website. The pocket of ancient parishes in the heart of London had been brandishing gold and autonomy for close to a millennium.

A state within a state, a City within a city. Its new website preserved the proud tradition, flaunting the City's history. But then it had a lot of it.

> The City of London is the oldest continuous municipal democracy in the world. It pre-dates Parliament. Its constitution is rooted in the ancient rights and privileges enjoyed by citizens before the Norman Conquest in 1066. From medieval to Stuart times the City was the major source of financial loans to monarchs, who sought funds to support their policies at home and abroad.

Loan shark to the warmongers. That gained you a fair bit of independence over the years. The website made some attempt at explaining the idiosyncrasies of City government. They retained a medieval structure of Aldermen, derived from the wise 'elder men' of Saxon London. They had a Remembrancer, responsible for ceremonies and protocol. It was a fine and solemn name, Belsey thought: London should have more of them. Then, of course, they had the Chamberlain.

> The Chamberlain is the Finance Director of the City of London. He is the financial adviser, accountant, receiver and paymaster and is responsible for the City of London's local and private funds. In addition, he is also responsible for making arrangements for the investment of the City of London and other funds.

The website gave Granby's CV: as a stockbroker, working through the usual range of investment positions, and as a climber in the Corporation of London, rising through the ranks of various City guilds: a Livery man, an Alderman, a member of the Worshipful Company of Makers of Playing Cards. In his spare time Milton Granby enjoyed travel, walking, golf and theatre. It didn't mention booze.

> Institutions for which he is responsible extend far beyond the City boundaries and include the Barbican Centre, Central

Criminal Court at the Old Bailey and ten thousand acres of open space including Epping Forest and Hampstead Heath.

This caught Belsey's eye. Apparently the Corporation of London took on ownership of the Heath following the abolition of the Greater London Council in 1989.

Granby didn't make many headlines. He made one in the last week, after an interview with *The Times*: 'CHAMBERLAIN EXPRESSES CONCERNS OVER CITY'S FINANCES': 'Very challenging, if not severe conditions lie ahead. The City Corporation's own finances have not been sheltered from the raging storms which have had a major impact on our investment incomes. There is little doubt that all of us face a very difficult financial environment for some time to come, and some equally difficult decisions.'

Belsey wondered what decisions Granby was making, as his car sped back through the night. The City desperate. Devereux ingratiating himself. What was that coincidence about?

Don't trust Buckingham. Kovar's solemn warning had stayed with him. It was the only name left unexplored. No Buckingham came up on any recent local crime reports. Beyond that was the full archive of the PNC which, as Belsey expected, swamped him with information. Seventy-nine Buckinghams had come to the police's attention in the last year in London alone. Two hundred and thirteen in the country at large. He didn't have the resources to sift that. He made a mental note not to trust any of them.

Belsey switched the computer off and left the police station. There was something he wanted to see. He walked to the Heath, onto the pale track that followed the side of the ponds into the blackness. Belsey could find his way without sight. He headed north. Bats swung erratic loops out of the trees above his head. Athlone House appeared as a deeper shade of night in the distance, on the horizon. Then he had passed it. He saw Kovar's smile, and he heard the voice of the Chamberlain: *The budget should be balanced, the Treasury should be refilled and public debt should be reduced.* Then he heard the Heath gardener: *I want to show you something . . .*

The yellow crosses appeared like a shriek from within the woods. They caught the moonlight. Belsey rubbed his thumb over the painted bark. He tried to follow their trail south, stumbling in banks of rotting leaves, but he got lost near the model-boating pond. He sat down and wondered about the crosses, and if there was any possibility that they connected to the moneyed world he had just passed through. He became cold.

Belsey climbed into the landscaped gardens by Kenwood House and crossed them, back towards The Bishops Avenue. The road was empty but for its heritage lamps. Everything was very still and silent. Belsey approached number 37 on the far side of the street. The gentle curve of the road gave him cover. It allowed him to see the house before it saw him, along with any cars parked up, the windows of the house opposite and the walls behind which someone might hide. The memory of Charlotte Kelson walking into the casino sobered him. Someone, somewhere, had been watching them. They knew he'd been investigating Devereux. Did they know he'd been sleeping in his bed?

Belsey opened the front door slowly and stepped into the hall. A photograph had been pushed beneath the door. He picked it up. It showed a naked male body on a concrete surface. The man's nose and ears had been removed and the face was veiled in blood. He assumed the exact identity may have been less important than the implication it carried for himself.

Belsey took a chopping knife from the kitchen drawer. He turned the CCTV on, then the alarms, and gave a bleak laugh. He was turning into a good little Hampstead resident.

He went to Devereux's study and found the correspondence from lawyers representing the Hong Kong Gaming Consortium. 'Subject: Project Boudicca'. *As agreed, 80 per cent will be paid direct to AD Development and 20 per cent to a/c K9767 with Raiffeisen Zentralbank Austria.*

Belsey took the paperwork and the knife to the living-room sofa. He turned the sofa to face the door. He held the knife and put Sky News on and let the adrenalin slowly leak out of his system.

What did he say you'd get here? Information about the Starbucks shooting. Someone called Nick Belsey . . . Exhaustion began to claim him. Through his half-open eyes he saw Jessica Holden. She filled the screen, looking at him. To the reporters she was Jess now, with that familiarity we assume with the young and dead. But it was just the same old photographs; a shot of her home, a shot of the devastated Starbucks. It was a tragic loss. It was a mystery. Hampstead was pulling together in its grief.

34

HE WOKE IN MID-FORMULATION OF A PLAN. IT GOT HIM TO his feet. The knife fell to the floor. He put it back in the kitchen and walked outside to the garden to breathe the dawn. He thought, in the half-light, he might be able to discern which of his ideas were dreams and which belonged to the daytime. It was a pitiless light: everything in the garden seemed carved from stone; the plants, the tennis court. He had expected the dream to disperse but what evaporated with the night was doubt. Doubt fed on options, and he could see only one.

Belsey went to the Somali brothers and bought all the newspapers he could find. Saturday 14 February. Valentine's Day. Front page of the *Telegraph*: a photo of flowers left among broken glass. A picture of Jessica on a school trip, beaming. They'd decided her hobbies were acting and dancing and that she wanted to be a teacher. The school was planning a special memorial assembly. Meanwhile the Chinese student was out of hospital. The Ugandan was having his immigration papers looked at. Police were looking for a young man described as being of Asian or North African appearance, but even the tabloids were hesitant about splashing this. There was a map of the supposed escape route; he would have gone straight past Belsey. He hadn't.

Along the side they'd pushed a separate, more personal feature: HOW A PEACEFUL MORNING TURNED INTO CARNAGE. 'Sharon Green was taking her two sons to nursery when she heard the shots . . .' It came with more quotes from the local celebrities, former models and political activists of

Hampstead, all of whom could imagine this happening anywhere but NW3. 'Leafy Hampstead', the papers kept saying, until you wondered if the leaves might have been in on it.

They hadn't pieced together a motivation yet. The red tops were still filling space with victim stories, getting itchy to switch on the hate. Police were giving nervous quotes about a culture of 'respect killings' among London gangs, and had released a dubious e-fit of a square-jawed, grey-skinned man with deep-set eyes. Someone was e-fitting their own nightmares.

Belsey found Kovar's business card. *Max Kovar*, it said, and didn't feel the need to specify a job or company. Belsey went into the CID office and spun his Rolodex of contacts. He called a friend in the Branch Intelligence Unit – a subdivision of Specialist Crime. Belsey used to play football with them. They played filthy. And they had connections; they played with men who weren't police officers, describing themselves as Civil Service which Belsey took to mean MI5. The unit's switchboard put him through to DS Terry Borman.

'Terry,' Belsey said. 'You're up early.'

'I'm up late. One of those weeks. How can I help?'

'If my paths crossed with a character called Max Kovar would you be interested?'

'I know the name.'

'Can you know more than that?'

'Let me call you back.'

Belsey had expected as much. He'd be checking the files, but he'd also be checking the heat. When they operated on the edge of a big grey shadow called the secret services even men like Terry Borman went suddenly quiet on you.

Borman called back in ten.

'Which bit of him are you interested in?'

'Give me a rundown.'

'Speculator. Throws his weight around. He made a lot of money in the eighties investing in copper mines. Comes up in various corruption inquiries: unsavoury connections in Peru, naughtiness on the Ivory Coast. Likes to put money in the bank accounts of government officials and ship guns to loyal friends. But his big love is horses. Kovar spends a lot of time over in the UK checking on his thoroughbreds. He runs a major stable, got a manor in Gloucestershire he uses.'

'What's he up to now?'

'No idea. The last couple of years he's been moving a lot of capital into new media and gambling.'

'OK.'

'Are you still playing football? I tried to call you the other night.'

'I'm between phones.'

'We've got a match against Vice on Sunday. We need your pace.'

'I'm not match-fit right now, Terry.'

'We're desperate.'

'Not this weekend.'

Belsey found the number for RingCentral. He had to move fast, while he had the CID office to himself. He rang RingCentral and gave Devereux's reference number off the invoice.

'Is that Mr Devereux?' a cheerful-sounding woman asked.

'That's correct.'

'How can we help you this morning?'

'I believe at the moment calls to AD Development are going to an answering service, is that correct?'

'That's correct, sir.'

'I'd like to divert them instead. Can you divert to this number?' Belsey gave the number for his extension at Hampstead police station.

'That's done for you.'

'Fantastic,' he said.

Kovar's card gave a mobile number, but Belsey decided on a more subtle approach. He found the number for the Lanesborough hotel. He spent a few minutes looking at it, then lifted the receiver. His finger hovered over the buttons and then he pushed them, slowly. A hotel receptionist answered. Belsey introduced himself as Alexei Devereux and said he was looking for Max Kovar. She put him through to the Royal Suite. Belsey let it ring once then put the receiver down.

Three minutes later a call came in. He answered: 'AD Development. Jack speaking.'

'It's Max Kovar. We met last night.'

'Max, good morning.'

'Did someone call me?'

'No, I don't think so. I told Alexei I met you. Maybe he called.'

'Mr Devereux? Well, I'm able to speak now.'

'He's gone. He's in a meeting. Everything's full steam here, as you can imagine – Boudicca, all that.'

'Yes. You seemed like he might be open to some conversation on the subject.'

'Oh, I don't imagine so. I don't see why. Well . . .' Belsey paused. 'Open to conversation?' he said.

'Yes.'

'I don't think it's possible. Alexei's a man of business, not conversation. But I wanted to thank you for your interest.' Kovar was silent. Belsey let whatever he was thinking go on being thought. 'I'll speak to him,' Belsey said finally. 'I didn't think you were serious.'

'Of course I'm serious,' Kovar burst out, then softened. 'Yes, I am serious.'

'My apologies. Our apologies. We'll call you if we get the chance.'

Belsey hung up. The game was back on.

Kovar was canny, but that was what a good con man looked for: someone clever, someone who knows good luck happens quietly if you're clever about it. Belsey called the answering service and told them to revert to the previous arrangement.

'Of course, sir.'

It took all of thirty seconds for his good spirits to sour. He went to the window. A man in an expensive overcoat looked up from a bench across the road and met his eyes. Belsey saw at once that it was the blond man from the Arabic newspaper cutting, the man shaking hands, the man who'd been banging on Devereux's door at midnight. He hadn't changed clothes. Hadn't shaved. Belsey stared at him and the man stared back. So it wasn't a tail operation. Belsey didn't know what it was.

Belsey checked the corridor. It was empty. He took the carrier bag of money from where he'd stashed it in his desk and stuffed the notes into his pockets. He left the station by the back entrance.

Ocean Wealth Protection was just opening up. The advisers were in a cheerful mood. The place smelt of fresh coffee.

'Come in, come in.' They had the bonhomie of men about to close a deal. 'Are you still looking for the same set-up?'

Belsey trimmed his ambitions. Five grand got him an office address in Liechtenstein, a checking account with the Bank of the South Pacific and a company called International Metal Holdings, registered in the Dominican Republic.

'It's a nice one. Records go back four years. You've got three directors. All yours to start trading whenever you want.'

It was enough to sink some money out of reach for the moment, and it left him with a grand to play with.

'Do you take cash?' Belsey said, and they laughed. 'I suppose you know where to put it,' he said. They didn't laugh at that.

Belsey took his new paperwork and left the office. He walked to a newsagent's on Belsize Lane. They stocked five Arabic papers in a rack at the front along with all the major European and American dailies. He compared his clipping of the men shaking hands to the newspapers on offer – *Al-Ahram*, *Alarab*, *Asharq Alawsat*. None quite matched.

Hampstead station shared a pool of Arabic interpreters with the rest of Camden Borough but none were around that morning. Belsey stashed the ownership documents for his new business corporation in his desk. He felt a pride at the hard evidence of his new life and its burgeoning infrastructure. Now he needed to get some money in it. Which meant taking on the mantle of Project Boudicca. He made some calls. There was an Iranian PC at Holborn station but the mosque was closer.

Belsey walked to the Regent's Park mosque. Since his first, tense visit, the day after the bombings, he had grown to like the place, and its imam Hamid Farahi in particular. The worn lustre of its golden dome rose above the bare branches of the park, facing the apartment blocks of St John's Wood. Through the doorway Belsey could see an expanse of red prayer mats, temporarily abandoned but for two men prostrate beneath the huge chandelier. The sunrise prayers had finished a while ago, early-morning devotees dispersed to work, to the coffee shops.

Belsey slipped his shoes off, went in and asked an attendant if Farahi was about. A moment later the imam appeared.

'Salaam, Nicholas.'

'Salaam,' Belsey said. They shook hands. Farahi was elegant in his white robes. Belsey had initially been surprised by how young he was. But he carried himself with the authority of his position.

'I've got some translation work for you,' Belsey said. 'If you have a moment.'

They walked into a library and cultural centre next door to the mosque and took a seat among the bookshelves. Belsey removed the clipping from Devereux's wallet and handed it over. The imam held it at some distance, as if it was safer that way.

'This is *Al-Hayat*.'

'Tell me about *Al-Hayat*,' Belsey said.

'One of the big Arabic newspapers: respected, pro-West, owned by a Saudi prince.'

'Do you see many in London?'

'Yes. Any shop selling Arabic newspapers will sell *Al-Hayat*. It prints in Europe.'

'What does the circled article say?'

The imam produced a pair of glasses from within his dishdasha and flicked them open. He peered closer and read: '"Hong Kong Gaming and its major stakeholder, Saud International Holdings, believes sport is a language we all understand. It is the model for a global community."' The imam looked up with a derisive smile.

'What is this project they're talking about?'

Farahi examined the article.

'Some investment in London. It doesn't say. It says "the UK entertainment and leisure sector". Some big project with these people, AD Development. It was agreed last Saturday. They have just agreed something. They are shaking hands.'

'It doesn't say what?'

'A development in the UK gambling sector. It will see big investment in London. That's all it says.'

'Who's the blond guy?'

Hamid read the article again. 'Pierce Buckingham. Representing AD Development.'

'Pierce Buckingham.'

'That's right.'

Belsey looked closer at the untrustworthy Buckingham. One more piece for the puzzle.

'Does it say who the other man is?'

'Prince Faisal bin Abdul Aziz, the gaming consortium's majority stakeholder.'

'Where was this picture taken?'

'It doesn't say.'

Belsey studied the spire in the photograph: it had a weathervane on the top, glinting: an arrow on top of a ball. The spire capped a square, stone tower. Between the men and the church was an empty space, like a courtyard, with modern buildings at either side.

'Have you heard of these people?'

'Not Pierce Buckingham. The other man, yes. The Prince is a great-grandson of the first king of Saudi Arabia. Not a good man.'

'Why?'

'He's a thief. He's draining the country of its money, state money, for his own projects. Many people there are suffering and he invests all the resources in Europe and America. This newspaper is owned by his cousin.' He prodded the paper.

'OK. Thanks.' Belsey took the clipping back. 'You've been a help.'

He dropped into Swiss Cottage Library on his way to Hampstead. The library kept old issues of the *Ham & High*: the last month's out on a rack, the last five years filed in a cabinet behind the issue desk. What had Charlotte said? There was a news story about Devereux moving to London but only the *Ham & High* ran with it. Belsey found last week's edition and turned through the pages until he saw the headline: NEW OLIGARCH IN TOWN UPSETS LOCALS.

Alexei Devereux is the latest in a long line of Russian billion-aires to set up home on Hampstead's luxurious Bishops Avenue. But local residents have expressed concern over his sudden arrival.

Devereux's investment company, AD Development, has courted controversy in the past with its aggressive approach to land acquisition, seeking room for an ever expanding gambling and entertainment empire. Now Devereux's new neighbours fear that the might of AD Development is in London for a reason. The Russian has made no secret of his wish to make an impact on his favourite European city. Nor is he short of political connections, all of whom refused to comment yesterday.

Belsey didn't have to go far to find the *Ham & High* offices. They took up a floor of the cream-coloured 1980s block beside the library. Belsey went in and said he had a meeting with Mike Slater and was sent up.

Slater's office went for a theme of organised chaos: a bicycle wheel and repair kit on the floor, half-empty mugs on top of stacks of books. The walls were decorated with old covers, various scoops, mostly concerning corruption on the council, and several awards for best local coverage: the environment, education, policing. Slater got up from his battered chair when he saw Belsey and grasped him with a double-handed shake. He appeared to be the one who'd had less sleep. One arm of his glasses was fixed with tape and his greying hair was a mess. His desk was covered with information on Jessica Holden.

'I was a bit short on the phone yesterday,' Belsey said.

Slater waved this away. 'All is forgiven. You couldn't have come at a better time. I've been trying to get my hands on a detective for five hours. It's a cock-up, right? The shooting. We're not getting any results from local gangs, criminals, police. I'm thinking it was one God almighty cock-up.'

'I don't know, Mike. Maybe. I'm here about Alexei Devereux.' Slater looked puzzled. 'You were interested in him,' Belsey said. 'At least you were last week.'

'It was a quiet week. Am I in trouble?'

'Why would you be?'

'Because of the article we ran: the petition.'

'Why would that get you in trouble?'

'Because something's wrong with it. And because he's suddenly dead.'

205

Belsey sat down. 'Talk to me.'

'I knew the name, Alexei Devereux.' Slater collapsed into his worn chair, hands gripping the arms. 'I knew he was one of the oligarchs, expanding his empire. I'd heard the rumours about his interest in the casino and gaming industry, and that he had a reputation for liking bribes, kickbacks, call it what you will. This was the first I'd heard about him moving to London. But I ran a check and it seemed right, he was on The Bishops. I never saw the petition until it was too late. A new boy cleared the story. I would never have run it without a thorough check. Not where someone like Alexei Devereux is concerned.'

'Then you heard he'd died.'

'Well, you can imagine I had mixed feelings. I got a tip-off from someone in the hospital that he was dead – that he'd killed himself. I imagine he had bigger things to worry about than the *Ham & High*, but at the same time it didn't fill me with a sense of good tidings.'

'In the article it mentions Devereux's political connections. Who are they?'

'Do you know anything about that?'

'No. I know Devereux was turned down for a visa two years ago because he was wanted on fraud charges. This time around he had Granby's name on the application and he was invited in. I know Granby helps those who help himself. And conveniently there are a lot of ways to help Milton Granby without your name appearing anywhere inconvenient. He's a local character. I can't pretend to know anything about his involvement with Alexei Devereux.'

'The petition was about racecourses.'

'Supposedly. It said he was a bad influence on the area. It was one of the vaguest things I've ever seen.'

'I'd like to take a look at it.'

Slater led Belsey into a back room crowded with box files. It had a safe in the side wall. The editor opened the safe, removed a file and after a moment produced the fax. It contained a list of 150 people who didn't like Devereux moving into the neighbourhood, but very little indication of their exact grievance. Slater had marked the list with question marks and crosses.

'What are these?' Belsey asked.

'After the event, when I started to get a funny feeling, I called around. I ran a check on these names. A question mark means they deny knowing anything about it.'

'What does a cross mean?'

'It means they're dead. Been dead two or three years in most cases.'

'Are you sure?'

'Absolutely. Dead and still indignant. That's Hampstead for you.'

'What do you make of it?'

'I don't know. Someone using an old tax roll. Someone with an axe to grind. A business rival, maybe.'

Belsey looked at the number from which the fax had been sent. It felt naggingly familiar.

'Have you traced the fax number?'

'No.'

'Send something through to it. A blank sheet.'

'OK.' They went back to the main office and Slater did as he was instructed. 'Now what?'

'Can I take this?' Belsey said, lifting the fax.

'I'll run you a copy.'

He used the same machine to run Belsey a copy of the petition.

'Did Devereux contact you about the article?' Belsey said.

'No.'

'Is that strange?'

'The whole thing's strange. It's going to get a hell of a lot stranger once news of Devereux's death becomes established. The rumours are just starting. Soon there will be a storm.'

Belsey wondered how that would impact on his own business. He had to get his plan in place quickly.

'Do you know of a Pierce Buckingham?' he asked.

'Rich boy. Helps Middle Eastern companies invest in Europe. Nasty piece of work as far as I'm aware.'

'How do you know about him?'

'I read the papers. It's part of my job. Why are you interested in Pierce Buckingham?'

Belsey produced the *Al-Hayat* clipping. Slater admired it but didn't have anything to add. It was a handshake about a London investment. That much Belsey knew. Something facilitated by Granby, was his guess. Something that brought a lot of money in, but not enough to keep Devereux or Jessica Holden above the ground.

Slater gave him a copy of the faxed petition. Belsey thanked him and headed for the door.

'Nick,' Slater said.

'What?'

'You haven't explained why you're here.'

'Haven't I?'

'No.'

'I appreciate you keeping me out of the paper, Mike. Thank you for that. I owe you a drink.'

Belsey walked to The Bishops Avenue and checked the fax machine. One blank fax had come through from the offices of the *Hampstead & Highgate Express*, forty-five minutes ago. The number on the machine matched the anonymous leak to the *Ham & High*. Devereux was briefing against himself.

He walked out of the front door, wondering why Devereux would do that. He grabbed Devereux's post as he left. It kept coming, more each day, eight envelopes of various sizes. Then he looked up to see Pierce Buckingham standing on the other side of the road.

Belsey crammed the envelopes into his jacket and started at a brisk pace away from the house. He let his stalker follow him back to Hampstead police station. Buckingham kept a steady distance of twenty or thirty metres between them. Belsey rehearsed what he knew of him. Buckingham and Prince Faisal connected – he had a newspaper clipping of that lucrative-looking handshake. Max Kovar didn't like that. Maybe he wanted to be the man in the picture. *Don't trust Buckingham.* Belsey didn't. But if Buckingham was going to hurt him he would have done it by now, surely. And maybe he needed the opportunity to speak. Maybe Belsey could ask him what exactly Project Boudicca involved that might have left a very empty home on The Bishops Avenue. And as he walked down Rosslyn Hill, thinking about the faked petition, he started wondering to what extent it had ever been occupied.

Belsey made it into the CID office and ran a full check on his new shadow. His colleagues were busy, heads down. Belsey tried to be discreet, nonetheless. There was more on Buckingham on the Internet than in UK police files, which said something about his profile and his legal team. The reports painted a charming portrait. Buckingham's first recorded misdemeanour was kidnap and false imprisonment of a stripper after an altercation in the Pussycat Lounge, Tel Aviv. That was four years ago. Buckingham played the diplomatic card; it turned out he was representing a UK government agency at the time, although it wasn't clear which agency concerned itself with the Pussycat Lounge. His father was Edward Buckingham, or Lord Buckingham of Tankerness to friends, former Shadow Defence Secretary. Edward Buckingham made a killing off the first Gulf War for reasons that may have involved the Kuwait Sovereign Wealth Fund. His son followed in his footsteps. There were a string of minor diplomatic incidents, rumours of assault, driving offences. Last year he had magically sidestepped a charge of aggravated violence and possession of cocaine. An incident two weeks later in which he ran over a journalist while trying to leave a Paris nightclub took an out-of-court settlement to reach a happy ending.

The CID phone rang. Belsey avoided it. It rang ten times before Rosen snapped and lifted the receiver and grunted. A few seconds passed and his bloodshot eyes slipped to Belsey. Belsey felt them. Rosen covered the receiver with his fat hand. He didn't say anything, just stared.

'What?' Belsey said.

'It's a Charlotte Kelson.'

Belsey sat up. He shook his head.

'She wants to arrange to speak to a Nick Belsey,' Rosen said.

Belsey drew a finger across his throat. Rosen slowly removed his hand from the receiver without taking his eyes off Belsey. 'He's not here,' he said. Charlotte must have said something else. Rosen grunted again and hung up.

'Thanks,' Belsey said. Rosen shook his head and went back to his papers. It was only then Belsey realised how much he had wanted to hear her voice.

He checked the window. Pierce Buckingham was there, on the pavement opposite. He had positioned himself behind a grey Saab, as if using it for cover. He was alert, scanning his surroundings. But his focus was the station. Skin infection – that was code for surveillance, for those on undercover ops. I've got a skin infection. I'm being watched. Now he felt why. His neck prickled. Something about the way Buckingham's overcoat was buttoned up seemed strange.

Belsey stepped out of the station. Buckingham watched him but didn't follow. Belsey walked to the Prince of Wales. The Prince had a public phone tucked away in one corner. He called the *Mail* and asked to be put through to Charlotte.

'Happy Valentine's Day.'

'How sweet,' she said with quiet caution.

'What have you got?'

'This Nick Belsey is a detective at Hampstead station. Do you know him?'

'I'll give you something to write about, Charlotte. But leave Belsey out of it. That's the trade.'

'Are you Nick Belsey?'

'This is a very complicated situation.'

'Apparently he's in financial difficulties.'

'Who told you that?'

'It's your turn to talk, Nick.'

While he'd been happily living Devereux's life, it seemed someone had been deciding how to use him. He had a vague vision of throttling them. But another, cooler part of his mind was profiling: someone sophisticated, controlled, with access to financial records. Someone who might have powerful friends. Someone Belsey had made nervous.

'Listen, Charlotte, the story's not about me. It's about how Milton Granby connects to the Starbucks shooting.'

There was a laugh. Then silence as she decided how to respond.

'You're joking,' she said.

'I'm serious.'

'Go on.'

'I will when I know more. Trust me, Charlotte.'

'You promised me a story. I get the feeling you're trying to distract me from one.'

'I have something. But I need time to get you proof.'

'I don't have that time, not on the promise of a bankrupt detective.'

'Charlotte –'

'We go to press this afternoon. I can't work with you if you're not able to tell me what's going on here.'

'Then you won't be working with me.'

Belsey put the phone down. He was being screwed with. So was Charlotte. The situation put him in mind of interrogation techniques – when you needed to undermine a hardened group of criminals you made sure every individual felt alone and betrayed. You built vast conspiracies going on beyond the interview-room door so that their values and identities collapsed.

But Belsey's mysterious foe had underestimated his resources. They had told Belsey he was on to something. Both he and Charlotte Kelson were on to something.

And they had made contact.

He returned to the station and called Vodafone.

'What the hell's going on? I faxed through a Section 22 last night and I'm still waiting . . .'

The police got deference from network operators. They made themselves a lot of Home Office money supplying call information. Belsey was holding twenty sheets of Charlotte Kelson's phone activity within ten minutes.

I got a call an hour ago. It said to come here. To tell the people on the door I was meeting someone in the restaurant.

He looked for calls the previous night, at approximately 10 p.m. There was only one: a landline number. Belsey ran a check and it was a public phone box in the middle of a residential street on the edge of Vauxhall. There wouldn't even be CCTV to pursue.

He called British Telecom. 'I want all calls made from that box yesterday evening.'

They sent the information through without protest. There was only one other call made from the phone box last night. It was to a Hampstead number: 37 The Bishops Avenue.

They called Devereux's home at eight minutes past ten. The call lasted forty-one seconds. Had he been in?

Something began to shift into place.

He called Les Ambassadeurs. A woman answered.

'Yesterday, a man called from your restaurant, confirming a booking. For Alexei Devereux.'

'Did they?'

'You tell me. He sounded maybe French or Italian.'

'I'm not sure about that, sir.'

'Why?'

'That's not our usual procedure.'

'What do you mean?'

'The table would be held for an hour, as a matter of course. After that we would try to seat the party where possible. We don't make reminder calls.'

'No one from the casino phoned yesterday?'

'I doubt it.'

Belsey put the phone down. He tried to cast his mind back to that voice, but a voice on a phone line was not a face, let alone a fingerprint. It seemed they wanted to scare him, but also to show him something. They wanted him to investigate. A lot of criminals liked the attention they got, but this was different. This one had something to show.

Belsey found Devereux's envelopes in his jacket and tore them open. Of eight letters, one was from a mental health charity and seven were demands for payment. In varying tones of politeness, obsequiousness and impatience they suggested it was time for the businessman to cough up: Carte Blanche International Yacht Charter, Sprint Domestic Cleaners, the Alan Cristea Gallery on Cork Street, the European Casino Association, Henry Poole Bespoke Tailors, Handford Wines in South Kensington, Les Ambassadeurs.

Finally there was an invoice from a courier company, Goldstar International. It was for a job the previous Saturday, 7 February; the day before Devereux died. But it was the amount owed that made Belsey take a closer look. The job cost £295. It involved three vans. Whatever required this amount of transportation had been collected from 33 Cavendish Square, 11.40 a.m; delivery to postcode EC2V.

Belsey typed the full drop-off postcode into his office PC and it came up as the Guildhall.

The Guildhall was the City's own grand banqueting house, its town hall, a fifteenth-century status symbol with roots down through the Middle Ages to Roman London. Most of the City admin got done in a modern building to the north, leaving the opulent space available for corporate hire. What was Devereux doing?

Belsey thought he might have better luck with the pickup address, but he was wrong. 33 Cavendish Square was a huge tower behind Regent Street, providing office space to twenty-seven separate companies, from Dental Protection Ltd, Coller Capital, Esselco Services and Sovereign Chemicals to Star Capital Partners, Advisa Solicitors, Lasalle Investment Management, MWB Business Exchange, TOTAL Holdings UK Ltd, Coal Pension Properties Ltd.

The names swam before his eyes in shades of corporate grey. The invoice didn't list anything but the address and there was no obvious place to start. None of the names looked familiar from paperwork he'd seen at Devereux's home or office.

Belsey called the couriers themselves.

'Goldstar.'

'Hi. I've just received an invoice for a job – but we don't have any record of it this end.'

There was a groan.

'Have you got the reference there?'

Belsey read the reference.

'Well,' the man said, 'we certainly did it, because I remember it.'

'What was it?'

'Very large, very fragile boxes. You tell me.'

'Which company did you pick them up from?'

'If it's not on the invoice I'm not going to know.'

'Can you remember what the event was?'

'The event? Look, we just delivered them –'

'How many boxes was it?'

'I didn't count. You were the one being secretive about it.'

'It's escaped me. Are there any of the drivers there? Perhaps they remember what it was about.'

'They're working. There's no doubt we did the job. Maybe it was so sensitive that's why you've forgotten all about it.'

Belsey hung up. He thought about the delivery address. Guildhall: the City. Milton Granby's domain. It was one of the few leads open to him. Belsey found a number for the Chamberlain's office and got through to a humourless woman with an affected accent who said that Granby was unavailable.

'When can I catch him?'

'What does the request concern?'

'It's personal.'

'Try tomorrow.'

'What's he doing today?'

'He's taking schoolchildren around the Barbican, for Community Week.'

'Is it Community Week?'

'Yes.' She hung up.

Belsey signed out an inconspicuous black Peugeot 307 and drove to the Barbican. It was all simple, really. He would discover what Project Boudicca was and how it killed Devereux, steer the Jessica Holden investigation in the right direction, use the knowledge to play Kovar, avoid getting killed, avoid falling in love, avoid whoever was playing games with his head, leave the country, re-establish some quality of life . . . Rain dripped down the surfaces of the grey complex. He cruised past Cromwell Tower, Shakespeare Tower, searching through the desolate shards of concrete for signs of Community Week. Eventually he found school buses parked beside the Museum of London and, a little further on, some security guards and a photographer from the local paper. Beyond them was Granby's entourage.

Milton Granby stood in the centre of a crowd once more, this time an adviser, PA, some interns and a make-up girl. Everyone was busy apart from Granby who looked a little queasy and unstable without the tuxedo. The make-up girl was putting life into his cheeks. The hangover made him irritable. Granby shouted something at the adviser and one of the interns, something Belsey couldn't hear. The schoolchildren kept their distance. This was going to be interesting, Belsey thought. The PA walked in his direction. He saw what was happening too late.

'Are you here for the shoot?' she asked.

'I'm a police detective.'

'OK.' It didn't seem to ruffle her. 'Follow me.' She moved him to the crowd in front of a sign that said *Building Communities Together*. 'We thought you'd be in uniform,' she said.

Belsey had his picture taken with the Chamberlain and the school-children. The children made a lot of noise and the Chamberlain gritted his teeth. After five minutes the photographer had what he wanted. The crowd broke up, with some words of wisdom regarding life opportunities from Milton Granby, and then he was being called away by his adviser. Granby made for the cars. Belsey caught up with him.

'Nick Belsey, Detective Constable from Rosslyn Hill.'

'Honoured to meet you, sir.' He shook Belsey's hand with the sincerity of someone who had to fake it often enough. Belsey could see, underneath the pomp of office, that Granby was a bruiser of a type you could find in any bar from Mile End to the Palace of Westminster. He strode along beside the Chamberlain. 'Police are central to my vision for the City of London,' Granby said.

'By necessity.'

The Chamberlain thought about this. He looked at Belsey again.

'Rosslyn Hill isn't in the City,' he said.

'I'd like to talk to you about a man called Alexei Devereux.'

Now Granby stopped and shielded his eyes against the winter glare to get a better look at Belsey.

'What is this?' he said.

'I'm worried that people are making trouble for you unnecessarily.'

'You'd be amazed,' Granby said tightly.

'I think I can help.'

'What do you want?'

'A chat.'

Granby waved the waiting car away and told the rest of his entourage to follow, saying he'd see them at the office. They left, casting suspicious glances in Belsey's direction.

'What about Alexei Devereux?' Granby said.

'He might have got himself in trouble. Before he did, he wanted a visa. He came to you. Do you remember?'

'I've never met him.'

'Is that right?'

'I've *tried* to meet him. If you know how I can meet him, please tell me. But contrary to what the *Ham & High* might claim, we remain strangers to this day.'

'But you don't deny sponsoring him.'

'He's an international figure. I was happy to encourage his presence in London.'

'Do you sponsor many applications?'

'No.'

'What did you get for it?'

'Nothing.'

'How's the Children's Fund?' Granby looked around, exasperated. 'Didn't Cicero once say be nice to policemen?' Now Granby fixed Belsey with narrowed eyes.

'I don't believe he did.' The Chamberlain's hands had developed a distinct tremor.

'Why don't we get a drink?' Belsey said. 'You can tell me about Cicero and explain the situation so I can make sure no one gives you trouble over this again.'

They ducked into a wood-panelled bar-cum-dining club on the corner of St John Street and were offered a table at the back. The staff seemed to know the Chamberlain. They seemed to know what he'd be drinking. Belsey ordered a vodka and Coke.

Granby fiddled with his cutlery while they waited for the drinks to arrive.

'Mr Devereux's a very successful and respected businessman interested in investing in our city. He's an asset. We should be bloody grateful.'

'How much did he give the Children's Fund?'

'I don't have to tell you that.'

'Tell me about Project Boudicca instead.'

'I've never heard of it.'

'It's the reason Devereux came to London. Not ring any bells?'

'No. But if it brings money in then I wish him luck. We need some new tricks around here. Listen, Detective . . .' A gin and tonic arrived and he lifted it and took a gulp before the rattling ice could draw too much attention. His voice emerged gritty and low. 'We are an inch away from disaster. We need to be very, very bloody resourceful.'

'You in particular?'

'No, not me in particular. Everyone.'

'What's Devereux's idea?'

'Who's your Sergeant?'

'What did he need to send to your Guildhall in three vans?'

'My Guildhall? That's nice. I don't know what you're talking about.' Belsey recognised a look of ignorance when he saw one. Granby had no idea. 'I've never met Devereux and I know remarkably little about him. I'm sure that's how he would choose to have it.'

'I think you've met Devereux.'

'No one's met Devereux. I don't need to lie.'

'No one?' Belsey downed his drink. 'Have another on me,' he said. He wanted another minute of the Chamberlain's time. They ordered two more drinks and stepped out to the beer garden, picnic tables on their sides against the wall, umbrellas dripping wet. The Chamberlain lit a cigarette. He didn't offer one to Belsey, but he'd softened.

'If I had my way I'd fill every house in this town with men like Alexei Devereux. And there's enough of them out there. One day they'll stop coming and we'll miss them, we'll wonder where all the money went.' He put a hand on Belsey's shoulder. 'Tourism. That's what Devereux understands. There will always be rich people and they will come to London if we give them reason.'

'Like what?'

'The thrills rich people seek. Have you seen the *Financial Times* today?

217

Devereux means business. Don't mess with him. Can I rely on you for that?'

'Of course,' Belsey said. 'I don't think anyone's going to be messing with him any more.'

35

BELSEY BOUGHT AN *FT* AND FLICKED THROUGH THE domestic and international news, glancing down the pages. Eventually he got to the companies and stock information. The lead headline declared: HONG KONG GAMING SHARES DEFY DOWNTURN.

> The Saudi-owned international gambling company Hong Kong Gaming Consortium has shrugged off industry downturn with rumours of European projects pushing up value. On Friday, stock prices for the company climbed 42 per cent to £30.45 from £21.39.
>
> According to the *Wall Street Journal*, HKGC, the world's second largest casino gambling operator, has a non-binding agreement in place with European investment company AD Development. It is known that HKGC has its sights on the UK market and is in talks with several developers to operate casinos, hotels and resorts in what is projected as a £3 billion London investment programme.

Belsey returned to the CID office and ran an intelligence search on the Serious Crime Inquiry System. He had limited security clearance, but high-urgency requests were sent through to senior investigators who might have an interest. He typed in the names 'AD Development', 'Alexei Devereux', 'Hong Kong Gaming', but got no results. Finally he fed it 'Project Boudicca'. A minute later a call came in from DCI Kosta of the Economic and Specialist Crime Intelligence Unit.

'What's this Project Boudicca?' Kosta asked. His voice had an edge of urgency.

'I don't know. I was asked to find out.'

'By who?' Kosta demanded. Before Belsey could invent an excuse, the DCI continued: 'Is it our friends in the City by any chance?'

'Our friends in the City?'

'We've had City boys calling every five minutes, asking whether we're investigating Project Boudicca, whether their investments are safe.'

'When was this?'

'The last few days.'

'Any guesses?'

'None at all. They clearly know more than me, which they seem quite happy about. There's something going on. How legal, I couldn't tell you.'

Belsey said he was unable to help, hung up and thought through sources. He had assisted enough City boys in his time to feel justified calling in a favour. He rang the offices of Sacker Capital Ltd and asked if Ajay Khan still worked there. Miraculously he did. Belsey declined to have his call put through and decided to pay the broker a visit.

Belsey had first met Khan in a West End nightclub, just days before the broker was arrested for insider trading. Belsey helped him with a defence lawyer and the case was eventually dropped. After that they played in a regular poker hand, together with some high-rolling City girls, a financial journalist and a cocaine dealer: an intense affair under a Fleet Street wine bar which blew itself out after a couple of years once they'd all bled each other dry. Khan always had a lot of friends in high and low places; he was a clearing house for information that wasn't always meant to be cleared – and if someone somewhere made a fortune out of it, Khan was rarely left out of pocket.

Belsey left the unmarked Peugeot in the car park on Limeburner Lane, next to the Old Bailey. Sacker Capital operated out of St Bartholomew's House, just across the road, angled so that its glass reflected the Central Criminal Court. Belsey walked into a reception with a lot of pale stone and a metal sculpture in the shape of an axe blade. He asked for Ajay

Khan. The guard was good enough to put a call through. He passed the receiver over.

'Mr Khan's out at the moment,' a woman said.

'When's he back?'

'That's hard to predict.'

'Sure.'

'Would you like to leave a message?'

Belsey checked his fake Rolex. 'That's all right.'

He walked out of the office block, down Newgate Street, to a doorway squeezed between a tobacconist's and the dusty shop window of a tailor's. It led straight onto a narrow flight of stairs which led down to another doorway with light escaping through coloured strips.

Inside the bookies were a handful of plastic seats and a thin scattering of afternoon punters. The air was close, heavy with artificial heat, winter sweat, lunches grabbed on the hoof. There were men in workers' fluorescent vests, and a pensioner in a scarf and hat, but most looked like they'd walked out of the investment banks. Khan stood in the centre, in his long overcoat and pinstripes, leaning against a ledge that divided the room. He had his black hair combed back and his eyes fixed on the 14:15 at Southwell.

Belsey stood beside him and watched the race. When it was over a couple of men balled the slips in their hands and dropped them to the floor. Khan took the newspaper from under his arm and flattened it on the counter.

'Detective Constable Belsey,' he said. 'I know what you're going to say.'

'I doubt it.'

'They were bad tips. It was a bad week, and I lost more than you did. I hope so anyway.'

'I'm sure.'

'I'll give you another by way of apology. This one's solid.' He lowered his voice. 'Malting barley.'

'How about Alexei Devereux?' Belsey said. Khan looked at him. 'How about Project Boudicca?'

Belsey passed one of Devereux's business cards. Khan read the card, then palmed it so it disappeared, then turned his hand and it was there again. He didn't say anything for a long while. He glanced around the rest of the room, at the men who may have been in earshot, and finally back to Belsey.

'What do you know about this?'

'What you're about to tell me.'

Khan went to a cashier's window and pushed a slip through. He watched the boy count out two hundred pounds in twenties and pocketed them.

'Think you can help?' Belsey said.

'Maybe.'

'That's enough to get you a drink.'

'If I'd said yes?'

'I would have bought it for you.'

The White Hart was one of those ancient, low-ceilinged pubs tucked into the fissures of the city like a parasite attached to its wealth. Workmen and suits drifted in and out of the pub's dark corners, lying into their phones, having swift pints and office affairs. City of hiding places, Belsey thought.

'It's got to be five o'clock somewhere, right?' Khan lifted his pint. They had a nook to themselves.

'And somewhere it's closing.' Belsey touched his glass to the broker's. 'To better cards.'

'Mine or yours?'

'Mine. Talk to me.'

Khan drank down half his lager and wiped his mouth. 'What do you know about Project Boudicca?'

'It's killing people,' Belsey said. 'What do you know?'

'Alexei Devereux's a big name. It's been about a lot recently. There was a deal about to be closed. That's all.'

'Project Boudicca.'

'Maybe.'

'Where did you hear about it?'

'A friend.'

'Which friend?'

Khan took another long draught. It seemed to embolden him.

'Emmanuel Gilman.'

'Who is he?' Belsey said.

'The golden boy.'

'Tell me about Gilman the golden boy.'

'Fund manager, reputation for being a bit wild. I knew him at Cambridge when he was rumoured to be a great classicist or something. But he couldn't sit still. Spent most of his time setting up crank websites about UFOs, farming details of the suggestible to sell to marketing companies. He was recruited into a hedge fund a month before his finals. A year after that he was running one of his own.'

'Doesn't sound so wild.'

'He likes to play hard. There's a party trick where he downs a shot and eats the glass. Something like that. He's been on fire the last couple of years, so when he started talking about Devereux people listened. He knows everything. Your round.'

Belsey got another pint in and a short for himself. City tongues needed lubricating. Khan picked up his drink and seemed to consider it, but he was staring into space.

'A couple of weeks ago Emmanuel started getting very excited about Devereux. Said he had a tip-off. And his tips are electric.' Khan sipped. 'Or at least they were. It's immaterial now. I tried to call him yesterday and got a message saying they'd stopped trading.'

'They'd stopped?'

'They fire-saled, it's all cash now. He got the staff in 6 a.m. on Tuesday and told them to sell everything. Said it was over. I heard they wrote off four billion, walked away with two and called it a day.'

'What was that about?'

'God knows.'

'But maybe you did some poking around for him. Maybe you phoned some of your precious contacts, asking about Boudicca. Maybe they were in Economic and Specialist Crime.'

'I made the usual calls. No one's as friendly as they used to be. I thought it was meant to be about community policing these days.' He sighed. 'The City needs help, Nick. One door closes and another door closes.'

'It's not a ghost town yet.'

'It's spookier by the day.' He drank. 'You seem OK, though. You always seem OK.'

'I seem OK?'

'You seem lively. Have you got goodies?'

'Only ChestEze.'

'You don't seem too wheezy to me.'

'God bless ChestEze.'

'You always seem to have things under control,' Khan said wistfully.

'Jesus Christ.' Belsey stared at the whisky in his glass. 'So what was the tip-off Gilman had?'

'I don't know. Why are you asking?'

'Alexei Devereux's left a few bills unpaid.'

'He's not the only one.' Khan downed his drink. Belsey considered his next move. Then he saw Buckingham walk in. His stomach turned.

'I was thinking of joining the police,' Khan said, oblivious to the new arrival.

'It's a nice thing to think about.'

'Recession-proof.'

Buckingham sat at the bar, watching them in the back mirror, with a new expression of intent. Belsey studied the arms beside the body. Buckingham didn't look like a man with a gun, but you could never tell.

'Do you know the guy watching us?' Belsey asked.

Khan glanced over, saw Buckingham staring and turned back.

'Never seen him before,' Khan said.

'He's been tailing me since this morning. His name's Pierce Buckingham.'

'He's staring right at us.'

'He's not a good tail. I'm going to leave. He's going to follow me. Stay here. If anything happens give the *Mail on Sunday* a call. Ask for Charlotte Kelson.'

'You've gone downmarket.'

'Take care of yourself.'

Belsey stepped out of the bar and saw the man get up and start behind him. Belsey slipped down the side of St Bartholomew's Hospital, around the blackened shell of the old market and then up to the Church of the Sepulchre. There was a packed service in Cantonese under way. He sat in the memorial garden; the tail stood by the gate. Belsey got up and found another gate to the street. He walked fast down Gresham Street, ducked into a wine bar and took a stool at the counter. Buckingham entered the bar a moment later.

He took a table directly behind Belsey, no drink, just staring with deadened eyes. The bulge didn't look like weaponry. It looked like body armour.

Belsey walked out again and they continued beside the Bank of England. Belsey kept close to the dirty, windowless stone. It was like walking in the shadow of an immense tomb. He wasn't running any more. He stopped and watched the street behind him in the black glass of a Japanese restaurant and saw Buckingham waiting. Belsey lost his patience. The best way to throw a tail is to follow them. He turned round and walked towards him. Buckingham backed off. But he wasn't running either. Belsey thought he saw the trace of a smile on the man's face. Buckingham walked calmly into a side street, and then deeper into the rat run of passageways; Change Alley, Pope's Head Alley. They continued like that, a few metres apart, across Cornhill, through the crowds of Old Broad Street to a drab, brown church abandoned beside London Wall. A dirty sign announced *All Hallows*. Buckingham pressed on a heavy, forbidding door and it opened an inch. He slipped inside.

Belsey followed, swiftly, before his prey had time to hide or prepare an ambush. It was dark in the church. What leaden light there was came from windows high above them. Dead leaves covered the floor. Buckingham continued to a pew at the front. He took a seat, staring up at a painting above the altar: a confusion of robed bodies before a blinding white light. Belsey sat in the row behind him, angled so he could see the man's face.

'What do you want, Pierce?' Belsey said.

It was freezing. A smell of cedar wood and incense remained. Buckingham spoke with a steady voice.

'I want them to kill you before they kill me.' Buckingham stared at the altar. The dirty windows lit his wide eyes. He had a dusting of fair stubble, and grime on the collar of his white shirt. Someone who hadn't been home for a while. Belsey saw the black Velcro fastenings of a bullet-proof Kevlar vest underneath his jacket. 'I want to know why I'm going to die.'

'Any ideas?'

'Who are you?'

'Not whoever you think I am.'

'Where's Alexei Devereux?' Buckingham asked.

'Dead.'

Buckingham absorbed this.

'Are you dead?' he asked. He wore that awful smile again. He still hadn't turned. Now Belsey saw a folding knife in his hand: box-fresh, with a stubby black handle and a three-inch blade.

'Not yet,' Belsey said.

Buckingham laughed. 'This won't be over for you when I die.'

'When will it be over?' Belsey said. He kept an eye on the blade. It was held carelessly. The muscles weren't tensed, and Belsey would be able to turn before it did damage. But it didn't seem very friendly.

'I don't know,' Buckingham said. 'Maybe they're saving you until last. I've told them you're the one they want.'

'Who did you tell that to?'

'You won't walk away. You know that. Whoever you are. When they get me, I want you to remember you'll be next.'

Belsey took out the page of *Al-Hayat* and unfolded it. 'What's this, Pierce?'

Buckingham turned to look at the clipping. 'I don't know.'

'You don't know?'

'Not any more.'

'You looked pretty happy about it.'

'Happy?' Buckingham said. 'Yes.' His breath stank. He looked into Belsey's eyes. 'Who are you?'

'Tell me what Project Boudicca is,' Belsey said. Buckingham's face creased with confusion and a terrible disbelief.

'Tell me who you are,' he whispered.

A motorbike choked to life outside. It was enough to startle Buckingham to his feet. He slashed wildly. Belsey backed out of reach as the blade cut through air. Then Buckingham was spinning on his heel and running out of the church, knocking a pew over, reaching through the darkness to the doors and crashing through them.

Belsey remained for a minute staring at the doors, waiting for a sound, waiting for a shot. When none came he stepped back down the aisle, through the dead leaves, into the cold diminishing daylight.

36

THE CID OFFICE SMELT OF GREASE. ROSEN HAD HIS NOSE in a bag of fried chicken. He put his meal down when he saw Belsey.

'So who's Charlotte Kelson?' he asked. Belsey looked at his colleague while he formulated a response. He couldn't read anything off the face.

'Just someone I had a thing with. It's a bit awkward.' They had never discussed personal lives. Rosen had fielded a few calls for Belsey in his time. Once, late at the pub, Rosen asked where he got his hair cut. That was as personal as it got: a fascinating glimpse, but no more.

'Why?' Belsey said.

'Listen to your answering machine.'

Belsey played his answering machine.

'Nick, this is Chris Starr from PS Security Consultancy. Been a while, I know. Got a favour to ask – a journalist, your neck of the woods – Charlotte Kelson. Looking for any previous, any goss, run-ins, controversies, et cetera. You know the score. Give me a call and I've got a twenty-year-old malt with your name on.'

Belsey turned to Rosen. He was concentrating on his food again. Belsey could never tell if he was feigning oblivion.

'Did you get one of these messages?' Belsey said.

'Everyone got one.'

'Did you say anything?'

'No.'

PS Security provided a second income for a lot of talented detectives

228

and a few senior uniforms as well. They did work for embassies, royalty, banks, Russian and American corporations and some high net individuals who wanted police without involving the police. It was run by Chris Starr, a former Flying Squad detective. According to one version of the story, Starr found a police officer's salary was never going to support his love of Italian cars so went private. In another version he made a quiet exit from the force, sidestepping the Directorate of Professional Standards and half a dozen charges of perverting the course of justice. But he retained a valuable address book, and rumour suggested that it included Northwood and those in the Chief's circle of influence. Belsey had met Starr briefly at a Drugs Squad birthday party. Starr had been out of the force two years by then, and he looked the healthiest person there. He was only a few years older than Belsey. Starr came over to him late in the evening. 'Got a minute?' His eyes shone. He led Belsey out to a car park with a yellow Alpha Romeo in it.

'Paid in cash,' he said, tapping the bonnet.

Belsey admired the car. He was expecting Starr to say that guns popped out of the indicators. Starr spent ten minutes detailing the specs then squeezed Belsey's shoulder and pressed a business card into his hand. *PS Security*.

'What's the PS?' Belsey said.

'Private Security.'

'Private Security Security?'

'You're sharp,' he said. 'I've heard good things about you, Nick Belsey. If you ever fancy a change of scene, give me a call.'

Belsey always fancied a change of scene. He went into the office the next week, in a flash new block between Baker Street and the Edgware Road, and was taken around and told about pay packages and given a cigar. Starr showed off a room of gadgets: hidden microphones, bugs and location devices. He was proud of these and they were far superior to anything the police used. But the investigator was too smooth. The job, it seemed to Belsey, was panty-sniffing: divorce work and insurance claims; Starr himself was a bully and an egotist. A few months later PS were investigated for links with an Essex property developer wanted for attempted murder. Starr was providing him with protection and

229

counter-surveillance, and happened to be slipping lucrative work to the very police detectives investigating the developer in the first place. It was a tangled web. Eventually the case against Starr was dropped with a lot of winks and drinks all round, but then the case against the property developer was also dropped, so everyone must have had a smile on their face.

Belsey played the message again, wiped it and called Starr back.

'Chris, it's Nick Belsey.'

'Nick, how's tricks?'

'Tricky. How's yours?'

'Getting by. You hear my message?'

'Charlotte Kelson.'

'It's a journalist, Nick. Works on the *Mail*, lives up near Archway. Just wondering if you had anything on her.'

'I don't think so. What's it about?'

'She's been getting nosy. But I think we're getting something anyway.'

'What do you mean?'

'Paying her a visit this afternoon. You might want to tell the boys to step away, just in case anyone whistles.'

'I'll do that.'

Belsey called Charlotte's mobile. No answer. He called her work extension and they said she was working from home. He ran downstairs and jumped into the station's fast-response car, trying to catch his breath. He made Archway in seven minutes: lights, sirens and leaning on the horn. He killed the sirens a block away, double-parked.

All the curtains had been drawn in Charlotte's home. The front door was a fraction open. That seemed a bad combination. Belsey stepped inside, slow and silent.

A corridor ran from the front door to a kitchen at the back. Halfway down was a beige-carpeted staircase. Charlotte lay at the top of the stairs. Her feet and hands had been bound behind her back and a strip of fabric stuffed into her mouth, but she was inching along the carpet to the top stair. She was struggling to breathe.

Belsey stepped silently up the stairs. Charlotte's eyes widened. Belsey put a finger to his lips and undid the binds and took the fabric out of

230

her mouth. Through a door at the end of the corridor he could see a man in a white balaclava going through filing cabinets.

Charlotte gasped for breath.

The intruder turned. Belsey launched himself towards him, landing a fist in his face. The man fell backwards into the study. He slipped a retractable baton from his pocket and swung. It glanced off Belsey's shoulder. He swiped at Belsey's arms and Belsey brought his right fist up, the impact snapping the man's head back. He brought his forehead crashing into the bridge of the intruder's nose. The man staggered. Belsey tried to get a grip on him but his right arm had gone numb. He threw a straight-arm punch with his left and caught the side of the intruder's mouth. There was blood now, a streak across the front of the silk bala-clava. Belsey tried to tear it off him but the man turned. Belsey grabbed his wrist and forced him halfway into a police hold, gripping him from the back, but the intruder knew police holds and wasn't ready to give up the fight. He slammed Belsey repeatedly against the wall, knocking vases and ornaments off a shelf to the floor. Charlotte grabbed an award that had fallen, a lead fountain pen set into a heavy block of wood. She smashed it against the intruder's head. He didn't like that. He swore and turned, flailing. Belsey sensed he didn't enjoy being outnumbered. Charlotte aimed another swing in the direction of his face. The intruder lost his footing and almost fell, before stumbling down the stairs towards the door.

'Let him go,' Belsey said.

'Let him go?'

Belsey watched the intruder jump into a blue Renault and drive off, still masked, grinding the gears.

'What the fuck was that?' Charlotte said.

'That was us winning. Are you OK?'

'Better than three minutes ago.'

They returned to the room where he'd interrupted the man. It was a study with a desk and shelves of files and reference books. Charlotte sat at the desk, still shaking. Belsey took her hands and checked her wrists where they'd been tied. Blood was returning. He released them.

'Should I call the police?' she said. Charlotte picked up her mobile, stared at it blankly, then put it down again on the desk. She ran her hands over her face and shut her eyes then opened them.

'No,' Belsey said. 'He'll be on first-name terms with whoever turns up.'

'Why?'

'He's a private investigator.'

Belsey went over to the filing cabinet the investigator had been so busy with.

'It's not where many people keep their jewellery,' he said. He slid a cabinet drawer out. 'What have you been doing to get them interested?'

'I've been told not to trust you.'

'Sure. There's been a lot of stuff thrown in your direction – do you know what I mean? I think trusting me might be your least worst option right now.' She turned to face him. 'This is your decision, Charlotte. You trust me or you don't. Tell me about the person who phoned you with so much to say about my financial situation.'

'It was an anonymous call.'

'What did they say?'

'That you were bankrupt.'

'The same person who told you to go to the casino?'

'I think so.'

'What does he sound like?'

'Male, English. Middle-aged, or thereabouts.'

Belsey pushed the cabinet drawer shut.

'Listen, someone's trying to tie us up in knots. The whole casino meeting was engineered to show us who was in control. They know we're on to them. Me and you. We're dangerous together because we're close to figuring something out. So they're playing games with us. I think they're using us to block each other and to slow down the rest of the people they've pissed off. That's not a very safe role for us. You might have to learn to trust me.'

'What's this about?'

'It's about them getting away with something. I think that something involves Milton Granby and the City of London. You said he was up to no good. What's he doing?'

232

'I haven't got the details yet. It's a scheme to bring money back into his accounts, that's all I know. You're bleeding,' she said.

Charlotte led him to a bathroom. His lip was bleeding where the old cut had been reopened. He couldn't lift his right arm very easily. He removed his shirt and inspected the damage. His right elbow had swollen. He cleaned himself up. He was more angry about the voice on the phone, fucking him over.

Charlotte sat on the edge of the bath watching him.

'Do you really think the Starbucks shooting is something to do with this?'

'I know it is. Jessica Holden was in a relationship with Alexei Devereux.'

Charlotte looked incredulous. 'A schoolgirl?'

'Is that the surprising part?'

She was silent as he put his shirt back on. He could see her thinking. Finally she said: 'Are you really part of a Ghost Squad?'

'Does it matter what I'm part of?' He splashed his face with water and leaned, dripping, over the sink. 'We're on to the same thing, and the same people are trying to get at us.' She passed him a towel. 'What else have you found out about Devereux?' he said.

'I've found out why certain Hampstead residents might not have wanted him moving in next door.'

'Why's that?'

'He was very into his gambling, his casinos and racetracks. Ran a lot of racetracks in Afghanistan and Russia. There was concern about animal welfare. The horses being run into the ground. There were races where the last one standing won. Big money, apparently. Not my scene.'

'The petition was sent to the paper by Devereux himself.'

Charlotte frowned. 'Why?'

'I don't know. He made it all up.'

'I don't get it.'

'Me neither. Maybe he did it to let people know he'd arrived. Maybe he liked trouble. Something else you might be interested in: guess who sponsored Devereux's visa application.'

'Who?'

'Granby himself. Devereux was meant to be at a party thrown by him

last night – a get-together for compassionate industrialists and finan-
ciers. Devereux made a donation to the City Children's Fund. Then, a
few weeks before he died, he had a UK visa sponsored by Granby. The
two might be connected. Granby denies ever meeting him, but he's not
shy about wanting his investment.'

'You spoke to him?'

'Briefly. It all concerns something called Project Boudicca. That's all
I know. That's why Devereux was in London. Are you going to be OK
here?' She seemed fully recovered. Her hair was still mussed from the
encounter. She looked like someone who'd been rolling in bed, which
made him want to take her there.

'I'm going into the office,' Charlotte said. 'It seems I've got quite a
story on my hands now.'

Belsey walked her to Archway tube station. You never knew when
another investigative thug was going to jump out. At the tube she kissed
Belsey on the mouth, which took him by surprise. She kissed hard and
he kissed back, ignoring the pain in his lip.

'Was that trust?' he said when they parted.

'No. That was me being stupid.' But she didn't say it like someone
who thought they were being stupid.

'Charlotte, do you have any holiday time left?'

'Why?'

'I thought maybe we could go on holiday. When all this is over.'

'Maybe. Where would we be going?'

'I don't know. Somewhere with no extradition treaties, relaxed banking
laws, a long, porous border.'

'Sounds nice,' she said.

The Archway Tower caught them in its winds, wrapping carrier bags
and old pages of newspaper around their legs. He was being stupid,
toying with the possibility of continuing to know her. But it had been a
while since he'd let himself feel like that. At least this relationship he'd
destroyed in advance.

'I want to find out what's going on first,' Charlotte said. 'Do you think
our escape can wait?'

'Sure it can,' he said.

234

37

PRIVATE SECURITY HAD GONE BIG TIME IN THE LAST eighteen months. Belsey walked into the PS Security office between silently sliding doors and saw they'd refurbished. Now there was a front desk with a logo behind it and a coffee table with copies of the *FT* and *The Economist*. The logo was a stylised take on Justice as she appears on top of the Old Bailey, with her blade out. There are PI agencies that play it very bland and there are ones that like to dazzle the client with gadgetry and framed black-and-white photos of European capitals. Starr had gone for the latter. In some ways it was a better front. It suggested espionage depended on sleek professionalism rather than the goodwill of a few crooked contacts.

'I'm here for Chris,' Belsey said.

'He's just with a client. He'll be with you shortly.'

Belsey took a seat and picked up a brochure. The cover had a picture of the globe being orbited by a laptop and a fingerprint. Inside it introduced PS.

> The premier private detective and investigation agency, based in the heart of London, operating throughout the centre of the capital for the past 25 years.

A lie.

Our private detectives and private investigators will undertake all manner of investigations, particularly in the financial, criminal, civil and commercial fields. We offer a confidential and sensitive telephone or office consultation, without obligation. You will find us understanding and professional.

Services included: Matrimonial/Domestic, Electronic Security De-Bugging, Adoption/Birth Parents, IT Crime and Forensics. There was a wing of subsidiaries that did more muscular protection: escort convoys, bodyguards, babysitting for billionaires on a city break.

Belsey put the brochure down and picked up *The Economist*. After five minutes a man in a beige suit came out of Starr's office, flushed, followed a moment later by a stocky man in a grey suit carrying a see-through bag of shredded paper. The second man had a goatee and a shaven head exposing rolls of pink flesh that cushioned his skull from his spine. It was a police look. He read Belsey with a police officer's undisguised suspicion. After another moment Starr appeared in the doorway with a grin and an outstretched hand.

'Nick, come in.'

Starr's sparkle had turned seedy, the healthy glow a little too defiant. But he still had the air of a showman. He wore a blue suit, matching tie and pomade. He was everything a well-dressed private investigator ought to be and he gave Belsey the shivers.

'What can I do for you?' Starr beckoned Belsey into his office and gestured to a seat. Belsey shut the door and sat down. Starr sat down. 'Have you remembered something about our journalist friend?'

'No. Actually I'm looking for my birth parents.'

'Who isn't? Mine owe me three grand.'

'How's business?'

'Truly unbelievable.' Starr flashed his white teeth. There was a fine band of perspiration beneath his hairline. He glanced at his watch. 'What can I really do for you?'

'You can tell me how you're involved with the Starbucks shooting.'

Starr's smile set like concrete. His fingers wove together on the desk as if to keep themselves from Belsey's throat.

'What makes you say we are?'

'I got a call from you asking for leads on a perfectly innocent young lady called Charlotte Kelson. Why are you interested in her?'

'Because she's interested in us.'

'She was looking at some business that I reckon ties to the assassination of Jessica Holden.'

'What do you know, Nick?'

'Still want to put me on the books? I'm cheap.'

'If you have information I suggest you share it. It might put you in a very awkward situation if you don't.'

'I hate awkward situations,' Belsey said. 'All I know is you've got very defensive all of a sudden. It was just a guess.'

'We've got nothing to do with any assassin.' He let the word hiss between his teeth.

'So what were you just shredding?'

Starr leaned forward and pointed to the door. 'Fuck off out of here, Nick. I don't need you around.'

Belsey stayed seated. He looked at the office and thought.

'Let me put it to you that you've been supplying information to a client who then used that information to carry out a hit. You didn't know they were going to hit someone, but it doesn't look good for a man with as many friends as yourself. Doesn't look good full stop.'

Starr sat back again and waved this away.

'Crap,' he said.

'But you got details of the girl,' Belsey said. 'Intercepted an arrangement to meet. Maybe you were bugging her phone.'

'Who we got details of is our business. Between us and our client.'

'Who's your client?'

'I thought you were a clever guy, Nick. That's why I asked you to work for us. I'm glad you didn't have the balls to apply. So don't push this one. It's a mess, and it's not one you're going to sort out.'

'Who was at Charlotte Kelson's place?'

'Why?'

'Tell him he throws a lousy punch. Tell him to leave her alone.'

'Why? Are you fucking her?'

'You tell me.'

Starr leaned forward again, face red. 'Go fuck who you want, Nick. But don't get caught up in this. It's not something you need to care about or can handle.'

Belsey considered his face, the tensed hands, the vein at the side of Starr's neck, pulsing. On a card player they would be the tells of someone ready to crumble. It began to dawn on him that things were far worse than he realised.

'What's going on?' he said.

'Why should I tell you?'

'Because I obviously know things that might help. I know things about Alexei Devereux.'

The name had its usual effect. Starr went very quiet and thoughtful. Eventually he said: 'Nick Belsey,' with a shake of his head and something like a groan, which could have been awe, Belsey thought, but was more likely frustration.

'Why are you interested in him?'

Starr sat back and took a deep breath. His eyes narrowed.

'We were paid to be.'

'And what's gone wrong?'

'We've lost one of our men,' he said.

'Lost?'

'Gone. I don't know where. But he was working on Alexei Devereux.'

'When was this?'

'A few days ago.' He looked down at the carpet, furious and reluctant to concede this fury. 'So, you see, it's our business and it's our business. Do you understand?'

'I understand.'

'Are you done?'

'No. Who was he?'

'Graham Dougsdale. Used to work in Covert. He was one of our best: a pursuit man, a watcher.'

Graham vanished. He was on a recce where he got photographs of Devereux. Do you know how hard it is to get photographs of Alexei Devereux? We get a call from Graham at 2 p.m. on Sunday saying he's tailing and he's had a result; he's following the Russian. Then nothing. No contact.'

Belsey thought about a strip of exposed subsoil in the corner of The Bishops Avenue garden. He wondered what time of year you were meant to plant bulbs.

'Where did you lose him?'

'Hampstead somewhere.'

'Did you get the photographs?'

'No.'

'Where was the call from?'

'Whitestone Pond. We're searching everywhere: the Heath, everywhere. We'll find him. And get the pictures.' It sounded as if he'd rather have the pictures than the missing investigator.

'Photos of what?'

'Devereux and whoever he was with. Some business going on. I don't know. Something Graham thought was significant.'

'Who are you working for?'

'Some people.'

'And Jessica Holden – did these people ask you to investigate her?'

'No comment, Nick. Tell me your side of the story.'

'Did you tell your client where they'd be able to find her? Did you know they were going to fill her with bullets?'

'We haven't broken any laws.'

'Oh, thank fuck for that. Let's all sleep easy. Who are they, Chris? Who's paying?'

'Clients.'

'Why are they upsetting my neighbourhood?'

'I don't know.' Starr looked sincere.

'Something they're angry about.'

'I'll say.' He leaned back and massaged his face, then removed his hands and stared at Belsey.

'I think that's why you were asked to gain information as to where Jessica Holden was going to be that morning,' Belsey said.

'Is that what you think?'

'Maybe I'll go to the police.'

This elicited a scornful expression from Starr.

'How popular are you with your fellow police these days, Nick?'

'What's that meant to mean?'

'I hear about you.'

'What do you hear?'

'Your luck's running out.'

'Where did you hear that?'

'Tell me what you know about Alexei Devereux,' Starr demanded.

'Tell me who's hiring you.'

'No way.'

'What do they want?'

'They want to know who's associated with this Devereux. They want to know everything about his life. What happened to Graham?'

'I'll get back to you on that,' Belsey said, rising.

'Don't fuck me around,' Starr said. 'Don't make me angry when you're in the line of fire.'

'I'm in the line of fire?'

'You're putting yourself there.'

38

DISPOSAL OF A BODY IS HARD. PEOPLE TALK ABOUT ACID, but even acid leaves teeth and gallstones. And who has acid? Burning anything in London is a nightmare, and you never get to a heat necessary to melt down bones, not even with petrol. Burial is just preservation. That's if you were lucky. Less than two feet down and nature's scavengers will reveal a body in a week or so.

Belsey returned the response car to Hampstead station, swapped it for the more discreet unmarked CID Peugeot and drove back to The Bishops Avenue. The winter afternoon had turned dark as night. He left the car on a side road and walked the last block to Devereux's. He let himself in, went to the garden and took a spade from the shed.

Graham Dougsdale, the days of man are as grass, as a flower of the field so shall he flourisheth.

The saplings came straight out when he pulled at them. They hadn't been properly bedded. Belsey tore the trees out, threw the bulbs to the side and began to dig. After a minute he hit something. He'd cleared a small hole, just over one foot deep. Crouching, he could see the unmistakable colour of bone down through the rich soil. He checked the spade edge and it had caught some blood and a scrap of flesh.

Belsey took a roll of bin bags and a fresh pair of rubber gloves from the kitchen. He put the gloves on and knelt beside the grave. After a minute of clawing at the soil he could see thick black hair. It didn't make much sense. Belsey dug around and the hair continued. He took the gloves off and felt the hair. It was coarse. He dug some more until he could see a tail. Eventually he was able to wrench the corpse free. He pulled out a mixed-breed Dalmatian-pointer.

Belsey stared at it for a moment. Then he used the spade to lift the dog into a bin bag and carried it to the kitchen, where he laid it on the breakfast bar. He turned the main light on. The dog was male, eyes misted, throat slit.

Belsey gave Isha Sharvani a call.

'Very funny, Nick,' she said.

'What's that?'

'The blood sample. You asked if it was the same.'

'It's dog's blood.'

'Right. I'm a busy woman –'

'Which one is the dog's blood?'

'Your package labelled "Safe Room". The other's human enough, the carpet fibre. But the safe-room sample's got canine antigens. Did you not know that?'

'Not until now.'

'There's no mistaking them.'

Belsey returned the dog to its grave and piled the soil back in. He stepped softly up the stairs to the safe room and stood there for a long time looking at the dried blood. He felt the logic of the world shifting once again. There seemed plenty of reasons why someone might murder Alexei Devereux but he couldn't see why they'd then go to the elaborate lengths of staging it as a suicide. That wasn't the MO for revenge killings. A crime of passion, maybe, but not a hit. He sat down at the control panel for the CCTV.

Belsey checked the system again, in case there were any early recordings that he had missed. He couldn't find anything before his stay. He watched the recordings of the previous night.

Each monitor gave footage from four cameras, the screen quartered. There was a camera at the front of the property, one in the hall, two cameras in the upstairs corridor, one in both the study and the living room, two in the garden. He watched himself sleeping on the living-room sofa. He had never seen himself sleeping before. One time they raided a man's home and found images of people sleeping, thousands of them over three hard drives, and had to figure out if there was anything illegal about it. Belsey sat watching the images. He thought about shutting himself in the safe room, drinking the mineral water, eating the tinned food and waiting for the emergency to pass. Then something appeared on the left-hand monitor.

The clock said 4.32 a.m. Belsey was lying on the sofa with one arm over his face. A man entered the room.

Belsey stopped and rewound. The figure walked in from the hallway, went up to the sofa and cast his shadow across Belsey's chest and arm. He had no face. Something obscured his features entirely. Then the figure walked out again.

Belsey felt the touch of that shadow cross him. A deep, superstitious instinct made him get up and walk through every room of the house, checking the windows and the doors to the outside world. Finally he could sit back down at the monitor and try to understand what he was seeing.

The hallway camera caught the intruder as he entered the front door – he went straight to the alarm and punched the code in. He wore a latex mask. Then he went through the living room. He knew the place. Belsey tried to see the figure's throat as if it might bear telltale scars: Devereux revisiting his past life, touching the surfaces, the furniture, looking for whatever it was that would allow him to escape limbo.

Then he saw Belsey.

The figure froze. Then very slowly he approached the sofa to look at the sleeping form. He continued out of the living room to the study.

The shadow stood a long while in the study, then crouched down. He disappeared from view as he crawled across the floor, reappearing beside the desk. 4.40 a.m. He searched the bin and the fireplace. He faced straight into the camera and still there were no features.

He must have seen the camera lights, Belsey guessed. A small red light beneath each camera told you the CCTV system was on. The intruder began to move towards the stairs. To the safe room, Belsey thought. He was on his way to stop the tapes. Then, suddenly, he fled. Some noise must have startled him into thinking Belsey was getting up.

Belsey watched the tapes again. Whoever they were, they were looking for something. They searched systematically, moving through all the rooms, but they lingered longest in the study.

He stopped the tape and went downstairs and retraced the ghost's steps. What was he searching for? Belsey crouched to the floor in the study, as the ghost had. When had he been crawling around here before? The watch. He straightened, looking at his wrist and wondering how valuable a fake Rolex could be. Worth breaking back into existence to retrieve? He took it off and looked for an inscription but there was nothing.

Something was closing in. This was clear now. His hours in London were numbered. Belsey wanted a passport in his pocket. He wanted to know he could move fast whatever happened with Kovar. The phone rang. Belsey unplugged it, then plugged it back in and called the B & B where he'd last been staying.

'Have you got a contact number for Siddiq Sahar? He was there last month.'

The B & B had a mobile number for him. Belsey called and the new wife answered.

'Oh yes, Nick.'

'Can I speak to Siddiq?'

He came on the line. 'Nicky, my friend.'

'I need papers.'

'You want papers?'

'A passport and ID.'

'You sound bad, man. Very bad.'

'I've been better.'

There was a brief pause; then, in a low, measured voice Belsey had not heard him use before, Siddiq gave an address on Green Lanes.

'Take two passport photos. Ask for a man called Hasan Duzgun. Say I sent you. You will need fifteen hundred in cash.'

'Fifteen hundred.'

'If he is not there, wait and he will come. I will tell them to expect you.'

Belsey had nine hundred pounds or so remaining but he was ready to haggle.

Belsey knew of the Duzguns. They were a sprawling family with ties to the Turkish mafia. Their London activities were a model of political tolerance, working with the Kurdish to import heroin and with the Greeks to trade black-market cigarettes. Belsey placed a call to Operation Mandolin from the Peugeot's car phone as he drove north. Mandolin was Haringey's specialist taskforce, given the job of monitoring the Turkish and Kurdish communities since a string of shootings a couple of months back. He got hold of DS Simon Walters.

'Hasan Duzgun,' Belsey said. 'Is he selling passports?'

'Yes.'

'Good ones?'

'Good as they come. Fresh from a printer's in Wolverhampton.'

'What's the going rate?'

'About two large for a full set of papers.'

'Is he currently under observation?'

'No.'

Belsey drove through Holloway to Haringey. He found a photo booth in Manor House tube station and drew the curtain. *Father, I have sinned.* He looked severe, the monochrome mirage in the glass reduced his face to bloodless skin and dark grey hollows. A sign said not to smile if it was for a passport. He had two sets taken, one with his coat, one without and with his hair messed up. While he waited for them to appear he took a torn envelope from a bin and transferred the last nine hundred pounds from the carrier bag to the envelope. It left two lonely twenties in his possession. He wrote a date of birth and a fake address on the back of the envelope. The photos appeared. He headed down Green Lanes.

The address he'd been given was a social club with brown shades over its windows and no apparent name. The interior consisted of three plastic tables, six old men, a pool table and not much else.

'Is Hasan Duzgun here?' Belsey said.

The men looked up. Belsey was nodded through a doorway into a back room. Card tables stood in neat rows, covered with paper table-cloths and lit by bare bulbs. Behind the furthest one sat an obese man with a full ashtray and the remains of his meal on a plate. He had large brown eyes. He gestured to the seat across from him and Belsey sat down. The table was small. Their knees touched. The man raised two fat fingers and a moment later two thimble-sized glasses of mint tea arrived. A grey curtain was drawn across the doorway to the front.

'You know Siddiq.'

'That's right,' Belsey said. 'He told me you could help.'

'How do you know him?'

'We shared some temporary accommodation.'

'How is he?'

'He's very well. He just got married. I need a passport and a driver's licence.'

The fat man nodded. 'Why do you want papers?' he asked.

'I lost mine.'

'Sure. It will cost you fifteen hundred pounds.'

Belsey reached into his jacket and took the envelope out and placed it on the table.

'That's nine hundred. I'll give you the rest when I see the papers.' Duzgun raised his eyebrows at this. 'I want them in the name of Jack Steel,' Belsey said. 'I want a UK passport, not Honduras or some crap from the Internet. I need something that will scan at an airport.'

Duzgun didn't look at the envelope. He dropped two sugar cubes into his tea using small gold tongs. He stirred and it sounded like a bell ringing. Belsey did the same. They sipped their tea in silence.

'This is a good country,' the man said.

'It's great.'

'Peaceful. Lots of money.'

'I love that about it,' Belsey said.

'To the British, two things are very important: politeness and respect.'

'You're kidding.'

'Where are you from?'

'Lewisham, originally.'

'Why do you want these?'

'There's nine hundred pounds on the table. I didn't think I had to have an interview.'

'How did you get here?'

'Here? I drove.' The conversation was breaking down. Belsey needed to leave. 'A good passport, not new, but valid for a while,' he said. 'And a driver's licence, ten years old. I want you to use the different pictures for them.' He got up.

'You know a lot about this.'

'That's right. When can I collect them?'

'Two days, maybe three.'

'I need them tomorrow. Get them to me tomorrow and I'll give you another seven hundred,' Belsey said. Duzgun reached into the breast pocket of his jacket and produced a toothpick. He thought about this.

'Come tomorrow afternoon. That is the earliest I can do. You come here.'

'Tomorrow afternoon.'

'I will be here, Jack Steel. You bring another seven hundred.' He watched Belsey leave. 'Seven hundred,' he said at his back. 'Or I hand you to police. They know me. It will cause trouble for you.'

39

BELSEY CHANGED A TWENTY AND CALLED MAX KOVAR'S mobile from a public phone in Archway Snooker Centre. The place was deserted. The speculator answered on the second ring.

'Is this line secure?' Belsey said.

'Yes.'

'Are you certain?'

'Absolutely.'

'Mr Devereux is back now. He says he was sorry not to have met you the other night. He sends his regards.'

'Well, tell him I'm very honoured. Is he there?'

'He's with someone. But he didn't want to waste a moment. An opportunity has arisen.'

Kovar controlled his voice. He wasn't a man to sound grateful or excited. 'Well,' he said, 'as I've made clear, it would be in your interest as well as my own.'

'Yes. That much is clear, I think.'

'I need details, however.'

'I'll get you details. But we need big-game players here, Max. Men not afraid to step up. You understand me?'

'I think we understand each other.'

'Meet me later,' Belsey said.

'Will Mr Devereux be there himself?'

'I hope so.'

'And he will tell me what I'm looking at?'

'Exactly.'

'Where will I find you?'

'The Rivoli bar at the Ritz,' Belsey said. The Rivoli was a mess of art deco glass and gold leaf. Belsey loved it. He had kept warm there plenty of times, wondering if he could afford a drink. He'd always wanted to do some business at the Rivoli.

'I know it,' Kovar said. 'I have a dinner appointment, but that can be rearranged.'

'Keep your dinner appointment. We'll be there around midnight.'

'Perfect.'

He hung up. Now he really needed to sort his act out. He called Ajay Khan.

'You said there was one guy who was talking up Devereux and Project Boudicca.'

'Emmanuel Gilman.'

'I need someone who can give me an indication of what Devereux was working on. I'd like to see what Emmanuel Gilman knows.'

'OK.' Khan sounded hesitant. 'But Emmanuel's in a strange place right now.'

'I need to speak to him. Can you arrange that?'

'Sure. I'll tell him you're a drug dealer.'

'And a policeman?'

'Exactly.'

'Where can I find him?'

He gave Belsey a Docklands address, a block of flats near Canada Water.

'Will he talk?' Belsey said.

'Oh, he's talkative all right. Be gentle with the guy, Nick. Be careful.'

'What's that meant to mean?'

'It means I don't know what you'll find.'

40

THE LAST TIME BELSEY SAW DOCKLANDS IT WAS FIVE IN THE morning and he was on his way home from a large, expensive night. It had appeared more impressive then, its cold artifice suiting his frame of mind. Belsey drove through the evening silence of Canada Water now and it still had the coldness with none of the glamour. Remnants of the Commercial Docks survived but most of that world had been destroyed. Half a century on, the place still felt Blitz-damaged: empty and stunned. Street lights glimmered on imprisoned squares of river while converted warehouses stared blankly across from Wapping. Endless ziggurats clustered to the mysterious luxury of water. Belsey wondered what he'd find.

Gilman's block was the most grandiose of a garish bunch. It was called Sand Wharf and preserved an iron hoist, painted red, above the entrance to its underground car park. Belsey left the Peugeot above ground. A concierge waved him towards a lift with mirrors on every side. Belsey took it to the tenth floor and knocked. Four locks were undone with what sounded like shaking hands. Finally Gilman opened it on the chain and stared blankly through the gap.

'I'm a friend of Ajay Khan. I think he told you I was coming. I think we can help each other out.'

The synapses connected. A wild smile lit the fund manager's face. The door shut and then swung open again.

'Nick, right? Praise be. Come in.' Gilman wore a running vest, shorts and trainers. He had the kind of blond good looks that wouldn't age, but just find the material of which they were made start to waste away. There was a towel around his shoulders and he was sweating hard. He led Belsey into a front room with a rowing machine in the centre of the bare floorboards and a Kalashnikov on the black leather sofa. It made Belsey start. The blinds were down. Deodorant had just been sprayed. A mound of scribbled A4 sheets spilled from a glass coffee table to the floor.

'Welcome,' Gilman said. He collapsed back into the sofa and lay the gun across his lap. 'Don't be freaked out.'

'Would you mind if I was slightly perturbed?'

Gilman laughed. Belsey took a good look at his eyes. Pinned and pale. He looked like someone who hadn't had their benzodiazepines today.

'It's a piece of history.' Gilman stroked the barrel with long, thin fingers. 'Have you ever used one?'

'Not since Leningrad. Can I see?'

Gilman handed it over.

'It's been through the ranks of the Red Army, the Soviet-Afghan War, the Taliban uprising. It's a history lesson in steel.'

'Where did you get it?'

'I can't say.'

Belsey tried to imagine the supply chain; maybe the gun came through coke dealers, the City's primary tie to the underworld, if you discounted the money laundering. Maybe there were entrepreneurial men doing a roaring trade selling AK-47s to disillusioned fund managers, like the Koreans who appear with boxes of umbrellas when it starts to rain.

'It's a beauty,' Belsey said.

'I've got a cabinet,' Gilman said, 'so you can't arrest me.'

Belsey unlatched the magazine, took the safety lever off and pulled the bolt back to eject the remaining cartridge. He put the bullets on the table and handed the empty gun back.

'I never share a room with a banker and a loaded assault rifle. It's one of my few rules.'

Gilman winced. 'I'm not a banker.'

'You're close enough.'

Belsey pulled up a beanbag and sat down. He saw, beside the sofa, a tub of Maximuscle protein powder and several blister packs of pills. The room had the cloying atmosphere of an infirmary.

'So, you're a detective,' Gilman said.

'That's right. I heard you lost your job.'

Gilman laughed. 'I was the job. I got lost.'

'You sold up.'

'The game was over. All that was holy had been profaned, all that was solid melted into air.' He sighted the empty gun on the glass door to the roof terrace.

'Or into new investments?' Belsey said.

'What do you mean?'

Gilman's phone rang. He checked and killed it.

'I'm curious about where it all went.'

'Where what went?'

'The leftovers. All the cash you got out.'

'Me too.' Gilman picked up the phone, rubbing the screen with his thumb, as if this might reveal the message he was waiting for. 'Have you heard of the potlatch?'

'Never.'

'Opposing tribes – this is a tradition across the world, but mostly among Native Americans – opposing tribes have gatherings where they try to impress their rivals by destroying the most extravagant gifts they can afford. It's a way of expressing honour. Could be anything from animal skins to burning their own village and killing all their slaves. That's the gift.'

'That's interesting.'

'Seriously.'

'It's not all in cash, is it?' Belsey said. 'Some of it got reinvested.'

'What makes you say that?'

'Alexei Devereux.'

Gilman stood up with the rifle and went to the next room. Belsey heard a metal cabinet close and a combination lock turn. He picked up some of the sheets on the coffee table but couldn't make out a word. Beneath them was a red hardback copy of Plutarch's *Life of*

Alexander. He placed the sheets back. Gilman returned, unarmed, and sat down.

'What's going on here?' Belsey said.

Gilman leafed through some of the dog-eared papers then appeared to forget what he was looking for. He stared at the mess.

'I'm writing a book,' Gilman said. 'The history of war and intoxication.' He glanced up as if expecting Belsey to laugh. When he saw that Belsey wasn't laughing he continued. 'My argument is that it is impossible to understand the history of war without understanding drugs. Not just recent war. Alexander the Great and his troops were drunk from day to day. They were winos. They conquered the known world and probably didn't remember they'd done it. The Aztecs drank pulque in the days before battle – it's a beer made from cactus. The Scythians, the fiercest bastards in history, had an awful, awful weed habit. I'm not kidding you. Now eighty per cent of the Afghan security force is addicted to heroin. History's a hangover. Eighty per cent . . . That's what I'm trying to say, Nick. Can I call you Nick? You seem like an intelligent guy. I want you to read it when I'm done, tell me what you think.'

'It sounds a good idea. How about a book on Alexei Devereux?'

'How about it?' he said.

'I'd like to read one of those.'

'Is that why you're here? Is he under investigation?'

'If a company called AD Development was under investigation, how badly would you be exposed?'

'What makes you think I'm interested in them at all?'

'Because you know about them. You were shouting about them. And to know them is to love them, right?'

'Devereux's the future. Everybody loves the future.' Gilman smiled.

'What does it look like?'

'You'd have to ask the man himself.'

Belsey stood up and walked over to the window. He moved a slat blind to the side.

'Don't do that,' Gilman said.

The view extended to Surrey Quays Shopping Centre, and across the black river to the Isle of Dogs. It struggled to live up to its price tag. What you actually saw looked like toytown, with the ghosts of a local community passing through dark, deserted squares. It was time to shake the fund manager up a little.

'You can't tell me about Devereux because you were shorting AD stock. You knew he was bankrupt and the whole thing was about to drop. A friend at the Financial Services Authority says you've stitched up half the Square Mile.'

Gilman laughed. 'You're good.' But he was unnerved. He stood beside Belsey at the window. His phone rang. He turned it off. 'Is the FSA saying that? I don't think so.'

'Tell me about Project Boudicca. Everyone was talking about Boudicca, weren't they?'

'Were they?'

'Sure they were,' Belsey said. 'You couldn't move in the Pitcher and Piano for it, the toilets of All Bar One, everywhere, talk of Devereux and his London project.' Belsey unlocked the door to the terrace and stepped out. He knocked on the window. 'Does every flat come with bulletproof glass?'

'Can you please come inside?' Gilman said. Belsey tried to read the situation. He came in and slid the door shut. 'Listen, Nick. The cupboards are bare. Do you have anything on you?'

'Not on me, but just minutes away.'

'Can we make that happen?' He took the Maximuscle tub from the floor, unscrewed the cap and checked inside. Belsey glimpsed thick, soft bundles of paper money. Gilman put the cap back on.

'If you're willing to talk,' Belsey said.

'I'm talking. I haven't talked like this for ages. It feels great.'

Belsey sat down again. 'Have you met him?'

'Who?'

'Devereux.'

'No one's met him.'

'What's he about?'

'Gaming. Racing. Casinos. I think he wants to have a casino in every city. Not just casinos but resorts. You know what George Bernard Shaw said? Gambling promises the poor what property performs for the rich.' Gilman gave a sly grin. 'Something for nothing.'

'Crime does that too.'

'I think Devereux would legalise crime if he could. Gambling's the closest he can get. He says gambling will be the heroin of the twenty-first century. He reckons by 2030 there will be fifteen Las Vegases, just as big, just as profitable, in all the new deserts of the world. A lot of his gaming websites are run out of Turkmenistan. That's the base of his empire, but the icing is the tracks. He races horses in deserts at night, across industrial wastelands, around Native American reservations. One of his more eccentric ideas was to race horses through gas pipelines. He films the races and broadcasts them. There was a London project in the works – a big one. A guy called Pierce Buckingham was trying to raise money for a stake. That's what I heard. That's the whole of it. He was gathering the right names together.'

'Who is he?'

'Pierce? He's a go-between. A slush puppy. He arranges weddings. You can usually find him at a place called Les Ambassadeurs in Mayfair trying to be a playboy and thinking he's untouchable. I went to a party at his house once and there were porn stars and a snake charmer. A few years ago he set himself up as the go-to financial adviser for individuals with money wanting a slice of the London pie.'

'What did you think Pierce Buckingham was raising money for?'

'I don't know. But I heard there was a French company coming in. If Pierce couldn't raise the ante then the whole thing was going to France. So he hustled. He went to his old friends, the Hong Kong Gaming Consortium – because quite frankly they could sink five billion into mud and not notice it's gone.'

'Let's say I needed to give someone details of Devereux's project. What sort of thing would I say?'

'I don't know. Pierce was being extra cagey about this one.'

'Why?'

'Local sensitivities.'

'Like what?'

'People. Sober people. Poor people. I don't know.'

'Did he get the money together?'

'The money was already together. It's called the Hong Kong Gaming Consortium and it's bottomless. The Consortium was bought last year by Prince Faisal bin Abdul Aziz. He operates Saud International Holdings, the main Saudi government investment fund. He gave his wife two fighter jets for her birthday and then built the most expensive house in Riyadh with the change. Buckingham negotiated his purchase of the Dream City Casino on Macao when the Prince wanted in on the gambling market. It's the only place in China where you can gamble. Imagine that. Then Buckingham arranged the takeover of an Italian gaming group called Gioco Digitale. But that was just a stepping stone. Everyone saw that. It was a foot in the European sector. They've got their sights on London. Prince Faisal thinks London is where it's at. He thinks Pierce Buckingham's their man because he's blue-eyed and vicious.'

'And you have no idea what he was working on with Alexei Devereux?'

'None at all. I imagined it was something to do with property or sport or a bit of both.'

'Why aren't you answering your phone?'

Gilman groaned and stretched. 'How much do you think you can get?'

'Let's say you tell me where Pierce Buckingham lives.'

'That's easy.' Gilman sat up and scribbled an address on the back of a property magazine. He tore it off and gave it to Belsey. 4 Queen's Gate Mews, a street in SW7. Belsey pocketed the address and walked over to the windows a final time.

'How much are you looking to score?' Belsey said.

'Anything. Everything.' He drummed his fingers on the tub.

'Give me an hour. I'll see what I can do.' Belsey cast a final glance around the apartment then left. He pushed the button for the lift. Something said: *Get out of London*. It said: *Look, a mirror deep enough to drown yourself in.* Maybe he could become a jockey. He tried to imagine how that would feel, horse racing in the night air of the desert.

Gilman's door opened. He leaned out, checked the corridor, then called after Belsey.

'What about Boudicca, Nick? What is it? Do you know?'

'I've no idea,' Belsey said, without turning.

'If you find out, will you tell me?'

'Of course.'

'If it's happening? If it's all good?'

The lift arrived. Its doors slid open and Belsey stepped inside.

41

BELSEY MADE KENSINGTON IN FORTY MINUTES. PIERCE Buckingham kept a bachelor pad on a small, very expensive road close to Kensington Gardens. The little house at number 4 had its lights on, windows fogged. Someone had been taking a hot shower. Belsey knocked on the front door but got no answer. He couldn't see through the windows. He pressed the door and it opened with a gust of steam.

The whole place was damp, condensation dripping down the white walls of the hallway. Belsey stepped slowly inside. He trod softly into a living room that had exploded. Someone had slashed the seats, torn up the carpet and emptied all the cupboards into a big pile of designer belongings. An imitation Wurlitzer jukebox lay in pieces on the floor. A projector screen had been pulled down and torn in two. Droplets trickled down the abstract surfaces of metal sculptures and the wall-mounted TV screen.

It didn't look like Buckingham was home.

Belsey stepped over piles of clothes to a steam room and sauna at the back. The shower was on and the sauna door was open and the tiles had been ripped off the walls.

He climbed the stairs to the bedroom and there was a lot of broken glass and a reek of amyl nitrate. The bed was huge, circular with black silk sheets on the floor, the mattress against the wall, slit down the side. Belsey found a few long blonde hairs on the pillowcase. The drawers from the bedside table and the cabinet at the side of the bedroom had been tipped onto the floor spilling condom packets and pharmaceutical bottles. One hardback book lay on the floor beside the bed.

The Kingdom: A History of the House of Saud. Belsey picked it up. It had an elaborately ornamented cover, inlaid with gold leaf. The pages were wilted and bunched by the steam. A note on the frontispiece said: *To our esteemed friend, with blessings for the future.* Inserted halfway through was a photograph of a man with his arms around two teenage girls. They sat on a red banquette with an array of glasses and bottles on the table in front of them. It took Belsey a moment to recognise Pierce Buckingham: grinning, shaven, the other side of whatever crisis had set him stalking Belsey in a bulletproof vest. On Buckingham's right was Jessica Holden in a silver, strapless cocktail dress; the other girl was the blonde friend who'd been crying on TV. She wore something tight and black that stopped short of her thighs. She had one hand on Buckingham's shoulder. Jessica smiled with her mouth closed. The blonde girl showed teeth.

Justice will be done, the crime scene flowers had said. Belsey called Miranda Miller from a cordless phone on Buckingham's bedroom floor.

'Have you got contact details for Jessica's friend, the blonde girl?'

'No. Well, yes, but they get through to an agent.'

'An agent?'

'She was trying to hustle for a five-figure deal. Now she's gone to Sky.'

'She's over the shock, then.'

'There's something about her, Nick. Other kids at the school don't remember them being that close. She was in the year above Jessica. Now she's left the school. I think she's on the make.'

42

ISHA SHARVANI SAW BELSEY AT THE FRONT OF THE FORENSIC Command office and groaned.

'You're going to like this,' Belsey said. 'I promise. I need image enhancement.'

Sharvani led the way through her lab to the photographic unit. The unit was two rooms between the toxicology labs and forensic dentistry; one of the rooms had a projector. Sharvani dimmed the lights and scanned the photograph. After a few seconds it appeared on a wall-size screen, enlarged to fill it and divided into a grid by thin red lines.

'Is that a waterfall in the background?' Sharvani said.

'It's a waterfall.'

'In a bar?'

'In a casino. It's called Les Ambassadeurs.'

'Nice.' She admired the image. Then her expression became serious. 'That's Jessica Holden on the left.'

'I'd say so,' Belsey said.

'What is this?'

'The reason she got shot.'

Sharvani stood back and folded her arms, casting a professional gaze across the enlarged image.

'Who's the man?'

'He's called Pierce Buckingham. Zoom in on his glasses.' She zoomed in. There was a lot of glare on the glass; lights from the slot machines. 'Reflected in them,' Belsey said.

'What is it?'

'It's whoever's taking the photograph.' She zoomed in further. 'You can see the figure?'

'I can see a shape.'

'Look, down in the wine glass you can see them as well.'

She filled the screen with a wine glass. The hazy form of a man raising a camera was clear enough. It didn't tell you much else.

'I can enhance it,' Sharvani said. 'I can't make it show you a face that isn't there. Who do you reckon it is?'

'A man called Alexei Devereux. He's also dead.'

'Well, this is cheerful.'

Belsey took out the clipping from *Al-Hayat*, and replaced the photo with the fragment of newspaper. It appeared on the screen.

'Same guy,' she said.

'Yes. Can you tell me anything?'

'The photograph's being taken from inside. It's a large doorway for a church. Maybe a cathedral.'

'Get closer on the buildings in the background. I want to know where they are.'

The spire came into focus, set on top of old, blackened stone.

'Recognise it?' she said.

'No.'

He switched the images back to the gaming scene and looked again at the blonde girl, Jessica's companion, on Buckingham's other shoulder. If they weren't close friends at school they certainly seemed to be running a tight operation outside of it. He needed to speak to her, the fourth party in this memento. He didn't want to get through to an agent. *Someone must have information*, she'd said to the cameras, in her expensive clothes.

'Is this computer online?' Belsey asked.

'Sure.'

Belsey sat down and searched for the Sweetheart Companionship website. It arrived with its parade of youth for hire. 'A girl with you in one hour!' There were a lot of blondes, a lot of girls from small-town Ukraine and Lithuania. All the beauty of the former communist world seemed to be on the game in London. And then there she was: Lucinda, 'our English Rose'.

Sharvani watched over his shoulder.

'Are you looking for a date tonight?'

'I just found one.'

'That's the girl.'

'Looks like her to me.'

He called Sweetheart on the Forensic Unit's phone and they answered on the first ring.

'Good evening, sir. Sweetheart Companionship.'

'I've seen a girl on your site and I'd like to arrange a date with her.'

'Yes, sir, which one?'

'Lucinda.'

'I'm afraid Lucinda's not available tonight.'

'I'll pay good money.'

'That's not possible. Can I recommend another girl, very similar?'

'An English Rose?'

'Yes, sir.'

Belsey hung up. Then all hell broke loose.

Engines roared into life down in the car park, sirens opening up. Individuals sprinted down the corridor outside. Sharvani took a call and pulled on her jacket, grabbing a murder kit from the desk.

'What's going on?' Belsey said.

'Showtime. I've got to go.'

Belsey stepped out of the office. 'What is it?'

'Another shooting. EC4.'

Belsey jumped into his car and joined the convoy. He tailed the Response Unit north across London Bridge into the City. They stopped at Monument. He jumped out.

A silver Audi sat abandoned at the junction of Cannon Street and King William Street, the passenger window smashed, driver's door open.

The burn of a motorbike tyre ran fresh alongside it. Red-and-white police tape entangled the junction. Six City uniforms guarded the scene, one on his radio – 'No, no sighting'.

But it wasn't the car that attracted the bulk of the attention.

The action was down in the darkness of St Clement's Court, outside the building that had housed AD Development.

'Move away,' someone shouted.

Belsey showed his badge and ducked through. Buckingham lay in the alleyway, beside an unmarked door to an empty office. He was still in his expensive overcoat and bulletproof vest. Most of his skull was missing, bone and brain splashed across the tarmac and up the adjacent wall.

'Someone cover him,' yelled a sergeant from the City Police.

Belsey walked back to the Audi. He found what was left of Buckingham's glasses twisted by the pedals. *When they get me, I want you to remember you'll be next.* He glanced up at the windows and roofs and ledges. Figures of Industry and Commerce stared down. An air ambulance cast its low growl over the Square Mile. He stepped out of the light and walked back to his unmarked police car.

43

SWEETHEART. HE NEEDED COMPANY.

Belsey drove west into Soho, senses open for his killer and flooded by the general brutality of Saturday night. Two cars collided at the junction of Shaftesbury Avenue and Cambridge Circus and everyone cheered. Glass broke outside a pub and everyone cheered. He never knew what they were cheering: the promise of violence, the physical fact of destruction. Shattered, he thought. It felt like he had shattered and now exhaustion had no place to cling. He had his second wind, pumped with the chaos. People moved loudly between pubs and bars, outrunning closing time; tourists marching to the strip shows, locals edgy with nine hours of drinking. Addicts weaved through the crowd. One woman lay on the pavement, unconscious, flanked by queues for cash machines.

He was ready to break into the escort agency's office if necessary. It might have been preferable. But as he approached the building he saw a light from the top-floor window. The front door was open.

The agency's receptionist tried to stop Belsey when he reached the top floor.

'We're closed.'

He put a foot in the door. The main lights were off. Light came from under the door to Freddie Garth's office.

'You left a light on.'

He pointed and moved past her as she turned. She ran to the phone and lifted it to put some warning through but was never going to connect in time.

Belsey opened the door. Garth sat alone, extracting papers from a file.

'I'm in the middle of something,' Garth said.

'This will be inconvenient then.' Belsey sat down.

'What do you want?'

'To speak to Lucinda.'

'No.'

Belsey leaned across the desk, picked up the phone, pressed speaker and dialled.

'Channel Five,' the phone said.

Belsey leaned over the mike. 'It's Nick Belsey, friend of Miranda Miller. Can you put me through to the news desk?'

Garth hit the phone and cut them off.

'She lives in north-west London,' he said. He opened one of the files and read a street address and shut the file again.

'Thank you for your cooperation,' Belsey said.

The address was a neat slice of property just west of Highgate Cemetery: a whitewashed home on a gated development. It was eleven o'clock and a new VW Passat was twinkling on the driveway, though the house lights were out. Bedtime. This was going to be fun, Belsey thought.

He rang the bell and waited, then tried again. After a moment, a man answered in a dressing gown. He had dark hair flecked with grey and looked like he might play a good game of squash.

'Is there a Lucinda here?'

'My daughter's Lucy.'

'That'll be the one.'

'What is this?'

'Police. It's nothing to worry about, but I need to speak to her. Is she home?'

'I think so.'

'Can I come in?'

The man led him into a very clean, pale, carpeted home. Belsey saw envelopes on a table in the hall addressed to Dr Howard Grant. The living room had pink and cream sofas.

'This is about Jessica,' Grant said.

'Yes.'

'Lucy wishes there was more she could do. It's been very hard for her. For us all.'

'I know. This must seem cruel. I just want to run one or two new developments by her.'

Belsey admired the sofas and matching armchairs with their pouffes. There were professional-quality shots of Lucy all over the walls, a copy of the *British Journal of Cosmetic Dentistry* on the coffee table, a magazine called *Smile*.

'Let me see if she's up.'

The father went upstairs and came down a few seconds later.

'She's in the bathroom.'

'OK. I'll wait. Could I get a tea?' Belsey said. 'I've been on my feet all day.'

'Of course.'

Belsey waited for the man to disappear into a newly fitted kitchen and then went upstairs. There was light from under a bathroom door. Beside it was a girl's bedroom: a wall of photos, A-level textbooks on a shelf, clothes on the floor. He opened the wardrobe, opened the bedside drawer: contraceptive pills, address book, a bottle of diazepam and two brochures for breast augmentation clinics. Belsey flicked through the address book then put it back.

He went back downstairs to the living room. His tea arrived a moment later.

'It's a terrible situation,' the man said.

'Yes.'

'Lucy's mother worries herself sick.'

Belsey leaned back on the plump sofa. He looked at the soft-focus shots of the dentist's daughter: in ballet gear, in ballroom gear. No one ever believes the threat is in their own homes. Even when it's them. Even as they're bludgeoning the members of their close family to death.

'We're going to find whoever's responsible,' Belsey said.

'How can they live with themselves?'

Lucy came downstairs in fresh make-up, skirt and knee boots with a fake fur jacket over her arm. It didn't seem like she was about to turn in for the night. She looked from Belsey to her father and back at Belsey.

'He's a policeman,' her father said. She frowned.

'I've told you everything already.'

'I think you might have forgotten some details,' Belsey said. 'I'm interested in the company Jessica kept. You know – sweethearts. That kind of thing.' The girl's expression changed rapidly to one of panic. She turned again towards her father to read his face but caught only blissful ignorance. 'Shall we talk somewhere private?' Belsey suggested.

This seemed to be a good idea. They went to her room.

'What do you want?' she said.

'Sit down.' Belsey shut the door. She sat on the edge of her bed. 'I want to talk. You ever get clients who say that? They just want to talk?'

'I don't know what you mean.'

'What did you mean when you lied to the police?'

'What did you tell my father?'

'That you're a cynical little whore. What did you tell Sky?'

'Fuck you. You don't care about Jessica.'

'Don't I? Do I care that you might be in a lot of danger yourself right now?'

'You're all incompetent.' She turned away, but not very effectively, and not without having heard his last words. He sat on the bed beside her. He gave her the casino photograph. 'I'd like to know about this – this night, this man. I think, the more I can find out, the safer everyone will be.' She spent a while looking at it. She seemed to be checking it was real, then it felt like she'd stopped looking at the picture and was trying to see its implications.

'He's called Pierce,' she said finally.

'What does Pierce do?'

'He's a businessman. Very rich.'

'How do you know him?'

'I only saw him that night.'

'Tell me what happened.'

'We were at this club, a casino.'

'Who's we?'

'Me, Jess, Alexei.'

It felt bizarre, in this teenager's bedroom, to finally find the person who had set eyes on him; to be at one remove from someone he had almost stopped believing ever existed.

'You met Alexei Devereux?' Belsey said.

'Yes.'

'When was this?'

'A week last Wednesday.'

'What was he like?' Belsey asked.

'Quiet.'

'Did he like to have two girls with him?'

'No. I don't know why he wanted me there. Then, when we met Pierce, I spent most of the time with him and Alexei stayed with Jessica.'

'They were close, Devereux and Jessica?'

'They were in love.' Lucy lowered her gaze to the carpet as she said this. Suddenly she seemed young, with her defences down.

'And what about Alexei and Pierce? Did they know each other well?'

'No. They just met that night. They got talking.'

'Really?'

'Really what?'

'They just met and started talking?'

'I think so.'

'About what?'

'Business. They wouldn't let us hear.'

'Do you think maybe Devereux knew Pierce was going to be there?'

'Maybe. Pierce said he was there a lot. He liked playing blackjack and a game called craps.'

'Did he pay you?'

'Mr Devereux paid.'

'Did Pierce know you were working?'

She shrugged. He figured there were scenes where everyone was working one way or another.

'What else do you remember about Pierce Buckingham?'

'He had cold hands,' she said. And she looked very young and very lost now. Belsey got off the bed and pulled a seat out from a dressing table. He leaned towards her but not too close.

'I think I can find out what's going on here, what happened to your friend. I can make sure that you're not in danger. But I need you to tell me what you know.'

She reached under her mattress and pulled out a menu: a single, printed piece of paper headed 'Villa Bianca'. She gave it to him.

'Did you go here?'

'No, they did. She gave it to me.'

'A menu?'

'Look on the back.'

Belsey turned it over. Someone had written a short note with an expensive pen. It was the same elegant handwriting as the suicide note.

'Dear Jessie

You have made me so happy. I know I can't tell you everything and that upsets you. You say we don't know each other. But does love always mean knowing someone? Maybe you could love someone you don't know very well at all. Is that possible? My snow tiger, my little fighter and dreamer – whatever happens, I think we know each other now.

It was signed 'A', with a single kiss. Belsey read the note again. *Snow tiger*. It was touching. It was odd. His vision of Devereux became more complicated once again.

'When did she give this to you?'

'The night before she died.'

'Why did she want you to have it?'

'In case something bad happened.'

He turned the menu face up again. It was dated Sunday 8 February. The day's special was salmon tortellini. It matched the receipt in Devereux's wallet. It seemed to Belsey something bad happened soon after.

'I think she would want you to help us find out who did it,' he said.
'That's all I know.'

'What did Mr Devereux sound like? What was his accent?'

'Something foreign. It's hard to say, he spoke so quietly. He didn't like speaking. He said his English wasn't good.'

'It's OK in the note.'

'I guess so.' She thought about this.

'Did Devereux mention a project?' he asked.

'What do you mean?'

'Something he was working on.'

'I don't know. They were excited about something. They got champagne.'

'Why?'

'Something had come up. An opportunity.'

'Do you think it was this opportunity that got Jessica killed?'

'She was worried something would happen. She knew it.'

'What did she know?' Lucy shook her head, empty of everything apart from confusion. 'She looked up to you. Bought the same clothes,' Belsey said.

'Yes.'

'She was a quiet kid. Then Mr Devereux comes along and sees in her everything she wanted him to see.'

'She wasn't quiet. Not inside.'

'What was she?'

Lucy thought about this. 'She was sad. Mr Devereux changed her. He was kind, wealthy. They were going to run away and live together.'

He was wealthy. It didn't tell Belsey much that he didn't already know. There are people who get called rich and there are people who get called wealthy. There aren't many who get called kind in the process.

'Why do you do it?'

'What?'

'Turn tricks.'

'I'm on my gap year.'

Belsey laughed. He felt bad for laughing but couldn't help it.

'That's a big gap,' he said.

270

'I need the money.'

He heard footsteps: two people coming up the stairs.

'But what do you want?' He looked at her. All he saw was a young girl who'd lost a friend, or as close as things got to a friend; saw she was all alone in the world with a nice home, too many clothes, and an endless supply of men who'd pay to sleep with her. 'Where were they running away to?' he said.

'I don't know. Somewhere far, Jess said. But she couldn't decide.'

'Couldn't decide what?'

'Whether to go with him.'

Belsey thought once more about the letter in the handbag. She'd decided. The question was why Devereux never made the rendezvous to find out. Lucy began to cry. She reached for a box of tissues beside her pillow. Her father opened the bedroom door.

'What's going on?' he said. The mother appeared beside him in a matching dressing gown, clutching a small white dog.

'Lucy?' she said. 'Precious?'

The mother had good teeth. The whole family had good teeth.

44

Belsey tore back into town to meet Max Kovar at the
Ritz. On Charing Cross Road he stopped and ducked into an adult video
emporium. Its ground floor was disguised as a bookstore. Most people
headed straight for its basement leaving the shelves of yellowing hardbacks deserted. Belsey found a glossy monograph with a painting of a
horse on the cover, shook the security tag onto the floor and walked out.
In the pub next door he asked for a pen. He wrote 'To Max Kovar' on
the first page, and signed Devereux's name beneath.

Details. A con rides on the details; the subconscious.

Belsey arrived at the hotel just in time. The Rivoli was shifting clientele, from dining tourists to late-night bar sharks. It was as splendidly
tasteless as he remembered. He called Charlotte's mobile from the bar's
phone.

'Hey, Charlotte. I know it's late.'

'I thought you'd forgotten about me.'

'I remembered you,' Belsey said. 'I got you a present. He's called Pierce
Buckingham and he died in EC4 this evening.'

'You shouldn't have.'

'It's being played quiet, so feel special.'

'I heard there'd been a shooting in the City. They haven't released a
name. I didn't hear any more.'

'You probably won't, unless you hear it from me. Pierce Buckingham:
that's your name. But move fast because they're going to try to suffo-

cate this. Buckingham connects to investors going by the name of the Hong Kong Gaming Consortium. He was drinking with Devereux a week last Wednesday.'

'Where do I look?'

'You could start with an investigations firm called PS Security. You've already met one of their operatives. Take a look at their working relationship with serving police officers close to Chief Superintendent Northwood. At the very least it will give you some leverage.' Belsey watched Kovar walk in. 'Listen, Charlotte,' he said. 'Do me a favour and call back on this number in three minutes, say it's Alexei Devereux.'

'What?'

'It would be doing me a huge favour. I've got to go.'

'Wait –'

Belsey hung up and told the barman he was expecting a call. Kovar had taken a table at the back. Belsey joined him.

'You're punctual,' he said. They shook hands. Belsey saw a few dark suits in the lobby outside who may have been security, and may have belonged to Kovar, but the speculator had come into the bar alone. 'Here.' Belsey gave him the book. He watched him open it and read the inscription.

'Well, that's very kind. Where's Mr Devereux?'

'There's been some trouble.' Belsey glanced around the bar with what he hoped looked like a combination of caution and impatience. 'He's sorting it out.'

'What sort of trouble?'

'You'll see. It might work in your favour.'

'What do you mean?'

Belsey fixed Kovar with a stare. 'The thing you told us about Pierce Buckingham – well, we acted.'

'What's happened?'

'You were right. And now we'd like to reward you with a proposal.'

'Like what?'

The barman came over. 'You have a phone call, sir. An Alexei Devereux.'

'Oh.' Belsey glanced at the watch. 'Would you excuse me?' he said to Kovar. The message had had an electrifying effect on the speculator. He excused Belsey. Belsey took the call at the bar.

'What is this?' Charlotte said.

'I think you're very special,' Belsey said. He hung up and came back. 'Well, the good news is he likes you or he wouldn't have phoned to apologise.' Kovar nodded. 'The bad news is that he sends his apologies.'

Kovar took this well, all things considered.

'The proposal,' he said.

'What proposal?'

'When Mr Devereux called, you were saying you had a proposal.'

'Thirty per cent. That was the slice Buckingham was responsible for and now we need it covered. That was going to be the Hong Kong Gaming share but they're out of the picture. A clean thirty per cent and it's yours if you want it.'

'Thirty per cent of what?'

Belsey rolled his eyes. 'Jesus Christ, Max. Mr Devereux told me you'd be hard, but now you're testing my patience.'

'Listen,' Kovar said. 'Before I put money into a project I like to smell it. Do you understand? I smell what I'm investing in. I touch it, I taste it. That's why I travel. That's why I'm here.'

'Delay your flight. I'll give you something in the next twenty-four hours and you can taste it or do whatever you want with it. I can get you another room if you need one. You can use one of our jets if you have a problem arranging travel.'

'Delay my flight? Can you give me some indication of what I can look forward to?'

'Do you really not know?' Belsey said.

'No.'

'I can't talk about it here. Will you be in London tomorrow?'

'I guess I'll have to be.' Kovar was exasperated. He looked like someone who'd never been played before. Now he was the one chasing, and that was the best way to remind someone they wanted something. When someone sees themselves chasing it's hard for them to believe they're wrong.

'Listen, Max, I'll give you a piece of advice, because I think you'd be good to work with. Buckingham was a crook, but he made Mr D feel loved. Do you know what I mean?'

274

'I think so.'

'The window of opportunity, the window in which to demonstrate your love, is becoming increasingly small. We'll be moving on from London in the next day or so.'

'I see.'

'So prepare yourself for a speedy handover. If there was anything you wanted to give Mr Devereux. And don't pay too much attention to what they're going to say on the news.'

'About what?'

'About Pierce Buckingham's death.'

Kovar looked bewildered. Belsey shook his hand and got up from the table, moving rapidly out of the bar, towards Piccadilly Circus.

City of London Police divided into two territorial divisions, with stations at Snow Hill and Bishopsgate, and an HQ at Wood Street. The shooting was geographically closest to Wood Street, and Wood Street was the base for Specialist Crime. Belsey guessed this was where he'd find them. He walked into the front inquiry office and there was a crowd of detectives lining up beside the reception desk, saying they'd been requested to attend by Chief Inspector Walker, regarding the shooting.

'He's in an urgent meeting with senior officials,' the Duty Constable explained. 'You can wait in the office.'

They shook their heads wearily and went up. Belsey walked around the block, found an empty box file in a skip and came back, flashing his badge.

'Nick Belsey for Chief Inspector Walker.'

'He's not taking anyone at the moment. Everyone's waiting in the office.' Belsey sighed. The door buzzed and he walked through to the stairs.

The Specialist Crime office was big enough to accommodate ten separate workstations, with three more offices to the side and a door to a conference room at the far end. It had already filled with officers, and the air was stale. Thirteen men and women gathered beneath harsh fluorescent strip lights: inspectors, sergeants, detective constables, waiting in the open-plan area. They leaned on desks or paced, gripping paper cups of coffee, all with one eye on the conference-room door. There were a lot of anxious faces.

'Where's the Chief?' Belsey said. One nodded to the conference room. Belsey headed for the door.

'I wouldn't if I was you.' This came from a DS with a moustache and a south London accent, restlessly tapping an unlit Benson on its packet.

'We're all waiting,' said a second man: a lanky grey inspector Belsey half recognised from the Money Laundering Unit. Belsey stood exasperated in the centre of the room.

'So what the fuck's going on here?' he said. He went and poured himself a coffee.

'Are you from Murder Squad?'

'Operation Fortress. City Gun Crime Unit.'

'Walker's in with brass. We've been told to hold tight.'

Belsey asked the frustrated officers what they knew. It seemed that something about Buckingham had set off a silent alarm. According to the waiting talent, two MPs, a civil servant and several officers from Special Branch were holed up in the conference room, with a total media ban imposed, which left a lot of elite detectives sitting on their hands and shooting theories.

'It can't be Buckingham,' Belsey said.

'It would be about time,' someone muttered.

'Bucking Bronco?' Another officer laughed. 'I always said he'd dig himself a hole.'

Belsey propped himself discreetly in a corner. He imagined going to sleep. He listened.

'Not exactly short of enemies,' one man chipped in.

'We were a couple of days from getting our hands on his Italian accounts when the judge fell out of a window.'

The phone rang. The tall money-laundering expert picked it up and then turned to the room. 'It's Bronco, no doubts,' he announced.

'Well, no one's going to be shedding many tears.'

'I am,' the DS said. 'This is going to be a bloody nightmare.' He picked up a lighter and headed out.

A DI from Snow Hill station flicked through a file. 'Financial adviser,' she snorted. 'That's a nice way of putting it.'

'Glorified arse-kisser to the criminal elite.'

They passed around Buckingham's sheets: a lot of work in West Africa and Egypt and finally the United Arab Emirates, where he was first linked to the Hong Kong Gaming Consortium. The DS with the moustache came back in, clutching his mobile.

'We might as well go home.'

According to the DS, staff from the FBI London bureau were on their way now. The rumour was rendered more plausible when the Snow Hill DI spoke.

'We got a request from the US Securities and Exchange Commission four days ago, saying they had an investor who thought Buckingham was up to no good. The next day the SEC call again saying the whole thing had been taken off their hands and we should forget we ever heard about it. Buckingham had connected to certain friends in the East. Key associates.'

'Maybe that's who was flying in,' the lanky Inspector said. 'I heard the Branch have got details of eight private flights into London last Saturday. Big boys. No one knows why they were here, but Buckingham's name came up as party organiser.'

'Can I see the file?' Belsey asked.

'Be my guest,' the woman from Snow Hill said tiredly.

Belsey flicked through the sheaf of notes and forms. He found the memo from a Lt Stephen Maynard of the US Securities and Exchange Commission, responding to a complaint by a Texan investor with 'significant concerns' over a deal between the Hong Kong Gaming Consortium and AD Development. There was a further memo regarding an Austrian Sparbuch account that might have been the sink for a lot of sweetener. He felt a jolt of familiarity at the account number. He gave the file back.

Still no one was touching the phones. The conference-room door remained shut. Seeing Devereux's account in the file had been like coming across something personal, details of a dream he had never told anyone. But this dream was shared.

The doors to the conference room opened and Chief Inspector Walker emerged, his face pale and strained.

'Can anyone tell me why Pierce Buckingham was running around last weekend, trying to raise thirty-eight million pounds in twenty-four hours?'

45

BELSEY LEFT THE ROOM. HE WALKED DOWN THE CORRIDOR
to a deserted office, picked up a phone and dialled 9 for an outside line.
When it connected he called up the Raiffeisen Zentralbank. *Thirty-eight
million*, he thought. He looked around the office: a chart of investment
banks and corporate ownership, a list of names and pending Suspicious
Activity Reports. He was in Economic Crime. He laughed. The bank
answered on the third ring.

'*Guten Tag*,' Belsey said.

'*Guten Abend*. Can I have your account number, sir?' It was a man this
time. Belsey gave the account number. For all his gall, he didn't feel reckless. What could be less conspicuous than a call to an Austrian bank from an
Economic Crime office? An office no one would ever know he'd been in?

'Is that Mr Devereux?' the man said.

'That's correct.'

'Can I have your password?'

'Jessica,' Belsey said. He spelt it for him. He waited.

'Thank you, one moment.' He didn't dare breathe. 'I'm just bringing
up your details,' the man said.

Belsey's heart soared. The door handle turned. Four officers walked
in. They frowned at the sight of him, and he hung up.

'The wife's not happy,' Belsey said.

* * *

He drove back to north London, buzzing on triumph. He could see his future and it was lavish. What a dumb password. People think their obsessions are the most secret part of them. But they are all the same. Nothing's more obvious than a secret – you learn that as a detective. That's why you attend to the mundane: the brand someone smokes, how they take their coffee; everything they don't think about.

He parked on the street and sprinted into Devereux's home, calling the Austrian bank from the study and giving the password.

'Yes, sir?'

'I want to make a transfer to a company account held with the Bank of the South Pacific.'

'How much?'

'Everything. In instalments of ten grand a day until it's empty.'

'Were you intending to pay a sum into your account first?'

'No. Why?'

'There is currently a balance of two euros.'

'Two euros.'

'Yes, sir.'

Belsey hung up. He poured a drink. The fantasy caved in and left an awful silence.

The US Securities and Exchange Commission operated out of Atlanta. It was 9 p.m. in Atlanta. Belsey thought of the memo of theirs he had seen in Wood Street and wondered what they knew about Devereux's secret Sparbuch account. After ten minutes being passed around the voicemail of various US departments he was put through to the Office of International Affairs and when he told them what he was calling about they gave him the number for Maynard's 'cell phone'. The lieutenant answered in a noisy restaurant.

'Who's this?'

'Lieutenant Maynard? I'm calling from New Scotland Yard. It's about Alexei Devereux.'

'Hang on.'

Belsey heard the lieutenant push through doors to somewhere silent.

'Who am I speaking to?'

'Detective Constable Nick Belsey. I work in the Financial Investigations Unit of New Scotland Yard, London. I came across your name in conjunction with AD Development and Alexei Devereux.'

'What's going on with him?'

'I think I can help,' Belsey said. 'What is it you're investigating?'

'We got a heads-up from an individual who'd been approached about an AD Development project. This is a very influential person coming to us in confidence. He felt something wasn't quite right so I agreed to look into the company. By the time I got there it had disappeared.'

'What do you mean?'

'The draw-down started 7 a.m. Monday morning, three accounts in the name of AD Development closed for good, funds emptied into eight shell companies on the British Virgin Islands. Half a million in cash is withdrawn. The person then opens two new accounts on the islands and splits the cash between them. Then he closes these down. We can only trace one half, which is moved over two days through eight front companies in Andorra. He uses one of those companies to buy twenty-seven more dormant companies stretched from Luxembourg to Delaware. That's where the paper trail ends. I think the banks he's using are ones he bought himself, offshore, licences paid in the last twelve months. That's why we're having no luck with them, and aren't likely to any time soon. Do you know anything about this guy?'

'He died last Sunday.'

'Well, he's been busy in hell.'

Every penny had been shipped out of reach. Someone a lot slicker than Belsey had drained Devereux dry. You can't take it with you, they say, but he was starting to feel like Devereux might have tried.

'Did you see London activity from him?' Belsey asked Maynard.

'No, I checked all EU countries and couldn't turn up one report.'

'There was one Suspicious Activity Report,' Belsey said. 'From Christie's auction house in London, dated 29 January.'

'There isn't any SAR from London. I checked.'

'You didn't see one? Five hundred grand cash.'

'I didn't see anything. I'm struggling over here. I'm saying this is one of the biggest frauds I've seen and no one gets it.'

Belsey hung up and called New Scotland Yard. The phone was eventually answered by a night duty officer for the Specialist Investigations Department. It took another five minutes to persuade him to run a check on the SAR. Ten minutes later he could confirm there was no Suspicious Activity Report. They hadn't logged any SARs from Christie's for eight months. It seemed Inspector Philip Ridpath was inventing his own excuses to chase Devereux.

46

Belsey found Devereux's last bottle of vodka in the freezer. He sat in the study in front of the bloodstain, drinking. No SAR, he thought; what the hell had Ridpath been playing at? And then he didn't care any more. He was exhausted; the raised hopes had led him to a crash. Now perhaps he could sleep. He raised a toast to Pierre Smirnoff; comrade, old friend. The phone began to ring. Belsey drank. He didn't want to see the antique furnishings any longer. The phone kept ringing and Belsey picked it up.

'What's going on?' a man said.

'Nothing,' Belsey said. 'It's fucked. Get out of here.'

'Who is this?'

'Who is this?' Belsey said.

'What's going on?'

Belsey hung up. He answered again when it rang a second later.

'Mr Devereux?' a different voice this time.

'Speaking.'

'Nothing you said was what you promised it would be.' The caller was struggling with the English; thin vowels, Latino or maybe even Chinese. Furious, which didn't help.

'That, my friend, is life,' Belsey said. '*C'est la vie. Así es la vida.*'

'No thing at all. Now a lot of people are unhappy.'

'A lot of people are always unhappy,' Belsey said. He put the receiver down on the desk.

'Hello?' it said. 'Don't fuck me around.'

Belsey lay on the floor and shut his eyes. When he opened them there was a man standing in the doorway.

47

'It was open.'

Detective Inspector Philip Ridpath paused with his black brogue raised where it had prodded the door. It took him a moment to recognise the individual on the carpet.

'Detective Constable Belsey,' he said finally.

'Detective Inspector Ridpath.' Belsey got up. There was no way of doing it elegantly. Ridpath had his hands deep in the pockets of his overcoat. He appeared more crumpled than before, and smaller than Belsey remembered, but with the same animal-like inquisitiveness. He stared at Belsey, then at the receiver on the desk, still cursing: '*You mother fuck, you die . . .*' then back to the front door, to The Bishops Avenue, his expression melting very slowly from suspicion to concern.

'Welcome,' Belsey said.

Ridpath stepped over the threshold of the study like a priest entering a brothel. He looked around the shelves, peered at the bloodstain, then went back through the hallway to the living room. Belsey dropped the phone in its cradle and followed. Ridpath nudged a fallen decanter with the toe of his shoe.

'Looks like he went out with a bang,' Belsey said.

'How did you get in?' Ridpath demanded.

'With a key.'

'Do you have a warrant?'

'No.'

The Inspector winced. 'Have you touched anything?

'Hardly at all,' Belsey said. 'What brought you here?'

Ridpath walked to the French windows and tried the handle. 'What have you learned about him?'

'He had a nice house and not much else, as far as I can tell. He liked his towels tied with ribbons.'

Belsey sat at the breakfast bar and tried to sober up. He watched the Inspector circulate the ground floor. Ridpath put on a set of forensic gloves to open the doors. At each door he turned the knob, paused, then opened it. Then he stood in the doorway, staring. Belsey watched him go upstairs, then he picked the cognac up off the floor, took a final swig and placed it back on top of the cabinet. He went up to the first floor where he saw the Inspector kneeling at the side of Devereux's bed like a child in prayer. Ridpath rose, stiffly, arms tensed by his side and walked to the master bathroom, looked along the line of aftershave bottles, then punched the door frame.

'Are you OK?' Belsey said.

'Yes.'

Belsey went back to the living room and half considered running. Running and never stopping. He heard Ridpath call.

'Look at this.'

Belsey found the Inspector in Devereux's garage standing beside the pile of leftover goods.

'Someone's tried to strip the place.'

'The Egyptians used to load up the dead with possessions, for the journey.'

'He wasn't Egyptian. And there's no car.' He turned a full circle, then seemed to fully grasp Belsey's presence for the first time. 'What are you up to here?'

'What's Project Boudicca?' Belsey said.

'What do you know about that?'

'I know you're going to talk to me about it while we have a drink, about why you're working a case in secret and faking SARs; you can tell me why no one knows you're working it and you're still chasing a man after his death. Then I'll leave you alone.'

Ridpath held on to an expression of righteous defiance.

'I don't drink on duty,' he said.

'I don't think you're really on duty,' Belsey said.

48

RIDPATH HAD A BATTERED VOLVO PARKED OUTSIDE
Devereux's home. They climbed in. 2 a.m. in the north-London suburbs
didn't present many options for a nightcap. Belsey directed them to West
End Lane, to a basement bar called Lately's, a divorcee pickup joint with
a shutter in the door through which they assessed your eligibility. The
detectives must have looked rich or desperate because the door opened
and they were nodded downstairs.

The nightclub was very dark and close to empty. Small tables nudged
a dance floor big enough for two or three. Sticky booths with UV lights
lined the side of the room. The lights picked out curling photographs
of previous partygoers, arms around the old owner. Ridpath scrutinised
the place.

'Is it safe to talk here?'

'It's about the only safe thing you can do.'

Belsey set up some overpriced beers and let the Inspector gather his
thoughts. When he spoke, Ridpath was still looking at the empty dance
floor, his eyes deep with memory.

'You want to know why I'm still pursuing Alexei Devereux?'

'Yes.'

'He ruined my life.'

Belsey nodded. Already he had the sense that this was Ridpath's big
moment, and he was providing the audience. 'How did he do that?'

'I've read every report on Devereux, every transcript. Not just ours, but those in Paris, Rome and the scraps that Washington will share. I'm saying this because I want you to know that I've been interested in Devereux for a long time.'

'OK. So what do you know?'

'Where do you want me to start?'

'Start at the beginning.'

There was a wicked twinkle in Ridpath's eye, like a man holding a flush when the world thinks they're bluffing.

'Born Alex Demochev, Odessa, 2 February 1957. His parents were local party stalwarts. Their loyalty wasn't repaid. They were killed by the secret police in 1963, after a show trial. By all accounts they were passionate about the cause. But it seems there were party wranglings. Loyal sacrifices to Stalinism.

'Under the name Alexei Devinsky he becomes a young ideologue. At sixteen he's writing speeches for local party Communists, very brilliant, tipped for top things in propaganda. But he got in trouble for organising a gambling racket among the local workers. They used to race rats. At seventeen, he escapes a reformatory in Leningrad and smuggles himself to Paris. He began forging connections in the banking community, worked for an underwriter, changed his name to Devereux. Became an entrepreneur.'

Belsey wondered at the obsession in Ridpath's eyes. They caught the coloured lights of the basement bar, as did his gleaming brow. His little moustache twitched. He looked a long way removed from his own life; alive, by proxy, through Devereux.

'Everyone who met him – in Paris, Prague, Amsterdam – they all say how intriguing he was. How charismatic.' Ridpath made the word sound glutinous. 'He had beautiful manners – apparently he bedded several wives of local captains of industry. That may be why he left both Paris and Prague at short notice. He went back to Russia in 1992. People say he funded perestroika from afar. But he got back in time for the kill. Do you know much about the oligarchs?'

'Tell me about them.'

'People in the right place and time for the sell-off of a superpower. Everything must go. The summer sale included its military.'

'Right.'

'The world's second largest military complex divided up between four or five individuals who happened to have the cash and connections at the right time. Dmitri Kovalevski got a lot of uranium, Vladimir Shchepetov the hardware. Devereux asked for the sports facilities.'

'The sports facilities,' Belsey said. Ridpath drank his beer and licked his lips.

'Hundreds of Red Army gyms, tracks, sports equipment. That's what he wanted. People thought he was mad. Then he bought up floodlights. The army had a lot of floodlights, first used in the film studios after the revolution, then to blind the Nazis on the battlefield. He bought them. No one knew what he was doing.'

'What *was* he doing?'

'He saw that you didn't need anyone at a racetrack except the jockeys and the horses and a camera. It meant he could run them through the night and broadcast live images to the UAE, Hong Kong, Singapore. He knew people who needed to sink money – money from embezzlements, money from sharp trades in weaponry and natural gas – and he persuaded them to sink it into these tracks. His first big international partner was the Iroquois tribe in New York State. They built a race-course for him on their reservation. Last year he bought up a stretch of the Margow Desert in Afghanistan for a combination mall, track and casino. That was when he got the reputation for disaster capitalism. The US still pay him to hold the land. Six months later he set up a casino resort on the site of an old Pennsylvania ore pit, which he bought for a cent.'

'And how did this ruin your life?'

Ridpath took a deep breath and a long swig of beer.

'I was investigating him. Once. This was two years ago. I wasn't always doing my current job. I was head of International Liaison. That was the capacity in which I met him.'

'You met him?'

'I interviewed him. As far as I know I'm the only UK officer to have done so, maybe the only European one. He visited London for a weekend in spring 2007 and I was told to pay a discreet visit. We met at a hotel. It was an interview of sorts, one I'll never forget, though I'm not sure who was interviewing who. Nothing came of it. Then, two months later, I was suddenly tasked with coordinating his arrest on tax evasion and theft charges. He was flying into City Airport on a private jet and I had forty men in place. That took a fortnight of planning. Devereux landed at Biggin Hill instead. He sent a decoy to City Airport – a team of gymnasts. The charges were dropped a week later. I don't know why, but I have a few guesses and most of them have noughts on the end. Subsequent to that episode, I was moved from the department. Sideways they call it. There's no such thing as sideways. I got a card from Devereux saying good luck in your new job.'

'What was he like?'

'Apart from a bastard? The most oddly charming person you'll ever meet. I remember that he spoke in an incredibly measured way, never raising his voice – and he'd meet your eyes and appear interested in all you had to say in turn. Because he *was* interested, you see. He thought he could profit out of everyone he met. But he revealed nothing of himself. You only realised this afterwards. It felt as if you might not have really met him at all.' The Inspector paused, as if still wondering. 'Then, two weeks ago, I heard he was here again. I wanted to know what was going on.'

'What did you find?'

'Nothing. So I knew he'd arrived.'

Belsey saw the Inspector more clearly now. All detectives know that you can fall into an investigation and get stuck. Sometimes, out of nowhere, a case you didn't even think you were that invested in starts spreading its tendrils – into your home, your bed, your dreams. At police training college, before every exercise, one of the instructors liked to say: *When you've finished, stop.* It was his only joke, and the best advice Belsey received.

'Ever thought of getting your revenge?' Belsey asked.

'What do you mean?'

'Cutting his throat, maybe?'

Ridpath levelled a stare. 'Are you suggesting I'm involved in Mr Devereux's death?'

'I haven't. But I could, I suppose.'

'I'm a police officer.' Belsey laughed. Ridpath said under his breath: 'I'm not like you.'

'What's that meant to mean?'

'What would you call it? Bold?'

'We see bad people get away. That's frustrating.'

'If they get away it's because we haven't built our cases properly.' Ridpath sat up straight. 'He lost me my job. I'm not going to have him lose me my freedom and my dignity. That's not my idea of justice.'

'Got an alibi?'

'Look –'

'Relax. I'm not serious.'

But the Inspector was fired up now. A red flush spread from his throat to his cheeks.

'What were you doing there? What the hell were you doing in his house, Detective Constable? On the floor. With *vodka*. Explain that.'

'Maybe I'm on an investigation of my own,' Belsey said. Ridpath snorted. Belsey persevered. 'What was Devereux up to in London?'

'I never got the chance to find out.'

'This wasn't just exile,' Belsey said. 'He came over with a plan.'

'He always said he loved England, the English countryside.'

'Sure, the sense of humour.'

'The sense of humour, the political freedom.'

'He wasn't here for the sense of humour. He's just over, moved in, barely back from IKEA when he's hustling. He's been cosying up with the Corporation of London who seem to like the idea of a new billion-aire friend. He came to London for a reason. I think he might have come to Hampstead for a reason.'

Belsey saw a reluctant admission of curiosity in Ridpath's eyes. Now they were doing business.

'I think you're right,' Ridpath said.

'How slippery was Devereux?'

'He was clever. But he was a man of his word.' Ridpath conceded this reluctantly.

'That's what they all say.'

'He told me he was a man of his word and that was why he used so few of them. He had a personal code of conduct. That's what set him apart from the rest.'

'Devereux met a man called Pierce Buckingham at a club called Les Ambassadeurs the week before last,' Belsey said. 'It was Buckingham's haunt but Devereux gets membership. In fact he's there with a couple of girls, one of whom he passes on to Buckingham while they celebrate a new business opportunity. Over the next few days Buckingham raises a lot of money for Devereux. Buckingham's a middleman, he runs between investors with bad names and investments with good margins.'

'Devereux had certain principles. That doesn't mean he wasn't sharp. He didn't let opportunities slip.'

'It looks to me as if he might have made them up himself.'

'Exactly.'

'I don't mean in an entrepreneurial way. I mean pluck them out of thin air. I mean persuade people to invest in projects that weren't as solid as they sounded.'

Ridpath considered this, before shrugging non-committally.

'That's not the Alexei Devereux I knew. You seem to have got an idea into your head. OK, you're not the first to come up with theories about Alexei Devereux.'

'Pierce Buckingham's on a slab now. So is one of the girls there that night, Devereux's one. She's called Jessica Holden. You've heard of her.'

'The Starbucks girl.'

'That's what they're putting on the headstone. Know of a firm called PS Security?'

'I knew Chris Starr when he was in Flying Squad.'

'They were keeping an eye on Devereux. My guess is that it was on behalf of some men who were passing a lot of money in the Russian's direction. Now the money's gone missing and so has one of their investigators. He was on Devereux's tail in Hampstead and took some photographs. I spoke to Chris at the agency yesterday. No sign of him or the precious photographs. Something's gone wrong. The blood around Devereux's body was from a dog, which makes me think the suicide was either rather elaborate or a fake. Devereux was murdered because of Project Boudicca. It would be useful for me to know what it was.'

'Why would it be useful to you?'

'That's my business.'

Ridpath digested all this. Belsey could see the cogs turning.

'Gangsters build their reputations on murder. That's what they are: the threat of violence. Why would they kill Devereux and then pretend it's a suicide?'

'I don't know.'

Neither did Ridpath, it seemed. He frowned, picked up his beer bottle without drinking, and after another minute of reverie said: 'I don't know what Project Boudicca is. But something's still going on now. Something survives him.'

'Like what?'

'Someone's been messing around with Devereux's belongings. A toerag called John Cassidy was picked up last night skipping bail in a hire company Porsche Cayenne that was last signed out to a Mr A. Devereux. I don't think he knew anything about the car but someone did. That might be the someone who's signing for Devereux's plastic – in a souvenir shop in Camden, a chemist's in East Finchley. All this might be low-level identity theft, but they've stolen the wrong identity. And I think they might know more than is good for them.'

This was a moment Belsey had been braced for, only he hadn't expected it to come from so close. 'What have you got on that?' he asked.

'The places these cards are being used, he'll be on one camera or another.'

'Anything else?'

'Yesterday a man called Max Kovar was still talking to people about an opportunity regarding Devereux, something he said he'd just heard about in the last twenty-four hours.'

Belsey felt a fresh injection of anxiety. But even as the new waves of misgiving rolled over him there was a quiet thrill at hearing of what he had set in motion, a morbid fascination with his predicament.

'How is that possible?' he said.

'It's as if the idea of Devereux is too powerful to die.'

A couple joined the dance floor. Belsey checked the time. Quarter to three. When he looked up, Ridpath was staring at the fake Rolex. An unpleasant thought occurred to Belsey. Had Ridpath seen the watch on Devereux? It was an eye-catching watch. Belsey had a vision of Ridpath and Devereux – Ridpath interviewing Devereux – in an anonymous hotel room with the watch as the only standout object in the place, Devereux hypnotising him with the watch.

'Very flash,' Ridpath said, still gazing at the dials. 'Do you even know what all those things do?'

'I don't care. I like the weight. It was a present from my father.'

'Good.'

Now Ridpath turned and stared at the dance floor, at the couple, with a passing look of regret. Belsey told himself he was being paranoid about the watch.

'Do you want to dance?' Belsey said.

'I want to leave here.'

'Nowhere else is open.'

'Do you drink whisky?' Ridpath said.

'I've heard of it. I don't mind giving it a try.'

'I think I have a bottle.'

'At yours?'

'I don't live far.'

'Then what are we waiting for?'

Keep your enemies close, Belsey thought. Keep them drunk. Ridpath conscientiously left his Volvo on West End Lane and they walked in silence towards Kilburn. A fine rain hung in the air. Sirens passed in the darkness and the two men glanced towards the sound with the half-interest of off-duties. They got slowly drenched. They didn't trouble with small talk.

The Inspector lived on the corner of a low, red-brick terrace. His hallway contained a bicycle and a basket of men's shoes. He led Belsey into a living room and gestured feebly towards a sagging sofa. There was an old TV and a lot of papers – work papers – and books on international finance open around the place. The house smelt of old fabrics and chip fat. Ridpath crouched down to turn on a lamp that sat on the floor.

Through a doorway at the end of the room Belsey could see a kitchen that hadn't been redecorated since the 1970s, a sink crowded with crockery, more papers on the kitchen table. He took a towel from a clothes horse in the corner and dried his hair. Ridpath opened a chest of drawers and produced a bottle of Scotch, half in wrapping paper, from among a china set. He went to get glasses. Belsey picked up the bottle. Stuck to the wrapping paper was a good-luck note from Specialist Crime, '*Wishing you well, Philip*'. No such thing as sideways, Belsey thought. Ridpath came back and filled their glasses and sat in an armchair that sank as he lowered himself down.

'I spent a long time wondering what it was that Devereux had,' Ridpath began. 'Then I saw it was secrecy itself. That's what he sells. There are no photographs of him known to exist. He once attended a party in Moscow for five minutes and his minders kept all the guests back until two in the morning, going through their cameras and phones. Secrecy. That's why you never meet him. He calls it the last resource. When all the oil's gone we'll still have our secrets.'

'What are we going to do with them?'

'I don't know.'

Belsey watched Ridpath. He thought about men with too much time on their hands. The devil finds work for them, but so, it seemed, do the angels of justice. What were Ridpath's secrets? They drank. Ridpath grimaced.

'Are you meant to have ice with this?' he asked.

'Do you have ice?'

'No.'

'Then I wouldn't worry about it.'

Ridpath swallowed another few mouthfuls, braced for the burn this time. 'Do you know what a great explorer once said? To be having an adventure is a sign of incompetence.'

'I know the feeling.'

'Devereux would never have started this violence. Violence is the failure of crime, that's what he said to me. Murder is the sign of absolute failure.'

'That's what he said?'

'It was a maxim of his. He was different.'

They finished their drinks and sat for a while. There was plenty of bottle to go. But Ridpath wasn't relaxed. Belsey watched him grip the glass. He thought of what the investigator had said and compared this Devereux, the Devereux of Ridpath's account, to the one whose life he had become acquainted with over the last couple of days.

'I think he'd become a fraudster,' Belsey said. 'He was conning people. Something had gone wrong and he wasn't owning up. That's how he met his end.'

Belsey felt a vague guilt at puncturing Ridpath's fantasy of the man. When someone's ruined your life it's important to respect them, to feel that whatever's destroyed you is worthwhile.

'I'm not sure,' Ridpath said.

'I think the whole London thing was a set-up.'

'Why?'

'Did you see all the catalogues at the house?'

'Yes.'

'What do you make of them?'

Ridpath made a show of considering this, although he was too good a detective not to know the answer.

'Someone setting up a front, trying to create the illusion that the house is occupied.'

'That's what I was thinking.'

'But it was him.'

'So he'd changed styles.'

Ridpath nodded, already onto the next thought.

'You know what the strangest thing is?'

'What?' Belsey asked.

'The girl.'

'Jessica?'

'Yes.' Just thinking about it gave Ridpath a look of bewilderment. 'A relationship. That's the real change of MO. Falling for her.'

'Even billionaires do that sometimes, I'm told.'

'I guess they must do.' Ridpath leaned back in his chair. Belsey refilled their glasses. Ridpath sniffed his drink and stared into the glass. 'I just ask myself: why *that* girl?' he said. 'Out of all the women he could have had.'

'Because she was no one,' Belsey said. 'A teenage escort. She was a blank slate. Maybe he could pretend he was young again. Maybe he felt he was. No one ever denied that fucking an eighteen-year-old could do you wonders.' Ridpath looked up from his glass. 'Maybe he even believed she loved him,' Belsey said.

'You don't think they loved each other?'

'I've no idea if they loved each other. That's not my business. I'm saying that if they did it wasn't by coincidence.' The Inspector considered this. 'She'd have been after rich men, a bit of glamour,' Belsey elaborated. 'Maybe she thought that would give her more of something, more life, whatever. She probably thought she deserved whatever he had to offer. Maybe she was right.'

They were silent for a long time.

'You belittle people,' Ridpath said.

'I haven't belittled anyone. I saw her. She seemed a nice girl.'

'You saw her?'

'I was there, nearby, when the shooting happened,' Belsey said carefully. Ridpath looked at him. Belsey hoped it wasn't with suspicion.

'Did she say anything?'

'Latte with vanilla. Not to me.'

'And you make it a professional job?'

'Forty-eight hours on and no one makes it anything. You don't get that without being professional. Letting off guns in central London, twice now. I think we're dealing with someone international, maybe not worked the UK before, but costs. Someone paid handsomely to get back at Devereux for something, employed by men who keep their fat, manicured hands clean, and give him the resources and intelligence product to perform.' Ridpath nodded. Belsey wasn't sure if he was talking to his friend or his enemy or both, but he felt that talking to the Inspector was getting him closer to understanding Devereux. Ridpath was very good at letting you do the talking, though. Belsey imagined he could be ruthless in an interview room. 'Are you chasing the credit cards?' he said.

'I've got contacts in Card Fraud. I've requested CCTV footage.'

'When are they going to move on it?'

'Soon.'

'How soon?' Belsey said.

'Soon as I can convince them that this is serious. We're meant to be speaking to people first thing tomorrow about getting hold of the tapes: councils, shop owners. There are certain parties who are beginning to realise the significance of someone using Alexei Devereux's identity.'

Belsey stood up and felt his heart flutter.

Bravo, Echo, Lima, Sierra, Echo, Yankee.

India, Sierra.

Foxtrot, Uniform, Charlie, Kilo, Echo, Delta.

A familiar, ominous dismay returned. The tension reached his muscles. He paced, looking along the shelves, thinking hard. Tucked under the old legal volumes were notifications of awards: Association of Police Authorities Award, Queen's Police Commendation. They were incredibly sought-after pieces of card, and usually framed in an office. Ridpath had not got around to framing them.

'You said someone called Kovar was under the impression that Devereux's still in business,' Belsey said.

'That's right.'

'What do you know about him?'

'Max Kovar? He crosses our radar often enough.'

'He has access to a lot of money, right?'

'Kovar is shady. If I was a businessman like Alexei Devereux I wouldn't have anything to do with him. I'm not sure Devereux ever did.'

'What do you think Kovar would offer in return for a bite of this London project?'

'To grease the wheels? I don't know. Why?' Ridpath gave a curious smile. 'Whatever he wanted, I imagine. Kovar and Alexei Devereux? Money is not an issue there.' He stood up and pointed a remote control at the TV set. News came on. 'City Shooting' with footage of the busy chaos that had descended upon the St Clement's Court crime scene. 'Met and City on Gun Alert,' they said. Then a picture of Northwood last Christmas, raising a glass with the Home Secretary, then footage of families criticising the police.

They watched in silence for a few minutes before Ridpath turned it off. He left the room and returned a second later with a blanket and threw it on the sofa.

'Crash here if you want. In a couple of hours we can go to Card Fraud and see if they'll help us find Devereux's identify thief.'

The hospitality took Belsey by surprise, even if it was offered grudgingly. It wasn't a bad idea. He felt a lot more likely to stop Ridpath getting his hands on the images by being with him. He pictured himself accidentally wiping a disk, dropping it down a hole.

'OK,' Belsey said.

'I'll be getting up at five,' Ridpath said on his way out of the room. 'I'm not a big sleeper.'

Belsey waited, listening to the Inspector upstairs, running a tap, closing a door, the creak of bed springs. Belsey lay down. He wondered what Charlotte Kelson was doing, and pictured her sleeping. He barely knew her but he knew what she looked like sleeping. *Does love always mean knowing someone?* What a strange note that had been. He felt mystery settling in layers, like snow.

He gave it half an hour, until he thought he could hear snoring, then tiptoed to the kitchen and lifted the phone off the wall. He eased the kitchen door shut. He dialled Kovar's suite. The man answered on the sixth ring.

'I know it's late,' Belsey said. He spoke very quietly, which was just fine. He spoke like someone in a house with people they didn't want to wake, which was how he imagined very powerful men might speak.

'Not at all.' Kovar cleared phlegm from his throat. 'I saw the news.' It was the first time Belsey had heard Kovar sounding less than commanding.

'You were right about him,' Belsey said. 'He brought us nothing but trouble.'

'I hope I haven't caused yourself or Mr Devereux any complications.'

'It's a world of complications, Max. You don't have to cause them, they're just there.' Belsey imagined he could hear the room Kovar was in; he heard the plush carpet, the wood. He could hear the smoke of the cigar ascending. 'The reason I'm calling at this hour,' Belsey said, 'was that it occurred to me you might need some more precise indication of what we need from you.'

Kovar coughed. 'I think it's best we are straight with one another.' His voice was thick with sleep.

'I've just been talking to Alexei, and I told him how discreet you are compared to Pierce Buckingham. Because now there are sensitivities as well as complications and these sensitivities are costing us.'

'I'm sure,' Kovar said.

'I'll be straight with you. Mr D loves presents.'

'I know,' Kovar said very carefully.

'Something to calm him down after the last few days.'

'I need things too.'

'Sure.'

'If I know this is going ahead, I will make sure that Mr Devereux is not left feeling unappreciated.'

'That's a good way of putting it, Max. We're talking hours rather than days. So long as you know that. I'm going to call you very soon, to finalise the handover.'

'I will need those details,' Kovar said.

'Of course.'

'If everything is in order, the gift will be ready.'

'Excellent.'

'Goodnight, Jack.'

Belsey returned to the living room and lay down, heart pounding, watching headlights cross the ceiling and thinking about the things that money can buy. He hadn't expected to sleep but the whisky must have done its job because at some point he woke up. The door was open. Belsey saw the Inspector's silhouette approaching slowly. Ridpath moved, one step at a time, towards him and touched the pile of Belsey's clothes on the rug and finally touched the blanket. So, Belsey thought, that was the score. It wasn't the first time it had happened. But Ridpath wasn't his type.

Belsey made a good deal of noise turning over, making like he'd been disturbed but not fully woken. It was enough to bring the blanket around him tighter, to say he was on the verge of waking and maybe even causing a scene. Ridpath backed off. After another second the door closed again and Belsey almost felt sorry for him.

That's how it works, Belsey thought. You dig down, through the layers of mystery, the crime and obsession, and you get someone trying to touch someone else's skin. A bit of warmth, a moment of contact all wrapped up in a lot of trouble and fuss.

He didn't go back to sleep. Ten minutes later he got up, dressed quietly and slipped out of the front door.

49

North again, across a silent West End Lane, over the deserted junction of Swiss Cottage to Hampstead. He collected the Peugeot from The Bishops Avenue and returned it to the police station. Then he walked to South End Green. Instinct had led him to Hampstead. Instinct now kept him away from Devereux's old home. Ridpath's appearance had infected Belsey's sense of The Bishops Avenue as a secure hiding place: that and the attention of Pierce Buckingham, the soon-to-be attention of City Police . . . He would not be sleeping on The Bishops Avenue again.

He walked into the Royal Free Hospital. It was hushed, the nocturnal city of vigil-keepers, A&E nurses, cleaning staff going about their businesses without noise. It always made him feel safe. He passed the cafe, the medical school library, the Radiology Unit, and arrived at the multi-faith chapel. Lights flickered on as he entered. Faith reduced to its common ground looked like the waiting room of an upmarket dentist's surgery: magnolia walls and fake plants in white vases. A single, carpeted step led up to an altar. Belsey knelt on the step with his forehead against the laminated wood and then he curled up behind the altar and slept.

He woke to the sound of trolleys rattling down the corridor. It was Sunday. It felt like the last time he would ever wake up in London.

He walked back through the ground floor, sliced the binding on a block of papers outside the hospital shop and stole a selection. *The Times* went with 'CITY EXECUTION KILLING' and a picture of Monument in a web of red-and-white tape. The *Guardian* led with 'DARK SIDE OF THE CITY: DEAL UNRAVELS WITH BLOODY CONSEQUENCES'. They had also got hold of Buckingham's name and had been busy untangling his associates. But only the *Mail on Sunday* made the leap, placing Buckingham's photograph side by side with one of Jessica Holden. The photograph of Buckingham showed him on a catamaran, smiling, in mirrored shades. They tagged him as an 'independent financier', which was polite. The headline declared 'POLICE: "SHOOTINGS CONNECT"'. Charlotte Kelson got the credit. But when you turned to the continuation on page 4 it became clear that not all police were promoting this link. In fact, within the story was another one of splits in senior command – and in the centre was Chief Superintendent Northwood.

Charlotte threw a lot of flak in his direction, using unnamed sources to suggest he was out of his depth and possibly compromised. It closed with a tantalising nod to 'Private investigations firm PS Security', who had refused to comment on their involvement. Belsey was impressed. It wouldn't have taken her long to see that Northwood lacked the necessary skills for true corruption. But his friends in PS and their lack of discrimination over clients had dragged him in. And Northwood was not a man to cast himself as the hero of a murder investigation on any reckoning.

At 8 a.m. on a Sunday he expected the CID office to be empty. But from the first-floor corridor he could see someone sitting at his desk. Belsey held back. It was Inspector Tim Gower, rifling through the drawers. He had Belsey's files open and their contents stacked across the surface. Belsey walked in.

'What's going on?' he said.

Gower looked up. His face bore the grey tension of someone who'd been woken by his bosses at 3 a.m. and wasn't going to get back to bed any time soon.

'City Police want you to go into Wood Street,' he said.

'Why?'

'This shooting yesterday. Have you heard about it?'

'Just the headlines.'

'It's an individual called Pierce Buckingham. He's been associated with a man who died recently in Hampstead called Alexei Devereux. I believe you dealt with the body.'

'That's right.'

Gower glanced up, then continued sifting.

'Well, I'm told this is going to explode in the next few hours, and they want to speak to you.'

'OK.'

'And there's some balls-up with the IPCC thing – I've not had anything from them in the internal.'

'I got a call from Nigel Herring. He said they sympathised with my position and were doing everything possible to keep me in my job.'

'OK.' Gower barely seemed to hear this. 'Wood Street want you to take any relevant paperwork in with you.' He shifted a pile of papers back into Belsey's drawer and sat back, wiping his brow. 'Nick?'

'Yes, sir?'

'Did we overlook anything? Was there cause for suspicion?'

'It was a straightforward suicide. I'm sure the coroner agreed. I'll check.'

Belsey took a squad car and drove by The Bishops Avenue. Two police cars and a forensics van sat outside Devereux's home. He sped up and continued down to East Finchley. He still had almost forty pounds of Cassidy's payment left. Forty pounds didn't seem the foundation for the new life he had anticipated. He imagined Kovar waiting for his call, with a million pounds in a case by the phone. Belsey just needed to know what Devereux had been selling. That was all the speculator wanted to hear.

He called Wood Street from East Finchley tube station.

'This is Nick Belsey. I believe you wanted to speak to me.'

'Yes. You know something about Alexei Devereux.'

'Very little. I found the body, that's all.'

'Can you come in?'

It was a male officer. He sounded reasonable, not suspicious; intelligent even. If they had something on Belsey they would jump him in the street, not play games. But it wouldn't be long now.

'You want me in today?' Belsey said.

'Immediately. We believe your suicide case connects to something called Project Boudicca.'

'Boudicca?'

'So does the man who got shot last night.'

'Oh,' Belsey said.

'We've found quite a few interesting things about Boudicca.'

'What are they?'

'When can you come in? Shall we send a car?'

Belsey drove himself to Wood Street, through the silent City, its gleaming monoliths abandoned to security guards and the occasional tourist. Twice he thought he saw a motorbike following; twice it disappeared. He concentrated on the immediate threat, and formulated a story to give the City detectives. It was that of a police officer who found a body; who felt something might not be right but didn't chase it. He hoped none of the men and women present at Wood Street last night would still be around to recognise him. If it came to it, he was ready to sprint.

In the event there were only five people in the Specialist Investigations office. None were survivors from the previous night's excitement. The man Belsey had spoken to, DCI Malcolm Gray, was in his thirties. He appeared alert and upwardly mobile. His colleague, DI Deborah Mullins, was short and fiery in executive pinstripes.

'Thanks for coming in,' they said. They shook his hand and ushered him into the conference room that had been so impregnable a few hours ago. It had been cleaned and aired. A varnished oval table occupied the centre of the room, crowded with overlapping copies of files. One dirty double-glazed window looked down over the City.

They had a map of EC4 up on a flip chart, with an X for the body. Beside it was a whiteboard with a name: Pierce Buckingham, caught in a web of individuals and corporations associated with the Hong Kong Gaming Consortium. On the right-hand side was a list of times from 2 a.m. the previous morning to the hour of his death – with known locations, calls, addresses, including sightings by Hampstead police station and one close to All Hallow's Church. Belsey felt the touch of Buckingham's hand.

On a separate board they had written the name Alexei Devereux.

Around it, they'd filled in some of his business interests – TGT, Polsky – but it was a work in progress. Finally, at the far end of the room, they had taped sheets with lists of flight details – times, countries of origin – and then hotels in London – Sheraton, Park Lane Hilton, Grosvenor. Everything converged on Saturday 7 February, where they'd written 'Location of London Meeting' and then a big, red question mark.

Gray opened a notebook.

'Talk me through what you know about Alexei Devereux.'

Belsey started with the missing person report. He talked about having an initial look at the property, getting called back, finding the safe room. He gave them a bit on his Internet research and the *Ham & High* article so as not to seem wilfully ignorant. He left out Ridpath's SAR, the faked petition, Milton Granby.

'What did you find in the home?' Gray said.

Belsey thought his way through. He told them. He talked about conspicuous wealth and the odd undertone of transience. He didn't say 'a vision of myself as someone better', or 'a way out of the insolvent cul-de-sac my life had become'.

'Anything make you suspicious?'

'The fact he'd hidden himself away, the note. There were some papers about a project.' He felt them freeze, their eyes on him. 'The name. You mentioned it on the phone.' He glanced around the flip chart and whiteboards.

'Boudicca,' Gray said.

'That's the one. What is it?'

The City officers hesitated, unsure whether to admit Belsey into their privileged circle. Gray gestured at the wall of flight details.

'These are the clues we have. A9C-BI is the Bahrain registration for a Gulfstream 200 jet belonging to Prince Faisal bin Abdul Aziz, head of Saud International Holdings investment group; B-KZB is a Hong Kong-registered Learjet known to be used by Young-Jin Choi, billionaire casino magnate and occasional colleague of the Prince. They were among eight private jets that landed in Farnborough on the morning of Saturday the seventh. Eight of the richest men in the world flying into south-east England. We believe they deliberately avoided the London airports so as not to draw attention to themselves: the travellers included two chief executives of Internet gambling sites and a lot of heavy security. They were personally met by Pierce Buckingham.'

'What for?' Belsey said.

'We don't know. That's what we were hoping you could help us with. A lot of these men connect to the Hong Kong Gaming Consortium. We believe they came in for a meeting.' He pointed at the question mark. 'The meeting was held eight days ago, Saturday afternoon in central London. I don't know what transpired, but two of the men present have died and a lot more have stopped answering their phones.'

Belsey nodded, studying the names. 'What's your money on?' he asked.

Mullins pitched in: 'Something messed up. In the two days following the meeting there are three hundred calls from Pierce Buckingham's mobile to numbers run by various call-forwarding services. It seems he couldn't get through. He then calls a lot of men with no official job titles in private rooms in Riyadh and Beijing and Monaco, all waiting to hear about a project he's putting their money into. I don't think they were very happy with what he had to say.'

'They were investors?'

'Not according to their lawyers. Let's just say there's a lot of people lying low, people who say they've never heard of Buckingham or Devereux. Half of them claiming they've never heard of themselves. Everything's gone hush, so I think Pierce Buckingham was shipping a hell of a lot of backers through to this Project Boudicca, and no one wanted to know how naughty it was. Now it turns out it was crooked to the core, people are writing off big sums and going on holiday.'

'And killing Buckingham.'

'Maybe.'

'Are there witnesses for the shooting?'

'No one saw anyone with a gun.'

'What kind of bullet?'

'A 7.62mm hollow tip.' There was another shared glance between the detectives.

'It's the same story as the Hampstead Starbucks,' Belsey said.

Gray and Mullins nodded in unison. They made a nice couple for a policing nightmare. The book of unwritten rules told every detective: don't say sniper, don't say gang war. Don't introduce the spectre of lawlessness that can reduce a peaceful city to war footing in one headline.

'Let's return to Alexei Devereux,' Gray said firmly. 'Buckingham called this a once-in-a-lifetime opportunity. It seems to have got people excited. Is there anything you saw or heard about Devereux that might suggest what it was exactly?'

'I'm not sure.' Belsey got to his feet and walked over to the chart. They didn't stop him. 'Can you tell what the project was from the people involved?'

'The list includes the IT people who helped Hong Kong Gaming set up their Snake Eyes website. There are also figures from architecture and construction who worked with the consortium in Dubai and Pennsylvania. But we don't know who was running the London project. The architect hasn't broken cover.'

'So Devereux was building something.'

'Something big. Shares in HKGC rocketed in the last week. The head of its European strategy, Vincent de Groot, was on holiday in the Maldives. He flew in especially. According to Special Branch, he visits London on the seventh of February, stays at the Grosvenor, sleeps with three lap dancers, spends nine grand on golf clubs and meets Buckingham. He and several other individuals and twenty security personnel go for a walk on the Heath. He wants in on the project. No one knows what the project is.'

'The Heath?'

'Ten hours later one of the attendees is picked up on intercept arranging a contract for three thousand cubic metres of concrete and two hundred tonnes of glass.'

'Jesus Christ.'

'I don't know what Buckingham said but serious sums of money transferred in the hours afterwards.'

'Transferred where?'

'To Devereux.'

'Where was this meeting?'

'We don't know. They used codes on the phone. It would be a help if we could find the venue. It would be a step in the right bloody direction.' Gray rubbed his face with his hands. Belsey tried to imagine where in London you'd take those people, if you wanted to impress them, people who had everything, expecting the best. What would dazzle? Deborah Mullins leaned forward.

'Buckingham used the meeting to raise thirty-eight million. This was a meeting where he asked for thirty-eight mil of other people's money just for a seat at the table. We need to know what they expected in return. This is where you come in. You looked into Alexei Devereux's suicide –'

She was interrupted by a sudden cacophony outside, as if metal objects were falling from the sky. The bells of St Paul's had begun to toll, endless and discordant. Gray and Mullins winced. Belsey sat back and listened. He was so close and so far. He tried to think of various tales he could spin to Kovar and none of them struck him as impressive as Boudicca must have been. He was insane for hanging about. Belsey gazed out of the window, towards the grey stone of St Lawrence Jewry, just visible above the nearest rooftop. Were the bells of St Lawrence ringing? Now they seemed to come from every church in the City, howling to each other like dogs. Belsey stared at the tower of St Lawrence, peeking above the concrete.

His pulse quickened.

He looked at the stump of spire, at its blackened bell tower and golden weathervane, and he saw the picture of Buckingham shaking hands with Prince Faisal. Beyond the tower he could just make out the turrets of the Guildhall.

The Guildhall. What had the courier's invoice described? Three vans, £295, last Saturday.

'I wish I could help you more,' Belsey muttered, getting up quickly.

'We have a few more questions.' Gray started to look suspicious. Belsey didn't hear the rest. He shared the lift down with a crowd of City detectives. One of them had a copy of the *Mail*.

'London sniper,' he said, with a note of exasperation in his voice.
'Northwood's blowing a gasket over those leaks.'
'You know his next move?' another said.
'What?'
'*Crimewatch* Special.'
Everyone laughed.
'Him and all the brass.'
'He fancies cosying up with Kirsty.'
'Who wouldn't?'
'Because he's fucked.'

50

An alleyway called Love Lane ran beside the police station, crowded with squad cars and riot vans. Belsey strode down it, into the courtyard of the Guildhall. He unfolded the scrap of *Al-Hayat* with Buckingham and the Saudi Prince. He turned, comparing the view. They were here. He spun 360 degrees. The Guildhall's doors were open, staff carrying last night's tables and chairs outside.

Belsey walked to the entrance and peered through the Gothic arch of the doorway into the banqueting hall beyond. It was immense. Stained-glass windows filled the walls. A rose-tinted light fell across men and women collapsing thirty tables beneath the soaring stone roof. Around the place stood monuments to Nelson, Wellington, Churchill, men who had hacked their names into history. It was a godless cathedral, consecrated to the City. To power. Of course he would, Belsey thought. Of course the bastard would bring them here.

A man with thin hair combed over his skull was leading two other suits through the hall, between the activity. He walked stiffly, and they turned as he pointed out details, taking photos on camera phones.

'The Great Hall hosts the Lord Mayor's Banquet each year,' the man was explaining. 'It's where royalty and state visitors have been entertained down the centuries. It lends an entirely unique stature to any event, gentlemen.'

'Excuse me,' Belsey called, walking towards him.

The man glanced at Belsey, spoke to his guests, and approached with his hands clasped apologetically.

'I'm afraid we're closed.'

'It's urgent. Are you in charge here?'

'I'm events manager.' His face had a bland pomposity that seemed to qualify him for the job. 'Do you have an appointment?'

'I've got a few questions,' Belsey said.

'Perhaps you could come back tomorrow.'

'It concerns an outstanding payment.'

'Payment's conducted through the Remembrancer's office.'

'Is he around?'

'Not in person.' The man smiled condescendingly. Belsey produced his badge.

'I think you had some men in here last Saturday that I'd very much like to know more about. Why don't you tell your friends to come back tomorrow?'

Something about this registered with the manager.

'Wait one moment.' He went to speak to one of his assistants. Belsey admired the statues and stone arches, the shields of the livery companies hanging down from brass flagpoles.

What a place to steal thirty-eight million.

An assistant took over the task of tour guide and the boss returned. 'What is this?'

'We're going to try to find out,' Belsey said. 'The hall was hired by an individual, for a small group of people, but he wanted the place to himself. You're still waiting for the balance to be settled.'

'How do you know about this?'

'You wouldn't believe what I know.'

The man led Belsey into a quiet corner.

'Who were they?' he asked.

'You tell me.'

'I don't know anything more about it. Except that they were very important figures in the City and internationally.'

Belsey couldn't help smiling. 'What gave you that idea?'

'They were, weren't they?'

'Some of them, no doubt. What happened?'

'I don't know. I wasn't there.'

313

'Who was working last Saturday?' Belsey said. 'Any of these people?'

'No.'

'I want to speak to someone who was there, who saw the meeting.'

'You have to understand, we get some very prestigious clients. We have to respect their confidentiality.'

The man seemed torn. Belsey decided to make it easier for him.

'Do you know what the sentence is for assisting terrorism?'

'Terrorism?'

'Has anyone reported ill in the last few days?' Belsey asked, a little louder. 'Rashes? Breathing difficulties?' Some of the staff turned.

'Follow me,' the man said. He ushered Belsey into a side office with wood panelling, a writing desk, an old clock. He spoke fast now. 'We weren't allowed to see. Men came in the day before, the Friday, to run a security check. They were armed. They covered the mirrors, sealed the windows, put up screens. We didn't know anything like that was going to happen.'

'Your caterers would have seen the meeting,' Belsey suggested.

'They brought their own catering. They brought their own security and drivers. I never knew anything about how out of the ordinary it would be until last week, when they contacted me with these requests.'

'But when was it booked?'

'Three months ago.'

'Under what name?'

'The Boudicca Society.'

Three months ago, Belsey thought. He had this pinned from the start – to the day, to the hour. Who exactly was weaving this elaborate con? To do it that fast, to know his targets inside out, to let it collapse around him as he walked away with thirty-eight million. 'The Boudicca Society. Had you heard of them before?'

'No. But –'

'You're happy for prestigious clients to use pseudonyms.'

'I had no idea.'

'Was there someone in charge of the Boudicca Society?'

'The man in charge came in two hours before everyone else. The man who organised it. He came early and then left.'

'Did he give a name?'

'No.'

'What exactly did he organise?'

'He needed a large table. I don't know why. He asked for the biggest table we had.'

'How large?'

'About five metres by five. We had to use three of our largest tables pushed together.'

'But you don't know what for?'

'A model of some kind, I imagine. We had to have the place emptied of our staff before it arrived.'

'Show me any paperwork you have.'

The man went through his files. He produced a booking form with the address for the abandoned AD Development office and a number that would get through to RingCentral. It also had the account number for Devereux's overdrawn Barclays current account.

'How does the parking work here?' Belsey asked.

'Why?'

'All this security must have required vehicles.'

'You register. We have our own car park.'

'Then you'll have records for the vehicles. Let me see the plates, the permits.'

'They didn't park. They were dropped off. They didn't want any records.'

Belsey thought. He looked around the office, searching for his final piece.

'The model, whatever sat on the table,' he said.

'Yes?'

'What happened to it afterwards?'

'It went back wherever it came from.'

Belsey racked his brains. Where was the pickup for the delivery? 33 Cavendish Square. He moved past the events manager to the phone on his desk. He called directory enquiries and asked for the office block reception. Eventually he got through to a sleepy-sounding security man.

'I need the names of any companies in your building that deal with construction,' Belsey said.

The security guard grunted. He looked through the building directory until he got to one. There was only one. They were called Kilgo Vesser Architectural Associates. No one was in their office that Sunday.

51

BELSEY DROVE TOWARDS CAVENDISH SQUARE, STOPPING AT an electrical goods store to watch the news through the window. There was a shot of The Bishops Avenue, then it panned back to a BBC reporter. Beside him was Charlotte Kelson. He thrust a microphone in her direction. Belsey couldn't hear what she was saying but it looked like she was laying claim to her scoop. A ticker flashed 'Live'. Devereux's home rose up behind her.

It made Belsey uneasy. She had his name. One wrong word, even off camera, and they'd be onto him before he had a chance to disappear. He wanted her by his side.

He pulled a U-turn and sped to Hampstead with the sirens on.

Sky News had parked beside the gates to Kenwood House. The media throng began a few metres down The Bishops Avenue. Police tape started soon after. Inside it, forensics officers were carrying bulging evidence bags out of number 37. News cameras jostled for a shot of the house. Charlotte Kelson stood apart from the crowd, across the road, reading copy down her phone.

Belsey screeched to a halt beside her.

'Get in.'

She stared at him, then at the Met squad car. It seemed to reassure her a little. He watched her weigh up the opportunity before speaking into the phone: 'I'll call you back.'

'Tell them to hold the front page while you're at it,' Belsey said. She put the phone away but didn't move to the car.

'They're taking your holiday home apart, Nick.'

'Want to see something?'

'What?'

'Project Boudicca.'

She looked sceptical. 'Where?'

'Kilgo Vesser Architectural Associates. Get in.'

She climbed in. Belsey breathed her perfume.

'Keep an eye out for motorbikes,' he said. 'If you see any behind us, tell me.'

'Why?'

'I don't like them.' Belsey put the blue lights on and drove towards Cavendish Square. 'What have you got?'

'Growing concerns about being in this car with you,' she said, putting on her seat belt.

'I'm the only one who's helped you on this. Remember that.'

'But *why* have you helped me?'

'Because you're great in bed. Tell me what you've found.' He swerved down Fitzjohn's Avenue, then weaved through the Swiss Cottage traffic.

'I looked into this Pierce Buckingham character. He was a prime bastard, with a long, dark history to his name. He was last seen trying to extract Saudi funds from the Hong Kong Gaming Consortium. It was the Gaming Consortium that hired PS Security. I have this from a chief inspector on Buckingham's murder inquiry. Buckingham thought he had a deal on with the Corporation of London, but they're denying everything. Meanwhile, some disgruntled investor has leaked correspondence between Buckingham and Alexei Devereux regarding what they call the 1871 Act.'

'What's that?'

'There's only two significant Acts passed in 1871 as far as I can tell. One was the American Civil Rights Act, the other was Victorian legislation that vested large parts of Hampstead in the Metropolitan Board of Works. My money's on that one. The worrying bit is the caveat: the Act

318

guarantees to preserve the natural beauty of the area in perpetuity, and to see that any future owners preserve it too.'

'What does Devereux say?'

'He says it won't be a problem. He has this on the authority of lawyers who work for Milton Granby, a firm called Charlton and Doubret who he claims had sent a confidential fax outlining loopholes.'

'Have you spoken to them?'

'They're denying everything.'

'Was the fax from this machine?' He told her Devereux's fax number. 'I think so.'

'The lawyers are telling the truth for once. They didn't send the fax.'

'So what's going on?'

'There was a meeting,' Belsey said. 'And the people in the room wired through thirty-eight million at the end of it. That bit's true.'

'What was it for?'

'I think we're about to find out.'

They slid down Portland Place, past expensive office space behind the department stores. Cavendish Square had a tidy Regency decorum apart from one glass-and-concrete colossus that dominated the south-east corner. Number 33. Revolving doors led into a smart reception with fake marble columns, sofas, a TV screen and security barriers before you got to the lifts. A guard slouched behind a glass-topped reception desk. Belsey checked the list of companies behind him: Kilgo Vesser were on the fifth floor.

'Someone reported a break-in,' Belsey said. The guard sat up fast. Belsey showed his badge.

'Where?'

'Fifth floor. Kilgo Vesser. Someone smashed the door.'

Now the guard looked unnerved. 'I don't think so.'

'Stay here.'

Belsey jumped the barrier. Charlotte followed. They took the stairs to the fifth floor. He found the door marked Kilgo Vesser Architectural Associates, picked up a steel pedal bin and rammed the lock until the wood splintered. Then he kicked it open. An alarm blasted. He walked in and turned the lights on.

The architectural model took up the whole of the front office. The ponds gave it away. It took Belsey a moment to recognise the painstaking details of trees and sloping parkland, because a racetrack looped around what had been the North Heath and was now a casino complex. The central structure rose up from beneath ground level like a long glass coffin, tiered on both sides, and beyond the track, to the west, was a new, artificial lake fringed by parking and a cinema. Tiny figures crowded the green space, some making for the casino, some walking dogs or setting out picnics and flying kites.

'Oh wow,' Charlotte gasped.

Belsey looked around the drawing boards and Macs and across crowded desks. He opened a drawer and tipped it onto the floor. Then he did another. He searched through rolls of plans and maps until he saw two relating to the casino design. He folded them into his jacket.

'Let's go.'

They ran back downstairs, past the guard, to the empty street.

'Where now?' Charlotte said.

'I have to do something,' Belsey said. 'I think you've got enough story here to be getting on with. I might need to run soon, though. To somewhere else.'

'OK.'

'Think you'll be able to find me?'

He held her hand and looked at her in the light from the reception. A red dot flickered like a firefly over her pale neck and up her cheek to her temple. Belsey thought it was from the guard so he looked behind him and the guard wasn't there. He watched it. And then a wave of dread rushed through his body.

'Get down,' he said, and the reception doors blew in.

52

BELSEY COVERED HER. THEY CRAWLED TO THE PARKED CARS and took shelter. He could feel blood on the palms of his hands. He didn't think it was his own. Charlotte started screaming, which was a good sign. If you can scream you can live.

The next shots hit the cars. Glass rained down. More screaming.

He moved to see her face: no head wounds, blood spreading across her blouse.

'Charlotte, listen to me. Where are you hit?'

'My arm.'

Belsey tore the sleeve. The bullet had taken a slice out of her left arm and grazed the torso. He took her scarf and balled it like a compress and fixed it to her body with the sleeves of her coat. They must have shot from an opposite building, he thought; the roof of one of the office blocks. He couldn't see any movement.

'I'm OK,' she said.

'Press this against you. Don't stand up. Don't try to go anywhere.'

'Why?'

'Because we're still alive.'

He crawled to the reception.

'Get an ambulance,' he said to the guard, who was flat on the floor. But just then an ambulance bike braked hard, a few metres away. The paramedic got off the bike with a first-aid case in his gloved hand.

321

'She's here,' Belsey said. Why hadn't they taken their helmet off? This was what he was thinking. What are they carrying on their back?

They opened the case and took out a handgun and levelled it at his face.

Belsey moved in towards the man. The mistake is always to back off. He moved closer, turning, and the gunman panicked and fired. A window smashed. Belsey moved into the cover inside, drawing him away from Charlotte. The gunman had the Dragunov slung across his back. But he had come prepared for close-range executions as well. Belsey took a fire extinguisher off the wall. A bullet sparked off one of the pillars. He pulled the pin on the extinguisher. The gunman was close now, a few feet away. Belsey aimed at the tinted visor and sprayed.

It worked. The gunman fired wildly, blinded, then backed out towards the road. Belsey aimed a kick at his kidneys and he went down but held on to the gun, desperately trying to wipe the foam off the visor. He got to his feet and raised the gun again. Belsey kicked it out of his hand. The man still wouldn't run. He had the rifle, so what did he want? Belsey stood between him and the ambulance bike. He wants the bike, Belsey thought.

Sirens approached. The gunman stiffened for a fraction of a second. He listened to the directions of the sirens and then ran in the opposite one, tearing his helmet off, but too late for Belsey to see his face.

Belsey walked over to the bike. He'd stolen it with the key in because the ignition box was intact. The key wasn't there now. The tail box was locked. Belsey found the assassin's handgun by the kerb, a Browning BDM that had seen some action. He picked it up using a scrap of newspaper, aimed it at the lock on the bike's tail box and fired. The box blew open. Belsey looked in the compartment and saw why the gunman was getting anxious. It contained a shirt and suit, spare ammunition, a conference badge on a length of ribbon and a swipe card for the Royal National Hotel.

He checked Charlotte was OK. She was pale, but with enough fury remaining that she'd pull through. If the shots had attracted any attention, no one yet dared show their face. They would soon. Belsey returned to the bike and emptied the tail box. He stripped and wiped the blood off his face and hands with his shirt then squeezed into the gunman's clothes. He waited until he was sure the approaching sirens were real. But he didn't want to be around when they arrived.

'Do me a favour, Charlotte,' he said. 'Don't mention I was here.'

She rolled her eyes. He gave her a kiss.

53

THE ROYAL NATIONAL WAS A SIXTEEN-HUNDRED ROOM hotel off Russell Square, a concrete maze of restaurants, corridors and migrant workers. It was a perfect hotel for an assassin. The gunman's conference pass said 'Ninth International HIV Research Conference' and gave the name Dr Antoine Pelletier. Belsey hung it around his neck and turned it so the name was hidden. The hotel was musty, all 1970s wood and 1980s fabrics in a jaundiced, subterranean light. He walked past the reception to the lifts. You needed a swipe to work the lifts. The gunman's hotel swipe card worked. The lift contained information about breakfast options and West End shows. Belsey took it to the first floor and back down to reception.

The receptionist's badge said 'Tasha'.

'Tasha, hello.'

'Hello, sir. How can I help?'

'There's another delegate here, from the HIV conference,' Belsey said. 'Dr Pelletier. Could you tell him Dr Steel is here?'

'Hang on.' She spent twenty seconds scrolling down her computer screen then lifted a receiver. Belsey watched her fingers. They dialled 561. She waited a moment.

'I'm not getting an answer,' she said, without hanging up. Belsey checked his watch.

'Maybe he's gone already.'

'Would you like me to keep trying?'

'No, that's fine. Is there a bathroom I can use?'

She directed him past the lifts to the toilets. He walked past the lifts to the stairs and took the stairs to the fifth floor.

Belsey found room 561 and knocked. No answer. He swiped the assassin's hotel card in the lock and got a green light. Belsey kicked the door.

The room was empty, bed made, three suit bags draped over a single chair. It smelt of stale smoke. There was a hotel ashtray and a box of surgical gloves beside the bed. The ashtray was the only object that looked used, although no butts had been left. The gloves suggested Belsey wasn't going to find any prints very easily. He kicked the bathroom door open. It was spotless, with a cleaner's seal on the toilet and the soaps still wrapped. Belsey searched the place. He turned the mattress, lifted the cistern. He lay down on the bed and stared at a very fine line on the ceiling, like a crack in the plaster, only it covered the edge of the ventilation grille. A hair. He stood on the bed and punched the grille and it fell out.

In the metal duct above it was a telescopic sight, rifle cleaning kit, harness, a carrier bag containing tactical grips and a scope mount, and a key for the hotel safe deposit.

Belsey took the key and a bag for sanitary waste and went back to reception. The safe-deposit boxes were stacked to one side of the desk. He sat outside the hotel's Big Ben Pub waiting for Tasha to leave her post. A screen above the bar announced: *Murdered financier was 'playboy fixer'*. Then: *Public warned to avoid Square Mile*. The Mayor was saying something to an assembled crowd. Then a ticker started flashing *Breaking News: New Shooting Central London*. They hadn't got the cameras to the scene yet. Northwood appeared, and Belsey could just make out his words: 'If these incidents are the work of one individual, and at the moment that's a big if . . .'

Tasha left her post, replaced by a tall man with a badge that said 'Yakubu'. Belsey walked up.

'Yakubu.'

'Sir.'

'Can I reset my morning call? I want it at nine tomorrow. Room 561.'

'Of course.'

'And breakfast in my room. The Continental option.'

'OK.' He made a note. 'That's done for you.'

Belsey laid the safe-deposit key on the counter. 'I'll grab something from my box.'

'Sure.'

The only thing in the box was a Canadian passport in Dr Pelletier's name. Belsey took it by the edges and dropped it in the paper bag.

54

EVERY INSTINCT, HUMAN AND POLICE, TOLD HIM TO PUT A name to the threat – the man who had killed Jessica, Buckingham, then tried to kill himself and Charlotte. He was still surfing on adrenalin from his near-death experience. By his own estimation he had ten hours to put the bastard out of action one way or another. This was non-negotiable. Secondary, but only just: find seven hundred pounds for Duzgun and get a passport of his own. Book a flight. Then put the final touches to Kovar. That had to be done soon so that the speculator could get the money ready. He would say his goodbyes to Charlotte, collect his winnings and take flight.

The attacker's passport gave the name Dr Antoine Michel Pelletier, born 2 June 1976 in Quebec City. The face was that of a Caucasian male in his thirties, clean-shaven, pale skin, receding black hair and small eyes. Organised Crime Forensics took a clean print off the back and came up with another seven identities: seven men all with the same fingerprints, all with hits to their name.

The Print Unit officer looked a little shaken when the results came through. He was young, not long out of training college.

'Where did you get this?' he asked.

'Why?'

'There's nothing in the UK before, but I checked the Interpol database and there's thirty-seven separate warrants.'

'Who is it?'

'Take your pick: Aleksander Boskovic, Niko Pacassi, Nathan Risboro, Carel Dupont. The first three pseudonyms come up in connection with a series of killings along the Amalfi coast between 1995 and 1997. Carel Dupont fits the same description, wanted for the murder of Swiss judge Carla Pinto in 1996. Never found. The Swiss think that Dupont is probably the pseudonym of someone of Croatian origin, connected with a number of killings while travelling on Belgian passports in the name of Christof Segers, Jens Thomas, Jean-Paul Claessens. Those were in Paris, Marseille and Stockholm. The Police Nationale call him *le chasseur*, the hunter.'

'That's cute of them,' Belsey said.

'From the weapons and tactics favoured, Swiss and Italian investigators profiled him as military-trained, probably with experience in a sniper unit during the Bosnian War. They narrowed it down to Milan Balic, a crack shot who helped take several cities across Herzegovina before going private, mostly for the Mafia in Naples. More recently he's murdered a Nigerian ambassador and an Egyptian banker who'd fallen foul of Prince Faisal bin Abdul Aziz.'

And from there it looked like he was on the HKGC payroll. It was in the pay of the Prince that he turned up as Christian Le Febvre in Macao, associated with a hit on two of the gaming consortium's rival developers in a bathhouse on the southern edge of the autonomous zone.

'Were the killings connected to the Dream City Casino?' Belsey said.

'That's right.'

Belsey made some calls. There was no Ninth International HIV Research Conference, it was a cover for a visa application. He called Emergency Services Central Command. Charlotte Kelson had been taken to St Thomas' Hospital.

55

No one in or near Forensic Command knew where Belsey might find a travel agent's. Eventually he found an independent package holiday firm on Kennington Road, with security grilles over the window and a sign that said 'Victory Holidays'. Inside were pictures of white beaches and two staff with fake tans.

'I need a flight tonight,' Belsey said. 'The cheapest you've got. Late as possible.'

'Anywhere?'

'Within reason.'

The girls laughed. There was a clatter of painted nails on computer keyboards.

'Thessaloniki,' one of them said.

She had a map inlaid on the desk and pointed with the end of a ballpoint to the south of Greece. It would work, he saw. Greece was EU, which meant there was no limit on the cash he could carry. It meant high-volume travel and low scrutiny; a low-suspicion destination, even for a wrecked man with no luggage.

'When's it going?'

'Eleven thirty tonight from Stansted. Air Berlin.'

He could travel down into Turkey via Kipoi. The border police would be looking for drugs coming west, not individuals heading east. The E90 highway became the D110 in Turkey, and he could follow it to Istanbul. Easy to get lost there, sort visas, put his head down in a cheap room for a while. With luck he'd have the money to lie low. From there any transport could take him south to Ankara, and from Ankara he could bus it east, to the Habur border gate, into Nineveh. Nineveh, for Christ's sake.

'Good for resorts,' she said. 'Might be a bit chilly at this time of year.'

'What's the total with tax?'

'Will you be checking baggage?'

'No.'

'Thirty-two pounds.'

'I'll get it.'

The flight was in just over ten hours. He took his ticket and said his mobile had died and asked if he could make a couple of calls on their phone. He offered the girls money, which they declined.

He called Kovar.

'Meet me at the House of Commons. St Stephen's Gate. Seven o'clock this evening.'

'The House of Commons?'

'Do you know it?'

'I'll be there,' Kovar said.

Belsey booked a Prestige car on Devereux's account for the same time. There was a serious risk that the booking drew unwanted attention. He had no idea how deep the police operation against Devereux was currently working. But he couldn't cut corners. He needed to set the scene perfectly, right down to the last detail.

'I want one of the limos,' he said. 'Something with space. Pick me up on Millbank, by Victoria Tower Gardens, seven o'clock. Next to Parliament; as close as possible to the no-drive zone.'

Belsey hung up. The travel agents stared at him. He thanked them again as he left.

56

Six hundred minutes to take-off.

Belsey left the car at the top of Kennington Road and bought some flowers near the Imperial War Museum. He walked to St Thomas' Hospital. It was the end of weekend mop-up, casualties off the battle-field. He stepped through bleeding couples, crash victims, the glassed and the glassy. He avoided two reporters, quick off the mark, waiting for news from A&E.

A uniformed constable sat outside Charlotte's ward. He looked up at Belsey with business eyes. No one Belsey knew. Belsey got the scan: face, fingers, waist, and an uneasy glance at the bouquet.

'Sorry, chap.' The constable raised a large hand.

'I'm a friend.'

'No visitors at all at the moment. She's sleeping anyway.'

'Is she OK?'

'I can't give any information.'

'Can you give her these?' Belsey offered the flowers.

'No.'

Belsey looked past him, through a small window with a slat blind. He could see some bedlinen – nothing else. He felt his fury return. He walked back down, gave the flowers to an old woman with tubes in her neck and called Met Central Operations.

'This is Detective Constable Nick Belsey from Hampstead CID. I was

331

present at the shooting on Cavendish Square. I have information about a suspect.'

'OK.'

'Which station is dealing with it?'

'Who's that?'

'Detective Constable Nick Belsey, from Hampstead police station. I have information about the shooting.'

'Go in to West End Central. Can you do that?'

'Yes.'

'Quick as possible.'

He made West End Central in less than fifteen minutes. A constable greeted him and led Belsey through the station to an interview room in which three men had apparently been waiting. It was badly lit: one of the strip bulbs had gone and most of the light came from a desk lamp. Sitting at a table was a thick-necked, shaven-headed officer with a goatee and a stained shirt tight across his beer gut. With him was a thuggish ginger-haired constable and a man in a caramel-coloured suit. It took Belsey a second to recognise the suit as Nigel Herring, Northwood's stooge.

Now he took a better look at all their faces. He didn't know the Constable. The goatee was the man he'd seen leaving Chris Starr's office with a bag of shredded paper. He didn't look much friendlier now. A uniform jacket with Sergeant's stripes hung over the back of his chair.

Belsey braced himself for the possibility that he had walked into a less than ideal situation. He could smell their sweat; they had been in the room for a while. But it wasn't an investigations team. A copy of the *Mail on Sunday* lay on the desk, among stained paper plates, cartons of Ribena and cigarette packets, a story connecting PS Security and Chief Superintendent Northwood ominously to the fore.

'What is this?' Belsey said.

'Sit down.'

'I've got a name,' he said. 'For the shooting.'

'A name.'

They all looked blank. Then the Sergeant laughed. The ginger Constable shut the door.

'You've got a name all right,' he muttered.

'Let's do this the easy way, Nick,' the Sergeant suggested. He had cagey eyes. Belsey surveyed the mess on the table, the newspaper, their smirks. Then he surveyed Nigel Herring.

'Sit down,' Herring said.

The young Constable put a hand on Belsey's shoulder. He forced him into the plastic seat and tapped the paper.

'What's this?'

'What does it look like?'

'Looks like someone talking crap.'

'You'll have to write them an angry letter then.'

The Sergeant leaned forward. 'You're not in a position to be a whistle-blower, Nick.'

'Sounds like you've got a guilty conscience.'

'What about your conscience?'

'Nothing I can't deal with.'

Herring threw a photo of Jessica Holden onto the table.

'Know her?'

'The face is familiar.'

'Anything to tell us about her death?'

'That the investigation's a fuck-up.'

There were glances between the three men.

'Maybe it is,' Herring said. 'When were you last on The Bishops Avenue?'

'For Christ's sake,' Belsey said, as a deeply unpleasant scenario began to gain clarity. 'Are you all PS Security boys? Is that what this is about? Have I fucked with your bonuses?' He wondered where it was all going. Now he studied the room more carefully, analysing his options: the layout, the three men, the desk.

'Answer the question.'

'No comment.'

'Had you ever spoken to this girl before the day she died?'

'No comment.'

'What about Charlotte Kelson?' Herring said.

'Never heard of her.'

'She was investigating you, Nick.'

'That's one way of putting it,' the Constable added. They all laughed.

'And now the poor woman's in hospital,' Herring said. 'She was investigating you and how on earth you tie in to all of this. I can see why you'd be coy.'

'Meet a young lady and don't tell her your name,' the Constable tutted. 'Cheeky.'

'Try to fleece a young reporter and then turn nasty on her,' Herring suggested.

'Get her phone number and then lie to her network operator so you can access confidential data,' the Sergeant said. 'That's love, Nick.'

Belsey sighed. 'And yet it's not me in the papers this morning,' he said.

'Oh, Nick. Why make enemies? Making enemies hurts.'

Belsey looked up in time to see the fist. It belonged to the Constable. It caught him square in the face and he lost vision for a second. There was a lot of laughter in the office now.

'A present from friends.' The ginger one punched him again. Belsey gripped the chair to stop himself being lured into the trap of fighting back. That was what they wanted; then there'd be three men on him, no holds barred, and the cuffs would come out.

'Fuck you,' Belsey said.

'Oh no! Best tell the IPCC.'

More laughter. Belsey tried to think. He could see this act going on for a while and didn't imagine it would become more endearing.

'She's made a statement against you,' Herring said.

'She wasn't making many statements last time I looked,' Belsey said. He licked his lips and tasted blood.

'You keep turning up where people die,' the Sergeant said. 'Looks like unlucky coincidence.'

'Is that what you're charging me with?' Belsey asked.

'Want to know what we're charging you with?' Herring said.

'Impress me.'

'Conspiracy to rob, conspiracy to defraud, perverting the course of justice and attempted murder.'

'Attempted murder of who?'

'Charlotte Kelson.'

'For Christ's sake.'

'Would you like to nominate a solicitor?' the Sergeant asked.

'Or how about you just try and explain yourself.' Herring stared at him.

'I've got no comment,' Belsey said.

'Any comments about this?'

They prodded the newspaper across to him: Charlotte's criticism of the mighty Chief Superintendent Northwood. Belsey scanned the desk under the pretence of studying the story – regulation-issue styrofoam, no cutlery. The only solid objects were the tape recorder and the desk lamp.

The Constable admired Charlotte Kelson's byline.

'She's nice. Did you get a shag for this?'

'Twat.'

The ginger thug came over and clapped him on the ear. So they were going to keep on playing roughhouse. That was West End Central for you. Belsey looked again at the desk lamp. They had the same make at Hampstead. It took a pin bulb.

'I asked you a question,' the thug said.

'Would I fuck you?' Belsey said. 'Was that the question?'

'You're a disgrace.'

'You're a credit to the police,' Belsey said. He could hear keys jangling. Which one of them had keys? The ginger PC had a chain from his pocket to his belt. Belsey brought a hand up to his face and felt the mess. 'Can I get a tissue from my jacket?' he said. They grunted. Belsey found a clump of tissues and dabbed at the blood.

'You've forgotten something,' he said.

'What?'

'You haven't read me my rights.' They smiled at this. Belsey stopped dabbing. He put his hands in his lap. He wrapped the bloody tissues around his right hand.

The Sergeant drawled laconically: 'You do not have to say anything, but it may harm your defence if you do not mention when questioned something which you later rely on in court. Anything you do say may be used in evidence. Has that been understood?' He raised an eyebrow.

'Don't you think you should cuff me?'

'Come on, Nick,' Herring said.

'Cuff me.'

The Constable moved towards Belsey. Belsey popped the bulb, smashed it on the desk and jumped up, elbowing the Constable hard in the face. He got a hand in the man's hair and wrenched his head back, fitting the jagged stem into the soft flesh beneath his chin.

Herring and the Sergeant froze. Belsey pulled the head back further so everyone had a good view of the shards. The Constable gurgled. Belsey pushed the base deeper until he stopped struggling. There was a smell of burning skin.

'Back off or I rip his throat out,' Belsey said.

'Don't do anything stupid,' Herring said.

Belsey moved the Constable backwards towards the door. He kicked the handle and continued out, down the corridor, dragging his hostage.

'Open the back,' Belsey shouted as he approached the desk. Blood was dripping off his elbow. He passed through the exit door out to the car park.

Belsey dropped the Constable hard, so that he was winded. He unclipped the keys from his chain. The car key had a Mazda logo on the ring. There was one black Mazda MX-5 in the car park. Belsey got inside the car, fired the engine and drove it through the barrier.

He checked the rear-view when he was on Chandos Way and saw their faces. His hand on the steering wheel was caked in blood.

Four hundred and fifty minutes.

57

HE RACED IT TO HAMPSTEAD, STOPPING TO WASH THE BLOOD off at a drinking fountain on Heath Street. There'd be an All Ports warning out in ten or fifteen minutes: to airports, ferry ports, international train stations. The borders were closing in. He had a couple of hours before the system fully connected. They would put out a bulletin with his name on, including calls to every patrol unit, but that didn't mean the stations would know until the next parade. He was counting on circulation lag, and got it.

PC Craig Marshall on the front desk nodded.

'Nick.'

'Craig.'

'How's things?'

'Ticking over.'

Belsey went up to the second floor, past the Community Support office, to the room they used for evidence storage. PC Drakeley, on guard duty outside, signed his name in the book.

'All well, guv?'

'Very well, thank you.'

Belsey walked in, opened the safe, removed ten grams of ketamine and a Sig Sauer P220 handgun. He stuffed them into the pockets of his jacket. He couldn't find any money. There were bullets for the Sig in a separate cabinet at the side. He emptied them all into his pockets and walked out.

'Have a good one, Nick.'

'See you around.'

Up to the CID office, which was empty. So this was it, he thought – a silent goodbye. He picked up a phone on Rosen's desk and called Duzgun.

'It's Jack Steel. Is my order ready for collection?'

'It's ready. Do you have the money?'

'I'm getting it now.'

Belsey called Emmanuel Gilman and it rang ten times then went to voicemail.

'You're in luck,' Belsey said. 'I've got something for you. I need seven hundred in cash and that's a bargain.'

Halfway down the stairs he bumped into Trapping: gangly, grinning.

'Nick.'

'Rob. Have to run.'

'I got a name for the assault on Thursday,' Trapping said.

'Good work, Rob.'

'Everything on the Halifax job is on your desk. Patrick Dent's given five alibis so far. The CPS called –'

'I'm in a bit of a rush right now.'

Trapping frowned. 'Are you OK?'

'I'm good. I've got to run, though.'

'Can you sign the forms?'

'Sure.'

Belsey went back up and signed them. He gave Trapping a wink and touched his arm. What did he want to say? Goodbye. Do not embrace the idea of being a policeman. Manage your expectations. Remember to move.

He ditched the Mazda in Camden, and stole an old Citroën estate from behind the market. It had a baseball cap under the passenger seat. He put the cap on, pulled it low and started driving. King's Cross, east on City Road, Commercial Road, into Docklands. At a red light he leaned down and loaded the gun. He breathed in the smell of polish and cordite. He put it back in his jacket and continued weaving between the office blocks of Canary Wharf.

338

There was no answer on Gilman's intercom. Belsey followed another occupant into the building. He went up to the top floor. Gilman's door was open. He took the gun out.

'Emmanuel?'

Silence is different with a gun in your hand. It seemed brittle. Blood had reached the living-room doorway and seeped into the hall.

Gilman lay face up in the living room with the AK on his chest. His mobile lay a few inches from his right hand. The body hadn't fully stiffened. Belsey removed Gilman's socks and put them on his hands. He tried not to look at the fund manager's head. He picked up the mobile and played the message.

'You're in luck,' he heard himself say. He wiped the message and put the mobile back.

Belsey flushed the drugs and took all the cash in the Maximuscle tub. It felt like close to a grand. He was halfway out of the door when he stopped and took a last look at the bleak tableau. The screen of the mobile phone was still lit. He went back and picked it up. One message remained, undeleted. He played it.

'Emmanuel, it's not good.' A man with an East Coast American accent. 'I made some enquiries and he hasn't been in London for a couple of years. The hotel says Devereux's been on the island six months. He's not investing in anything and doesn't know the Hong Kong Gaming Consortium. His lawyers flew over the day before yesterday and they're ready to sit on anyone who says otherwise. He's in a wheelchair, Emmanuel. He's devoting himself to environmental charities: marine conservation, coral reefs. I don't know who you've been talking to . . .'

Belsey counted the money in the lift on the way down and it came to nine hundred and sixty.

He tore north through east London, through Hackney to Green Lanes. Old men crowded the front room of Duzgun's social club watching a TV mounted high in one corner: *London Sniper Panic*. It was rolling news now. Reports kept cutting back to a computer-generated map with four crosses for four crime scenes: Starbucks, St Clement's, Cavendish Square, The Bishops Avenue.

'Here.' Belsey slipped twenty pounds to an aproned man. 'Is Hasan around?'

He was nodded through the doorway into the back room. It hadn't changed. The fat man was behind his table. The passport was on the table, with the licence inside it, jutting out.

'I'm in a bit of a hurry,' Belsey said. He placed the seven hundred on the table and picked the passport up. It was UK, backdated a couple of months, which was a nice touch. He checked the driver's licence and the passport photo and moved the holograms under the light. They were fine. There were whole factory towns in northern China devoted to producing black-market holograms. One day he'd like to go to those places. It was one of the best fakes he'd seen.

'Good job. Thanks.' He was on his way out when Duzgun said, 'Sit down.'

'I can't stop.'

'I have something that might be of interest to you.'

'What's that?'

'Work.'

'Work?'

'If you want to work,' he said. 'I can get you good work, minimum wage.'

'I'm not looking for work at the moment,' Belsey said. 'Thank you.'

'Good employer.'

'I'm fine,' Belsey said. 'Maybe another time.'

He stashed the Citroën at the back of Smith Square, close to the river, with the gun and baseball cap in the glove compartment, put his jacket on with the Kilgo Vesser architectural plans inside it, then walked up Millbank to Parliament. Westminster was extra jumpy, snipers on the mind. He could see endless protection officers: stopping vehicles, keeping tourists moving along. A gathering of protesters was being shaken down, scattering pictures of burnt children and Palestinian flags. The Palace of Westminster loomed over them, lit for effect and vaguely monstrous. Its yellow stonework dripped down over the scene. It kept the tourists distracted. Belsey showed his police ID to the officer on St Stephen's Gate and went inside, into St Stephen's Chapel. He sat for a moment in the musty lobby area admiring his new passport. He bent it, ground it beneath his heel, roughed it up a little. Then he walked back to the entrance and saw Kovar beyond the gates.

'Max,' Belsey called. He wanted him to get the full effect. Kovar looked up. Belsey stepped out of Parliament, thanking the police guard. He grabbed Kovar's hand with both of his own. 'Treasury on a Sunday,' he said. 'There are places I'd rather be. I'm sorry to keep you waiting. Can we walk?'

'I hope you haven't had to cut anything short.'

'It's sewn up. Now they just need to drink the champagne. Alexei's got them swooning. He's a dangerous man.'

Belsey led Kovar across the front of Parliament onto Millbank.

'So you have the information on Project Boudicca?'

'Sure,' Belsey said. 'But I've been having second thoughts as to whether this is fair on you, Max. The sort of money being thrown around is distasteful. Once people know something like this is a sure thing, they go crazy. Now we've got the Treasury on board, and we're putting up another ten mil of our own. Mr D says this kind of project is the future. What can I say to him? He's never lost money before and I'm not the man to turn around and tell him now might be different. But a casino on Hampstead Heath . . .'

'A casino on Hampstead Heath?'

The limo was right where it was meant to be, waiting beside the entrance to Victoria Tower Gardens. They'd even sent the same driver.

'Evening, sir.'

'Here we are,' Belsey said. 'Would you get in? It will be more conven-ient.' He opened the car door for Kovar. They got in. There were four rows of seats, turned to form two booths, each with a shiny black table, a rack of cocktail glasses and its own minibar. They slid into the back booth.

'I hate these things,' Belsey said. 'But they're useful if you want to work. Alexei calls it his portable office.' He pulled the crumpled plans from his jacket and spread them across the table: a map of the new-look

Heath and a design for the central structure itself, in aerial and cross section. They hung over the sides of the table and across the men's laps. 'There it is. Project Boudicca.' He let Kovar drink it in. 'The Mayor's desperate for it, the City's desperate for it. We've got tax breaks that make me blush. Now people are talking about Hackney Marshes, Clapham Common. I'm thinking, is this real?' Belsey fixed them both a brandy. Kovar pored over the plans. He couldn't contain a smile. 'If it's the start, then it's just the start,' Belsey said. 'The beginning of the start.' He checked the window. Two men in paint-flecked overalls watched them from beside the park railings. 'Let's go round the block,' Belsey said to the driver.

They joined the traffic and Belsey thought one of the men might have lifted something to his mouth. Keep calm, he thought. When you're on the black, close the game.

'In Pennsylvania – did you see what we did there? I personally made half a million in the first month after I invested. With this we were hoping for sixty per cent market share. It's looking more like eighty. It's printing money. It makes me sick.'

They approached Buckingham Palace and stopped as a crowd of tourists crossed the road, cameras flashing in the darkness. The driver hit the horn.

'Tell me,' Belsey said. 'Why do these people come here and take photographs?'

'I've never understood,' Kovar muttered.

'It's because they don't have anything better to do. They've finished shopping, their show's not until eight. Why do people go to see the *Mona Lisa* when they're in Paris? They have no idea what else to do. That's what Mr D knows. London's a resort town now.'

'Yes.'

'By 2030 there will be fifteen Las Vegases, spread all over the world. God willing, London will be one of them.'

'I expect so.'

Belsey watched the rear-view mirror. 'How long's that Mondeo been behind us?' he asked the driver.

'I don't know, sir.'

It was hard spotting tail techniques in London traffic. The Mondeo was making late turns; one man driving, one passenger in the back.

'Make a left here,' Belsey said to the driver. 'Don't signal.'

'Pardon, sir?'

'Turn here. Don't signal.'

'The road's closed.'

'That's why I want you to do it.'

They swerved around the Queen Victoria memorial, cutting up a lot of angry drivers, and turned onto Constitution Hill.

'Now keep going to Hyde Park Corner. Put some speed on it.'

'Is there a problem?' Kovar tore himself away from the plans as the limousine accelerated.

'No, no problem. What do you think?'

'I think it's impressive,' Kovar said.

At the Hyde Park Corner roundabout Belsey told the driver to go round twice. It seemed they'd lost the Mondeo.

'I've got a good feeling about you,' Belsey said, sliding low in his seat. 'That's rare for me. There are people I want you to meet now: the IT boys, the MPs. I told Devereux how I feel. We're men of instinct.'

'I can cover whatever Hong Kong Gaming were covering.'

'That's a thirty per cent stake.'

'It won't be a problem.'

They were on Park Lane, beside the monument to Animals Killed in War, when a silver Skoda Octavia pulled up beside them, two men, making a point of not looking at the limo, but not looking at anything else either.

'Take us back to Parliament Square,' Belsey said.

'What happens next?' Kovar said.

'Well, we're at Stansted in three hours. Mr D wants you to come over to St Petersburg in the next few days, thrash out the fine details. But I know he'd hate to go home empty-handed. I said I could pick up your gift at Stansted.'

'Stansted?' Kovar looked uncertain.

'Is that a problem?'

Steer it home, Belsey thought. All the dots had been connected, all the boxes ticked. He needed the pay-off. He could see Kovar thinking.

He could see the Skoda close behind them as they ran lights back towards Whitehall. It was a police surveillance unit, he was sure now. The Skoda Octavia was popular for discreet jobs – unadventurous looks, high performance. The Yard owned a few. Belsey made a mental note of its registration.

'Is the airport the best place?' Kovar said.

'It's the only one that works. It'll be secure – we'll make sure of that. I need you to bring the gift to Stansted for quarter to eleven tonight and I'll see to the rest. Ten forty-five on the dot, in front of the main terminal building. I'll be there to collect it.'

'That's possible.'

'It's possible. You'll do it.'

'OK. I'll get out here.'

'Stop here,' Belsey told the driver.

Kovar shook his hand and climbed out. Belsey watched him cross the road, back towards Parliament.

'Hold on one second,' he said to the driver.

There were two men outside Westminster Abbey, one of them talking on a radio handset. They watched Kovar cross the road and continue down Millbank where he hailed a cab. Then the men climbed into a black hatchback, swung a violent U-turn and began to follow.

58

Belsey used the phone in the limo and called the Coordinating and Tasking Office. The Tasking Office made sure police didn't end up crashing each other's operations. He ran a check on the Skoda Octavia using his colleague Derek Rosen's ID code. It came back SCD10: Covert Unit.

'One of ours?'

'One of ours.'

'Who set it up?'

'It's tied to the sniper. Northwood thinks he knows how to catch him, and it involves tailing this target, Kovar.'

'Why?'

'I don't know. Everyone's in Vauxhall drawing up a plan. Rush job.'

Belsey punched the back of the passenger seat hard.

'Where did Northwood hear about Max Kovar?'

'Financial Development.'

'Philip Ridpath?'

'I don't know which officer. Someone started talking about Kovar yesterday.'

Belsey cursed. Vauxhall meant Citadel Place, the headquarters of SOCA, the Serious and Organised Crime Agency. He could make it in five minutes, but what was he going to do apart from get himself arrested?

'Which units is Northwood requesting?' Belsey said.

'Operational Support, Armed Response, CO19, Territorial. Leave's been cancelled. He sees this as his last shot.'

Belsey slammed the phone down. They were calling up every unit in the south-east with guns and wheels. He lifted the phone again, called Ridpath's office and got Midgley.

'He's on his way out,' the officer yawned.

'Tell him it's Nick Belsey. I've got something about tonight he needs to know.'

'Seriously, he's going.'

'Tell him to take the surveillance off Max Kovar. This operation won't work.'

'OK. I'll pass that on. Thank you.'

'Where's he going?'

'Maybe it's private.'

'He's going to SOCA.'

'What if he is?'

'Tell him to wait.'

'Tell him to wait?'

Belsey left the limo parked on Whitehall for any surveillance to watch and walked the four blocks to New Scotland Yard. He caught Ridpath as the Inspector was leaving, clutching files to his chest, heading towards a taxi.

'Any luck with the CCTV?' Belsey said. 'Sorry I ran. I had an appointment.'

Ridpath blanked him, continuing past.

'I need to talk to you about what you're trying to do,' Belsey said.

'You're a wanted man.'

So, Belsey thought, it had arrived.

'I'm being set up,' he said. 'The whole thing's bullshit. We're both being played.'

'I don't know what your situation is, but I think I can get the sniper. That's what I care about right now.'

'The whole thing's a fraud.'

'You were right about the Corporation of London. They're selling off the Heath. The Hong Kong Gaming Consortium were coming in with Devereux but now Max Kovar is preparing to deliver his entry fee and take their place.'

'No one's selling the Heath.'

They reached the taxi. Ridpath fixed him with a stare.

'Why's Kovar been on the phone all day preparing to deliver what he calls "a gift"?'

Belsey felt the money, felt the longing for the money in his heart.

'I don't know,' he said.

'It's for Devereux. Kovar thinks he's delivering something to Devereux.'

'Kovar is a joke,' Belsey said. 'He's nothing to do with Alexei Devereux. Devereux's sat on an island somewhere, saving marine life. Our Devereux, the one on The Bishops Avenue, was a fraud. This was a con man who used us as his props. The set-up was pure theatre: the petition, the rumours about Milton Granby, French companies competing for the contract. He almost walked off with a cool thirty-eight mil, leaving them to fight among themselves, except someone got a blade to his throat. It was going to be a perfect long-con, played out over three weeks and closed down in less than an hour.'

Ridpath climbed into the taxi. Belsey went round to the other side and got in.

'Don't start,' Ridpath said to the driver. 'He's not coming with us.'

'Yes I am.'

The driver started. They drove down Victoria Street onto Vauxhall Bridge Road.

'There's still a murderer on the loose,' Ridpath said, looking straight ahead. Belsey sensed the terrible force of a small man given his day.

'Kovar has nothing to do with the sniper,' Belsey said.

'So who is Kovar meeting? Who is he delivering this gift to?'

'I don't know.'

'He will lead the sniper. He will lead us to the sniper.'

'No.'

'It's our best chance.'

'And you're going to take him down in the next few hours? Wherever he ends up? That's crazy. That's inviting a bloodbath.'

'It's now or never.'

'But none of it's real,' Belsey said finally, quietly.

'Jessica Holden was real,' Ridpath said. He wouldn't look at Belsey. 'I will find whoever killed her.' They were at lights waiting to cross onto Vauxhall Bridge, with the stream of traffic endless and grey around them. Ridpath stared out. Belsey tried to see his face. The traffic lights turned amber and caught pain far back behind the Inspector's eyes. And it struck Belsey as odd. It looked like grief.

'Stop the car,' Belsey said.

59

HE DODGED TRAFFIC, WEAVING BACK TO THE PAVEMENT, RAN along Horseferry Road and took a stack of empty cardboard boxes from outside a newsagent's. A fluorescent vest hung over roadworks at the next junction and he took that as well. He was attracting a few stares now. He continued to New Scotland Yard.

An estate maintenance vehicle sat parked across the road from the main entrance. There would be plenty of flammable products in that. Belsey found a hubcap in the gutter and used it to smash the back window. He was right: the van was filled with various tins, plastic bottles, rags and tools. He took his Zippo and set light to the cardboard boxes then dropped them in. They smouldered with paper and clothing. For a moment there was just thick black smoke, then something went up with a roar. Thirty seconds later the vehicle was engulfed in flames. Guards ran out of the front of New Scotland Yard, then back in to raise the alarm. Belsey put the vest on.

'Everybody out,' he shouted, walking into reception. Police and civilians streamed out of the gates. He moved through them. 'Evacuate the building,' he said, badge out. He ran up the stairs to the fourth floor, past Cheque Fraud and Computer Crime to the Financial Development Unit. Midgley was pulling his coat on. Belsey walked past, to Ridpath's office, and tried the door. It was locked.

'Have you got keys to Inspector Ridpath's office?' he asked.

'Yes. Have you got permission to enter?'

'Yes.'

'I don't think so. Because maybe there's pictures of you in there. You with someone else's credit card.'

Belsey walked to the officer's desk, took the drawers out and emptied them on the floor.

'What are you doing?' Midgley reached for the desk phone and Belsey punched him hard in the face so that he fell to the floor, out cold. He took Midgley's keys and opened Ridpath's office, went in and shut the door. CCTV images of himself with Devereux's cards lay on top of a white envelope stamped 'Camden Council'. Belsey pocketed them and searched the desk. Inside the top drawer was a dog-eared sheaf of photocopies: *Specialist Crime Directorate – UK Eyes Only: Pierce Buckingham*. It contained full intel reports on Buckingham for the last seven years, stapled to a printout from the *Moscow Business Gazette* website: '*Fortunately, Devereux has established bases in Paris, London and New York and would probably be welcome in any of them. . .*'

On top of the pile was a copy of an email from Chris Starr: '*I appreciate your concern. Unfortunately, for reasons of security, I cannot disclose information regarding any equipment PS Security utilise in their operations. . .*' It was clipped to printouts from espionage websites, pages torn from catalogues of hidden cameras, miniature cameras, cameras in lighters and jewellery and fake cans of drink.

Belsey called PS Security from Ridpath's phone. Starr sounded tense.

'Nick? Where are you?'

'Where am I meant to be, Chris? The cells of West End Central?'

'What's going on?'

'When exactly did Graham Dougsdale go missing?'

'Sunday, around 3 p.m.'

'He's five eleven, broad, balding.'

'That's right.'

'He's at St Pancras Mortuary, tagged as Alexei Devereux. My condolences, Chris. Better luck next time.'

Belsey put the phone down. The fire alarm was still going. He checked the time on his fake Rolex. Two hours to get to the airport. Everything was in place and he was fucked by a tail team. Then he looked at the watch again.

Very flash. Do you even know what all those things do?

He saw the figure on CCTV moving through the house, searching the study, and then he saw the same silhouette standing over him at Ridpath's, touching the blanket, after something. He lured me back there, Belsey thought. He was trying to take the watch.

Belsey stared at the watch face, the fake Rolex hands, the stars and buttons. He took it off. Then he pulled it apart.

The lens was a pinprick in the 'o' of 'Rolex'. The buttons operated the device. A third unscrewed to reveal a port for linking to a USB input.

It wasn't Devereux's watch. It was PS Security's.

Belsey barged out, stepping over Midgley, down the stairs, out through the back of the Yard.

He searched for an Internet cafe. The first place he found with PC access was a convenience store that advertised laptop repairs and money transfers and had six monitors along one wall. It worked. The owner had a box of wires and adapter cables and the second one they tried connected the watch to a hard drive. There were a couple of people making long-distance video calls and a group of teenagers listening to ringtones. The watch attracted a crowd.

'How much does that cost?' the teenagers asked. They gathered around Belsey.

'Where did you get it?'

They stopped smiling when the images appeared on the monitor.

It was obviously surveillance, hurriedly taken from a variety of angles, none very close. They showed a middle-aged man and an eighteen-year-old girl in embraces, obscured by parked cars, spied through the window of a restaurant, leaving the restaurant and kissing.

The images were time-stamped to 2 p.m. last Sunday. The couple had then been tailed back to the house on The Bishops Avenue, photographed leaving it again an hour later, then Dougsdale made his way inside. There were photographs of the living room and the bedroom and finally the study. Then there were no more photographs.

Belsey clicked back to the kiss. The couple stood between the Porsche

Cayenne and the front windows of an Italian restaurant. Villa Bianca. Ridpath held the girl's coat and she had her face raised, eyes closed, both with their eyes closed, looking like they knew it was their last.

Belsey printed a copy. He found his flight details and checked in online, printed his boarding pass, then slit the lining of his jacket and slipped the watch inside.

60

CITADEL PLACE HAD GOT ITS NAME FOR A REASON, AN UGLY 1980s block on an armoured business park by the river, all black gates and caged turnstiles. Belsey approached with caution, glad for the area's industrial gloom. Cars swept hurriedly in and out, past crumbling warehouses and rusting barbed wire. This evening they were parked up the street as well: marked and unmarked, all under the eyes of four security guards and fifteen cameras. Belsey recognised Northwood's silver BMW from the driver waiting in the front.

They would be putting a plan together, huddled around a big table in the Operations Centre. They needed men moving to Stansted in the next thirty minutes. There was no way he could get into the place unnoticed. If anyone was going to have his picture up, ready to pounce, it would be the Serious Crime team.

He went to the pub.

The Rose occupied a corner at the riverside end of the street. There was a man behind the bar, stacking glasses, and one customer: a ten-year-old boy in a Chelsea kit putting someone's money into the fruit machine. A train passed over the adjacent bridge and the pub rattled.

'Evening,' Belsey said. He found a telephone beside the toilets and checked it for a dialling tone. The back seats were beside a window with a sight onto the entrance to Citadel Place. From the seats you could also see anyone entering the pub without being immediately noticeable yourself. A doorway in the corner led to the beer garden, which contained

353

two wheelie bins, a parasol and empty kegs. Belsey went out. He climbed onto the kegs. On the other side of the wall was a row of storage spaces under the railway arch, leading back into the Lambeth housing estates. It was a getaway.

He bought a pint of Guinness and took a sip. Then he went to the phone and placed a call.

'Organised Crime Agency,' a man answered.

'I believe you've got people in a meeting at the moment,' Belsey said. 'I need to speak to one of them quite urgently. His name's Inspector Ridpath, from Financial Development. Could you put me through to the Operations Centre?'

'Who should I say it is?'

'A friend of Alexei Devereux.'

The voice disappeared for a moment then came back.

'He's not taking calls.'

Belsey swore under his breath. He thought about this. He tried to control a mounting frustration.

'Tell Inspector Ridpath it's his snow tiger,' he said finally.

'His what?'

'Tell him. Say it's his snow tiger. He'll understand.'

The line went silent. Belsey thought they'd gone for good. Then a few seconds later he heard the faintest of clicks as a receiver was lifted.

'Yes?' Ridpath's voice was absolutely still.

'Step outside the building,' Belsey said. He hung up. Belsey found the printout of the kiss and admired it. It was a fine shot. Dougsdale must have been sitting in a cafe on the other side of the street. Playing with his watch. The barman disappeared into the back. Belsey called the boy over from the fruit machine.

'Want to make some money?' Belsey held up a twenty-pound note. 'A man is about to come out of the offices across the road. Give him this.' He passed the print. 'Tell him his friend is waiting for him here.' He reached into his pocket, got a tenner and handed it over. 'Half up front. Half when you've given it to him.' The boy took the money and looked at it, then at Belsey. 'Easiest money you'll ever make. Yes or no?'

The boy took the picture and the tenner and walked out. Belsey watched the window. Ridpath stepped out of SOCA HQ. He stood alone on the street, looking up and down towards the blind end of the road and then the river. Then he saw the boy, the sheet in his hands. The boy gave him the picture and pointed at the pub. Ridpath looked at the pub, then at the picture.

Belsey settled away from the window. The young gambler returned and Belsey gave him his money. 'Go spend it somewhere that's not here.' The boy left quickly. Ridpath walked in a moment later.

He looked around, saw Belsey and walked over. For a moment they just stared at each other.

'You're a cute bastard,' Belsey said, with awe.

'What do you want?'

'Stand them down.'

He could see the Inspector thinking through his diminishing options. So, Belsey thought, here he was: the man who created the fiction I inhabited. The man who was prepared to destroy me. And yet he couldn't help feeling a reluctant bond, as if they had shared an obsession.

'I can't,' Ridpath said.

'Northwood can. He's following whatever you tell him. Say you want to hold off for now. Say something's not right.'

'I want justice.'

'You want justice? You got her killed.'

Ridpath threw himself at Belsey. He wasn't a natural fighter. He ended up with a hand in Belsey's face and one holding his collar. Belsey was ready to take it.

'I didn't kill her,' the Inspector said, eyes bulging. 'You know that. You know who did.'

'Take the tails off Kovar,' Belsey said. 'Let him get where he's going, then do what you want. There is an alternative and it's not pretty.'

Ridpath released Belsey. 'When are you meeting him?'

'An hour.'

'You won't do it.'

'I'll do it.'

'Give me the camera.'

'Call it off. Tell them it's switched to tomorrow morning.'

'It will make a complete fool of me.'

'So will the photos I have.'

Ridpath hesitated for a few seconds then backed away. Belsey watched him leave. He went to the window and saw the Inspector cross the road to SOCA HQ and stop at the entrance. Ridpath stood there for another moment with his head bowed, then he showed his pass to the guard and walked in.

Fifty-eight minutes.

61

B ELSEY WENT OVER TO N ORTHWOOD'S BMW. T HE DRIVER
sat in the front, studying a manual on pursuit technique. Belsey knocked
on the window and the driver jumped then rolled the window down.

'Yes?'

'Is this Chief Superintendent Northwood's car?'

'Yes.'

'He's asked for his shoes. From the boot.'

'His what?'

'His shoes. In the boot.'

The man got out, frowning. He went to the back of the car. Belsey
climbed in, started the engine and drove.

Everything was fine.

At ninety miles per hour he was out of central London in four minutes,
past Bethnal Green in seven and onto the A12. He found a detachable
police light on the passenger seat and stuck it on. He flicked the switch
for the sirens.

A low suburbia peeled away. The woods of Romford flashed past. The
boarded-up houses that flanked the route out of town were briefly beautiful in the sodium light, then they were gone.

He found the police radio and lifted it. He called in a sighting of the
BMW heading in the opposite direction down the M20 towards
Folkestone.

'Received,' the call room said.

He swung onto the M25 and eased it to one hundred. It took him back to his night-racing days. Gallows Corner, Pilgrims Hatch. His sirens split the darkness. The world itself seemed to divide to let him through. At Junction 27 he joined the M11 heading north. Now all he had to do was follow a straight course for the airport. It was perfect: total peace. And then the police arrived.

The first to give him attention was a Traffic Police Land Rover. They thought he was on a chase and wanted to help; Belsey could see them in his rear-view mirror, radioing through. They were trying to make contact.

Belsey lifted the two-way. 'It's all fine. Back off. This is a Met operation. Please back off.'

He could outrun a Land Rover Discovery, and he accelerated away. That was a rush. He enjoyed it for all of twenty seconds. When he checked his mirrors, he saw two red pursuit vehicles with the swords of Essex Constabulary on their side doors. Mitsubishi Lancers. Belsey swore. That was all he needed: a pair of Essex boys up for a race. The front-runners pulled level and eyeballed him. Two young, gelled-up constables. They turned to each other and spoke. Then the officer in the passenger seat lifted a radio to his mouth and Belsey knew they were running a check on his plates. Next they'd be radioing a block.

Belsey took it to a hundred and thirty.

The response unit tried to box him. Belsey felt the force of a side slam. But Northwood's BMW had weight advantage. He slammed back and they lost control for a moment. He weaved out between them.

They were close to the border with Cambridgeshire now. The clock said a hundred and thirty-five miles per hour. Reality doesn't keep up at that speed. He felt calm. He could see his pursuers a few hundred metres behind him. On either side, Essex fields were preparing to become Cambridgeshire fields, level and grey, divided by pylons and hedgerow. Cambridgeshire Constabulary would provide the backup for a block. They also had their own air support. He knew he had to do something before they got the helicopter up.

Junction 7 passed in a blur. If they set up a block it wouldn't be before Junction 9. He could see planes coming in, low, to the north, the lights of the runways reflecting off the underside of clouds. Then the Essex cars were joined by a Motorway Police bike. The three gained on him, appearing suddenly large in the rear-view mirror. Belsey put his seat belt on and moved towards the hard shoulder. The car directly behind him nosed his bumper with a clang, and the LED signs above the road flashed across all six lanes: *Stop Now. Block Ahead.*

Belsey moved his passport from his breast pocket to inside his jacket. He slowed to ninety, then eighty, which confused them. The bike raced on ahead. The nearest car smashed his back bumper again. He could see a line of blue lights flashing in the near distance. Two hundred metres to go. Belsey wrenched the wheel to the left. The car scraped across the hard shoulder and was suddenly free of the ground. It came to earth a second later with an almighty crash. Then he was upside down and he thought he'd fucked it. Lean, he thought. He was still conscious. The car landed heavily back down on its wheels. Horns screamed above him, fading into the distance. He was alive.

He found the door handle, jumped out and plunged into a field of crop stubble. He checked himself as he ran; nothing was broken. He could see. He climbed over an electric fence onto a golf course, crossed the golf course, climbed a brick wall beyond the clubhouse, then stumbled past farm equipment and a barn. Now he could hear the helicopter. It had missed his evacuation though, which meant even with thermal imaging they were unlikely to have a lock on him. Walk calmly, he thought; he couldn't be the only person on the ground, walking, although it felt like it amid the thin sprawl of countryside that Sunday night.

He followed a road with no pavement, walking in the storm drain, following signs to Bishop's Stortford. A fleet of Dutch lorries passed him. Then there were just fields swaying beneath moonlight. I've made it out of London, he thought.

A few scattered cottages became a cluster of pale Barratt homes. Bishop's Stortford was locking up: tables upturned outside pubs and cafes, a group of youths by a war memorial, one man walking his dog. He'd lost the sound of sirens now. Even the helicopter was distant. Walking through the town was like entering another world, with smells of Sunday roast, white cider, fresh tarmac. And he knew he could make it then.

The airport appeared as a box of light on the horizon. He'd lost precious time. He thought about the hour, about the security on the gates. Who walked into Stansted airport with no luggage and a nice, new passport in the middle of the night? He knew the anti-terrorist precautions. Now he was on the edge of the village, almost on the last stretch of road. A train released a long mournful note, slowing as it passed through Bishop's Stortford station. The Stansted Express. Belsey crashed through a back garden to a field, and down the muddy slope of the field towards the tracks.

The train rattled by, throwing sparks, lighting the branches behind it. Belsey eased himself down the embankment. Something caught his leg and tore through the trouser fabric. He kept going. He pushed through the brambles and rubbish to the gravel of the railway sidings and felt the force of the train. He reached a hand out, tried to grab a handle at the back of a carriage. The metal was torn out of his hand. He'd have to make a clean jump. He prepared himself. Three more carriages passed. As the last arrived he grabbed the handrails of the rear cab and leapt.

Suddenly he was clear of the ground. Belsey felt a wave of agony as his entire body hung from his fingers. His feet kicked frantically for support, then found the buffer bolts. He wedged himself flat against the metal as they roared into a tunnel. The sound was deafening. The back of the cab slammed against his face and knees but the pain was trivial beside the fear of falling. After another minute the train began to slow again. Then, like a dream, the concrete shell of the airport's train station appeared. Families stood waiting beneath neon lights. Belsey stepped clean from the back of the train onto the platform and walked to the escalators, checking for security, brushing himself down.

Welcome to London Stansted. The low-rise labyrinth of retail outlets and food concessions stretched towards passport control. Some travellers already lay prostrate on the bench seats. Two airport police were getting money out of cash machines, Heckler & Koch sub-machine guns loose at their sides. All was peaceful. Belsey checked the departure boards.

11.30 Thessaloniki YK954 – Proceed to Gate 16.

He had ten minutes to check in, five before the local police force arrived. He ran to the front of the terminal. Signs said *No Stopping* but cars were stopping, families hugging and throwing suitcases into boots before the airport security approached. The glass terminal leaked a cold, synthetic light over the scene. Where was Kovar? Belsey checked the road and listened for sirens. And then he saw Kovar moving towards him and his heart kicked.

'Max,' Belsey said.

62

KOVAR GRINNED, HAND OUTSTRETCHED. THE FLOODLIGHTS lit his teeth. Two members of his own security hung back beside their vehicles, stalling the airport staff in yellow vests who were trying to move them on.

'Jack,' Kovar said.

Behind the security guards were two long trailers, each attached to the back of a jeep. They blocked the road. Belsey moved towards Kovar, his own hand extended, looking past him to the trailers and the men guarding them. It wasn't a cash truck.

'Here they are,' Kovar said. And then the hand Belsey was about to shake wasn't there and he was walking through a fine spray of blood.

Belsey saw Kovar pirouette before he heard the shot. Then he processed the sound: it wasn't a police Heckler or airport security. It was the sniper.

Kovar's guards took a second to react. Then they ran, covering him, moving Kovar back towards the jeep.

'The money,' Belsey shouted.

A second shot brushed Belsey's arm and clipped the trailer. He was the target, it seemed. He dived for cover, behind the concrete anti-terrorist slabs. There was a sudden commotion as the trailer seemed to shake and a new noise filled the air. It sounded awful – bestial and terrified. One of the guards angled a handgun uncertainly at Belsey but a third shot came between them, from the roof of the terminal, and the guard swung wildly in that direction.

The first jeep roared into gear and tried to pull away as a shot punctured its side. Sirens started now, police coming in from the motorway and airport security closing in, one vehicle speeding towards the back of Kovar's convoy. The jeep reversed suddenly and its trailer slammed into the airport security van. The trailer toppled over. Horses spilled out.

There was a blur of panicked muscle, glinting hooves and eyes. One horse freed itself from the tangled mass, rose up and ran wild. The rest followed. They galloped across the tarmac in all directions, five horses, colts and yearlings, black and grey. A second police car swerved to avoid them, then a third crashed into that one.

Belsey crawled forward. There was violent whinnying from the second trailer. He could see it rocking with the panic inside. At the sound of another shot, the cargo burst the doors and leapt out, dragging ropes. The flat glare of the lights shimmered blue on their coats. They bolted across the runway towards the fence and then circled back to charge the airport security. The sound of hooves on tarmac filled the air.

The sniper shot again.

Two horses ran inside the terminal. Then a third and fourth. Belsey watched someone climb down the outside of the building and move calmly inside, pulling on the yellow jacket of a baggage handler. A fire crew crashed onto the scene – three engines, blocking up the terminal entrance but not enough to stop horses stumbling past. Belsey moved under cover of the horses, past the fire engines and inside.

Screams filled the air, along with the shrill stench of perfume and alcohol. Bottles of duty-free vodka and aftershave lay smashed across the floor, abandoned as passengers ran for cover. There was a horse jammed in the revolving doors and another charging at the Krispy Kreme stand, spilling aluminium tables and chairs. Families piled into the airport pub and the Burger King, trying to barricade whatever doors they could find. People had rushed to the sides and there was suddenly a void in the centre, a no-man's-land in which the horses circled frantically.

The man in baggage-handler kit swung himself up onto the roof of the Burger King concession. Belsey watched, considering his options. A shot breezed past from outside. It came from the airport police. He reached for his badge, then thought better of it and ran for the back of the terminal.

Now a shot came from up high, aimed at the front entrance where the security were taking up positions. I've brought him an army, Belsey thought. Through the glass walls he could see Cambridgeshire police clattering in, and the Met behind them: riot vans and area cars, men and women from SOCA screeching to a halt, spreading a wall of vehicles across the front concourse.

The terminal had begun to smell of the horses now. They'd urinated as they ran and scattered manure across the ground. When the sniper released another barrage of rifle fire, one horse jumped the passport control barriers and one kicked through the windows of a souvenir shop. A third careered into the Ryanair desk, slipping on perfume, its hooves tapping madly for a second. Then it was on its side, slamming into a bank of plastic seats. One of the horses had been hit. It splashed blood, looking for an escape route. The horse sounds were unearthly. Somewhere someone was still making announcements: *This is a final call. Could passengers for flight YK954 to Thessaloniki please proceed to Gate 16.*

Belsey took one of the spilled tables from outside a coffee shop and used it to climb onto the top of a unit being used as a Tie Rack. He pulled himself up slowly in time to see the sniper fifty metres in front of him, skipping across the top of the concessions to a bureau de change where he had cover behind one of the structural support pillars.

Belsey pulled the Sig and took the safety off.

He checked again. There were three stores between them, a jumble of roofs, vents and structural supports. Beyond the sniper he could see the entire scene at the front: plain-clothed officers running, airport security taking up positions, SOCA led by Northwood. The Borough Commander looked lost. None of them could see the gunman.

Belsey had one advantage: he was behind the action. He had been the last officer to dare attempt a run through the terminal before the sniper began laying down fire. Now he watched the gunman's back, up on the roof of the bureau de change, wedged in behind his roof truss, sliding another magazine into the rifle. The gunman was focused on the ground.

He hadn't seen Belsey. He locked the catch, then slung the rifle over his shoulder and jumped to the roof of the check-in desks. He secured himself again, aimed, let off another burst.

Ten-round box magazine, Belsey thought. He counted five shots, now six. He hauled himself up to the roof, keeping low, using vents for cover as he crawled forward. The police returned fire, shattering a panel of the terminal's glass roof, and Belsey ducked. Splinters rained down. The sniper brushed the glass off. He was taking his time: sighting, firing, still protected by the support columns. The idea was clearly to keep the police at a distance, and so buy himself an occasion to escape. The smashed roof offered one possibility.

The sniper crawled to the edge of the check-in roof to angle another shot. The recoil almost knocked him off his perch. Belsey waited. His tenth shot hit a security guard in the arm. Now came the reload. The sniper fumbled with the bolt, let the empty magazine fall and reached into his jacket for new ammunition. Belsey jumped across.

'Milan,' Belsey said, moving in fast. He crouched to avoid any cross-fire. The gunman looked over his shoulder, still searching for ammunition. He seemed startled, as if he hadn't heard the name in a while and had to think what it meant. He was younger than Belsey expected. The gunman must have underestimated the distance between them. Belsey put a boot in his face and watched him fall.

63

MILAN BALIC WAS STILL ALIVE WHEN BELSEY REACHED THE ground, sprawled in the centre of ten armed officers with his rifle lying a few metres away. Belsey had enough time to see that the man was moving. Then a group of officers turned in his direction.

'I'm OK,' Belsey said. Someone pepper-sprayed him. He was thrown to the ground and cuffs closed around his wrists. 'Hey . . .'

They hauled him into a secure room, eyes streaming.

'Take the cuffs off,' he said. No one did. 'Get some fucking water on my face.'

Someone threw water on him. Eventually he could breathe. A little after that he could see. They were in an immigration custody suite, with maps of Africa and Central Asia on the wall. A select crowd had gathered: Northwood, the head of the Armed Ops Unit, the acting airport Superintendent. In the background he saw Chief Superintendent Barry Marsh, head of SOCA, Commander Ashfield from Anti-Terrorism. They closed the doors.

'I know him,' Northwood said.

'Sir,' Belsey said.

'Talk.'

Belsey took a moment to gather his thoughts. He had a captive audience. He had quite a story to tell.

'The man you've got is a Croatian, probably born Milan Balic. Most recently he was travelling on a Canadian passport in the name of Antoine

Pelletier. International Crime know him. So do Paris, Geneva and Rome. Balic carried out the hits on Jessica Holden and Pierce Buckingham. He was hired by a group called the Hong Kong Gaming Consortium after they got roped into a con game and wound up handing over thirty-eight million pounds to someone who wasn't a Russian oligarch called Alexei Devereux.'

Belsey let them digest this. Finally Chief Superintendent Marsh spoke. 'How was Jessica Holden involved?'

'Jessica met the con man through an escort agency. They fell in love and she helped him. The money was tied to Project Boudicca. It was meant to be a casino and racetrack on Hampstead Heath. The con man set the scene to perfection. He did everything you'd expect from a new oligarch in town, including getting friendly with the wrong people. He used Pierce Buckingham to rope the investors in, because that was Buckingham's mission in life. There was a meeting at the Guildhall last Saturday in which Buckingham gave Project Boudicca the hard sell and a lot of money transferred before the day was done. Then it disappeared. Not surprising as the real Devereux is on an island somewhere and doesn't know the first thing about any of this.

'As a result, the gaming consortium hired an investigations firm – PS Security. On Sunday, the man posing as Devereux killed a PS Security operative named Graham Dougsdale. I found his body at The Bishops Avenue address. It was left so that anyone coming across it would assume he was the Russian and he'd taken his own life. The con man bought a dog and cut its throat and the mess contributed to the overall effect. Dougsdale had caught him off guard. That was where the problems started.'

Belsey took a moment to savour the scene. The handcuffs bit into his flesh, but his audience was hanging on every word.

'The con man made two mistakes,' Belsey said. 'He got blood on his hands and he fell in love. Both slowed him down. He missed the right moment to die. The fact that he got Jessica to ID the body as Devereux suggests he wanted to buy a day or so to get away. When he found he had a body on his hands he thought he could use it to his advantage, to distract the victims of his sting. But the consortium were already busy with revenge.'

'Who is he?' Commander Ashfield said.

'The con man?' Belsey looked around the flushed faces of the senior officers, then at the maps on the wall. 'I don't know.' He shook his head wistfully. There were a lot of sighs and a few curses.

'Any ideas where we'd find him?' Ashfield asked.

'Where would you go to disappear forever?'

Silence. Apparently none of them had ever considered it.

'Give Johnny Cassidy protected informant status,' Belsey said. 'Tell the judge he's provided significant assistance.'

'John Cassidy?' Northwood said. 'He's involved?'

'He's helped me, yes. I'll be able to reveal how at a later date. And take a look at the escort agency, Sweetheart Companionship. They use underage girls. And I believe the only reason they haven't been shut down is because the boys at West End Central have a working agreement and take part in orgies, sometimes filmed, with animals and drugs involved.'

'West End Central?'

'Check their hard drives. Can I get some air?'

They unlocked him and he got up, rubbing his wrists. The Command team were already at action stations, radioing instructions, calling up the Yard. It was going to be a busy night. Belsey moved between them, out to the terminal. Jesus Christ, he thought, surveying the scene. Then Northwood was beside him, grim, still furious, but very faintly vulnerable.

'What are you going to say?' he demanded.

'To who?'

'To anyone.'

'Nothing.' Belsey sensed a shift of power, small but significant. They faced each other beside the trashed and bullet-pocked Burger King.

'Going to tell more lies to your friends at the *Mail*?'

'I'm going to do what I can to ensure no serving officer is brought into disrepute,' Belsey said. Northwood digested this sceptically.

'There's going to be a lot of issues,' Northwood said.

'I thought, given the number of issues, I'd leave it to you.' Belsey's eyes glinted. 'How does that sound?'

'That would be the first sensible thing you've done in a while.'

'Do I have a job?' Belsey asked.

'I think we can arrange something.'

'Then I should probably get some sleep.'

Belsey was assigned a chaperone: a young, serious-looking constable who walked beside him to a panda car. They were closing the airport, stringing tape across the front. One horse lay on its side receiving medical attention. The rest were being rounded up. The flashing lights of seventeen emergency vehicles lit the animals and a line of shell-shocked travellers being marched to the Premier Inn.

The Constable gestured for Belsey to take the passenger seat of the police car.

'What are you meant to do with me?' Belsey asked.

'Ensure you go straight home,' he said.

Straight home. Belsey laughed. He heard voices behind him: Northwood sorting the press conference, forensics arriving with expressions of disbelief. Then, once they had started to drive, the wind blew all their voices away and it was quiet again.

64

IN THE END HE TOLD THE CHAPERONE TO DRIVE HIM TO Kilburn. The young Police Constable dropped him off on the High Road but didn't leave immediately, watching from the parked car as if Belsey might explode into sudden insubordination. Belsey turned into a residential cul-de-sac, waited to hear the car drive off, then walked in the direction of Ridpath's home. He didn't know what to expect.

The Inspector's car was still there. It was low on its suspension, with a heavy boot. A light glowed dimly within the house.

Belsey rang the bell. He heard someone approach the door and stop. 'Let me in,' Belsey said. There was no answer. 'I'm alone, unarmed.'

After another moment Ridpath opened the door, checked the street and walked back into the house. Belsey saw him return a knife to the kitchen drawer. It passed through Belsey's mind that he had already killed a man, not so long ago. But Belsey didn't feel in danger. He entered Ridpath's home and closed the door. He collapsed onto the sagging sofa. 'Thirty-eight mil,' Belsey said. 'That's quite a haul.'

'How long have I got?' Ridpath said.

'Six hours, tops. I wouldn't stop to take any pictures.'

'You didn't tell them about me?'

'It slipped my mind.'

Ridpath stared at him. He gave a small nod. Finally he said, 'What do you want?

'Maybe I want to say goodbye.' Belsey looked around the room. He got up and found the rest of the Scotch in the cupboard, took a mug from the sideboard and poured a drink. 'Do you really think you can get away?' he said.

'It's still a big world.'

'Maybe.'

Belsey offered the bottle to Ridpath but it was declined. A life on the run, Belsey thought: was that anything to envy? Watching your back every hour of the day? But then thirty-eight million could make for some slick running.

Ridpath turned the gas off and found his coat. Belsey poured himself another whisky. The Inspector rummaged beneath the sink and produced a stack of documents and a clear bag of hair dye, scissors and glue. Belsey watched him standing very still in the kitchen with the getaway kit.

'Was there a passport on her?' the Inspector asked suddenly.

'A passport? On Jessica, you mean?'

'Yes. Was she going to come with me?'

He said it like someone painfully aware of themselves, exposed to ridicule and stiffened against it. How had Jessica's friend described Devereux? *He was kind, wealthy.* Belsey wondered if the transformation could ever be repeated. Maybe Ridpath was already planning his next billionaire. He would be omnipotent again. Maybe Devereux and his charm were gone forever.

'I don't know,' Belsey said. He thought about the farewell note, about the passport in the girl's locker. 'Sure. Why not?' He reached into his pocket and brought out the watch. 'Do you want this? It still has the pictures on it.' Ridpath looked at the watch for a moment, then took it from Belsey.

'Wait here.' Ridpath went upstairs. Belsey stared at the kitchen, the washing-up still to be done, then at the awards lying on the shelves: *In recognition of DI Philip Ridpath's diligence and resourcefulness in the course of duty . . .*

The Inspector returned with a thick A4 envelope.

'What is it?' Belsey said.

'This explains everything.'

Belsey took the envelope. It felt heavy in his hand.

'What's there to explain?'

'In case you have any trouble.'

They both left the house. Belsey watched him lock up for the last time. He waited to see Ridpath look round and drink it in, feel sorry for himself, but the Inspector just got into his car and started the engine. No goodbye for Belsey either. Ridpath reversed out fast. He drove off towards Willesden Lane, into exile.

65

BELSEY DIDN'T LEAVE IMMEDIATELY. HE WASN'T GOING anywhere. He sat on a garden wall across the road, watching the house, which seemed very small now, crouched to the earth, as if everything on the planet was resting low on its suspension. He was tipsy. It had been a long day. He watched the house and the sky above it, searching for stars. Finally he looked at the envelope in his hands. How much did he want explained? He stabbed the packet and tore it open, took out a bank-sealed wad of notes. Then he took out another. There were wads of crisp fifties and twenties. Belsey crouched by the side of the road and made neat piles on the pavement, trying not to laugh or cry. Twelve piles. He estimated eighty grand, maybe ninety. Well, he thought. He stuffed some in his pockets and the rest back in the envelope and sat there, breathing.

Well, he thought again. And, after another moment: that's a start.

It deserved a celebration. He took a cab to the Dorchester hotel and hit the bar. The place was lively, polished tables occupied, bar staff doing brisk service. The bar was long and curved and there were a lot of mirrors and men and women who looked famous. Belsey ordered a bottle of Krug Grand Cuvée. He watched the ceiling lights, the glass sculptures, the velvet. He drank the most expensive champagne he had ever tasted. But it wasn't a drink to enjoy on your own. After half a bottle Belsey slipped a band off one of the wads and caught a cab across the river to the Wishing Well.

'My round,' he announced to the bar.

'Nick!'

The Well's infamous Sunday-night lock-in received him warmly.

'What am I done for now, officer?' He took friendly blows to the shoulders and pretended to fight back. He bought a round. The crowd seemed to swell when he started getting drinks in.

'What are we celebrating?'

Men got on their phones and spread word of a party. Belsey bought the two dusty bottles of Cava that had been behind the bar for as long as he had drunk there. He downed a lot of sambuca and some stale beer. Eventually he went to a public phone box on the street outside.

He called St Thomas' Hospital. Charlotte Kelson had been discharged. The hospital refused to give him any details. Belsey tried her mobile but she didn't answer. He stood in the phone box and thought about visiting her house.

He went to Lorenzo's.

'Nicky, you're back.'

'Nicky, what are you having?'

He arrived in time for the shambolic end of what must have been a birthday or a hen party, with a paralytic DJ and women dancing on tables who looked like they weren't hired entertainment. The floor was sticky. The landlord was bandaging his arm.

Belsey bought a lot of rounds and made some new friends. He found himself behind the bar, fixing people drinks. At one point he was talking to a girl and she said, 'What do you do? Are you a barman?' And he said, 'I'm a police detective,' and it felt OK.

He moved on to Roxy's, then across the road to the Blue Eyed Maid: tourist traps and pubs for people who didn't go to bed. Then, when even the stalwarts closed on him, Belsey caught a cab to Soho, to the Spanish Bar. There was a man who worked for a ferry company and they were drinking vodka Martinis and watching shop assistants set light to shots. After his fifth or sixth Belsey must have left because he was walking up the Euston Road. Even without a home he had the sensation of walking away from home. The night was young. London restrained a smile, finding him still there. So, it seemed to say, the two of us again.

Acknowledgements

Many thanks to Judith Murray for making it happen; to Alex Bowler for making it a pleasure. The excellent people of FIE provided good times and accommodation, both of which were invaluable. Charles Harris has been a huge source of inspiration and advice; Elaine Harris supplied pretty much everything else. Emily Kenway was the book's first reader and her comments improved it greatly. It's dedicated to her for less literary reasons.

HR 7|"
SC "|"